Dirty Water

Dirty Water

TOM KRATMAN

DIRTY WATER

A Baen Books Original

Baen Publishing Enterprises
P.O. Box 1403
Riverdale, NY 10471
www.baen.com

ISBN: 978-1-9821-9300-3

Cover art by Kieran Yanner

First printing, November 2023

Distributed by Simon & Schuster
1230 Avenue of the Americas
New York, NY 10020

Library of Congress Cataloging-in-Publication Data

Names: Kratman, Tom, author.
Title: Dirty water / Tom Kratman.
Description: Riverdale, NY : Baen Publishing Enterprises, 2023.
Identifiers: LCCN 2023030373 (print) | LCCN 2023030374 (ebook) | ISBN 9781982193003 (hardcover) | ISBN 9781625799371 (ebook)
Subjects: LCGFT: Science fiction. | Time-travel fiction. | Short stories.
Classification: LCC PS3611.R375 D57 2023 (print) | LCC PS3611.R375 (ebook) | DDC 813/.6—dc23/eng/20230703
LC record available at https://lccn.loc.gov/2023030373
LC ebook record available at https://lccn.loc.gov/2023030374

Printed in the United States of America

10 9 8 7 6 5 4 3 2 1

To my new grandson, Nicholas James Barton III

And to:
My late father-in-law, Delfin Miranda
28 April 1929 to 7 September 2022

Prologue

Boston Gaol, Prison Lane, Boston, Massachusetts
16 November 1688

Though it was cold, bitterly cold, and windy, it wasn't the weather that set the creature to trembling. Oh, no; the Q'riln trembled with anticipation as the old, worn woman—the Q'riln thought of her as "the pursuer"—bound in cold and rough iron chains, was hustled from the jail and pushed into a crude wagon, drawn by a single horse. Forming a circle around the short passage from jail to cart were some scores of catcalling, sneering, garbage- and mud-hurling men and women. Those emotions were spice, perhaps, but the main meal, the "juice," as the Q'riln termed it, was still to come.

The old woman about to be mounted on the cart was not so old as all that, not as her own people measured things. But, since being assigned to Earth, along with her mate, everything in her assignment had gone utterly wrong. First there came a hard life of war, capture, deportation, and sale as an indentured servant to Barbados. In the course of all this, she'd lost her mate, a loss that pressed down upon her soul like a stone block. This, more than anything, was what made her *seeming* seem prematurely aged. Indeed, she'd grown old at heart and soul, these last fifty years, even as her people measured things.

Worst of all, the old woman going to her miserable death was further agonized by the knowledge of failure. Sent to track down and eliminate the Q'riln, she, instead, had been arrested. Worse, the Q'riln had somehow managed to deprive her of sensible local speech. All she had left was her own native Galactic Common III, and nobody here spoke that, not even the Q'riln.

The pursuer's name here and now was Ann Glover but among her own people she was, and to her late mate she had been, called something that meant "Topaz," for her smoky yellow eyes. Those eyes sought desperately for an open human she could transfer to and inhabit to continue her pursuit. But no, no, *These are as closed-minded a bunch as Sinesquotian War Tarts, no hope of even a temporary home with them.*

But where can I find shelter? I've set up the cat, but that's not my first choice of a future.

Around the cart, a group of halberdiers and arquebusiers, the latter with their long matches smoking, formed a secure ring, three of each to each side. The driver flicked the reins, causing the horse to begin its slow trek to the town gallows, which stood near to a muddy, stinking, corpse contaminated pool, out on Boston Neck.

Chapter One

∽∾∾✣∾∿

The most serious charge which can be brought
against New England is not Puritanism but February.
—Joseph Wood Krutch

Interstate 81, Shenandoah Valley, Southwest of Stanton, Virginia

The car, a late model Avalon, black in color, with leather seating, more or less vibrated with the music coming from four throats and rather more speakers than that. The song was Shel Silverstein's "Dirty Water," a cultural icon of Boston and, especially, its sports teams.

As if on cue, everyone shut up for a moment as the Old Man reached over and turned down the volume so that the youngest member of the party, his granddaughter, Cossima, eight years old, olive-toned, and tiny, except for her voice, could sing out, with The Standells, a particular line that was, in the family musical lexicon, hers. The line concerned, among other things, the personal qualities of the muggers and thieves strolling, much like the lovers, late night, along the River Charles.

The volume shot up again, the lyrics changing immediately to a discussion of the nature of the water—formerly, as in when the song was first written, so filthy it had been a health hazard if not even a fire hazard. But did the Roman still revere Father Tiber? Did Londoners have the Thames flowing through their hearts? So, too, did Bostonians feel about their river, the Charles, their "Dirty Water."

The song then was suddenly but briefly interrupted by the noxious aroma of a pig farm, just west of Interstate 81, emanating

3

from more tons of pig manure than a human being's nose ought to be subject to.

Pig crap notwithstanding, through coughs and some gagging, the song continued all the way through to the final dedication to the Charles.

The Old Man, while gray and a tad worn, wasn't actually *that* old, mid-sixties, perhaps, and looking a bit younger since he carried more weight now than was comfortable, which extra lard kept the skin taut. Between the weight and some serious mileage, he was more worn than he looked, despite that little bit of looking a little younger than his true age.

There were many names by which he was known. Officially he was Sean F. Eisen. Unofficially, people often appended, "that son of a bitch" to the name.

This was not, to be honest, entirely undeserved; when one grows up in as Irish a place as South Boston, Massachusetts (where one cannot throw a beer bottle of a Friday night without bouncing it off the heads of three Doyles, two Hanrahans, and a Quinn before it hits a Mahoney and then a Delany, mid-chest, or possibly two before finally falling to the ground) with the last name of Eisen . . . well, Johnny Cash pegged it pretty well in "A Boy Named Sue." Eisen had grown up fast and he'd also grown up with a mean streak, keen of wit and with a fast punch.

Some of the names were more or less special, just between him and his grandchildren. These ranged from the commonplace, "Grandpa," to "Old Man," to "Grumpy Old Man," and points beyond.

Eisen, "The Old Man" had, unofficially, taken up the cause of the cultural education of his grandchildren, as well as keeping them in touch with their Boston roots. This had become rather more difficult since terroristic levels of property taxation, aided by an influx of overpaid yuppies and dinks, had driven the extended family entirely from the city limits out into the suburbs of Braintree, Quincy, Plymouth, Hanson, and even such *terra incognita* spots on the North Shore as Salem. Yes, *that* Salem.

"Hey, Old Man," asked the grandson, Patrick, "Can we get some lunch?" Patrick looked *exactly* like the Old Man had at the same age. Indeed, he'd once found a picture of his grandfather as a seven-year-old and asked, "Hey, how did I get in this picture? And where did that old uniform come from?"

"That's an interesting question," observed the Mean Old Grandpa, referring to lunch, not old photographs. "Should I feed you three or develop your characters by letting you go hungry for another twenty-four hours or so? Building character is *so . . .*"

"GRANDPA!!!" cried all three.

"Oh, all right." He glanced up at a road sign and asked, "Snivel, snivel, snivel. German work for you spoiled brats?"

"YYYEEESSS!!!"

"Edelweiss, it is, then."

The food smelled simply wonderful. Even so, the Old Man rested his head on the fingers of one hand and shook it, when the accordion player in the background began unwittingly playing the "Horst Wessel Lied." Eisen considered calling him over to explain his musical faux pas, then decided, *Nah, let him figure it out for himself.*

The plates being presented, the Old Man and the kids ganged up on the *Goulasch*, ingested the *Jaegerschnitzel*, reduced the *Rahmschnitzel*, slaughtered the *Sauerbraten*, and veritably wiped out the *Wiener Schnitzel*. The *Spaetzle* and the red cabbage hardly stood a chance.

"And there's about that good of a chance of me buying you little monsters dessert, either."

"We don't want any," said the eldest, twelve-year-old Juliana, who had, within family circles, a rather pungent nickname. That, however, was only for within family circles.

Twelve years old was an important age for a girl, it being the last year for her to remind everyone how sweet she was before puberty turned her completely—albeit hopefully temporarily—psychotic.

In any case, for now, Juliana was very sweet, very short, and very, very pretty, with brown hair and eyes, and a fairly regal bearing, inherited from her grandmother, Eisen's much mourned, desperately missed, late wife.

Thus, a very sane—at least for the nonce—Juliana asked, "You've never really shown us South Boston; what was it like?"

Nodding, the Old Man answered, "I'll show you this trip. It was a magic place, really, back then. There's even a song about it, 'Southie Is My Home Town.' 'I was born down on A Street, raised up on B Street...' In fact, though, I was born in the Boston City Hospital, and raised up on *I* Street, right across from the Gate of Heaven church."

He mused aloud, "Ah, the Gatey. Maybe the most beautiful non-cathedral in all of Roman Catholicism.

"It was odd," Eisen continued, "an odd way of living, compared to today. Though we were not nearly as involved in church affairs as many, you still lived your life to the rhythm of the church and the church's bells. Mass in the Gate of Heaven was an every-week event, and holy days of obligation were rarely if ever missed. Even if you didn't go to Catholic school, religious education for those of us in public school was essentially mandatory, weekly, and well organized. We'd traipse over to the Gate of Heaven School for it."

The Old Man started to laugh.

"What's so funny, Grandpa?" asked Cossima.

"Well... when I was about seven the nun teaching our catechism class explained to us that, were we boys to be killed in action in battle for our country and against communism, it would count as baptism by fire and we'd be translated straight to Heaven. Makes for an odd outlook; makes boys want to sign up to fight. Makes some of us even go to Army Ranger School.

"Yep, that sort of thing was effective," the Old Man continued. "Even South Boston's criminals would eagerly sign up for combat if there were a war in the offing. My uncle the cop's friend, Pat Nee, interrupted his criminal career to join the Marines and do a tour as a grunt in Vietnam. Note, too, that if the rest of the country had volunteered for Vietnam at the rate boys from South Boston did, we could not possibly have lost; the Viet Cong and NVA, both, would have been extinct.

"For that matter, Stevie Flemmi, who worked for Whitey Bulger and killed a number of people, had the Silver Star from fighting as an infantryman in Korea. And Jerry Angiulo, a high-ranking mobster, underboss in the Patriarca crime family, also fought with the Navy all through the war in the Pacific. Although he was from the North End. Still, the principle holds. Hell, the head of the Winter Hill Gang, Howie Winter, lied about his age to enlist in the Marines when he was fourteen years old, and fought through the last half—and, for the Marines, the worst half—of the Pacific War."

"That's pretty wild," said young Patrick who, as a nine-year-old, already had, indeed had always had, firm intentions of following his father and grandfather into the service.

"It is. Like I said, 'strange place,' especially by modern lights. At age five, even four, I could go anywhere I wanted on my own, in the sure and certain knowledge that anyone, *anyone*, who saw me in trouble from someone older than me would spring to the rescue. It was *much* safer than Boston is today.

"And, though as a boy of perhaps seven or eight on up you had to be prepared to fight at any time, anywhere that wasn't sort of common, like the shopping areas on the two Broadways, there wasn't any street crime as such. Can you guess why?"

Seeing the blank looks on the kids' faces, the Old Man knew they hadn't a realistic clue. "I'll tell you why; because the real and really serious criminals would hunt them down and kill them, quite possibly in inventive ways. Why Willie Delaney, the family hit man . . ."

"'Family hit man'?" asked Patrick, incredulously.

"Well, yeah," Eisen shrugged. "Willie had been dragged into court on something fairly trivial and the old man, the *other* old man, posted his bail. From then on he was on call if needed. We never, so far as I know, anyway, needed him.

"But I'm telling you, Willie was loyal! I remember this one time— the old man had forgotten a Mother's Day gift and mentioned the fact to Willie after hours. So Willie went to the electronics store on Broadway and L, threw a rock through the plate glass window, and brought back a toaster for a present. I only met Willie a couple of times, well, okay, maybe half a dozen, but he seemed like a good sort to me. For a multiple murderer.

"Anyway, Willie got himself killed. There's the official story and then there's the story the old man, the other one, told me. He said that Willie was first tortured with both a blow torch and electricity, then bent into a C-shape, backwards, with his neck and ankles connected with piano wire. Then they threw him into the harbor's polluted water to either drown or half cut his own head off. The torture session before that was serious, as I said, involving a propane torch, a pair of pliers, and electricity. Me, I believe the old man; he was in touch with the kinds of people who did things like that."

"Ummm . . . Grandpa," Juliana began, brown eyes gone quite wide, "were we . . . criminals?"

"'The *Murphia*,' we used to call it, as a joke. Well, *I* wasn't. When I used to blow up vending machines that cheated me I never kept any more than the money they'd stolen. That would have been wrong! But I can make no vouchers for anyone older than me except for my Uncle Billy, the cop, my Uncle Tommy, who was blind, my mother, her sisters and their husbands; oh, and my grandmother, too, of course. Billy was an honest man even though he had a number of dishonest friends, like Pat Nee whom I mentioned."

"Did you know any criminals when you were young?" Cossima asked.

"Fair number or, rather, I met a fair number, like Willie. Pat Nee, I think it was, came down to the cottage in Brant Rock for a couple of weekends when I was seven or eight, before he shipped over to Vietnam with the Marines. Then, too, Whitey Bulger . . ."

"Him, *too*?"

"Just once. I couldn't have been more than ten or so and was with my mother—you may recall she was a very beautiful girl—when she went into Whitey's liquor store to buy some . . . mmm . . . rum, I think it was. Whitey had a taste for beautiful girls so was plainly hitting on her. When we left she said, 'Well, that's the last time I go in there.'"

"Why?" Cossima asked.

"Because women involved with Whitey's gang had a tendency to disappear, I suppose."

"But you said there was no street crime."

"And there wasn't; Whitey would kill them or have them killed in the privacy of someone's home, then bury the bodies in the cellar. He didn't kill randomly, except once by mistake; he shot the entirely innocent twin brother of the guy he was supposed to kill. But some women who really didn't understand the situation would threaten to go to the cops over what they knew, and those he'd kill. And business rivals. And people on the other side of the gang war."

Eisen's brow furrowed as he thought back to those days.

"Same with Pat Nee," he said, "come to think of it. Come to think of it, too, I think at least two and maybe three of Whitey's victims were *buried* in Pat Nee's cellar. Still, no street crime, to speak of. If you stayed away from that kind of life, it would generally stay away from you."

"No, wait a minute," Juliana said. "Your uncle, the cop, was an 'honest man' and he was friends with a . . . with a *murderer*?"

"Well, an accessory to murder, anyway. Hmmm . . . well, usually just an accessory. There was one occasion, though; the murder of Bucky Barrett. Pat was in on that, I understand. Even there, though, Pat was caught dead to rights on so many charges, and was let out of prison so readily and so early, that you have to wonder who he was really working for. A lot of folks are pretty sure he was working for the U.S. government all along, even while working for the Irish Republican Army.

"But, in any case, my uncle was a cop in *East* Boston, not Southie. Made all the difference in the world, you see; Eastie was Eastie and Southie was Southie. To put things in perspective, Robert Mitchum, the actor, while filming *The Friends of Eddie Coyle*, is credibly alleged to have dined nightly with local gangsters, to *include* Whitey Bulger."

Sighing, wistfully, the Old Man added, "And then there was Slocum's Toyland, though we never called it that. It was just Slocum's, or Slokie's, or Sloke's, the best toy store in the world by density per cubic foot. Closed now, sad to say; been closed for, oh, it must be about thirty years. The place was magic."

Raising one eyebrow, a trick he'd picked up from his grandfather, Patrick asked, "What was magic about it?"

Without missing a beat, the Old Man answered, "It was magic how every store and toy department in the big department stores, like Jordan's and Filene's, could be completely out of the key toy of the year and yet Slokie's would still have it. It was magic in the sheer volume of the toys inside, tiny as the place was."

"How tiny?" Cossima, the tiny one, asked.

The Old Man pushed his chair back onto its two rear legs, looked up, and scoured his memories for facts. "Well . . . understand, I haven't been in there in . . . pushing fifty-five years or so now, but I think it must have been maybe . . . oh . . . twelve or thirteen feet or so across. Yes, that was about it, I think, twelve or thirteen feet across. Certainly not more than eighteen feet across, anyway, counting the space of the shelves that were filled with toys.

"It was divided into two sections. On both sides of the left-hand section, where the front door was, and in front of you were toys on shelves all the way up to the ceiling. On the right side of that area, too, sitting on the floor, was a glass case with various goodies, a sort of stand with baseball cards, gum, candy and such, the cash register, and an opening to the other half of the store. Old Slocum never let *anybody* into that half. At least neither I nor any of my friends were allowed on that side, and we were all pretty regular customers. It wasn't barred or anything; it's just that if you tried to wander to that side you would find Slocum, himself, barring the way. No matter where you thought he'd been standing, he'd beat you to the gap. For that matter, the plate glass window on that side was blocked by something or other. Or maybe it was painted dark. Hard to remember, at this point in time."

The Old Man laughed again. "It was a widely held theory among my then peers that on that other side was an interdimensional portal and that *this* was why Slocum never ran out of toys and never let us back there. Nonsense, of course."

Paying the bill and standing up, the Old Man said, "Time to get back on the road, brats."

All three started to scramble for the car, but Patrick was the one with the presence of mind to call out the time-honored and sacred cry: "Shotgun!"

"Grandpa?" whined the two girls with a single voice.

"He called it; he's got it. Now shut up and get in the car."

"But I'll get carsick," claimed Juliana.

"Nah; after pigging out the way you did you'll be asleep within half a mile of leaving the parking lot."

Indeed, bellies full to bursting, both girls had fallen asleep within twenty minutes of leaving the restaurant.

Half an hour after that, however, both the girls began to mumble and moan in their sleep. This had happened before, more than once, on trips that took the crew north past the town of New Market, Virginia.

"Females are odd," the Old Man told his grandson, who remained awake. "I do not understand the mechanism of it—I doubt any man can—but they seem somewhat attuned to a different reality. They know things that they should not know or, at least, that no one has told them. And they know it all together. Think, for example, of the drop in birth rates everywhere in the world. Here we claim it's the result of birth control and education of women and girls. But what explains the Islamic world, or Africa? No, the women—or their bodies—have simultaneously decided to have fewer kids. And we haven't a valid clue as to why.

"And it hardly stops with reduced birthrates."

They passed a dog, patiently standing by the side of the highway for a safe opportunity to cross over. That sparked a thought in the mind of Patrick, riding up front. He spared his sisters a glance before asking, "Tell me about the dog, Grandpa."

"Which dog?"

"You *know* which dog."

"I suppose I do. My boxer, Suzy?"

"Yes, that one, please?"

"Well, she was supposed to be a male. My uncle, the cop, took it upon himself to provide his sisters' families with one dog. Period. If your dog ran away or died he was not going to buy a second one.

"I was, I suppose, two and a half or three, but I can still picture the enclosure where the family that had bred their own female boxers kept the puppies. It was in a corner. The walls were a dark knotty pine, much darker than the knotty pine in my grandmother's kitchen that I wrecked; did I ever tell you about that? No? Well, maybe later.

"In any case, my uncle William and I walked in and the family opened the gate to that enclosure to let a veritable sea of boxer puppies pour forth. They were all cute, of course, but there was a little female and between us it was basically mutual love at first sight. She was tiny, easily the smallest of the litter, but she knocked me over on my back, even so, climbed onto my chest, and proceeded to give my face a good washing. Maybe I needed it; I don't know.

"Uncle Billy tried to prod me to another dog, a male, but—and I can still hear my probably not quite three-year-old voice saying it— I answered, 'No Unca Billy; I already foun' my own frien' doggie.'

"And so it was; she became my dog and I became...well... approximately, her baby. We were inseparable for the next two years.

"Then kindergarten started and I wasn't able to be with her all the time. No matter, she was always waiting for me outside the school gate when kindergarten, and later first through third grades, got out. Then we'd walk home or maybe go to the beach, or M Street Park, or down by Farragut Circle to play before going home."

Suddenly Cossima screamed, "Noooooo!" and sat bolt upright.

"What's the matter, Cossie?" the Old Man asked. Cossima screaming was unusual; she was a gymnast and, for all practical purposes, knew no fear.

Or at least I didn't think she did, thought Eisen. *Well, barring the bees and such.*

She looked around like a trapped rat, obviously confused, until she realized she was safe and in her grandfather's car. After a few deep breaths, she said, "Nightmare. I was hurt...bleeding. They carried me to a filthy table...then I was being held down on a table by four big men...and somebody was trying to cut my leg off with a saw. WITH A SAW!"

"Hmmph. Must have been from some history talk or other I've given you. No matter, go back to sleep."

"Not a chance, Grandpa. I'll sleep when I'm in Boston. Yes, even though you *are* the only one I trust enough to sleep while riding with."

"Suit yourself, bratso. Any musical requests?"

"Billy Joel," she answered instantly.

"'Only the Good Die Young,' it *is*."

New Market spurred a set of depressing thoughts in the Old Man. Ignoring Billy Joel, he mused, *"Die young?" That civil war, compared to the one that's coming, would count as mere. No huge armies maneuvering across the countryside this time, if we can't avoid it, but a combination of Argentina's Guerra Sucia and 1980s Beirut, written across a continent and written by people with a much greater penchant for mass, organized violence than either Arabs or Argentines.*

And I have no idea if we'll be able to avoid it or how we even might. I don't think anyone does, because nearly everyone else who's even aware of the possibility is actively, albeit ignorantly, trying to cause it or looking forward to it with drooling chops. I wonder how many on the left know that, in the phrase, "zombie apocalypse," they are the zombies.

Billy Joel being, for the nonce, finished, and with the music off, the Old Man, as usual for these trips, tallied the votes on what they were going to see and do over the two weeks he was planning on spending in the Boston area.

"These are the options," he said. "Just think about them and then we'll go down the list of priorities and preferences: Gardner Museum. Museum of Fine Arts. Aquarium. Duck Boats. Freedom Trail, which is an all-day event, too, by the way, especially if we both walk it and stop for lunch. Quincy Market. Downtown shopping. South Shore Plaza, which is a large mall. Brant Rock. Southie. Fort Independence and Castle Island in Southie. Lexington and Concord Battlefield. Bunker Hill. USS *Constitution*. Plymouth. Plimoth Plantation . . ."

At that, Cossie piped up with, "I want to see the cows again at Plimoth Plantation."

"Hold your horses, shorty," said the Old Man. "Let me finish the possibilities. Italian food in the North End . . . geez, you know I don't even know what's still open. Durgin Park . . . oh, never mind; it closed permanently. Shithead city should have taken it over and kept it open but noooo. Aiming further afield, the 'cottages' of Newport, Rhode Island. Mystic Seaport. Salem, as in witchcraft . . ."

"I want to see Salem," interjected Juliana.

"Even though the witchcraft was bunkum and the witch trials complete miscarriages of justice?"

"Yes," she replied, "even though."

"Maybe, then." Continuing on, he added, "Boston Common, Public Gardens, and Swan Boats. Copley Square Library. Newbury Street fashion district—"

That elicited a groan from Patrick along with some exciting jumping in their seats and hand clapping from the girls.

"Boston Latin. Boston College. Harvard and Harvard Square. Harvard Museum of Natural History. Harvard Art Museums, especially the Fogg Museum. Harvard Museum of the Ancient Near East. Peabody Museum of Archeology. The Enchanted Village of Saint Nicholas, whatever is left of it, at Jordan's Furniture which, by the way, has nothing to do with Jordan Marsh."

Sighing again, the Old Man said, "I swear; I wish I could show the three of you the old Enchanted Village, along with the stores as they were, and the Old Arch Street Inn, where treason was plotted and where my mother and I used to eat after shopping in Jordan's and Filene's. Oh, well.

"So, Juliana, what's your first choice?"

"Newbury Street," she answered, without hesitation.

"In favor?

"Aye," answered Cossie.

"Opposed?"

Patrick scowled. "What's the point, Grandpa? I've already lost that vote."

"True; isn't democracy a bitch? Your turn, Patrick."

"Bunker Hill and the USS *Constitution*. They go together, right?"

"They do. In favor? In FAVOR?"

"Oh, all right," answered Cossima, "But only if he won't vote against my first choice."

"I won't," agreed the boy.

"Plimoth Plantation and the cows."

"Fine," said Patrick, with ill grace. Meanwhile, Juliana had kept quiet. She intended to trade her future agreements to get to go where *she* wanted to go.

"My turn," said the Old Man. "I want to see the Gardner Museum and you don't get a choice on that. Juliana? Your turn . . ."

The sun was long down and the traffic thinned out to near vanishing. Despite Cossima's words, she was dead asleep on the rear seat, as was her older sister, Juliana, the former with her head to the right, and the latter with hers to the left. Patrick had his seat leaned back and was equally dead to the world.

At least none of the kids were snoring.

Meanwhile, the Old Man drove on, more or less blankly, aware of the road with one part of his mind but effectively on autopilot with the rest.

West Virginia and Maryland were well and long behind them. Now came the interminable slog thorough Pennsylvania. Before hitting Scranton, the Old Man slid a Harry Chapin CD into the player and advanced the music to "Thirty Thousand Pounds of Bananas."

All right, he thought. *So I'm superstitious. So I'm really superstitious. No matter how bad the traffic around Scranton, how*

abominable the weather, how much ice there may be on the roads,
playing this song as I pass through has kept me alive and out of the
hospital so far. And I'm not going to go against obvious success.

There was a twenty-four-hour diner just off Interstate 88, west of
Albany, New York, that the Old Man knew served a good breakfast.
Better, the waitress was young and pretty. He'd let the kids have
whatever they wanted, but ordered light on the food, heavy on the
coffee, for himself. Thus, while a slow eater, he'd finished before them
and, given the coffee, stood, groaning, to find his way to the toilet.
The fact that all three of them had had their noses stuck to their cell
phones probably delayed their finishing.

"This whole getting old with backaches thing," he said, "means
that when my time comes, I intend to have a serious talk with the
Almighty." Taking out a credit card he passed it to Juliana, telling her
to, "Pay the bill if you can get the waitress's attention. In the
meantime, I need to hit the can. Don't talk to strangers while I'm
gone."

In the few minutes he was gone, attending to business, the three
set to talking in low whispers. "When do you think the accent will
come back?" asked Cossima.

"Which accent?" queried Juliana. "He's got two, no, three;
Brahmin and Southie, plus his usual non-accent."

"Doesn't matter," observed Patrick. "We've seen it before, first
tollbooth on the Massachusetts Turnpike and he's dropping Rs all
over the place."

"No," Juliana insisted. "Sometimes it's not until the second or
third or even fourth tollbooth. Remember, in western Massachusetts
a lot of them sound more like upstate New Yorkers than Bostonians."

"Betcha," said Patrick.

"What do you want to bet?"

"First, when do you think it will come back?"

She thought about that for a moment, then said, "I'll go long; fifth
tollbooth. You're betting the first one?"

"Yep."

"Cossima, what's your call?" Juliana asked.

"I'm with Patrick, first tollbooth."

"Okay, so which ever one is closest? For a dollar each. That means if you guys are right, I pay two dollars, one to each of you. If I am, you each pay me one. Is that fair?"

"Deal," said Patrick, offering his hand to shake on it.

"Deal," Cossima repeated.

"What's a deal?" the Old Man asked, having returned unnoticed from the toilet.

"It's a secret," Cossima said.

"Oooo, a secret. Well, I won't pry, then."

"Did you manage to get the bill and pay it, Juliana?"

"Not yet, Grandpa."

"Okay, then give me the card back and I'll pay it."

The four walked to the cashier's station where Eisen noticed they had some higher end chocolate bars—Godivas—for sale. He turned over his credit card, bought one bar, and walked the few steps back to where they'd been eating. The waitress, that same young and pretty one, was clearing the table.

"I'll put a monetary tip on the card," he told the waitress. "But it pains me that you have to pay tax on it. So—since no girl can resist chocolate—please take this to make up for the tax bite."

Smiling, the waitress answered, "You're right; we can't. Thank you."

"Very welcome," The Old Man replied, adding, "Now if only I were forty—even thirty—years younger, miss."

That got him a bigger and better smile, still.

"Age is only a number," the girl said.

"True," Eisen agreed, "but in my case it's a really high number."

In western Massachusetts the Mass Pike was actually a scenic and generally stress-free drive, with continuous trees behind neatly trimmed grass, few or, for long stretches, no billboards, and all of that over gently rolling terrain. It didn't become even slightly difficult until one approached the outer half-ring road around the landward sides of Boston, Interstate 495, while traffic became quite dense and often quite slow once one hit Route 128, the inner half-ring road.

The Old Man's back just kept getting worse. It wasn't anything he'd actually *done*, though, just the normal wear and tear of a pretty hard and energetic life.

Every time I do this it gets worse. The day's coming when I'll have to take the train. And lie down all the way. And that day's coming fast.

As they'd passed across the Massachusetts border, the Old Man thumbed his nose at the "Massachusetts Welcomes You" sign.

"I used to enjoy doing that more," he told the kids. "Back in the seventies and early eighties there used to be signs up at all the entrances to the state—at least all the ones I ever saw—threatening anyone who brought an unlicensed pistol into the state with a mandatory year in jail. The problem, from the state's point of view, was twofold, though there were three problems, in fact. In the third place, it deterred tourism, and Massachusetts makes a lot of money from tourism. And in the second place, it was sometimes hard to get a conviction. People accused, so I've been told, would demand trial by jury and the juries would often tend to nullify the law and vote not guilty no matter what the law and the facts. But in the first place, it isn't obvious that it did much, if anything, to deter crime.

"Oh, and remember not to say a word to the police about the guns I've got locked up in the trunk. We're going to New Hampshire if we get stopped by a cop. We're *just* passing through."

"Why should ... ummm ... I don't understand, Grandpa," said Juliana.

"In 1986, I think it was, Congress enacted a law, duly signed by President Reagan, to allow someone to carry his gun risk-free, even through anti-gun states, provided it was locked up, unloaded, and in an inaccessible part of the car. This was also the law that forbade putting more machine guns into the civilian stream of commerce, thus driving the price of those to astronomical heights. There'd been all kinds of silly crap going on before that, to include, so I understand, arresting people on aircraft with their guns checked as baggage."

"Oh," she said. "But you always carry a gun. Are you not going to on this trip?"

"Oh, I'll be armed, I assure you," he replied. "And I don't 'always' carry a gun. When I fly it goes into checked baggage and I carry a cane. Only deadly weapon, if you know what you're doing, you can get away with carrying on a plane, no questions asked.

"Let me tell you a story," he continued, "true story as it happens. The moral of the story is that you can get away with whatever you act like you can get away with.

"Once upon a time, maybe forty years ago, I took your grandmother to lunch at a restaurant in Chinatown, in Boston, the China Pearl. Number Nine Tyler Street. It's still there, I think. Huge, long staircase to get up to the restaurant. It was pretty good food; maybe we'll go there."

At the mention of his late wife a tone of grief crept into Eisen's voice. He deliberately suppressed it in favor of the more jovial tone he usually used around the kids.

"Well, I was packing, of course; a Smith and Wesson Model 659 in a Bianchi shoulder holster. I was wearing a very nice suit, an excellent gray herringbone tweed I'd bought at Kennedy's, downtown. It's not there anymore, sad to say; I'd take Kennedy's over Brooks Brothers any day. It was a three piece, with a vest. Probably cost the equivalent of three or four thousand today. Fit perfectly.

"I didn't want to stain the suit so I took my jacket off. Forgot all about the gun."

The Old Man gave a little chuckle. "Your grandmother's eyes got really wide and she tried to tell me my gun was showing. There was, after all, that mandatory year in jail to worry about. And she'd seen the signs more than once.

"I realized three things, more or less instantly. One was that my pistol was, indeed, showing. The other was that if I put the jacket back on, people would know something was wrong and the cops would be along to arrest me in minutes. The final thing I realized was that I was young, clean cut, fit, tanned, and wearing an expensive suit, so anybody who saw the gun, provided I acted perfectly normal, would assume that I was either an undercover cop or a no-doubt properly licensed Mafioso.

"When I paid the bill an hour and a half later, the waiter tried to get me to take the 'police discount.'"

The kids all howled with laughter over that one.

"You're not serious?" said Juliana.

"Oh, yes, absolutely serious. But, since my uncle the cop never took the police discount, I figured I shouldn't either. I'm sure the waiter decided at that point that I was a properly licensed Mafioso. Your grandmother was so breathtaking, too, that I could see someone taking her for a high-end gun moll."

"Hey, Grandpa," Juliana asked, "shouldn't we have hit a toll booth by now?"

"They don't have any more toll booths," he replied. "You probably missed that because you were all dead asleep the last couple of times we came. Why?"

"Oh, no reason." *Dammit.* "How do they collect the money then, or is it free?"

"Free? In Massachusetts? The state give up the chance to hold you upside down and shake you until money stops falling out of your pockets and onto the ground? Never gonna happen; they take pictures of your license plates, get your address from your state DMV and then bill you. The bastards."

"If you dislike Massachusetts so much," asked Patrick, "why do we keep coming here?"

"In the second place, because Boston probably has the greatest level of culture, *per capita*, in the world but, in the first place . . ."

"Yes?"

"Because no matter where I've travelled, where I've lived, it's still where I'm from. It's still home."

As the traffic continued to thicken, Juliana looked out the window at the scenery. Her mind wasn't really on it, though. Instead, she was thinking, *Another trip to Grandpa's hometown. I don't know why he does it, it makes him so angry to see the changes, all his favorite familiar spots gone forever. And now, with our grandmother, his mother and the last of his aunts gone, I know it's changed for him completely. And yet, still, he comes back.*

He describes Boston as a magic place when he was growing up, the department stores, five or six of them that I know he's mentioned, Christmas shopping, common restaurants that were still really special, lights on the Common, which I guess they still put up. But it's not those things; I know better. He misses his mother, his own grandmother, his uncles William and Thomas, his aunts, Maggie, Lucy, Grace, and Celia. And, of course, his dog. Even his wife, they were first married in Boston, and he probably feels closer to that up there.

Yes, I suppose he keeps coming back because this is where he remembers them all best.

Or maybe that's half the reason; we count to him a lot, too. He wants us to know our roots and maybe continue to love the city for him after he's gone to join his ancestors. And he lives through us a little, too, when we see something new just as he first saw it when he was a kid.

Do I like it? A lot of it I do. He picks good restaurants and indulges me when I want to dawdle over something, in particular at one of the museums. Indeed, I can't recall him ever hurrying us along on any of our trips unless we had a particular showtime—he calls it "LD time;" I don't know why—to meet. And I do like shopping the fashions. With a little luck he'll buy me something nice to take home with me. Well . . . very little luck, because he always buys each of us several things to take home, wherever he takes us.

Her attention was caught by a McDonald's sign at one of the service plazas along the Massachusetts Turnpike. She wasn't hungry, but did feel the slight stirring in her bladder.

"How far to Lulu's house?" she asked.

"Bit over an hour," Eisen answered, "If the traffic doesn't jam up. Are you already hungry?"

"No, but I could use a trip to the bathroom."

Wordlessly, he turned into the plaza, then eased into a parking spot. "The rest of you brats go with your sister, and empty out. While it's a theoretical hour to my cousin's, traffic here can back up in an instant. I'll be here waiting when you get back. *Watch out for cars!*"

The sun was already about half up to noon when the Old Man took a couple of rights and eased his car onto the street leading to where his cousin, Lulu, and her husband, Sully, lived.

Interlude

Her parent had to help the new Q'riln and her cube—she being young and weak, both, and the silvery, crystalline cube brand new, hence with little power—to establish her own portal, through the web, to her own planet. The mechanism of the opening of gates was the cube, descendent or clone of the missionary cubes that had arrived some thousands of years before. They were allegedly grown in various places around the planet. The process was very secret; even her parent knew nothing of the inner workings.

It was the cubes, too, them and the other shapes in which they appeared, which synthesized the ambrosia, the *juice*, that made life, for a Q'riln, truly worth living.

The cube interacted directly with the Q'riln's nervous system—indeed, it was partially organic, itself—apparently drawing energy from the body to perform its various functions. The newly weaned Q'riln lacked that energy. This is what required the mother to also touch the cube, adding enough of her power to it to activate the gate. Upon the touching, the mother felt power flow from her own cube to her daughter's.

Mother, herself, would be heading back to her own foraging ground as soon as her daughter had departed the home world.

There was an inviolable rule, no more than a single Q'riln—the word meant "huntress and gatherer" in their own language—per planet except for home. Rather, it was one of two inviolable rules, the other being that the Q'riln must return to her own planet to breed, because, in the first place, this was where all the semi-sentient males were and, in the second, no one would want to be so much as seen with a male outside of breeding time.

The gate appeared in the air, an initially shimmering oval of about seven feet in height, and perhaps a bit over three across, the bottom hanging a few inches above the ground. The mother mentally worked with the daughter's cube to clear the shimmer so as to see the vestibule, and then to move the gate on the other side of that vestibule, the net's nexus, to a likely looking spot.

The spot chosen for the far side of the gate was at an area by a small ocean that fed into a larger one, which fed into the planet's world sea. Her mother chose this spot for her because of the extremely powerful waves of anguish that came from that general area, a sure sign of incessant warfare or some other mass suffering, plague, perhaps, or slave raids on an unusually large scale. There would be more than enough psychic anguish for the cube to harvest for the young Q'riln to feast on, without having to try too hard, while she built her powers and her cube's.

The natural shape of the Q'riln was vaguely insectlike, an oval body, hairy, with five equally hairy jointed legs and three shorter arms, each ending in a different kind of grasping member. The five lower limbs came in two classes, one of which could do double duty as a tail for balance while running. Her three eyes rode atop stalks, which were evenly spaced about her tripartite mouth, at the juncture of the lips. They were capable of seeing in darkness that no unaugmented human could hope to see in.

The gate itself, and its vestibule, served four main functions. In the first place, until fixed in place it could be moved around a bit to get the lay of the land as well as the shape of the prey. Secondly, it served to transport the physical Q'riln to the planet. Thirdly, using the shape of the prey as model, it modified the shape of the Q'riln to fit in nicely with the dominant species. It could also do very specific changes on demand. The Q'riln could choose to obtain the appearance of a male or a female, for example, and could set its age and apparent level of physical fitness. The process of shape shifting was, however, extremely unpleasant, and the more so as the shape varied from the natural shape of the Q'riln.

The vestibule demanded power as its payment.

Finally, when there was enough power in the cube, multiple gates could be opened to ease foraging by cutting travel time.

Once it had enough *juice,* the Q'riln's cube could also do what the gate did, shape-shifting-wise.

"This one is going to be very bad," advised the mother. "I'd tell you not to take it, to petition the Congregation"—the assembly that passed for a government among the hyper-individualistic Q'riln—"for a different planet, except that the feeding on this one will be very rich, indeed."

"I can handle it, Mother," the young one said. "I shall make you and the Congregation proud."

"I am sure you will, child. Now take the cube and go to your new grazing and hunting ground."

The change had been, indeed, agonizing, with three of her legs and one of her arms having to be absorbed into the new body, a changeover from fur-covered chitin to soft skin and hair, realignment of organs to produce two ridiculous lumps on her chest, and warping of her exoskeleton into internal bones, among myriad other, lesser changes.

The Q'riln had screamed and screamed throughout the process.

The spot her mother had picked for her to begin her independent life was only a few hours' walk from a major river. She consulted her cube and was informed that the river was called the "Dâmbovița" in the local tongue. Moreover, the town from which she was receiving already so much energy was called "Târgoviște." The cube further suggested that she get closer to the town.

It never occurred to ask the cube how it knew all this. Cubes just knew a lot; it was common knowledge.

She followed the cube's advice. With each step closer to the town, she received even more ambrosia than from the previous step, each jolt carefully refined by the cube into something that made her steps as light as the tufts that grew from a food plant on her home world, picked up and carried on the wind. And then she saw it, a rising forest of . . . no, not trees. What were they, she asked the cube.

"Mistress, they call them, locally, 'stakes,'" answered the cube. "They are a fairly frequent method of execution in this part of this world, as well as some other parts."

Oh, it was wonderful! She watched, enthralled and enriched, as a short and plump female of the local species had a stake driven up her reproductive organs, then out one side of her right shoulder. Even better, one of the infants, likely the woman's own, was then forced onto the stake. She screamed as the baby screamed, then both screamed still more as the stake was lifted to the vertical and placed into a hole in the ground. The female slid down the rough bark to a cross piece, and the baby to her mother's shoulder. Both screamed and suffered gloriously. A team of the locals then proceeded to fill the hole with rocks, dirt, and wedges of the local wood to hold the stake upright.

It was better than wonderful, unlike insects pinned for display, in this case the local species...

"They are called 'humans,'" said the cube. It vibrated even more vigorously than it had when they'd given the Q'riln's father the death of a thousand cuts.

...continued to wriggle and wave their arms and cry out for an aid that never came. Indeed, the only aid they got was in the form of 'misery loves company,' as still more men and women and children and babies went up on stakes.

In all, there were thousands, so many thousands of foodcreatures writhing in wondrous anguish.

"And they'll be suffering for days," said the cube. "I shall eat my fill for us both."

Chapter Two

I'm drawn to New England because that's where my roots are,
and I miss it. I come from many generations of New Englanders,
and so, in my writing, I've been drawn back there to the landscape
and the light and the type of personality that's revealed.
—Elizabeth Strout

Braintree, Massachusetts

The Old Man awoke in a spare bedroom of his cousin's house, in
something highly analogous to agony from an abused back, the result
of his roughly thirteen hours driving his car coupled with two hours
still sitting in not especially comfortable—and certainly not lumbar-
supporting—seats.

"I've *got* to do something about my back," he said with a groan.
"Well, nothing to be done about it now. Time to get the brats
moving."

Breakfast went pretty quickly, as breakfasts will tend to when
they're really good. The kids were ready to go within fifteen minutes
of finishing that.

"You get to ride on the subway today," the Old Man told them.
After the "Weees!" and similar expressions of boundless joy had died
down, and he had them strapped into the car, he said, "Okay,
geography test. I hope you weasels took careful notes.

"Where, Cossima," he began, "is Boston?"

"The center of the known universe," answered the youngest girl,
"at least according to Bostonians it is."

"Correct. And this is why they call it . . . ?"

"The Hub!"

"Very good. Now, Patrick, where is the very center of The Hub?"

"Roxbury," he answered, without hesitation.

"And what do we find *north* of Roxbury, Juliana?"

"The South End, of course, because everyone knows that the South End would have to be north of the actual center."

"Precisely. Now, Cossima, what is north of the South End?"

"East Boston," she replied.

"Very good. Now for extra points, where is the North End?"

"South of East Boston."

"Which is, again, of course, exactly where one would expect, right?"

"Yes, Grandpa," the girl replied.

"Okay, Patrick, what school is on School Street?"

"There isn't any."

"Very good; Juliana, what court is on Court Street?"

"No court, Grandpa."

"Also good. Cossima, back to you; what dock is at Dock Square?"

"No dock, Grandpa."

"And, Patrick, what body of water fronts Water Street?"

"Maybe a small puddle if it rains, otherwise none, Grandpa."

"I can see that you brats have captured the very Platonic essence of Bostonian geography. Let's work on accents. Repeat after me: *Cah, Pahk, Bah, Beah...*"

Braintree MBTA Station, Braintree, Massachusetts

"Yea, though I walk through the Valley of the Shadow of Death," thought the Old Man, *"I will fear no evil,"* for a Sig P365, with modified magazine spring for twelve rounds, plus one in the chamber, sitteth in my right pocket and a spare mag of another twelve resideth in my left. Moreover, stuck in the small of my back is an even smaller Walther PPK, in .22, with an Itty-Bitty suppressor, just in case.

Behind the thought was the now-slowing red, white, and silver painted subway train pulling into Braintree Station. The Old Man just didn't trust public conveyances, neither the crews, nor the passengers, nor the buses, street cars ("trolleys," locally), and trains, themselves.

He'd paid for two CharlieCard passes, good for a week, for himself and Juliana. The two littler ones rode for free.

Funny, as a young man I never gave any thought to the risk of a mugging on the subway. Is it the paranoia of old age in action here, or the paranoia of defending my brood of grand-brats? No matter, the fact is that I am prepared to defend my brood of brats and look far too well to do and even distinguished for the police to even think about stopping me to see if I am packing. Besides, better to be tried by twelve than carried by six.

The train stopped with a hiss of brakes and a *whoosh* of opening doors. He hustled the kids in and directed them to seats.

One of the advantages, he thought, *of picking up the train at Braintree is that you get to pick your defensive terrain while the train's still empty. Jesus, I have become paranoid, haven't I?*

"We've got ten stops to go to get to Park Street," he announced. "I'd get us off at Downtown Crossing, what used to be called 'Washington Street,' but since the closure or changing of the two department stores, Filene's and Jordan Marsh, I'm not sure how that station works anymore."

The doors *whooshed* shut again. Almost immediately the train began to move forward and to pick up speed.

"Is it okay to stand, Grandpa?" Patrick asked.

"Sure, but it's a bit of a skill, not too different from riding a surfboard. Unlike a surfboard, though, you've got those metal poles to hang onto. So go ahead but keep a good grip. You'll see more that way, anyway."

All three of them, then, stood up, uncertainly and unsteadily, took death grips on the silver poles, and began to enjoy the ride.

Weeeeee! thought Cossima.

Boston Common, Boston, Massachusetts

Down in the underground parking garage, someone male walked that little bit too close, causing the Old Man to nonchalantly slip his right hand into his trouser pocket. Cossima was the only one to notice it.

"Why do you do that, Old Man?" she asked, as soon as there was no one close enough to hear.

"Do what?" he asked, innocently.

"Get ready to shoot anyone who gets within ten feet of us?"

"Because I'm not as quick as I used to be? Because I'm paranoid? Because better safe than sorry? Besides, these folk are so unused to people carrying concealed that it would never occur to them that I'm reaching for a pistol. Moreover, it's not anyone. Were it a girl I'd flirt rather than grab my pistol."

She just shook her head, repeating his, "Paranoid. And flirt."

"Guilty on both counts," he admitted. "Come on, let's go topside. And stop worrying about my being paranoid.

"There's a common myth," the Old Man said, as they emerged from Park Street Station onto Boston Common, "pardon the pun, that they used to hang witches and Quakers here on the Common. Didn't happen or, at least, not often. The executions used to be down by Boston Neck, on what were called 'the common lands,' hence the confusion, which was southwest of here. We're not sure anymore exactly where the gallows was, but it was somewhere near where Holy Cross Cathedral stands now.

"The town was almost an island then, and the Neck was really narrow, about one hundred and twenty feet across. It had an earth and wood wall and fort, and a gate. The gallows was on the other side of the wall."

"Pretty brutal people," Juliana observed.

The Old Man nodded, slightly. "It was a brutal time, yes. But I would not judge them, were I you. People are entitled to be judged in accordance with their own place and time. Moreover, who knows; maybe there was a witch or two in amongst them."

"Grandpa! You know you don't believe in witches!"

"This is New England," he replied, with a shrug. "Steven King doesn't set his books mostly in New England for no reason."

"You're laughing at me!" Juliana exclaimed. "You're laughing at me because I *do* believe in witches!"

"Yes," he agreed with a smile. "Now let's walk down to what used to be Washington Street. Ah, but first . . ."

He led them to a small stand which sold souvenirs and such. "One item each," he said.

They each settled on sweatshirts, two of which, for the two girls, read, "Love that Dirty Water."

"You know," said Eisen, "the slogan is from the song, 'Dirty Water,' that we sang in the car. The song comes from the Charles River, which is pretty clean now, though I'm not sure I'd care to drink it, but was an appalling flood of dangerous industrial chemicals, untreated human waste, gasoline and fuel oil, and just about any other pollutant you can think of. It still can get pretty brown after a hard rain but they've mostly cleaned it up. Hell, you've seen it from the car, and more than once."

"I remember," said Cossima. "Looked fine to me."

"You should have seen it fifty or sixty years ago," her grandfather said. "Okay, let's head to the shopping district. For what it may be worth, these days."

The four made a quick dash across Tremont Street, then passed onto Winter Street with the Capital One Café to the left and a small branch of Bank of America to the right. Winter Street was purely pedestrian now, with brick replacing the asphalt of the road, itself laid over cobblestones, and with stone strips marking where the sidewalks' borders used to be.

He noticed that Frank's Custom Tailoring was still in business. Though not especially old—it had been founded in 1974—it was one of the few places in the city one could have something like true bespoke clothing made.

They teed out on Downtown Crossing, formerly known as "Washington Street" or, as he liked to think of it, *The corner of Jordan's and Filene's*. It wasn't until they reached that area that anyone realized how quiet it was there, compared to the cacophony of the traffic elsewhere in the city.

Sadly, Filene's was merely a shell, gutted from the inside, the bottom four floors filled with an Irish, as in from the Republic, department store, Primark, then built up and up, above that, and stuffed to the rooftop with condos, while Macy's had demolished most of Jordan's and chopped several floors off the one building they let stand. On the other corner, opposite Macy's, was what remained of Gilchrist's, now a mall bearing the name, "The Corner."

He directed the kids to the inside of Macy's by the main entrance on the corner of Summer Street. The makeup department began right on the other side of the door. An escalator led from that floor on up.

Cossima noticed the old man straining to keep from slipping his hand into his right pocket.

"You want to hear a story about your grandmother?" he asked, careful to keep from choking at the mention. "It has to do with this makeup department."

"Sure," said Juliana. "Why not?" asked Patrick. "Yes," said Cossima.

"Good enough. This was back when it was still Jordan-Marsh. One day your grandmother needed to be made up for a formal event we had to go to. My mother made her an appointment to come here for it. They used to do it, still may, for all I know, for free as a sort of advertising thing.

"I dropped her off at the door, then went to find a parking garage farther down Washington Street, which wasn't pure pedestrian at the time. By the time I walked back to here, the girl doing the makeup was about a quarter done. There was a solid wall of people, literally hundreds of them, standing around your grandmother, just watching this incredibly beautiful girl get made more so.

"I'm pretty sure she found the attention appalling. She was even more shy than she was beautiful."

"You still miss her badly, don't you, Grandpa?" said Patrick.

It took Eisen a moment to answer, and even then his voice was the essence of sadness and pain. "More than words can convey, every day and almost every minute . . . nothing to be done."

Changing tone, he then said, "Let's go see what this establishment has for a toy store. I'm sure it's crap. And then, lunch?"

"Where?" Juliana asked.

"I'd prefer Durgin Park but it's been terminated with extreme prejudice. The Old Arch Inn is gone, too. I'd consider walking to the Parker House. It's quite good, as I recall, but also quite pricey. Let's not be greedy; we can walk to Number Nine Tyler Street and eat at the China Pearl."

"This time, Grandpa," said Patrick, "leave your jacket on."

"Why?" the Old Man asked. "I keep my pistol in my pocket or in the small of my back now. They've gotten smaller, you know."

Braintree, Massachusetts

He sniffed the air then, picking up the distinct aroma of yet another cousin-cooked expansive breakfast. "No, they'll be up for that already. My job is to hustle them through breakfast, then get them in the car and we're off to . . . well, let's do the drive- and walk-around in Southie today. See the old church, the houses we lived in, Big and Little Broadway.

That last distinction referred, respectively, to West and East Broadway. The former was "Big" because the larger stores, the bulk of the banks, most of the restaurants, and the theater with the sticky floor from generations' worth of spilled drinks had all been there. "Little" had also been heavily commercial, but with smaller establishments, formerly Quinn's Fruit Stand, Slocum's Toyland, the local branch of the public library, Victory Meats, The A&P, more formally The Great Atlantic and Pacific Tea Company, a grocery chain and at one time the world's largest retailer, the odd hairdresser and barbershop, more than a few local bars, Federico's Bicycle Shop (though that was technically a little bit off Broadway), that kind of thing.

That was all in the past, though; hardly any of those businesses remained.

Indeed, in thinking about it, the Old Man had to admit, *You know, the old library may be all that's left. Hmmm . . . thinking about it, I'd best look into parking. Fewer people there now, but more adults, hence more cars, hence . . . nightmare fuel. Double hmmm; I'd better call.*

The phone rang only once before he heard, "Gate of Heaven/Saint Brigid's, Karen speaking."

"Hi, Karen," Eisen said, assuming an accent somewhere between Southie and Brahmin. "You don't know me from Adam but I used to live across the street from the Gate of Heaven. I've got my grandchildren up here, to keep them in touch with their Southie roots, and I was wondering if it would be possible to park in the lot where the Poor Clares convent used to be, at the corner of I and Fifth Street. I had in mind parking and then covering the highlights of Southie on foot. I'd be more than happy to make some donation to the church . . ."

"Well, those spots are all rented," she answered, "But if you just want it just for one day in the daytime, sure, no problem. Not that we'd turn down a donation, mind. The churches don't maintain themselves, after all and, despite the millions poured into it, the Gatey still needs work."

"Great! I'll be pulling in about nine-thirty. Mail the donation to the parish offices? Say, twenty dollars?"

"Sure, that would be fine."

Boston, Southeast Expressway, Northbound Lane

The Old Man barely glanced right, then began easing the white Avalon off of the expressway and onto Morrisey Boulevard. He said, "Now if you'll look to your right, you will see the latest rendition of one of the least credible lies ever told by a nun. That blue splotch on the gas tank is Ho Chi Minh, in profile, the leader of North Vietnam during the key parts of the French Indochina War and our war—well, campaign, really—in Vietnam. The original was another gas tank, with the same design. A Catholic nun, one Sister Corita, pretty obviously in sympathy with the communists, painted it. Personally, I consider it giving aid and comfort to the enemy and would have liked to have seen the bitch stood against a wall and shot.

"Note, here, that I admire Ho Chi Minh, communist or not. But the nun I loathe."

South Boston, Massachusetts

"It used to be a lot easier," the Old Man said, "driving through South Boston. There were more people but more of them were kids, and the rest mostly working class, so there were a lot fewer cars and almost none during the working or school day. Driving was almost never one way; the streets hadn't been narrowed by parking on both sides."

He steered the Avalon left, off of Day Boulevard, across the gap between the green strips fronting the beach, then right onto Columbia Road. Traffic was light, what with most of the Yuppies who had in recent years come to infest South Boston out working downtown or within striking distance of Route 128.

The Avalon went two more blocks to Hamlin, where he took a left, then another left on Eighth and a right on Winfield. Winfield was entirely row houses, uniformly well kept up, with narrow alleys between them.

"I couldn't live here," Cossima said. "Too crowded."

"It's not as bad as you may think," the Old Man said. "There's a little yard down at the end of each of those little alleyways, and even Southie, densely packed as it is, has a lot of open green space, plus about a mile of beach *and* Castle Island, which isn't actually an island anymore, not in a long time. And people are, or at least were, emotionally close."

He took a right on Seventh, then another one on Sanger.

"Patrick, remember that picture of me you thought was you?"

"The one with the old-style fatigues and toy submachine gun?"

"That one. It was taken at Number Twenty Sanger, where my Aunt Lucy and her husband Pasquale Farulla—we called him 'Patrick O'Farrell'—lived when they were first married. He was from Southie, too; a part of Third Street used to be an Italian Enclave. May still be for all I know."

"Oh, wow," said the boy, looking left at Number Twenty, as they passed. "It hasn't changed at all."

"It was a nice little first floor apartment," said the Old Man. "Made nicer still by the presence of my Aunt Lucy, who was, if a little high strung, still a total sweetheart *and* a fine cook."

"We remember her, Grandpa," all the kids said, as one.

"Please continue to, all of your lives."

Gate of Heaven Church, I Street, South Boston, Massachusetts

They all piled out of the Avalon just south of the imposing, cathedral-like, Gate of Heaven Church.

"This parking lot," the Old Man said, "used to be a convent. Poor Clares, they were. Before that it was a school my grandmother attended, over a hundred years ago. Now it's just . . . this." He shook his head. "It was history, physical, manifest history, for generations. It should have been preserved and repurposed."

He found himself sighing again. *I seem to be making a habit of this.*

"Never mind; this is only one little loss among oh, so many. Let's go look inside."

Of the three kids, only the eldest, Juliana, had seen the inside of the church, and that had been for her great-grandmother's funeral mass, several years before.

"Wow!" said Cossima as she entered via the rear entrance, facing Fourth Street. Before them was spread a vista of gleaming white marble, old gold, carved wood, fine statuary, and an overall glimpse of what mortal man could imagine the other side of the doorway to Heaven might look like. "I never imagined..."

"Trust the Irish," said the Old Man, "to give all they've got when *The Faith* is at issue. It's actually not as old as you might think, given appearances. There was an older church at one time on this spot but this one only goes back to the 1930s."

He led them in genuflecting, for him a painful matter, given the appalling state of his back, hips, and knees, then led them forward, from the narthex, up the nave, and toward the altar.

"This," he said, gesturing, "was actually the last spot I saw the face of my grandmother, my mother, and my aunts Lucy and Grace. Someday, with luck, it will be the last spot you see me."

"Don't talk like that, Grandpa," the boy said. "Everyone knows you're too mean to die."

"There is that theory," he conceded. "Come on over here."

He led them to the right, to a place on the western transept in between a smaller assembly of pews and a very lovely statue of the Virgin Mary.

"When I was very little, we'd sit over there," he said, pointing to a central location just to one side of the nave. "But when it came time for formal religious instruction, you—all the little kids of about five—got moved here. Odds were poor you would be sitting with friends, too. So here you were, five years old, and for the first time maybe in your life you are involuntarily separated from your loved ones.

"Wasn't just me, I think." He pointed toward to the west, saying, "This statue of Mary was about the only comfort you had as a lonely and intimidated little kid in this huge and intimidating church, too."

"That's why you've always felt close to Mary?" Juliana asked. "Why you went to her statue in the church back home when our cousin Julia looked like she was dying?"

"Exactly. I've felt very close to Mary since I was five. Had enough, kids?" he asked.

They looked around before answering, gradually coming to

understand why the building should have been so intimidating to their grandfather when he was a little boy.

"The whole thing," Juliana said, "it's just so . . . so . . . so *much*."

"As I said before, you lived your life to the rhythm of the church back then," he repeated, wistfully. "Let's go."

From the Gate of Heaven they walked back to I Street.

"That one, over there to the right of Minnie Court, Number 110, is where I was a young boy," the Old Man said. "Number 106 was where *my* great-grandmother lived, but she died before I was born. To the right from 110 were a bunch of mostly Federicos—yes, as in the Bike Shop—and, when married, for some of them, their husbands and kids.

"You would have to see it to believe it, but, trust me here; Federico girls don't start to age until several days after they've died. They both trend good-looking and they *stay* young. Mind, my mother was better looking but she aged and they never did."

With that paean to the immortal Federico girls, the Old Man led them to the intersection of I and Broadway, stopping at the southeast corner. Pointing left, up toward what was known as "Pill Hill," he said, "Over there was where my friend, Brian Moakley, was killed by a truck while riding his bike. He was seven, if I recall correctly. School, the Benjamin Dean—that's another fine old building gone—gave us some time off to walk to his wake. He was a little coppertop, covered with freckles. I can still, even today, picture him clearly in his coffin, wearing his white first communion suit, the red hair just standing out from the white cloth—satin or silk, I suppose—of the coffin. I've looked for him online and found nothing. Someone really ought to remember. I suppose that someone would be me and, now, you.

"There's a very old Marine Corps boot camp yearbook in my library. It came to me from Brian. I think it was his uncle's. Make sure whoever inherits the books takes care of it."

Turning to face just slightly more to the left, the Old Man said, "Over on the other corner, back then, was a pharmacy. We called it 'Morrey's.' I don't remember if it had an official name. Next to it or—no, I think it was two doors up; it's hard to tell with all the facades having changed, and my memory getting vague—was Kostick's Deli. That's where I first got turned on to *halvah*, New York style cheesecake—food of the gods, that was—and the joys of an overloaded pepper loaf sandwich on a bulkie roll."

"Grandpa," asked Patrick, "what is a bulkie roll?"

"Hmmm...how to describe? Well, it's a regional, as in New England, variety of sandwich roll, derived from Jewish baking. It's got a satisfyingly durable crust, and is usually topped with poppy seeds, but is essentially just white bread inside. No, don't ask me how they make them."

"I wasn't going to," said the boy. "Can we...?"

"If I find a Jewish deli that serves all those things, yes, of course, we'll have some. Just try to stop me. Now look across the street. Just in from Broadway, along Emerson, were Tom English's pub or tavern, I misremember—and, no, I never did know how an Irishman gets the name English; rape, maybe?—Federico's Bike Shop, where I bought your grandmother her first bike, and the Krause and O'Toole Insurance Company somewhere in there. Farther up was 'Pill Hill.' They called it that because in the second place, it was a hill, but in the first place it was replete with doctors and dentists. I had two dentists on this side, Swibalus, who had a really attractive blonde wife who served as his assistant and receptionist, and with whom I flirted when I was seven and eight, and Walsh, who unquestionably saved my life when I was nine."

"A dentist saved your life?" asked Cossima.

"Oh, yes," Eisen answered, with a deep nod. "This guy was old time, so much so that, while he had a modern electric drill in his office, he also had a foot pedal-powered one. Oh, yeah; he really did.

"I had cellulitis as a result of an incompetent quack's pulling an abscessed tooth. Picture my cheek swollen to about five times normal size, maybe bigger, and growing. Penicillin, for whatever reason, wouldn't work. The modern dentists all told my mother to take me home, make me comfortable, and let me die."

"Let you *die*?" Cossima asked, eyes wide as saucers.

Eisen nodded seriously, saying, "Oh, yes. There was nothing modern dentistry could do, apparently. But old Walsh was *not* modern. He told my mother he could save me, but it was going to *really* hurt, because Novocain also wouldn't work.

"So every day, two or three times a day, for ten or twelve days, I had to go in, open my mouth, hang onto the dentist's chair and scream like a damned soul while he slashed the inside of my cheek and my gums with a scalpel."

"Oh, my God," said Juliana, looking mildly ill.

"No matter," he shrugged; "I survived it. And it definitely made me more or less immune to pain. But I can *still* hear my little cousin, Lulu, outside, screaming louder than I was, 'What are they doing to my Sean?' Let's turn east."

Thereupon, the Old Man stepped off to cross Emerson. Just before crossing, he said, "My Aunt Grace lived down there for many years. I had at least two decent fights there, though in one I was badly outnumbered and had to conduct a fighting retreat for me and my cousin, that same Lulu. In my less Christian moments, I would still like to find the two kids that jumped us and shoot them. Fortunately, so far I've been able to resist the urge."

None of the kids thought for a moment that their grandfather was joking; he was just the type to hold a grudge that long and, without making an effort to control himself, also the type to act on that grudge.

Thumbing in the direction of the battery of shops on Broadway between the intersections of Emerson and I, the Old Man said, "Fact is, I don't recall too much about these stores. I remember my mother telling me that, during the Second World War and rationing, that was where you picked up your lardy margarine masquerading as butter and the yellow pills you mashed and mixed into the stuff to make the masquerade a little less obvious. Also there was a package— that means liquor—store. I want to say 'Johnson's,' and . . . maybe . . . Maguire's Jewelry."

On the other side of Emerson, he continued with, "There was a heating oil company here, M&T. Hah; the sign is *still* there, so maybe they are, too. Also Kiley's real estate. There was a travel agency here, too . . . maybe All Points, though I suspect that all points led to Shannon Airport, in Ireland. And Kearn's Insurance was in there somewhere."

"A travel agency?" Juliana queried. "Where did working class folks get the money for much in the way of travel?"

The old man shrugged. "Pretty prosperous working class. They went to Ireland and Ireland alone. Think of it as a kind of *Hajj*. I suppose someone had to arrange flights back to the *auld sod*, after all."

"Hey, is that the same library?" asked Patrick.

"The one where the librarian tested me on *The Battle of Midway* and then gave me an adult library card at two and a half? Yes. We should—I should—go over and get a copy of the record, if they have it still."

The Old Man pointed again, into the middle of the street. "There used to be a streetcar that ran up Broadway. The tracks are, I think, still down there under the asphalt. I saw a section of it dug up when I was a kid and there they were."

They walked a few hundred more feet, the Old Man pointing to this and that, when they came to a pizza place, the Olympic.

"Wow, a pizza joint in deepest, greenest South Boston," said Juliana.

"What's weird about that?" the Old Man asked. "In the second place, it's not very green anymore. But in the first place, we used to have the IA, the Italian-American Restaurant, down on Third Street, that had excellent pizza. I think I mentioned that Third Street was something of an Italian enclave. You brats hungry?"

Whether they had been hungry or not remained an open question; the smell of pizza *made* them ravenous, though. They went in.

The pizza had been first rate. This meant, in addition, that lunch had been long. That, in turn, meant that the Old Man's back was a horror story when he stood up.

"It's the calcification of the ligaments in my spine," he told the kids. "May as well call it 'fossilization,' I suppose." Getting his back straight enough again to stand upright, like a human being, took a while and was, in addition, accompanied by a lot of muttered swearing.

Once he was able to walk upright again, the Old Man said, "Let's go look at the place where Slocum's was and then head back to the car. I'm about backed out and walked out."

"What's there now, Grandpa?" Patrick asked.

"I think—*think*, not sure—that it's some kind of gift shop or home decoration shop. At least that's what it looked like to me the last time I drove by."

"Well, so much for that theory," the Old Man said, looking in the window of the former Slocum's Toyland. It was not, as it turned out, either a gift shop or a home decoration shop. Instead it was a . . .

"Well, let's look it up," he said, pulling out his cell phone. "Aha . . . WHAT? They have a massage therapist? Be still my heart. Ah, but they want you to text for an appointment. Well, no problem with that."

His fingers flew over the phone's keyboard, asking for both the earliest appointment available and if they had a waiting room. "I have my grandchildren with me and they are very well behaved, especially when I threaten to drown them if they are not."

The answer came back very quickly. "Yes, we have a waiting room in towards the back and Dijana, our massage therapist, can fit you in for an hour in forty-five minutes. Will that work?"

"You betcha," the Old Man sent back.

"Okay, brats, let's go see if the library has records going back sixty-three years."

As it turned out, the library did have those records. The Old Man got a copy, nosed around a bit with the kids, commented that, "This building was something like eleven years old, very midcentury modern, when I first set foot in it. It's held up and held on rather well."

After consulting the time on his iPhone, he said, "Okay, let's head back across the street."

"Can I stay here for a bit, Grandpa?" Patrick asked. "You know how much I like to read."

661b East Broadway, South Boston, Massachusetts

As it turned out, Dijana wasn't quite ready when the Old Man and the two girls arrived. They went to the rear, to a small waiting room perhaps eight feet on a side, and sat.

Initially, the girls played on their own cell phones. This continued even after the Old Man was called to the massage room. Juliana considered telling Eisen, "and please don't flirt with the masseuse," but decided it was a hopeless cause.

Eventually first one and then the other of the girls lost interest in her phone and began staring at the rear wall.

"You see it, too, don't you?" Cossima asked.

Juliana nodded, while commenting, "If you mean a shimmering oval spot on the wall, a little bigger than Grandpa, I see it, yes."

Cossima, the fearless, stood up and walked to the spot, then reached out to touch the wall. Imagine, then, both her and her sister's surprise and shock when her hand and half her arm disappeared into it.

"Holy crap," said Juliana, "it's true. What Grandpa thought of this when he was a kid? It's true!"

"I'm going in," Cossima said.

"Don't," Juliana, the eldest, ordered. "Wait for Grandpa."

"Nah, he'll never let me go. I'm going in."

Shaking her head, Juliana said, "That whole gymnastics thing was a terrible mistake. You were bad enough before that but you're so much worse since."

"Keep watch," Cossima said. "Don't leave without me."

With that, the little girl lifted a leg up and stepped over and through the bottom of the oval, and then into . . . she didn't really know what, yet.

While, across the street, his elder sister was fretting and his younger one was exploring God knew what, Patrick wandered about the library, looking over the offerings and just trying to feel the connection.

So the Old Man really did have an adult library card when he wasn't even three yet. I'm not exactly shocked, but it does feel a little weird, even so.

Walking to the desk, inside of the doorway and to the right of it, Patrick asked if they still had *The Battle of Midway* in their holdings.

"No, young man," the librarian had answered after checking on her computer. "That one was sold off, as near as I can tell, more than forty years ago. We do have an historical section . . ."

"No," he'd replied, "thanks, anyway. It wasn't history I was looking for so much as a book my grandfather had read when he was very young, too."

He didn't mention how much younger. While his grandfather had been able to get the record of his first library card, it had only had a date of issue in the record, not his age at the time. For that one had to know his birth year.

"Sorry, then; why don't you look over in the juvenile section for something that might interest you?"

"I'll do that," Patrick agreed.

Interlude

The city floated on anti-gravity, among clouds and above a planet surfaced mostly by water. The denizens of the city came in many shapes, spoke many languages, and were from all over. The lingua franca of the city was Galactic Common II, which was at least minimally intelligible to speakers of Galactic Common I and Galactic Common III. The differences in the three were not so much in either vocabulary or grammar, but based on the sheer ability of vocal cords to make particular sounds.

The planet had just a few substantial islands, occasionally visible below, as were a rather larger number of coral reefs. The surface of the planet, itself, wasn't uninhabited, but the amphibious inhabitants had no more use for galactic society than that society did for them. The traded a little, here and there, for precious gems, especially glowpearls, some exotic seafoods, local art, and chemicals, going up, and waterproof finished products, generally of fairly high tech, going down.

A certain law enforcement agency of the Galactic Confederation made its headquarters in the floating city, largely because it was out of the way, but still only one jump away from a busy nexus of interstellar gates. This allowed a certain amount of control over comings and goings, as well as providing a reasonable degree of cover for necessary movements of the agency's employees. That it was far from the seat of power was a definite bonus.

"There's another Q'riln loose," said the department chief, looking much like an enormous ambulatory mushroom with clusters of oysterlike, blue eyes around its cap, and half a dozen evenly spaced arms ending in four-digit hands. The chief spoke in Galactic Common II to a pair of well-tested agents, standing easily in front of his desk. These were Topaz and her mate, whose name translated to "Mica." They were both humanoid, albeit a little larger than the human norm, with enormous eyes of green and gold, barely noticeable noses, and light blue skin. Some tendrils, graceful things, grew from their heads, as did full caps of something like yellow or golden hairy feathers.

"It's been loose for quite some time, but we just found out."

"It got through our interdiction and went through a gate on a planet called Earth or Terra or, like all the rest of them, something that, to the locals, means Home."

"Oh, dear," said Topaz. "One Q'riln can . . ."

"Wreck a planet, given time. If they just went around feasting on pre-existing misery, it wouldn't be such a problem. Sentient beings can almost always create enough sheer torment and anguish to keep any number of Q'riln fed. But . . ."

"They're never content with that," said Mica. "A greedy species; they'll start manufacturing trouble to keep themselves fat and happy."

"Precisely," said the chief. "What I want you two to do is to go to Earth—the fact that you're both approximately humanoid will help keep the shifting pain down—find the Q'riln, and terminate it."

"We have to *kill* it?" gasped Topaz. "I've never had to . . . we've never . . . Seriously? *KILL* it?"

"One of them we'd caught and deported back to their planet got loose again and went back to the planet it had previously been feeding on. It manufactured a nuclear war. Since then, the orders have come down to kill any Q'riln found off of its own home planet."

"A nuclear war?" said Topaz. "Well, in that case, I suppose . . . I suppose that termination is all that's left, isn't it? I still hate the idea."

"No matter what you hate," said the chief. "Just so long as you do your duty."

"What can we take with us?" asked Mica.

"No modern weapons. You'll have your teardrops"—artificial intelligences not dissimilar, so far as was known in principle or in practice, to the Q'riln's cube—"a primitive single shot pistol each, a sword and a dagger, each with elemental *forjin* in the blades, and a mobile Grade Five AI that we've already named 'Mary,' who will act as your child. She will grow, as needed and is equipped with a full suite of detection, decontamination, and unarmed self-defense capabilities."

"That's not very much to deal with when we're talking about a well-fed Q'riln," observed Mica.

"No, it isn't," the chief agreed, "but the Authority is getting very touchy about introducing 'inappropriate technology' to extremely primitive worlds. There's even talk of cutting off trade with the amphibians, below, the Shreee!%$^nnn, though we've sent a few crates of local marine springtails to certain key members of the Authority, to keep them on side. This place would be dreary, indeed, without trade with the amphibians. That's part of why this mission is important, too; if we can stop this Q'riln, then the Agency is enhanced with the Authority. If the Agency is enhanced, then trade is somewhat more likely to continue. Remember, too, that the sale of glowpearls pays about six percent—a very large chunk—of our budget!"

"We'll do our best, chief," said Topaz.

"I know you will. I've got to warn you in advance that this is a very dangerous and primitive world you're going to. You'll stop off at Subsector five, Department &^*, for immersion before you gate to Earth.

"Also," the chief added, "if it helps any, there's a large psychological hardship bonus in it for you after you've terminated the Q'riln."

Chapter Three

⌒⌒⌒

If you hear an owl hoot "to whom" instead of "to who," you can make up your mind that he was born and educated in Boston.
—Anonymous

661b East Broadway, South Boston, Massachusetts

Weird, thought Cossima, *does not* begin *to describe this. Whatever "this" might be. No matter; I am Cossima and I am afraid of nothing . . . except for bees, wasps, and hornets.*

"Here" was, indeed, weird. It was neither light nor dark, but a sort of twilight, lighter towards the down and darker toward the up. The floor was spongy, just a little, and, if there were walls, she couldn't see them. Several hundred glowing balls floated around above any level she could reach, even with a high jump. If there were any pattern to the balls, she couldn't discern one. She had the impression that any sound she heard was coming from elsewhere; it was distorted and distant.

Far and near, there were ovals, much like the one she'd come through, which was . . . she turned around completely to ensure it was still there.

Whew! Gingerly, she put a foot out to ensure it would penetrate the oval from this side.

But, in any case, there they were, the ovals . . . the . . . well, *doors, I guess they must be. I wonder . . .*

Suddenly, a hairy arm shot out from one of the nearer of the doors. A voice said, in an accent much like her grandfather's when he was in Boston, "Now where did I put that GI Joe?"

45

Automatically, the little girl crouched down to make herself as small and unnoticeable a target as possible.

There came a sound something like the crack of electricity, though tinnier and fainter. She looked toward the sound and saw one of the balls of light begin to change shape and color. Pulsating, it became a flat square, an oval, a rectangle, before finally settling on an elongated box, about a foot long and maybe three inches on a side.

As soon as the box was formed, it shot into the hand pushed through the other door, which hand grabbed the box and pulled it through.

"Holy crap," she whispered to herself.

Cossima thought she heard some conversation coming from the other side of that other door, but it was far too faint to make out, except for one sentence. Someone, not whoever had put their arm into this place, said, loudly, "Thank God!"

Again the arm—well, this time, *both* arms—came through the other portal, as the voice said, "I'm sure I put that last Chatty Cathy here . . . some— Aha, here it is."

Again, one of the light balls began to pulsate, to change shape, to expand, to contract, to spin and twirl until, finally, in the form of a box with a picture of a doll across the front, it flew across the twilit space into the hands sticking out from the door. Then it disappeared into the portal.

It was terribly difficult to get a sense of scale in this place, but Cossima's impression was that the box had been about two feet long.

Carefully, gingerly, she duck-walked to the door into which the boxes—*A GI Joe doll, that must have been; Grandpa has a few of those stuffed in a box in the garage*—and looked out. There, not as plain as day, rather fuzzy, in fact, she caught a glimpse of a woman seated on tall stool next to a cash register. There was a man with her, speaking in tones too low to hear.

Just in front of the gate, Cossima felt something uneven on the floor. She bent down and felt around, then picked up a metal disc.

A tiny silver coin, maybe a paper clip's worth? Still more weird and there look to be quite a few of them down there.

She tucked the one she'd picked up into a pocket and then gave what she could see past the gate her full attention. "Narrow?"

Cossima asked herself. "Check. Division in the middle? Check. Oh, jeez, that's about sixty years ago . . ."

At that point the man who had been talking to the woman at the register turned around and looked right at her. Three long strides and he was there, climbing a short stepladder. In another moment, his face—only his face—stuck through the door, causing ripples not unlike one might get from tossing a stone in a pond.

He looked directly at her, his face fierce. Despite the fierceness, when he spoke he whispered, "Go back where you came from, little girl; you do not belong in there!"

With that, Cossima turned and ran for the door she'd come through, stepping gingerly through it.

"You just left," Juliana said. "Like two seconds ago. Your foot popped out and disappeared just before you came back. Nothing there?"

"Something's there," the little girl said. "Something . . . I don't know what." She felt suddenly faint. "And I was there longer than that. I need to sit down, then I'll tell you about it."

Saying "If you weren't already married, Dijana, I'd propose on the spot," the Old Man came into the waiting room looking, feeling, walking, and talking a good deal more sprightly than when he'd gone in. Both girls stood up as if they'd done something terribly wrong. Juliana nudged Cossima with her elbow, saying, "Don't just stand there with your teeth in your mouth; tell him."

Instead of telling, Cossima walked to the portal which was invisible to the Old Man, put her arm right into the wall and said, "Now where did I put that GI Joe?"

In a fraction of a second, she withdrew her arm, clasping in her hand an absolutely mint GI Joe box. "America's *movable* fighting man," was emblazoned on the box in a rectangle at the lower right. This she handed over to a slack-jawed, nonplussed, utterly shocked grandfather.

"We need to talk, Grandpa," Juliana supplied.

The Old Man didn't really look at the box. Indeed, he let the hand holding it just drop. Instead, he reached up to touch the spot he'd seen Cossima's arm disappear into. It was solid, just another wall.

"Put your arm in it again," he said. When she did, he was able to put first his own arm, and then his head it. He looked briefly, then pulled his head out.

"It was real? You mean it was REAL? You're telling me this was REAL? Holy crap . . . real . . . it was real. Let's go get your brother.

"Tell NOBODY!"

Braintree, Massachusetts

His cousin, Lulu, and her husband were both out working. They had the house to themselves.

In the dining room, the kids gathered around the Old Man while he worked on his laptop, the laptop resting on an antique, white painted, round table. Looking up from his laptop, the Old Man held up the GI Joe and said to Cossima, "This is worth about four thousand dollars. That means about three weeks of college, I suppose, is paid for.

"Now the question is, what are we going to do with this knowledge. No, that's not quite right; we need to first figure out just what we know.

"So, Cossima, once again, go over everything you saw, felt, and heard."

The girl did, for the second time.

"Hmmm," said the old man. "GI Joe and Chatty Cathy. Let me check . . ."

Fingers flew over the laptop. "Aha, GI Joe means it is not earlier than 1964 on the other side of the portal you described. And . . . let's see, Chatty Cathy; she wasn't produced after 1965, though, Slocum's being Slocum's, people might expect him to have one stashed away for another year."

Cossima said, "He said so, Grandpa; the man who put his arms through the door said, 'I'm sure I put that last Chatty Cathy here somewhere.' Something like that, anyway."

The Old Man went to a Facebook group, Originally From Southie, and hunted around until he found a particular picture of the front of Slocum's Toyland. Out front, sitting in a folding chair, was a man.

Motioning Cossima over, her grandfather asked, "Does he look familiar to you?"

"Grandpa, that was the face in the other door."

"So we know where the other door is, for certain; it's here, only well in the past. And we can be pretty sure we're looking at a potential two-year window, I think.

"It's a pretty good time, back then. The United States is just getting heavily involved in Vietnam, and the war is still pretty popular. Well, it *stayed* pretty popular in Southie until we lost.

"Anyway, crime is fairly low, the streets are pretty safe, most places. Employment was high and unemployment was low, in fact and not just in statistics. And Boston . . . Boston was a great city to grow up in. And, yes, safer, then, too, than it is now. A *lot* safer.

"Would you like to see it?"

"Yes," said Cossima, "but the man in the other door—Mr. Slocum?—told me I didn't belong there."

"He might have been worried about competition," mused Eisen.

"I'm in," said Patrick.

"Somebody with some sense has to watch out for you," Juliana said, resignation replete in her voice. "What if we change something important and destroy our own universe?"

"That's a concern," the Old Man agreed, "at least in theory. I can see a few possibilities.

"One possibility is that what Cossima saw, and where we'd be going, is not, in fact, our universe, but some parallel one. In that case we could not possibly change ours.

"A second is that it is ours. But tell me, how could we change our universe so substantially, in the past, and even be here to go back to the past from our present?"

"I don't know," Juliana admitted.

"I think it's a given that we cannot change the past in any way that would change the present, or we couldn't have gone back to the past. Example; let's imagine there were some way I could save your grandmother. Now imagine that I tried. If I'd succeeded, then I'd be with her right now and we'd not have come to Boston. But since we have come to Boston, obviously enough I did not try or succeed in saving her."

"I guess," the girl conceded, with ill grace.

"There's another way to look at it, too. You may not be able to change the world, but you could screw it up for your own family or some other individual. Small events, small consequences. So we'd need to avoid that.

"And, then, too, there's the obverse of going back to save someone. I would want to use my time back there to make a lot of money. A lot. Trump-weeping-for-envy levels of wealth. How can I do that since, if I had that money, I'd never have bothered to go back?

"Easy; I'd set it up so the money was not in my hands until *after* we came back from our trip. Hence no temporal paradox. Yes, I think there's a very subjective element to the classic temporal paradox."

Finishing, he said, "Lastly, though chaos theory might wax lyrical about the end of the world from a crushed butterfly, I think it's a fraudulent notion. You make one little change and it changes everything? It changes everything when an entire world's facts are arrayed against it? Not a chance; it's simply outweighed. Physics forbids, as does logic. The world forces the—let's call it 'the path'— back to where it would have been anyway.

"Now, any other objections?"

"Other than stinging, flying insects, I'm not afraid of anything," Cossima agreed. "Count me in."

"All right," said the Old Man, "there's a lot that has to happen. For one thing I'm going to rent us a mail drop and find us a hotel room not too far away. Then we're going to go to the computer store to buy three more laptops. Yes, they'll be yours to keep. Then we're going to check into that hotel room so we can do our work there. Most days we'll go visit things in and around the city. But for the next three or, if necessary, four days we'll work on this. When our time here is done we all go back to Virginia and continue our preparations. And I'll need to go see a company I do some consulting for up in Vermont."

"This is going to be *so* cool," said Patrick. "But, Grandpa, how are we going to get through locked doors?"

"How do you think? We're going to break in."

"See?" said the boy. "I knew we came from criminals."

"Shut up, Patrick. Breaking and entering, to be a felony, requires the intent to commit a felony therein. Even assuming Massachusetts law counts the business as an occupied dwelling, which I doubt. We're not going to commit a felony; we're going sightseeing."

"Yessir."

"Oh, one other thing, Grandpa," said Cossima. She pulled the silver coin from her pocket. "There were a bunch of these scattered around the far gate. I didn't *see* any at the near one, but they might be there." She shrugged. "Honestly, I didn't even look."

The Old Man took the silver coin and examined it from all sides. On the front was a Saint George's Cross inside a wreath, all rather off center. Turning it over, he saw two shields, one containing another Saint George's Cross, and the other the Hibernian harp, complete with bare-breasted woman's bust, with a Roman number I at the top, flanked by two dots.

"Hmmm . . . this is *old*. Way out of my skill set to say just how old, but that it's old I am certain."

50 Royall Street, Canton, Massachusetts

The hotel was decent for the price, some two hundred dollars a night plus the usual outrageous taxes. Given what hotels were often used for, Eisen consciously decided to forego his usual flirting with the girl at the counter.

"We'll work here days, then go sleep at my cousin's in the evening," the Old Man said.

If the clerk thought it odd that three kids and one old man checked in without much in the way of luggage, she said nothing. Indeed, all they brought in was a single suitcase, which happened to be full of office supplies, though the clerk had no way of knowing that, and four computer bags. Had they not looked enough alike to be presumptively relatives, the clerk would probably have called the police anyway, just to be safe.

The Old Man divided up the work. "I want each of you to get on eBay. Juliana, your job is finding four outfits each, two summer, two winter, for yourself, Patrick, and Cossima. They must be 1963, 1964, 1965, or 1966 appropriate. Make sure your brother and sister approve what you order. Have them sent to the mail drop. You'll need to get the sizes before you start.

"Don't worry about me, I'll take care of my own clothes.

"Patrick?"

"Yes, Grandpa?"

"I don't want you to order anything yet, but search through eBay and online, generally, for currency. It must all be from *before* 1966. I won't say it has to be American, because you might find some bargains with foreign currency. Just remember that, even though most of Europe uses the Euro now, back in the 1960s Germany used the Deutschmark, Italy used the Lira, and France used the Franc. Then, as now, the United Kingdom used the Pound Sterling, though then it wasn't decimalized, the pound having twenty shillings of twenty-four pence each.

"Bookmark everything you find and then we'll go through it together."

"How are you going to pay for it?" the boy asked.

"I'll raid savings and retirement if I have to. But I probably won't since your grandmother left me a fair amount, too.

"Now, Cossima?"

"Yes, Grandpa."

"We're going to need ID once we get there. I want you to hunt through death records for the Massachusetts area for someone who died, as a baby, in 1915, and 1953 through 1956. If it's not obvious, we need a girl's death for the oldest and newest, and a boy's for the middle."

"I don't understand," she said.

"Back then," he explained, "records security in cities was awful and no office really talked to another. We're going to get birth certificates either now or when we go back, possibly both. If we do go for back then, the birth registry isn't going to know about what's in the death registry, because they never talk, so, with those, we can get social security numbers and I can get a driver's license. Got it?"

"Not really, but I can at least look for the records."

"Good girl! Spread it out, too; stay away from small Massachusetts towns, everybody knows everyone else in those; go for the cities there, along with southern New Hampshire and Maine, as well as Rhode Island and Connecticut.

"In the meantime, I am going to contact those people in Vermont I mentioned, order a parts kit for a Sterling submachine gun, and get an eighty percent complete frame for an M1911. And then I'll start work on assembling a list of everything we're likely to need that isn't as obvious as clothes, ID, money, and arms."

"Grandpa?" asked Juliana, the sensible one.

"Yes?"

"If it's so safe back then—you insist it was safe—why the armaments? Yeah, I'm not stupid; I *fired* your Sterling. You're not ordering a parts kit to be a club."

"Well...hon; it *is* safer back there than it is now. But if I could get away with it I'd be carrying a Sterling *here.* The short version, little one, is that I am getting something, a weapon, made up because I can, because it doesn't hurt anything to get it, and because, as your sister agreed in the garage under the Common, I'm paranoid."

"Hey, Grandpa," asked Patrick, "if there's a chance we get there in winter aren't we going to need winter coats?"

"Good point! Juliana?"

"I'm on it," said the eldest, "but this is a lot harder than you think."

"Why?" the Old Man asked.

"Because so much of this stuff is downright hideous."

"Nothing is hideous, Juliana, if it makes you blend in."

"I am *not* wearing that crap," Patrick said, vehemently. "It's totally hideous."

"But there's nothing else for boys on eBay from that time period," his elder sister insisted.

"Grandpa," the boy complained, "you *can't* expect me to wear green corduroy shorts with suspenders in public. You just *can't.*"

"No...no, I don't blame you. I wouldn't have worn that in 1965 even if every other boy in the city was wearing the same thing, which they were *not.* I suspect what's going on is that boys' clothes wear out, then get thrown away or given to the ragman. Yes, there were such things as ragmen; I can remember watching the horse and cart of one of them, the horse dumping a load on I Street back when it was still cobblestones. In any case, that means that what's left is what nobody would wear that their maiden aunt gave them. Picture the bunny suit Ralphie's aunt bought him in *A Christmas Story.*"

"Try Etsy, Juliana," the Old Man said.

"Now that's a little better," Patrick said after a few minutes. "At least it doesn't make me want to hurl. But there's not that much of it in my size."

"Suggestion, Juliana," said the Old Man.

"Yes, Grandpa?"

"Find the 1965 Sears catalogs, preferably the summer and Christmas ones, and see what boys were wearing then that we can find something like now."

"Good thought! I will."

"Okay," said Eisen, "at vast expense—mine—Juliana has acquired for us two Sears catalogues, one summer, one Christmas. I've made a phone call to an online acquaintance, one Heather Knight, down in Rhode Island. She does sewing, has patterns, and can get fabrics. So we're all going to board the car and drive to East Warwick, Rhode Island, to get you mob measured and outfitted, two outfits each, hot weather and cold.

"You can look at the catalogs on the way for some things you think you might like. So, boots and saddles, brats; into the car with you.

"And *bring* the Sears catalogues!"

The door was opened by someone Eisen knew from Facebook was not Heather. The confused look on his face, coupled to the quizzically tiled head, prompted the woman to say, "I'm Jo, Heather's . . . friend. I'll go get her. She'll be out in a minute."

"And very lovely, you are, too," Eisen said, and meant it. The woman was short-haired, but had fine bone structure and extremely cute ears. *Because just because a girl prefers girls it doesn't necessarily follow that she doesn't like a compliment from any corner.*

"Oh, Grandpa," whispered Juliana, "flirting with a lesbian is just too much."

"You think so," he whispered back. "Remind me to tell you about the hot blonde lesbian psychiatric nurse practitioner, paired up with a lesbian psychiatrist, back home. Although who was flirting with whom, in that case, was an open question . . ."

It was, indeed, a minute before Heather popped out from a back room, looking rather matronly and showing a wide, friendly smile.

She spoke with a good Rhode Island accent, showing more New England to it than had become the modern wont. "Are these the ruffians of whom you spoke, Sean?"

"The *same*. How long to outfit them?"

"I can do the measurements today for all three. Call it three more days to sew them. Do you want to bring them back to check and redo?"

"No, there's really no time for that. If things are a little off . . . well, they're supposed to be dressed more or less off the rack anyway."

"Let's get to it," Heather said. "This will be fun!"

"Can you FedEx everything to an address I'll give you?" Eisen asked.

"Sure, easy."

"We've brought some Sears catalogues. They've dog-eared the pages of things they like."

"Funny thing about Sears catalogues," Heather said. "They tend to be somewhat regional. Let me see these."

The kids passed those over and, in less than a minute, she had judged, "The Summer edition is Dallas. It will have a lot more western wear and less that's suitable here. Christmas is the Philadelphia edition, and that will be fine.

"Is this for some kind of costume thing or play?"

"Something like that," Eisen agreed, "but they're for more than one wearing."

"Okay, kids," said Heather, bending slightly and slapping her hands against her thighs, "let's look in the catalogue for things you actually *like*."

"I think I've got our dead people, Grandpa," Cossima announced, the next day, back in the rental room. "A whole family was killed in a fire in 1965. Six kids killed and three of them match our ages or close enough to them. But I'm having trouble with yours. Seems the parents weren't home."

"Sad and creepy, both; poor kids. Well, get their names and . . . I doubt it's possible but see if you can find social security numbers for the ones we'll be using."

"Grandpa," said the boy, "I think I've got a line on our currency, but how much did you want?"

"Thirty-five to seventy thousand pre-1966 dollars' worth."

"I only see one dealer who looks like he can do that, Sam's Coins of California. I think you had better call him, though. This is going to be serious money."

"Why him?"

"He seems to have a lot of older currency, his prices are lower, and buying from one man means less shipping to be paid. Shipping and handling will kill you here."

"Clever lad. All right, send me his ad from eBay and I'll handle it from there."

"Just go to samstraus.com," Patrick said. "All the info is there."

Eisen dialed the number. "818 . . . 404 . . . . . ."

"Sam Straus," came the answer. The voice sounded younger than expected, but that didn't matter.

"Sam," the Old Man began, cheerily, "you don't know me from Adam. My name's Sean Eisen . . . yeah, I'm an associate member of the tribe but only that; my mom was a *shiksa*, grandmother, too, for that matter. In any case, I'm looking for a fairly substantial quantity of old United States paper currency, preferably mostly in larger denominations."

"How much of it are you looking for?" the young voice asked. "And how old?"

"How much am I looking for? Something between thirty-five and seventy thousand. I need it to be pre-1966 but I don't really want any of the older, oversized bills. Can you come up with that much?"

"If pressed," Straus answered, "I could probably come up with fifty thousand and it would cost you on the order of seventy thousand."

Eisen said, "I was looking at some of the old gold certificates. I understand that, even though you can't exchange them for gold, they're still legal tender. I even saw where you could get the ten-thousand-dollar ones for less than ten thousand dollars."

"Oh, no, Mr. Eisen; those ones are worthless. Oh, yes, they're real but there's a story there. You see, they'd just about all been redeemed and the Treasury had cancelled them; you can tell because they've got punch holes in them, most of them. Well, a bunch of them were sitting in a post office in Washington, DC, near the Treasury, awaiting destruction, when the building caught fire. This was back in the mid-thirties. The postal workers saved what they could by throwing boxes into the street. Some of them burst open and at least one of those was full of the ten-thousand-dollar gold certificates. People who were making twelve bucks a week saw those, stuffed their pockets, and ran with them. But they were worthless. They're all, in fact, stolen property but the Feds won't go after anyone for selling them because they're worthless. And the lesser denominations cost, oh, a *lot* more than regular currency because of the rarity."

"Kills that theory," the Old Man said. "Shame. How quickly can you come up with the fifty thousand? Oh, and I need a roll of silver quarters, a roll of dimes, a roll or nickels and a roll of pennies, all from that time period."

"The coins are easy. Currency's somewhat tougher. Give me a month? Maybe I can get it all within three weeks, but I can promise it for a month from now."

"Done. Do you need an advance to help you buy? Some earnest money?"

"Send me five thousand as a deposit and as earnest money. I can work with that."

"Done. Give me your snail mail address."

"Could you Venmo it to me?" Sam asked.

Eisen sighed. "If you didn't guess it, I'm technologically challenged. But, yeah, I can send you the five grand via Venmo."

It took the full three days, plus an extra one, for the Old Man and the kids to find and order, if not everything they might need, everything that could be found online that they might need. While waiting for things to arrive at the mail drop, the Old Man rented a storage space in Quincy. The people running it struck him as greedy swine, but it wasn't like he was going to keep it for very long. He put a very heavy, extremely strong, and highly lockable trunk in it, even so. His gay cousin, Danny, the dancer, who was a hell of a lot stronger than the Old Man was, and had a deeper voice, to boot, helped him move it.

A few items for Patrick and himself he ordered at the downtown tailor's shop, Frank's, on Winter Street. They'd be delivered to the drop.

Among the last items to arrive at the mail drop were the Sterling submachine gun parts kit and a complete kit for an M1911. Once these were in hand, he made a phone call to a certain custom arms company in Vermont, called, appropriately, Vermont Custom Armory.

Vermont Custom Armory, and its subsidiary, Brattleboro Air Repeating Arms, were perfectly capable of making conventional small arms; they had the design capability, the machinery, and the skill. But their particular niche was pneumatic, ranging from hunting arms to fully automatic—but legal, because pneumatic—weapons, to crew-served weapons and, possibly soon to be, military training simulators. The Old Man had been a consultant for them for about a year at this point, generally pointing out the rocks and shoals of trying to get a defense contract on a military ecological niche that was already filled, and pointing out niches that could be filled.

The Old Man's phone already had the number on speed dial.

"Jake? This is Sean. I need to ask a few questions."

"Shoot," answered the voice on the other end. "I'm all ears."

"I bought a couple of kits. The first one is a remarkably complete, the kind you can hardly ever find now, parts kit for a Sterling. No, of *course*, I don't want you to make me an actual submachine gun. I didn't buy a templated tube for it just in case BATFE follows those things more closely than people think. What I want is to convert it to pneumatic, make ammunition that can use the magazines as they are, and add a permanent suppressor to it, welded on so it can't be removed, hence the Bureau of Alcohol, Tobacco, Firearms, and Explosives can't bitch."

"That's all pretty doable," Jake replied. "But I've got a couple of caveats and suggestions to it."

"Go on," the Old Man urged.

"In the first place, it's going to need a largish air storage tank, maybe four inches in diameter by eighteen or so. So it won't be as pretty and would have limited capability. It would also be ungainly. We could weld one on in place of the folding stock, make it like an old-fashioned Girondoni, if the collapsing stock doesn't matter. Limited shots with that, though. Otherwise, it has to be attachable either above, below, or to one side. If it absolutely *must* go *on* the gun, I'd recommend putting it to one side, for reasons I'll explain in a minute. That said, I don't think that putting it on the gun in any position is your best solution."

"I will want to keep the collapsing stock," the Old Man said.

"All right, then," Jake replied. "Then, if it's to go on the gun, then the tank probably needs to go on top or to the right side. Why? Because the magazines . . . well, to make them work, we're better off just making big, solid, cast nine-millimeter bullets, the width of the casing and the length of a complete cartridge, and boring out the barrel and chamber. That's going to be heavy, much heavier than a standard magazine. Close to three times more. It will throw you off without a compensating weight on the other side. Hence, we should put the tank there. That, however, means we'd better attach a handle to the gun, underneath."

"I can deal with the extra weight," the Old Man assured him. "Don't sweat that. Though a handle might be nice, yes, if we go that route."

Jake continued, "Okay, the other reason to make the bullets like that is because air is unavoidably slower than an explosive propellent, so you want to hit with a heavier bullet to keep something like the same level of energy on the target. The weight of the bullet won't change the velocity much and it will tend to keep more velocity—well, a greater percentage of velocity—at range. Hmmm . . . let me do some figuring . . . okay, if we went with a solid slug, of pure lead, with a domed front for feed purpose, it would run around three hundred and sixty grains, which is maybe too much. If we hollow point it, and I think we should, we can get it down around two hundred and maybe eighty grains, which is still too much. But if we swag the bullets, using soft lead, and add in two aluminum balls, one each front and rear, we can get it around two hundred grains, hollow-pointed, and that's plenty. And at that weight we can push it out of the barrel at twelve to thirteen hundred feet per second. That's about seven hundred to seven hundred and fifty foot-pounds of energy at the muzzle. That's right in there with a non-fancy, lower end Remington forty-four magnum. Which is, you know, not *bad*. However, I don't think we should do that. Instead, we need to keep velocity down to under eleven hundred feet per second."

"To keep the bullet from breaking the sound barrier? Okay, makes sense. Go on."

"At a thousand and sixty feet per second, that gives around five hundred foot-pounds of energy at the muzzle, which is still good, roughly .357 Magnum levels of good. The suppressor could be a problem; we don't have a license for those and, if we did, the turn around on the form four can be lengthy."

"That's not a problem," the Old Man said. "The trick would be to weld the exterior can to the Sterling and the barrel to the tube before putting in the internals. Or . . . maybe . . . you on your computer? You are? Good. Look up the L34A1; that's the Brits' suppressed version. Can we do that? But with the same deal; we weld the barrel to the tube and the can to the barrel before filling it so there's no question but that it was never legally a suppressor."

The was a momentary pause while Jake thought about that. "Hmmm ... so it never could have been a suppressor because it was always affixed to an air rifle? I can see that. And, yeah, I see the L34 ... we can do that. Port the barrel, too. But BATFE is often inconsistent and sometimes fairly lawless, and will screw you by process if they can't screw you at law."

"Can you keep something perfectly legal a secret, Jake? I can."

"Good point," the arms maker conceded. "So, in any case, yes, we can modify your parts kit into a functioning, pneumatic, suppressed submachine gun. It will take about three weeks.

"But let's get back to the pneumatic tanks. If you really insist on it being part of the gun, I could make something here that can hold nine thousand PSI. But you would probably have to come here every time you wanted to fill it; that kind of capacity is pretty uncommon. I could make you a hand pump but it would never get that high and would take a thousand strokes to get anything decent. Instead, I suggest getting a plate carrier and mounting two tanks in it, front and rear, connected to each other and to the gun by hoses. Give you five hundred shots, easy ..."

"I don't need nearly that much."

"Probably not," Jake agreed, "but you want the balance, don't you? And besides, they really will be highly bullet resistant."

"Ah. Good points," the Old Man conceded. "Okay, front and rear tanks on a plate carrier. We'll go with that, though if we can save some weight by reducing the number of shots to the two to three hundred range ..."

"And a third, smaller tank, those two will feed into."

"Okay," the Old Man agreed. "My other project is to create an M1911, in .45 caliber, from a kit."

"Now *that* we can't do," Jake said. "That would be 'manufacturing' and we have no license for that, in the first place, while, if we did, we'd have to serial number it, which kind of destroys the point, no?"

"Puhleeze," said the Old Man. "Give me some credit here. I don't want *you* to make it. I want to show up with the kit and have you and your people talk me through using your machinery for *me* to make it. Indeed, I'll pay a whole ten dollars on the rental of the machinery and give you the jig, to boot."

"That would work," Jake agreed. "Except you can't pay us a dime for it. ATF, again, and their, shall we say, *nuanced* view of the law. Has anyone ever told you that you are a wicked, evil man?"

"Yes," said the Old Man. "Very frequently."

USS *Constitution* Museum, Charlestown, Massachusetts

"You know," said the Old Man, leading the kids through the Museum, "USS *Constitution* was funny. Leaving aside that it was the first instance of a massive cost overrun in American military or naval history, it was also an example of a cost overrun proving to be worth every penny. In addition, it was, in practice, one of the most powerful warships afloat, arguably more powerful even than HMS *Victory*, Nelson's flagship at Trafalgar. This is even though *Victory* had twice as many guns."

"How can that be?" Patrick asked.

"It was because, in the first place, *Constitution* carried mostly heavy guns, while *Victory*'s guns included a lot of twelve-pounders, while, in the second place, not being intended to patrol all the world's seas, as HMS *Victory* was, and so not needing so much food and drink aboard, *Constitution* carried enough crew to man both broadsides at once, where *Victory* could only man one side or the other, but not both. Mind, if *Constitution* had met *Victory*, *Victory* would have blown her to bits, because even if you can man both sides' guns, you can only use one at a time. One *Victory* against one *Constitution*, *Constitution* loses. But, if you put three *Constitution*s, four effective broadsides in all, against two Victories, I'd give odds on the *Constitution*s."

They came to a short pillar with a poem inscribed on one side.

"Okay, brats," said the Old Man, "watch this."

With that, he turned his back to a poem, Oliver Wendell Holmes, Senior's, *Old Ironsides*, and began to recite:

"Aye, tear her tattered ensign down;
    Long has it waved on high . . ."

He finished with:

"And give her to the god of storms,
    The lightning and the gale!"

The Old Man felt a gentle tapping on his shoulder. He turned around to see one of the museum's workers or supervisors standing there, holding out a deformed penny, oval, flat on one side and, on the other, emblazoned with "USS *Constitution*," a silhouette of the ship, and "Old Ironsides."

"You didn't make any mistakes," said the man, wonderingly. "I know the poem, too, and I know you didn't make any mistakes. I've worked here for fifteen years. In all that time I've never seen anyone do that. I've never seen anyone even try. Take this as a memento, please, as a gift from me."

"Thanks," said the Old Man.

"Can I have that?" Cossima asked.

"When I'm dead, it's yours," he agreed.

"I meant now."

"Yes, I gathered that, but *I* meant 'no,' not until I'm dead."

"How do you *do* that, Grandpa?" asked Juliana.

"The memory thing? I can't take any credit; it was a gift from my parents, a genetic gift. I've just always had it. Unfortunately," he said, with a sigh, "while long-term memory remains excellent, short-term memory has just recently begun to go. And I will be very much lost without it. What is commonly considered intelligence is often just a good memory, you know. Same with humor. It wasn't, I assure you, intelligence, in the main, that had me reading so young; it was memory.

"You brats ready for Bunker Hill, or are you hungry, as usual?"

"I'm a growing boy," said Patrick, which explained his position on the matter perfectly.

"I could eat something," said Cossima, "provided there's no pork in it." It wasn't that the eight-year-old girl was contemplating embracing Judaism. Oh, no; she'd just decided that a) pigs were people, too, and b) she was not interested in cannibalism.

"Sure," Juliana agreed.

"Okay, no sense in tackling on an empty stomach the hill it took the British Army nearly all day to take. Let's hit the Warren Tavern;

it doesn't go back to the battle, itself, since most of the town was burnt down in the course of the fighting. But it's either the oldest or, at least, one of the oldest buildings, in Charlestown, built about five years after the battle. Ought to be interesting."

Bunker Hill Monument, Charlestown, Massachusetts

"We won the Revolution here," the Old Man said to the kids. "Oh, it wasn't obvious at the time, but we won here nonetheless. 'How?' you may well ask."

"Yes," agreed Cossima, "how?"

"We won here, little weedhopper, because here we broke William Howe's confidence that he could overrun us and drive us from any fortifications. Oh, yes, they drove us from the fortifications here, but they did it at a cost they were never again willing to repeat. Never, not even once. After that, they had to be fancy, to maneuver us out of one position after another. And, sure, they *did* maneuver us out of one position after another, but because of it, our army always got away to learn, to train, and to fight again.

"You would have thought Howe would have taken advantage of our position at Valley Forge to exterminate Washington's army there. But, no, the memory of this battle, right here, froze Howe's mind and stayed Howe's hand. This saved the army, thus saved the Revolution and the country. You would also think he'd have assaulted Dorchester Heights when John Thomas set up an overnight defense for the guns Henry Knox brought from Ticonderoga. But, no; Howe was terrified of a replay of Bunker Hill.

"In terms of its ultimate effect on the world, this may well be the greatest pyrrhic victory in history."

"Grandpa," asked Patrick, "what's a 'pyrrhic victory'?"

"It's one that costs the winner so much that defeat, provided it was early enough, before too much blood had been spent, would have been preferable. It's named after an ancient king, Pyrrhus of Epirus, who fought the Romans and discovered they could bleed him white, as we did to the Brits, here, and replace all their own losses in an instant."

Interlude

The place was called "Magdeburg," and, even before the cannonade on the walls ended, the Q'riln, via her cube, could feel the terror of the townsfolk.

You really can't beat this area they call "Europe" for first class ambrosia, thought the Q'riln. *Not only is it varied but the servings are just too much. Well, not too much for me.*

The Q'riln had, some considerable time earlier, attached herself to the army that had now become the army of Graf Pappenheim. Feeding had been so-so, at best, since then. Indeed, so much so that she and her cube had occasionally had recourse to tampering with the minds of groups of soldiery, convincing them to desert in particular directions, then informing the authorities where to look for the deserters.

The hangings, even the mass ones, hadn't been much; it was all over too quickly. *But a girl has to keep her hand in,* she thought, as the cannon ceased their bombardment and blocks of Pappenheim's foot began their ponderous march to the breaches in the walls.

Now, after all those cycles of poor rations, here, at the city of Magdeburg, the Q'riln was finally going to be able to . . .

"Mistress," the cube announced, "there's been a new gate opened, and the pattern is not one of the people."

"Who?" she asked.

"It is consistent with portal technology from several of the law enforcement agencies of the Authority."

"*Those* meddling busybodies?" the Q'riln sneered. "How many?"

"Just two, plus some kind of artificial life form. I surmise from the power patterns that they're at best lightly equipped."

"Where did they emerge?"

"Behind us, near that place where all those people were impaled, when we first arrived."

The Q'riln thought about that for a moment, before saying, "The coincidence is too great. It's *me* they're after."

"So I would surmise, Mistress. Well, you *and* me, most likely."

"What's the distance on foot and horse to get to me, here, and how long should it take them to travel?"

The cube buzzed slightly for a moment, consulting its onboard maps and what it knew of transportation, here and now. Finally, it answered, "No less than three of the local moons, even assuming they can connect you to this. But here and now, there is no shortage of anguish anywhere. Neither do I sense that the instances we have feasted on are anything too very special. I think you can continue to graze here, in the area they call 'Germany,' for at least five moons before they show up. And then, perhaps you should go to the islands to the northwest for a while."

"All right, cube, I agree. And now, I see that the troops are at the first breach. Let us follow them in."

Chapter Four

ᘓᓍᓏ

Here's to New Haven and Boston
And the turf that the Puritans trod.
In the rest of Mankind
Little virtue they find
But they feel quite chummy with God.
—Walter Foster Angell

Draper's Meadow, Virginia

They'd driven back from the Boston area in fifteen hours, after which the Old Man had retired to his whirlpool to try to at least reduce the pain in his back. It helped but...

Not enough; the massage therapist is just so much better.

While the whirlpool was doing its thing, swirling and bubbling away the very worst of the aches and pains, the Old Man stared up at the ceiling, mentally reviewing various findings he'd come to in terms of where to put his money, in 1965 or wherever the date led to, to maximize profits here and now.

I know of ten potentially really good investments, with huge rates of return: Philippine Telephone and Telegraph, Apple, Dell, Microsoft, Amazon, Berkshire Hathaway, Google, Facebook, Bitcoin, or crypto, more generally, and Tencent, in Hong Kong.

But how do I get a brokerage house—no, can't be one, has to be one each or someone will start to notice a pattern... no, even that's bullshit. When you leave instructions in 1965 to buy something that won't exist for thirty or more years, that is a pattern, all on its own, a crystal ball pattern.

And what that means is that I cannot be one hundred percent sure that they'll even follow my instructions, since who, after all, believes in crystal balls?

There's only one really outstanding investment that I know of, that already exists, doesn't need any highly suspicious letters of instruction, and has a huge rate of return. Berkshire Hathaway is pretty much it; it already exists in 1965, has minor ups and downs but overall huge rates of growth, on the order of twenty-nine thousand times over, and doesn't need any crystal balls in operation. Warren Buffett, it is.

And what that means is a return of about a billion and a half or so on fifty thousand. No, wait, more than that, especially with instructions to reinvest the dividends. Oh, wait; no, Buffett doesn't pay dividends. If you want money you sell stock. Still ... pretty good rate of return.

But it's not as good as it could be. I don't necessarily want to stay back there long enough to play the futures game, but horse racing? Why not? It's legal enough. Fun for the kids. It's also corrupt as hell and everyone knows it. But with a bunch of small bets, on win, place, and show, without showing off with Trifectas or any of the fancy stuff, I ought to be able to increase my fifty thousand a good deal. Hmmm ... no, the IRS is extremely interested in people who win at the track. No horses. No dog races, either.

Play the number, the parimutuels? My first thought is no, I don't think so; that's all Mafia and Murphia and they're likely to take a personal interest in anyone who does too well at what ought to be a losing game. Well ... maybe a couple of minor plays there. But only that. Or one serious one? This requires thought.

So there's that part of the plan, no horse or dog betting to increase my capital, but maybe a little side betting with the bookies, parimutuels and sports, to avoid taxes on winnings, and then dump it all into Berkshire Hathaway before we come back.

But before I write off futures, let's see about what was hot back then.

He stopped thinking for a while, as the jets and bubbles eased away his pain. When he resumed thought, it was with, *And let's be honest about the whys of the matter. I don't really need the money, not to live comfortably enough for the years I may have left. But the consensus for maintaining the country, even the consensus for civilization around the world, is breaking down. Crassus suggested it, count no man wealthy who cannot maintain an army at his own expense. And forty percent of the country expects to have to take up arms against the government; talk about a self-fulfilling prophecy! But if I can squeeze as much out of this foray as I think I can, I can afford the private army—big brigade, small division's worth—and the kernel of civilization that will keep my children and grandchildren safe, fed, and healthy. This I could not do with what I have.*

"Hmmm . . ." he muttered aloud. "Best add a trip to hit up the *Boston Herald* for the numbers for 1964, 1965, and 1966. Fortunately, I don't have to find horse racing results for that long a period of time.

"Back to the computer, I suppose. But then, is it wise to do much off-track betting when there's perfectly legal betting in the form of futures options, and those allow margins? Nope, have to limit it. Note to self; pay for access to the *Wall Street Journal*'s archives. Yeah, commodities futures."

Draper's Meadow, Virginia

Before leaving again to continue preparations, the Old Man took them all out for ice cream. This was merely pretextual, though; he really wanted to give them final instructions away from any prying eyes and overly eager ears. His son-in-law was currently deployed to Afghanistan, and his daughter was staying at his house both to take care of her widowed father and, frankly, to save some money on housing while her husband was gone. He didn't want his daughter figuring out what was going on with her children.

"Okay, kids," he said, once they were in the Avalon and alone, "I'm heading back to New England to gather material, money, and information. In the interim, I've sent Juliana a number of links for online instructional material on lockpicking, which is—and I cannot overstate this—*critical* for our little trip. I've ordered material, pick sets, a snap gun, a half dozen transparent training locks, and a couple of real ones. They'll all be coming in Juliana's name. Got it?"

"Yes, Grandpa," they all said.

"You've got to learn to pick locks quickly and quietly. I expect you to spend most of every day until I get back working on this. Am I clear here?"

Again, all agreed.

"If it gets tedious," the Old Man said, "just think about how much fun we'll have when we do this.

"Oh, and don't show the material to your mother."

Ithaca, New York

The Old Man was on the road, legging it trippingly for a place where they normally had nine months of winter followed by three months of very poor sledding. It was not for nothing that the United States Army had put its cold weather test center not in Alaska, but in upstate New York.

The kids were still, albeit temporarily, back in Virginia, with their mother. The Old Man had purchased a number of locksmith courses and training aids, on which he'd put the three kids to work. So far, Patrick looked to have the greatest potential for it, with the girls not too close behind him.

Here, in Ithaca, there was a table, a chair, a satchel. And two men, one younger, one much older. Otherwise, the room was empty.

"I can't tell you there's not a single counterfeit bill in there," Sam Straus said. "I can tell you that, if there is, whoever made it was damned good, good enough to have me fooled."

The Old Man took a cashier's check for the remainder of the cost, sixty-five thousand dollars, and laid in on the table holding the money.

"Would you be insulted if I looked it over?" the Old Man asked, perfectly prepared to take the cashier's check and leave if the coin dealer objected.

"No, I'd count it, too, and look it all over, for counterfeits, were our positions reversed."

The Old Man smiled. "Haven't done this since pulling pay officer as a second lieutenant."

He pulled the chair out, sat, and proceeded to sort the bills into piles preparatory to going over each of the roughly two thousand, one hundred of them.

"I'll leave you alone while you count," said Sam. "You don't need the distraction."

The Old Man found it a little odd that the coin dealer was more trusting than he was, but took it as a good sign.

"You gave me a little more than I paid for," said Eisen, finally.

"Don't sweat it and don't cry for me," said Sam. "I've made enough on the deal for my trouble."

"'A workman is worthy of his hire,'" Eisen quoted. "Good doing business with you."

Brattleboro, Vermont

It was, in many ways, a quintessentially New England town, Brattleboro, Vermont. Beyond that, the town had more than a few claims to fame, despite its size, and not even including the Vermont Custom Armory.

For one thing, it had been the home of Rudyard Kipling, who'd married a local girl in 1892, written many of his most famous and revered works there, and built a large house just over the town line, in neighboring Dummerston.

For another, it had once been home to the largest organ maker in the United States, the Estey Organ Company. America's first social security check had gone to a woman of Brattleboro. America's first female auctioneer had, likewise, been of the town.

It represented a good deal of history for what was, after all, still just a small town.

Here and now, though, on a different table, in a different room, in a different state from New York, lay another treasure. This was, to almost all external appearances, a British Model L34A1, a suppressed Sterling sub-machine gun. The only things to distinguish this, at first glance, were the absence of a wooden foregrip and the hose leading from it to a plate carrier with, apparently, two SAPI plates installed in the front and rear pockets, and one on one side.

Picking up one of the magazines, the Old Man found another distinguishing feature; instead of regular nine-millimeter rounds, the magazine was filled with solid lead slugs. He thumbed one out and felt the front end for the hollow point, then returned it to the magazine. It was only a bit over half the weight one might expect of a solid lead slug. He assumed that the difference was both in the cavity and in the two aluminum balls Jake had mentioned.

"Have we tested to see whether this will expand at the velocities we're getting?" he asked.

"It will," Jake answered. "The bullet's actually travelling faster than any number of hollow points that expand routinely. And this is just soft lead, with those additions I mentioned. Even so, we test fired it in standard ten percent ballistic gelatin. It goes from nine mil to about seventeen, routinely, and sometimes a little more. The lead's *really* soft."

Jake pulled a fired bullet out of a shirt breast pocket and passed it over. The thing was a nearly perfect mushroom, and about twice the size at the expansion as it was at the nine-millimeter base.

Examining the nearly perfect shape, as well as the width, the Old Man said, "I'm genuinely impressed."

"The swager we're giving you has dies to use to make the hollow points," Jake cautioned. "We're also tossing in a mold that has inserts to make hollow points. They fit in from one side, where the mold's got openings. That's all we're charging you for—well, that and the lead, the aluminum balls, and a good deal of spare lead and balls. The slugs from the mold will be heavier, over three hundred grains, but will still mushroom nicely—very nicely—at seven hundred and twenty or so feet per second.

"We also put two hundred rounds through it without a failure. It's a pretty good product. The bullets do leave a thin coating of lead, which could build up, so you'll need to clean them out. Remember, lead is poisonous.

"As you can see, we've welded a Picatinny rail to the bottom and attached a green laser to it. Green's a little easier to see in higher light. It's zeroed already for one hundred and twenty-five meters."

"Nice," Eisen said. "Thanks, muchly."

"We've made you four hundred and fifty projectiles, over and above what we used for testing and what we've got for you to test, yourself, here. The tanks are full. You want to try it out?"

"Just try to stop me," the Old Man said, with a smile.

The entire rig, plate carrier, three tanks, front, rear, and on the left side, hoses, all of it—less the Sterling, itself—together felt like a bit over twenty pounds. Jake confirmed it as, "Twenty and a half, with enough air for nearly three hundred shots."

"I've worn heavier," the Old Man said, after sliding on the rig.

Even with the suppressor on it, the Old Man hadn't expected it to be quite so silent. Indeed, it was almost "Hollywood quiet," so called for Hollywood's penchant for making suppressors in movies seem a lot more effective than, in fact, they generally were.

Mind, there *were* suppressors that quiet; the U.S. Navy SEALs had used some during the Vietnam War, called "Hush Puppies," which were amazing. But, still, that kind of quiet was very rare.

In this case, though, "The cycling of the action is louder than the report," he said. "I'm impressed."

"So are we, frankly," said Jake, asking, "How's the recoil?"

"It feels like a little more than an actual Sterling, but gentler. In general, it's nothing bad."

"I test fired a full magazine," said Jake, "did a complete mag dump, on the opening of a commercial truck tire. I could keep every round inside the opening at seventy-five feet. I suspect I could do the same at seventy-five yards. It just vibrates a little; the recoil, as you say, is nothing bad."

"Let's get back to the shop," the Old Man said. "I want to start work on the M1911 in the certain knowledge that someone, somewhere, in Boston, Albany, Sacramento, Baltimore, and DC—to say nothing of the Left Coast—will lose sleep over the fear that someone, somewhere, has made their own untraceable firearm."

Jake nodded, then added, "You'll also want to see if the foot pump we've got is good enough. Takes six hundred pumps to fill a tank. Call it fifteen hundred or a few less to fill all three."

"Hmmm...let me think...call it thirty pumps a minute, fifty minutes to fill? That sounds fine. It's two and a half miles' worth of walking and I won't have a heavy pack on my back."

Draper's Meadow, Virginia

Juliana, as it turned out, was a far better lockpick teacher than she was ever going to be a lockpick. Reading, more or less, from *The MIT Guide to Lockpicking*, by Ted the Tool, she said to Patrick, "The trick is to find the pin inside the lock that's binding the most, and push it up, feel the lock move a little when the key pin gets above what they call 'the sheer line,' and move the tumbler slightly to lock the key pin above the sheer line. After that you go to the next pin that's binding the most."

Nodding, the boy manipulated his pick in the simulated, transparent lock, while staring intently.

"No, Patrick, she said; "you need to close your eyes and do it by *feel*, alone."

"All right," he said, "I'll try." Shortly after that, a pin moved and the simulated lock shifted.

"See?" said Juliana. "I *can't* visualize the inside of the lock. You can. I'd say it's a girl thing except that Cossima is getting it somewhat and I just am not."

"Give me some time," said Cossima. "I'm little. In a year I'll be better than *him*."

The simulated lock Patrick was working on suddenly sprang open.

"Okay," he said, "let's get the hard one and see if I can use the snap gun."

661b East Broadway, South Boston, Massachusetts

He'd shown up rather early for this appointment. It wasn't because he was OCD about timeliness, even though he was. Oh, no; Eisen wanted to case the joint, check for electronic security, and get the exact model of the lock on the back door, to get a copy of that to let the kids practice on.

Security, he was pleased to see, was minimal. *And, then, why not? They don't keep cash here, most of the capital value is in individual expertise, and insurance likely covers anything that's pilferable. A lock to keep kids out—well . . . most kids, anyway—is probably all they need. Makes perfect sense. And there's no camera system.*

Now, tonight, I'm going to see about getting back in after hours, either from the alley to the west or in from Emerson Street. But for now, let me get a picture of that deadbolt . . .

"Mr. Eisen?"

"Yes, Dijana, I'm more than ready. Shall we go shopping for a ring afterwards?"

"Flirt!" she said, with a smile.

There were narrow alleyways to either side of 661 East Broadway, 661a and 661b. To the west, by 661a, there was a handled door covering the alley. To the east, nearer to the next-door store, Bringing Up Baby, there was no door. Each alley was only as wide as needed to take out a full barrel, weekly, for trash pickup.

While there were no apartments above 661, both east and west of it there were two floors' worth.

Probably six apartments, in toto, the Old Man thought.

This only really mattered because the more apartments the more people, the more people the more combined nosiness, likelihood of having a sharp-eared dog, or chance of someone taking the trash out to dump in the can.

It's a pretty close call, he thought, walking down Broadway late at night, affecting a slight sway to simulate having had one too many. *There's more of a chance of being discovered to the right of the place, on the Deluxe Nails side, against what the map suggests is the location of 661's gate for trash removal, on the Bringing Up Baby side. I'm going with Katharine Hepburn on this one; Bringing Up Baby, it is.*

While there were overhead street lights on many of the lettered cross streets, none of the streetlights here on this section of East Broadway were overhead. Indeed, they gave every impression of having once been gas lamps, later modified for electricity. While, individually, not all that powerful, the sheer number of them made the place quite bright indeed.

And one of them, go figure, is right at the alley I want to duck into. Well . . . nothing to be done for it. And . . . here!

The Old Man glanced across the street to ensure that no one at The Playwright was dining *al fresco*, in front of the place, then abruptly turned into the alley by Bringing Up Baby. He followed the alley into the bowels of the block. His nose was assaulted by the very strong odor of urine, presumptively human.

Well, there's my excuse if the cops saw me and follow me in. "I needed to take a piss, officer"—which, come to think of it, is true—"and thought this was a better choice than whizzing right out in the open."

But no policemen seemed to have noticed or, if they did, they likely thought, *Just another drunk who needed to take a leak. Nothing to see here.*

He didn't have a flashlight with him, figuring that, if the police did stop him, the cell phone was innocent while a flashlight was inherently suspicious without some excuse. Instead of saying aloud, "Hey, Siri, turn on torch," he flicked his cell phone's light on manually. Then he followed the light down the narrow alley, mentally counting the paces to where the backyard of 661 should begin.

There, to his right, was a gate within a fence. He opened it, gently, then stepped inside. There was a shed directly to his front, with a couple of reeking trash cans inside, sheltering from rain and sun. Past that was a wall and, in that wall, a door.

Bingo.

From 661 East Broadway, the Old Man walked back to his car. From there he got back on Broadway, driving west and then northwest, after the intersection with Dorchester Street, before finally stopping and parking where he could see the police station, formerly Station Six but now called "C-6," at 101 West Broadway. Parked, he waited until "cruisers," the local term for police cars, started coming in and unusual numbers of uniformed officers began showing up.

"Okay," he said to himself, "now we know when to make our move, when the police are at the station, not on the streets. Twenty-three forty-five it is. Now to catch a little sleep and then tomorrow, 30 H Street to rent a parking spot."

Draper's Meadow, Virginia

The boy was blindfolded, with his tools in a folding leather case in his pocket and his snap gun in his left hand. In his right, he held a small tension wrench, basically a thin bar with each end twisted to ninety degrees. In front of him was a used deadbolt lock, sent by the old man from Boston, of the same make and model as the one at the place on Broadway.

Juliana stood by, ready to start the stopwatch feature on her phone. "On three," she said. "One...two...three."

Instantly, Patrick felt for the lock, then slid one end of the tension wrench into the bottom of the keyway. He held it there, with one finger of his right hand, while his left hand transferred the snap gun to the bulk of his right.

He inserted the needle of the snap gun into the lock, then pulled the trigger several times, while keeping pressure on the wrench. Nothing happened.

"Crap, need more force," the boy muttered. Leaving the wrench still in the keyway, he withdrew the needle and spun the notched wheel of the snap gun several turns. Then he reinserted the needle into the keyway, resumed pressure on the wrench, and tried again. At the first pull of the trigger he felt a tiny bit of movement in the keyway. Six more pulls and all the pins had been driven up above the sheer point, allowing the lock's cylinder to rotate freely.

Juliana stopped the clock on her phone and said, "Not at all bad, little brother. The Old Man will be pleased."

"How long did it take?" Patrick asked.

"Twenty-three seconds," she replied.

"I think you're ready for prime time, Big Brother," said Cossima.

"Maybe I am," Patrick agreed, smiling.

Eisen pulled back into his driveway after a week away. After a demonstration from Patrick of his newly acquired skills as a lockpick— "Well done, Grandson; I am impressed!"—he grabbed a bird-headed and very short semi-automatic twelve gauge, a Remington Tac-13, a .380 pistol, Czech, a .32 pistol, Beretta, and a Walther PPK in .22. Along with these he packed sixty rounds of number four buckshot for the twelve gauge, forty of the shortened twelve gauge, and a hundred for each of the pistols, plus another hundred for the newly made M1911 still in the car. The Sterling and its slugs remained in the trunk, with full tanks. The ammunition all went into an ammunition can, along with three magazines per pistol. He finished loading the range box, which had pretty much everything needed, from targets to digital earmuffs, to similarly digital ear buds, to eye protection.

Juliana, who had watched and helped with the loading asked, on their way out to the public range at Jefferson Forest, "Grandpa, if it's going to be dangerous enough to need all this firepower, maybe it's too dangerous to actually go through with."

"Fair observation," the Old Man conceded. "But I still think we should go. One thing is that, no, old Slocum never told your sister it was very dangerous but only that she didn't belong. These are different issues. Moreover, yes, while Boston is a good place and Southie maybe more so, still, you never really know about *anywhere* at *any time*. And, despite the general situation and higher level of safety there and then, if it did turn out to be dangerous, well, frankly, *I'm* dangerous, too, old or not, and even more so when I'm properly armed. Which, with these little goodies, I will be. As for any dangers there may be to the gate, itself, your sister went in, spent some time there, and came out fine, so I'm not worried about that.

"As to why we should go, in the first place, I want to show you the Boston I came from, which I remember as very beautiful and very happy, before the malls killed downtown and then Amazon killed the malls. But in the second place, we're going back not just with cash, not just with arms, but with knowledge. I intend to turn that knowledge into a very good life for all of you, your parents, and your aunts. We're going to expand the fifty thousand we're bringing to several times that, at least, and then we're going to put it into something that will grow massively, so that when we pull it out, we'll be very comfortable, indeed.

"Finally, I expect a breakdown in order and civilization here. Security then will depend not on individual arms, but armed organization. I intend to get enough to pay for that . . . for *your* safety.

"But if you still don't want to go, Juliana, you can stay behind with your mother, though you have to keep quiet about it."

The girl's brown eyes flashed angrily. "I didn't say I didn't *want* to go. I'm just concerned about the risks."

"Have you ever seen a risk I couldn't handle?"

"Well . . . no," she conceded, "but isn't there a first time for everything, Grandpa?"

"Not for this," the Old Man assured her.

Jefferson Forest Rifle and Pistol Range, Montgomery County, Virginia

Neither of the girls, it turned out, was quite up to using the short Remington twelve gauge. They both tried, with only one shell in the shotgun for each, and the recoil was just too much for them. Patrick barely managed it. From there, the Old Man tried mini-shells from Aguila, but those simply would not feed reliably, even with him behind the twelve gauge.

"Okay, this one is mainly backup for me, then. Let's go to pistols. Patrick, take the M1911, the box of ammunition, and load your magazines. Juliana, it's the .380 Czech for you. Cossima, yours is the .32 Beretta..."

"And now for the fun part," the Old Man announced. "C'mere, Juliana, and let's rig you up with the Sterling..."

There was a Fish and Game officer with delusions of grandeur who occasionally haunted this particular range. Upon seeing what was obviously automatic fire, and not hearing it, he sauntered over to inquire about paperwork from ATF.

"We don't need any," said the Old Man. "This is pneumatic, not a firearm. The suppressor is integral to it, hence cannot be removed to use on a firearm, hence doesn't need a tax stamp, approval, or anything along those lines."

"Oh, a *lawyer*, are we?" Fish and Game sneered. "Well, we'll just..."

"You want my Virginia State Bar number? Do you want to arrest me? Arrest me for having perfectly legal weapons? Are you that eager for me to publicly humiliate you in court? Ready for the lawsuit to follow, and the letter of reprim—"

"All right! All right!" said the wannabe with delusions of grandeur, holding his hands up, palms out, as if fending off a threat. "I was just curious, is all."

Calming down, Eisen asked, "Would you like to try it out?"

Thought Juliana, *And that's what actually makes him dangerous. As far as the old man is concerned, nobody but God outranks him.*

Swaging more ammunition, cleaning the firearms and the Sterling, and pumping the tanks full again occupied the rest of the day and a part of the night. They then packed an old military duffel bag, packed the car, and got a night's sleep. Moreover, to fool the kids' mother, they also filled the trunk of the Avalon with camping gear and food, both freeze dried and canned.

"Be back in a couple of weeks, honey," the Old Man told his surprisingly young-looking daughter, just before taking off.

"Try to stay out of trouble," she said.

Rest Area, Interstate 81, Southwest of Carlisle, Pennsylvania

"Rehearsal time.

"Okay, brats, I'm going to stop. When I do, Juliana and Patrick, both of you get out *instantly*. Juliana, you close your door and help Patrick pull the duffel bag. Cossima, you push from your side...."

"Too slow. Get the bag back in and we'll do it again...and again."

They drilled this until the kids could have the duffel bag, which wasn't yet quite as heavy as it would be, out of the car and dragged to cover in under seven seconds.

"Okay, back in the car and get some rest. I'll get you up when it's time to stop for chow. And now it's time to 'make' my blue eyes 'brown.'"

With that, the Old Man took out his normal contacts, which were clear, and flicked them out the window. He then took out a double pair of brown-colored prescription contacts and deftly put them in. He had two sets of replacements for both brown and clear.

"That's going to take some getting used to, Grandpa," said Juliana.

Quincy, Massachusetts

There wasn't all that much in the trunk in the storage locker the Old Man had rented. Some of what there was the kids and he put on, making them properly clothed for 1965. The rest was carried to the car and carefully stowed into the duffel bag, after taking out the .380 and the M1911. Even without those, the duffel bag was now *quite* full.

The current year *was* dangerous, much more so than 1965. Because of this, the M1911 was to go into the small of the Old Man's back. The Czech .380 was Juliana's, to guard herself, her siblings, and the bag until the Old Man returned from parking the car, the spot being already rented, at 30 H Street Place, less than half a mile to the west of 661 East Broadway.

Patrick had his locksmithing tools in his pockets.

The Old Man took a spin by 101 West Broadway. He circled the building, or maybe better said, rectangled it, just to make sure the new shift was gathering as the first half of the old one was turning in. They were.

No last-minute changes to SOP. Good. "Watch carefully, kids," he ordered.

From the South Boston police station, he turned right again on West Broadway, following it to the East and West Broadway, Dorchester Street, intersection. There he bore left to follow East Broadway. Up Pill Hill the Avalon went, past the courthouse on the right and the old Gavin mansion on the left. Keeping a strict eye out for police cruisers, he drove past 661, past K and L Streets, and then took a right on M Street, at the southwest corner of what was now known as "Medal of Honor Park."

From there he went to Fourth Street, taking a right just before Emerson, then following Fourth until it met Emerson again. Bearing right on Emerson he went back to Broadway, which he crossed, turned left, then right again, to follow I Street to Third. On Third he again took a right, travelling east to M Street and the park. There he went right, then right again at Broadway, which he followed past I Street to H Street.

"Anybody see any police cars?"

"No, Grandpa," they all answered.

"Me, neither."

On H the Old Man turned left, went to Fourth, then to I, and left again to East Broadway.

"Okay, everybody, we're about one minute out. Get ready."

He turned right on East Broadway again, then slowed even more than the speed limit required, coming to a complete stop at the old-fashioned, probably formerly gas-powered, lamppost right by 661.

"Go! Go! Go!"

Rehearsals paid off. Terrified half out of their wits, the kids had themselves and the duffel bag outside of the car and hidden between two parked cars in mere seconds, faster than they ever had in rehearsals.

"Be back in a few," Eisen said. "Remember, Juliana's in charge."

With that, he turned back onto East Broadway, then left on K, and via as direct a route as possible, to the rented parking spot at 30 H Street Place.

Getting out of the car, he stuffed the M1911 into the back of his trousers, shut and locked the doors, and then began walking briskly for 661 and his grandchildren.

"Hey, old timer, got any money?"

There in the shadows, and in the vacuum that criminals knew would be left by the police change of shift, were two rather scruffy looking sorts, probably eighteen or nineteen, each wielding a knife.

The Old Man said, while reaching behind him, "I really don't have time for this. If you want to see the morning, get out of my way."

The scruffier looking of the two laughed. "Oh, an old fart who thinks he's tough. We'll show you tou—"

The old fart was surprisingly quick. One second, he was several feet in front of the thugs; a split second later, after what seemed like a blur, he was not. Instead, he was right in front of one of them, with his left hand gripping the boy's hair and the right forcing the muzzle of his .45 through his lips and teeth. Somewhere in that lunge, the young man heard the safety being flicked off.

"Drop the knives, boys."

Twin clatters on the concrete said the toughs had obeyed.

After a sharp intake of breath, the street tough said to his colleague, around the pistol "Don' do any'hin', Mi'ey." Then to the old man, he said, "We wuh jes jokin', yah know, zir . . . jus' 'avin a li'le . . . sir . . ." The pistol withdrew, only to be pressed against his nose. "Please don't kill me, sir." The street tough started to snivel. "Please don't . . . I have a mother. . . ."

"Shut up. I told you I don't have time for this." Roughly the Old Man spun the punk around, ordering, "Get on your knees. Yes, you, too," he told the other one, pointing the pistol in his direction.

"If you believe in God, start praying."

Then, because the 1911 wasn't suppressed, and *only* because it wasn't suppressed, the Old Man decided to spare their lives. He raised the pistol on high, then brought it down with close to skull-splitting force onto the head of the main would-be mugger. Blood, hair, and some flesh stuck to the magazine and the mag well.

In the old days, I could have just shot them and nobody would have seen anything even if they were standing right here. Now the place is full of never sufficiently to be damned yuppies and dinks, and they can be counted on to complain and possibly provide eyewitness accounts.

Sensing the other one, Mikey, was about to bolt, he said, "Don't even think about it. Your friend will live, though I don't envy him his headache. You will live, too, unless you make a run for it. If you do, I'll shoot you to bring you down—and, no, I rarely miss and never at this range—then shoot you again, in the head, to make sure. Then I'll shoot this asshole who saw my face."

Mikey just nodded, repeating, as his friend had, "Just please don't kill me." Then the boy started blubbering.

"What the hell is wrong with Southie, these days, anyway?" the Old Man asked, disgusted. "In the old days you'd have already done your time in the Army or Marines and not be such a little wimp. Oh, well." Eisen raised the pistol high.

Wham. Mikey's unconscious body melted to the concrete sidewalk.

I so did not have the time for this.

With that, the Old Man began to jog. *And I am way too old for running, too. GodDAMNED knees! And moving quick for those thugs didn't help any, either.*

"Grandpa's running late," Cossima said, voice beginning to break. Just because she wasn't afraid of anything for herself didn't mean she didn't worry about those she loved.

"Don't worry," Patrick reassured her. "Don't forget that the old guy in *Secondhand Lions* was modelled after our grandfather . . . or should have been."

"Grandpa says it wasn't and that he's not that strong."

"Doesn't matter," Patrick replied, "he's that mean and then some."

Hearing footsteps pounding up the street, Juliana tightened her grip around the Czech .380. If someone was pursuing her grandfather, she was going to put a stop to that.

And then came the voice, a little out of breath. "Had a bit of trouble. Not too much. You brats ready to go?"

Interlude

It was the dead of night when Topaz and Mica came through their own gate. They wore local clothing, and carried arms considered appropriate to their sexes. Additionally, they carried between them a considerable quantity of *trelve* and *forjin* to ease their journey. Possibly most importantly, they'd all been immersed in what was believed to be the latest version of writing, here and now, something called "Sacred Writing."

The pair plus the AI, who had been given the name Mary, the better to blend in, came out not far from where the Q'riln had, by a spot that had once hosted a forest of stakes and abused corpses. The stakes and the bird-eaten bodies were long gone, now, centuries gone; only the faint traces of their psychic agony remained.

"It would have grown fairly powerful here," Topaz said. She was, as a female, considerably more attuned to such things than her mate, Mica. "So many sentient beings, so much agony, so long to finally find surcease. And . . . even little ones, who had no idea what they'd done to deserve a horrible death and who hardly knew what death was until it came for them."

She shuddered from the sheer horror. Her people just didn't do that kind of thing. They never had.

"It may be worth remembering," said Mica, "that the Q'riln didn't do any of that; at worst it fed upon it."

"Yes," Topaz agreed, "yes, I know. But, if we don't take it, then it *will* cause things like this. Or, as the chief said, 'worse.'"

"I'm aware," Mica said. He wrapped a comforting arm around his mate, just as he would have if they'd still been in their natural, somewhat similar, forms. "Remember, though, our job is not to take it, but to kill it."

"I know," said the female, with a deep sigh.

Mary, their mobile artificial intelligence, encased in and controlling a largely brainless, cloned body, turned in one direction, head and eyes concentrating like a pointer's, and one arm raised somewhat like one, too. She said, in a voice that still sounded metallic and artificial, "The Q'riln had gone that way but is no longer there, of course. Now she is.... computing.... sensing.... recalling.... right now she is ... a place called ... 'Germany.' I have this language but you will have to learn it. Shall we advance?"

"Yes, Mary," Mica said. "Lead on. Teach us this language as you do."

Language had been the first shock. While Mary, the AI, insisted that the writing they were seeing was mostly founded in the "Sacred Writing" they'd had implanted in them, they just couldn't see the connection. Now they'd have to learn an entirely new writing system but without the advantages of deep immersion their agency could provide.

"No way," insisted Mica. "There is no way that their vowel, 'A,' comes from a hieroglyph for a beast called an "Ox.'"

"Yes, there is," Mary insisted. "Here, look." With that she began to trace out what she thought was the evolution of the letter on a spot of bare earth.

"Madness," Mica said, "sheer madness."

"The Q'riln was here," Mary said, as they stood on a hill looking at the ruins of the sacked and burnt town. "Here she feasted on the death agonies of twenty thousand sentient beings."

"Why did this happen?" Topaz asked. "Do these people do this for fun?"

"Not fun," Mary replied. "They have different interpretations of their writing about and proper approach to the Universal Creator. It made them hate each other enough for massacre."

"Did the Q'riln cause all this death?" Mica asked.

"No," said Mary, "they came up with this conflict entirely on their own. And it was more than death. There was forced, unlubricated reproductive behavior, pain infliction for amusement, robbery, and arson. A LOT of arson."

"How many people did you say died here?" asked Topaz.

"On the order of twenty thousand. And not so much died as were murdered."

"Creator!"

"Oddly enough," said Mary, "many of the dead called upon the Creator, too; their echoes are still vibrating in the scorched stones of the town. He did not, apparently, listen to them."

Mica asked, "Where has the Q'riln gone now, Mary?"

"She has crossed the sea to that place they call 'England,' here and now. We must go west and cross an area called 'France.' Yes, it means another language for France, and yet another for England."

"Is there another way to go?"

"By sea, all the way, but I do not recommend it. I do recommend buying some of those quadrupedal riding animals."

"I don't know how to ride one," Topaz said, doubtfully.

"They seem to me," said Mica, "to be a lot like *chisnar* at home. Sure, four fewer legs and less fur, but the principles seem the same."

"Could we instead get a cart?" Topaz pleaded.

"I'll find out at the next town."

Chapter Five

~~~~~

One of the brightest gems
in the New England weather is the dazzling uncertainty of it.
—Mark Twain

661 East Broadway, South Boston, Massachusetts

The night air was still and very, very quiet. That is, it was quiet right up until the first peal of thunder, followed by a sudden downpour to make even Panama blush.

It is noteworthy, the Old Man thought, *that the narrowest alley still provides no shelter from the rain in the absence of even the slightest breeze.*

It was still summer, so none of the four were wearing coats. That meant they had to stop midway down the alley, halfway unpack the duffel bag, get out their winter coats, which were clearly too heavy for the weather, and then repack everything before continuing on. Even then, there were no hats for any of them. The chill rain was kept from their bodies directly, yes, but it gathered in rivulets, anyway, before running down chests and backs.

"Grandpa, I'm cold," Cossima whispered.

"I know, shorty. It will be better once we're inside. C'mon, brats. And *no* sniveling."

Trying their best not to snivel, the kids followed the Old Man into the depths of the alley. In moments they came to the gate that led into the back of 661. He opened the door for them, then directed the girls to get under the shed with the trash cans.

"Okay, Patrick, you and I will open the locks. By that I mean, of course, that *you* will open them while I stand next to you for moral support."

"Yes, Grandpa," the boy answered, miserably.

There were two locks on the door, Patrick could see by the glow of the streetlamps reflecting off the clouds above. He decided to dispense with the harder one, the deadbolt, first.

"Grandpa," the boy whispered, "Do we care if we break the lock?"

"Not really. I can always send them a little money to cover the cost of replacing it.

"All right. In that case, I'm going to use the snap gun. Might damage the lock, might not, but will probably be a lot faster."

"Go for it, Grandson."

First Patrick drew from his pocket and put in the torque wrench, which didn't set torque but applied it. This went into the bottom of the keyhole. From another pocket he drew the snap gun, which he inserted into the lock fully.

A dozen pulls of the trigger, none of which exceeded the sound of the rain hitting rooftops, streets, and sidewalks all around, and the wrench turned the cylinder well to the right.

"That won't reset itself," the boy explained. "We can lock it behind us if I haven't completely broken it."

"Get the other one," the Old Man said, impatiently.

Without a word, Patrick applied the same procedure to the bottom lock, a lockable door handle. It fell before his assault very quickly, but, as he said, "I'm pretty sure I broke that one."

"Don't sweat it; I'll send money or, better, increase my tip next time I come here. Don't go in yet."

"Why not? It's wet out here."

"I've got a section of blanket and a poncho in the duffel bag. I'm going to get them out and put them down so we can shake off and not leave a highly suspicious mess."

"Oh, okay, Grandpa. I didn't thi—"

"Don't sweat it; you haven't had the schooling yet for this kind of thing. Yet."

"C'mon, Old Man," the boy said, "even if there was such a thing as breaking and entering school, you never went to it."

"Army Ranger School, youngster, will teach you the most important aspects of any crime, security, planning, reconnaissance, and control."

With that, the old man went around to the other side to bring the girls and the bag.

"Don't even think about putting on any lights," the Old Man said. "Just stand here until we dry off enough. Wipe your feet very thoroughly and then take your shoes off, tie the laces, and hang them around your necks. Quietly!"

It's something of a lucky break or, at least, fortunate, that this building has no apartments overhead, hence nobody positioned to hear us.

"I'm ready, Grandpa," said Cossima. She, after all, had the least surface of any of them to dry.

"Juliana?"

"I guess I am. I'm still scared."

"That means you're bright, so long as you don't let it get control of you," said her grandfather. "Patrick?

"I'm ready."

"All right; follow me."

In the darkened back spaces, the Old Man led them forward around a corner and into the waiting room.

"Girls, can you see the gate?" the Old Man asked.

"Clear as day," said Juliana.

"It glows, Grandpa, but it casts no light on the room."

"Okay, Juliana take point and lead us to it."

It wasn't forty steps combined from all of them before they were at the oval portal. At this point, the grandfather once again reached into the duffel bag and put on his plate cum tank carrier, taking the Sterling in his hands.

"I go first," he said. "Cossima, put your arm into the gate."

"It is, Grandpa. You should be able to go now."

"Follow me at about two-second intervals; count 'one one thousand, two one thousand,' and follow, Juliana first, then Patrick, then Cossima. Here I go."

With that, the Old Man lifted his left leg and thrust it into the wall. It passed with less resistance than one might get from stepping into the ocean. Getting the right one in was trickier; his toes caught on the end of the portal, causing him, on the far side, to fall face forward with an audible "oof."

Fortunately, he knew—his body knew—how to roll into a firing position. This he did, though a stiff neck meant he had to hoist himself higher on his elbows. That hurt, too.

Juliana came through next, and almost fell on him. She didn't fall though, but stepped gingerly to one side to allow Patrick to pass. He came through, looked around, said, "Wild!" and then stepped out of the way. Last in was Cossima, who resisted the urge to show off by doing a gymnastics routine on the way through.

"That's everybody, Grandpa," Juliana said.

"All right." The Old Man looked down as, grunting painfully, he forced himself up and saw a largish number of small silver coins on the foggy floor. They weren't in any particular pattern, purely random, it seemed, but they did form a kind of constellation.

The same glowing balls of *something* were still floating randomly overhead. He watched for a while, then noticed that the number of balls was not constant; two formed from nothing in the short time he watched. There were also a number of gates visible, some lit and glowing, others dark. "Cossima, show me the other gate you saw the arms and Slocum come from."

"Over here, Grandpa," the girl said, pointing, "this one."

"This one" was darkened on the other side, which the old man took as a good sign.

"Stay back from it," he said, then duck walked—*Oh, Jesus this is for a younger man*—over to it. He looked through and saw little while hearing nothing. There wasn't even the sound of any traffic which led him to think, *early morning, three to four AM*. And the light, what little there was of it, was just a reflection from the streetlamp, bouncing off indistinct boxes and cellophane.

There was more light here, wherever "here" was. Looking down, he saw precisely the same constellation of silver coins on the floor. Instinct told him to ask, "Cossima, have you got that silver coin?"

"Yes, Grandpa."

"Let me have it, please. Don't worry; I'll buy you a bigger one to make up for it."

Wordlessly, she passed it over. He examined it again—*Sam Straus could probably identify it*—then put the coin down on the constellation of coins. He then walked back to the gate they came in through. That gate's coins now included one more, in the precise same relationship as the one he'd just placed.

"This is some weird crap," he muttered.

The gate was considerably higher on the toy store side than on the massage salon side.

"I'll go first," the Old Man said, muttering, and tossing the duffel gently through the gate. "I only wish I were about forty years younger."

He never saw it, but his grandchildren saw one of the glowing balls suddenly flash to life, begin to fly across the open space, and strike their grandfather squarely between the shoulder blades as he began to step through the gate.

Insensate, he fell forward to clatter heavily on the floor on the other side.

The kids barely restrained themselves from screaming. They formed a kind of miniature human traffic jam at the gate, each trying to get through to their grandfather. Cossima, being the smallest, was the least blocked one, hence the first to get through. Her brother and sister followed almost as quickly.

On the other side, their grandfather lay as if dead, on his stomach. Juliana checked for a pulse and found one but . . .

"There's something wrong here."

"He's . . ."

"My God, he's . . ."

The old man, awakening, started to choke. It took him a moment to realize that there was no room in his mouth for implants, minus the posts and his own teeth. Desperate, he clawed at his mouth until he managed to extract first the lowers, then the uppers.

"I'm *what*?" asked the grandfather, who then sucked air in at max capacity.

"Umm . . . Grandpa . . ." Juliana began.

"Your hair," began Patrick, ". . . it's . . . it's."

"It's not gray anymore," Cossima finished. "And there's a lot more of it."

The grandfather rolled over onto his back and, despite the extra thirty pounds holding him back, sat right up without any problem.

"No, wait," he said. "That's supposed to hurt. It always hurts. Usually a lot. What the . . ."

The three grandchildren, meanwhile, peered very closely at their grandfather. Not only was the gray gone, and the hair more plentiful, but his face was unlined, his nose straight, where he'd broken it several times previously, his skin was tight and he looked, oh, a lot thinner and yet still more muscley.

None of the kids screamed, though they all wanted to. "Grandpa, what did you say before you went through the gate?"

He had to think back. "I was dreading the climb down, and wishing I was . . . oh, hell, how old am I now?"

"Mid-twenties," said Juliana. "Maybe twenty-eight at the most, twenty-four at the least."

"It grants wishes," Cossima said, wonderingly. "You ask for something and it gives it to you. Not just small toys but any material things. Or changes."

"We've got to get out of here," Patrick reminded. "Grandpa, are you all right?"

"I seem to be . . . let me . . ."

The grandfather stood up, then bent again to put the false teeth into a pocket. His coat and jacket hung around him like a woman's muumuu. That was bad enough, but then he felt his trousers and underwear beginning to slip and . . .

"Oh, hell." Holding the Sterling in one hand, he found he had to hold up his trousers with the other. "This is *so* not according to plan. Okay, let's get the Sterling and Juliana's .380 packed up. Quickly now. Then we're getting the hell out of here."

What the hell do you do when your waist plummets from thirty-eight inches to twenty-seven or twenty-eight and your belt doesn't have any hole for that size. Why didn't I use the ratchet belt? I could have used one from the Army and nobody would have thought twice about it. Crap.

Maybe I can actually tie this thing.

Ten minutes later, with the bag repacked and on the Old Man's back, the belt tied, after a fashion, and the grandfather thoroughly embarrassed to be seen in public in what now looked like scarecrow clothing, the four walked out and emerged onto East Broadway from the narrow alley on what turned out to be the Victory Market, a butcher shop, just east of what was now, again, for the first time in decades, Slocum's Toyland.

"Now where do we find a taxi or . . . Aha, a pay phone!"

Cossima asked, "Grandpa, what's a pay phone?"

"You'll see."

"What are you going to do there, when you find one?"

"Turn into Superman? No, I'll just call us a taxi to . . . I know where; we're going to a place where service actually matters."

110 I Street, South Boston, Massachusetts

The dog, a smallish boxer with cropped tail and ears, one of the ears being floppy, awoke with a start. She normally slept where she could keep guard over both the front and rear entrances to the row house, which is to say at the head of the stairs to the bottom floor.

Baby? the dog thought. She was experiencing something she never had before, the presence of two copies of her baby, the eight-year-old boy, asleep upstairs, and another one, in the direction of what she thought of as *warm season sunrise big street stinky cars.* How this could be she didn't know, being, after all, just a dog. But it was a fact, nonetheless.

Unsure of matters, she padded the fewer than a dozen steps toward the front door, then ascended the steps to the third floor at a gallop. She nosed open the door to the right of the top of those steps and walked in as quietly as possible, lest she awaken her baby. She tugged a little on the covers to make sure that it was her baby sleeping there.

Satisfied that it was, the dog, Suzy, walked back down to the main floor, then sat by the steps, puzzling over how there could be two of her one baby.

I will cross street in the morning to big rock house of Great Being and ask, Suzy thought. *Maybe answer, maybe not.*

Parker House, Tremont and School Streets, Boston, Massachusetts

The air was warm, but, as Eisen well knew, this didn't prove anything in Boston. The place could go from bitter cold and fiercely windy to almost balmy, even in December, after a rain. And the sidewalks were, in fact, wet, while the typical water and small bits of trash flowed in the gutter.

"I'm obviously too young to be your grandfather now," Eisen said, after tipping the taxi driver and sending him on his way. "You're going to have to call me by—and you cannot imagine how much I detest the idea—Sean? No, that's too close. Shortened version of my middle name, call me, 'Fitz, Uncle Fitz.' That means that, unless I can find some other way, I'm going to have to hunt the graveyards for a boy who died around the right time, who has the right name or, at least, middle initial. No help for it since I got whacked over the head with the ladle from the fountain of youth. But for now, speak as little as possible."

He stopped for a moment to conjure both a story and a name from thin air. Once he had that, he said, "Now follow me on in. Remember, be quiet. And *don't* gawk."

The lobby was, indeed, opulent and then some, from the custom rugs on the floor, to the regency sofa in the center, to the massive, two tier, crystal chandelier hanging from the ceiling, to the clerks' desk, itself, to the ornate gilded panels behind it.

And yet, and yet . . . there are serious signs of decay in out of the way corners, a stained rug here, a broken light socket that hasn't been replaced there. It's nothing that can't be fixed, but I see much that does need fixing.

Walking to the lobby desk, the newly self-christened "Fitz" told the clerk, in his best quasi-Brahmin, "Suffice to say that what appears before you here and now is the result of the intersection of incompetent BOAC baggage handlers, a clumsy stewardess, a formerly full bottle of scotch, and the kindness of an overweight stranger. I have hopes to see my baggage again, someday, and even my travel clothing, perhaps before the sun runs out of hydrogen. In the interim, I need a room, no, a suite, I suppose, for one adult, myself, my two nieces, and a nephew."

All of the things he said were true, but not recently so.

"Sir," said the clerk, "the best I can do is a two-bedroom suite, with a convertible sofa. Would that do?"

"The boy can take the sofa, so, yes, it will do very well, thank you."

"Very good, sir. Note, there is a second sofa—well, more of a love seat—but it is not convertible. Now if you will just fill out this card . . ."

Eisen looked over the card and saw almost nothing he couldn't, with a clear conscience, fudge.

"Since I am here," he told the clerk, "and since my home number is unlisted, and since, finally, I live alone, the number won't do you much good. And, moreover, I like my privacy."

The real reason for his reluctance to put down a number was that Eisen didn't have the tiniest recollection of the format for long distance numbers in 1965. *There's always* something *you forget*. He did write down the name, S.F. Maguire, on the theory that, this being Boston, finding a prematurely deceased Maguire boy shouldn't be all that hard.

"That's all right, sir," the clerk replied. "The management occasionally likes to call to inquire as to our guests' satisfaction with the hotel. That usually doesn't happen until after you leave. But if you prefer not, that is entirely acceptable.

"If I may inquire, sir, how long can we expect to enjoy the pleasure of your company here?"

"Two to three weeks, though just possibly longer," Eisen replied. "Shall I pay it now?"

The clerk filled out a couple of lines on the card, which allowed Eisen for the first time to catch a firm day and date, Sunday, November 28, 1965.

I think this is the first moment I really, deep down, believed this was happening. Hmmm . . . Thanksgiving would have been . . . no, was, three days ago. And tomorrow, all the stores will be open.

"If it's quite convenient, sir. Three weeks would be . . . let me see . . . five hundred and ninety-five dollars, and thirty-five cents, including the commonwealth's old age tax."

While, at an intellectual level, Eisen was quite aware of the effects of fully ripe inflation in his own time, at an emotional level, he was somewhat shocked. *Sounds so cheap though, of course, it really isn't, not when average salaries in the United States are about that a month or even a bit less than that.*

Eisen passed the card back, then took six one-hundred-dollar bills from his wallet, laying them on the counter. The clerk gave the card a very cursory once over, before placing it into an unseen card holder. The money went into a silently opened cash drawer.

"Here are your keys, sir, one for you and one for the young miss. Shall I call the bellhop?"

The bellhop, Eddie by name, didn't bother with a cart, but carried the single, surprisingly heavy, bag to the human-operated elevator and the room. He carried the duffel as if one well used to this kind of military luggage.

Eisen couldn't help himself. "Army or Marine Corps?" he asked.

"Sergeant, sir, Army, Third Infantry Division," the bellhop answered, without a pause.

"I wouldn't give a bean..." Eisen began, to be met by the bellhop with, "to be a fancy pants Marine. This is your floor, sir." The bellhop then led the party past the open elevator doors and to their room.

The suite fully matched the quality of the lobby, both in its good side and its bad. It did so without going, as the lobby did, all the way to the very border of gilded tackiness. In the suite's parlor, wood and leather abounded. There was a desk, a central table already graced with cut flowers, two chairs plus an office chair, and a fireplace which appeared to be functional. Over the mantel was a painting. Two carved busts rested upon it. Other paintings and other sculptures graced other walls, tables, and shelves. Besides the main overhead light there were also reading lamps behind the chairs and a desk lamp upon the desk.

The suite also stank of tobacco smoke, something that disgusted the kids. They were too smart to mention their disgust though.

The bellhop didn't waste time on describing the visual, possibly so that he could avoid the obvious areas of deferred maintenance without outright lying about them. Instead, he showed the features, the only one of which that interested Eisen was, "And here's a lockable closet, sir. It has an extra pin or three. Your key and the young lady's will open it, but the service staff's will not."

And there's a load off my mind, how to hide some of our out-of-time impedimenta *and armaments from prying eyes. Not to mention the money, until I can expand and then deposit it.*

"This place *reeks*," said Cossima, making as if to put a finger down her throat to throw up.

"Get used to it," Eisen advised. "Damned near everyone smoked back then...back now...whatever. There are few or no non-smoking rooms, non-smoking sections in restaurants, all that. Indeed, in college, fifteen years from now I smoked in *class* and nobody said a word."

"Even so," said Juliana, "this place really smells *bad*."

"Yep," agreed Patrick.

"Trust me," their grandfather insisted, "you *will* get used to it."

"Could I speak to the concierge, please?" Eisen asked, in his quite credible Brahmin accent. "Ah, yes. I need someone to contact a local store to have them send someone to measure me for clothing. All of mine is somewhere . . . no, no, not Brooks; I've never forgiven them for selling shoddy uniforms for the troops during the Civil War. Filene's or Kennedy's? Yes, I agree with you; Kennedy's is the superior choice if one is in a hurry or looking for men's clothing. While I'm waiting, I'd like to order breakfast for four. Yes, certainly; transfer me to room service."

The kids were in normal clothing, normal for 1965, while Eisen, himself, wore a bathrobe from the hotel.

They were in the middle of a sumptuous breakfast, though one that left out some of the more exotic Parker House breakfast fare. No broiled honeycomb tripe ($1.50), for example, was present. Neither were there any broiled lambs' kidneys with bacon ($1.65). Broiled mackerel ($.90), too, could wait for lunch. But there were omelets ($.70 to $.80, each, for a total of $3.00), bacon ($1.10 times two), sausage ($1.32 times two), English muffins ($.96, total) with copious marmalade ($.32) and butter (gratis), corned beef hash ($2.20 for two orders), cinnamon toast ($1.04 for four), four glasses of orange juice ($1.32, total), and two pots of—it being, after all, 1965 Boston—tea ($.90).

In all, the entire feast came to fourteen dollars and fifty-eight cents, exclusive of taxes and tip to the room service staff.

They were just finishing up the last of the tea when there came a knock on the door.

"Hmmm," said Eisen, "I don't recall them actually ever coming to take away the mess until you call or leave it on the floor outside."

Wearing that hotel-provided bathrobe, he went to answer the door and found, not room service, nor even maid service, but, "Mr. Maguire? I'm Larry Southard, Kennedy's. You wished to be fitted for some clothing?"

Southard looked to be about fifty, with light blue eyes, and hair gone completely gray. He had a trimmed beard, good teeth, and ears nearly flat against his skull. He was not small, by any means, at six-foot-two, and maybe two hundred and twenty-five or thirty pounds.

Not small, but not gone to fat, either, thought Eisen.

"Oh, very much, yes. I am, as they say, a victim of fate, sartorially speaking."

"No, problem, sir," said Southard, placing a loose-leaf binder on the table and reaching into a pocket for a tape measure. "We'll fix you right up. May I suggest something?"

"Please."

"Well, first, how much of a wardrobe and what kind, generally speaking, are you looking for?"

"Hmmm . . . let me think. I'll need two suits, I imagine, three- or four-piece. My preferences run to tweeds, herringbone and Harris, and colors . . . mmm . . . grays, blues, browns, along with dress shirts, ties, pocket squares, cuff links if the shirts call for them. Then I'll need day-to-day clothing, shirts, trousers, underwear, socks, and by all means a couple of good belts. I'm partial to chinos, jeans, and flannels. Oh, and a good men's overcoat, plus gloves, peccary if available. And a decent shorter cold weather jacket. I suppose, a couple of sports coats, four or five pair of casual trousers. And a raincoat." Eisen just barely remembered to add, "And, I think, a good hat or two; I'm thinking a Fedora or a Trilby or a Homburg."

God, but I loathe hats.

"Oh, and I suppose I'll need a wristwatch."

"I think we can handle all of that by the end of the day, sir. But for the watch you might want to try Joseph Gann's or, better, Shreve, Crump, and Low."

"No," Eisen answered, "I don't need something Swiss. Just a good, decent wristwatch. Does Kennedy's have a selection?"

"Yes, sir; I'll bring half a dozen you can pick from. For the clothing, what I'd suggest is that I take your measurements, then run back to the store—it's not but a five- or six-minute walk—sort out a selection I think might do, wheel the lot back here, and let you decide which suits. Then I rush everything to and through our alterations department, and return here with your clothing, in about two and a half hours from when I leave. Maybe three and a half if there's a serious backlog at alterations, but there wasn't when I left."

"Let's get to it, then."

☙❧

While waiting for Larry Southard to return, Eisen contemplated the problem of getting an identification card suitable to get a driver's license, or the license itself, and rent or buy, preferably rent, a car.

It would have been a good deal easier if I'd not been, so to speak, Youthanized. We had a dead candidate who could have become me or, rather, whom I could have become. Moreover, finding those records was easier back where we came from, because of the internet. Here? Finding what I need here? Wandering graveyards until I find a dead kid's grave?

I don't like the idea of any of that. So what can I do? What do I know? Where can forgers be found?

I'd be willing to bet the bulk of them can be found in prison somewhere. No help th—or is there? Yes, yes, yes! Forgers may go to prison, but they get out again. How often do they change jobs? Do they ever really lose their old skills? I'd bet not much and never, respectively.

So there are forgers out there, somewhere, and probably not far away. But how do I find them . . . let me think . . .

I went to law school. I know how to Shepardize and do the casebook hunt. So I find a law library and look for cases involving forgery. Then I find the cases and the disposition, see when the forgers were due to be released, and track a likely one down.

But will they trust me? Well, my quasi-Brahmin accent is just that, quasi. I can do Southie or just Boston, Superior perfectly well. And credentials . . . money, money is my best credential.

Now, which law library? BU? BC? Harvard? Harvard is likely to be difficult and it wouldn't do me the slightest good to tell those Johnny-come-latelies that their school was founded to give the first graduating class from my high school a place to continue their studies. BC, I think. I can go up the street to Park Street Station and take the Commonwealth Ave Line to Saint Thomas More Hall. Old home week; the Boston College stop should let me off right there.

Note to self, while at BC check the Martindale-Hubble for a good lawyer.

And, at some point soon, I am going to need a car. A dealership would be a major pain, lack of identification-wise. So a private sale? And for that I need . . .

He reached for the phone. "Yes, concierge? Do we have a copy still hanging around of yesterday's *Globe*, especially the classifieds sections?"

Better than his word, Larry Southard returned in about two hours with ten suits, a dozen shirts, half a dozen sports coats, and adequate amounts of everything else "Mr. Maguire" had ordered. Fitting, checking, and marking for alterations followed, quickly and efficiently. Then, leaving the items that didn't need alterations in the slightest, Mr. Southard took off, legging it, for Kennedy's in-house tailor shop.

"All right, brats," said their new "uncle," Fitz, now clothed completely, if somewhat casually; "I need to go hit a few places. Juliana, you're in charge."

You know, it occurs to me that someone, say, my apparent age now, coming back here, to this time and place, would be totally lost. They wouldn't know where to look for anything, how to do anything, or how to bend and, when needed, break rules. This is a cheering thought.

It occurs to me, too, that without the preparation we put into this, I'd be screwed. If we'd just charged right in, I'd still have wished to be younger, still been zapped by whatever makes the changes, and then we'd be here with no choice but to head back.

Green Line, Commonwealth Avenue, Boston, Massachusetts

He'd left the .45 and the Sig behind in the suite, just in case, and taken Cossima's assigned .32 Beretta as a pocket pistol. It was a crap caliber, of course, ordinarily, but using those new-fangled Underwood copper jobs, machined for maximum wound cavity and faster because lighter than lead, it would just about do. The suit from Kennedy's, one of two, fit surprising well, for off the rack. *But, then, Kennedy's, after all.*

So strange to be riding this thing fifteen years before the last time I rode it, which was, subjectively, about forty-two years ago. Not much has changed in those—one way to look at it—fifty-seven years. The cars are different; a few of the stores lining this section of Commonwealth Ave are, as well. But on the whole, the place is the same as the last time I saw it, fifteen years from now.

He didn't need a guidebook to recognize Saint Thomas More Hall, the Boston College Law School. The thing was a modernist visual and architectural atrocity, of light-colored bricks, generally square and with much glass. It in no way fit the rest of Boston College's quite traditional neo-gothic campus.

It didn't have any bearing on why I didn't go to law school there, even though I was accepted. It was more that I didn't want a law degree from the same place that granted one to that orange-faced buffoon, that same windsurfing gigolo who threw other people's medals from Vietnam over the White House fence. But it's still a remarkably ugly building and one I hope they tear down . . . or perhaps have already torn down, in the future.

Now, should I introduce myself at the desk or just saunter on in? Fortes fortuna adiuvat; *walk right on in, boldly.*

Copley Square Public Library, Boston, Massachusetts

He was familiar with a law library, but less so with the reference desk at Copley Square. Indeed, Eisen had never used the general reference desk, though he had used—or would, in a future year use—the equivalent one in the rare books department.

At the desk was a very presentable young woman, hair in a pixie cut, simple top over what was likely a mid-length skirt. Her only jewelry was a single strand of pearls. She had a warm and very pleasant smile, and an intelligent look. The eyes were blue, but shading over to gray.

"Miss?"

"Willard, sir. Jane Willard."

He hadn't really asked that but he was, as usual, in automatic flirtation mode, so perhaps that was what she'd responded to.

"I'm looking for the White Pages for the city, older ones. I probably also need to look for some past years for the Yellow Pages."

The smile grew broader and, just possibly, deeper. The woman's nose flared slightly, as if she were taking in and analyzing Eisen's Caswell-Massey *Jockey Club* aftershave.

"Just follow me, sir."

She stood to reveal herself as about five-eight, slender, and rather small breasted. Her posterior was . . . not hard to follow.

You know, this girl may be a better and more automatic flirt than I am. At least she didn't ask me to "walk this way"; I just couldn't have stopped laughing over that one; Aerosmith and all.

Parker House, Boston, Massachusetts

That was, well, no, not fun, but interesting, certainly. Nice young lady, too, at Copley Square.

With the trip to the public library, at Copley Square, to check the White Pages for earlier years, now, as he returned to base, Eisen had the names, phone numbers, and addresses of various forgers going back to 1875. He didn't expect that last one to be alive, let alone still in business, but he may have left a talented son or daughter behind him, and may have left the house to the same. Failing that, the son or daughter might just know who was still in the business and free.

But he really didn't expect any of those to be needed. He had his contact and, in fact, had met him recently, for certain objective values of recently.

Whitey Bulger. Funny how one's own life keeps intersecting with the same people, over and over.

He didn't stop at the lobby to check messages. He did stop to see if the bill from Kennedy's had come, which it had. He asked the desk to contact Kennedy's to send Mr. Southard back to collect.

"Of course, sir, be happy to."

He stopped to pet the hotel's cat, currently lying on the counter, and kept on staff most likely to help control the rats that, if not as great a problem as in New York, were still problem enough, especially downtown and the Back Bay and *especially* any place food was sold or served. It was a beautiful creature, a calico, very fit and healthy looking, with a small, teardrop-shaped bangle hanging from her collar.

The cat purred as Eisen stroked it, then looked at him directly and with something like intelligence in its eyes. It was female, of course, calicos were only rarely anything but. As such, it purred while being stroked and studying the presumptuous human.

When Eisen left off his proper worship of the representative of the feline god, the calico lifted her head, glanced around, and followed him to the elevator.

Noticing, he pressed the button for his floor and, glancing down, asked in his best *Meow*, "Looking for some free chow you don't have to hunt down, kitty? Well, come on, the kids will love you and there's likely some leftovers you can have.

"Besides, since you are a 'money cat,' and I am in search of money, treating you well may be of some assistance."

"Oh, wow!" said the kids, or some version thereof, when the door opened and the cat, accompanied by their grandfather, strode in. "Can we keep her?"

"I'm pretty sure she belongs to the hotel, but I don't see why you can't feed her and make a fuss over her for now. Besides, who knows; she may be lucky."

Not that I intend to rely on luck, of course.

As the Old Man showered, the kids chatted in the suite's living room. The conversation was mostly centered on the calico, with which critter all the kids had fallen in love.

Stroking the cat, who lay across her lap, Cossima observed, "She's really *such* a nice cat."

Juliana agreed, saying, "She's very well-mannered and intelligent. She sat with me for three whole hours watching, if you could believe it, a weird show on TV called *Voyage to the Bottom of the Sea* and then *The FBI*. After that was a lawyer show called *Perry Mason*. She seemed a lot more interested in *The FBI* and *Perry Mason* than in the submarine. I can't say she understood any of it; but she seemed really interested in those two."

Patrick shook his head. He agreed about the cat; it was the television he was least impressed with. "I want my cell phone back," the boy said. "I want the internet. I want YouTube again. I want Snapchat, Instagram, and Facebook. This place sucks!"

"Yeah," Juliana agreed. "I miss my cell, too. But, you know, when we go back, we'll go back to almost the same instant we left, based on how long Cossima was gone on your first exploration. So we really won't be missing out on anything."

Patrick swung his head from side to side. "Maybe true," he conceded, "but we're not getting our calls and messages here and now."

"Don't sweat it," said Cossima, looking up from the cat. "Tomorrow Grandpa—whom I just cannot think of as 'Uncle Fitz'; can either of you?—is taking us shopping for new clothes. I'm looking forward to it, because the ones we have look old and used."

"You're a girl," Patrick countered. "Of course all you care about is clothes. I want my phone back."

"We're also supposed to see something called 'The Enchanted Village of Saint Nicholas.'" said Cossima. "I wonder if Santa Claus minds them using his name for a village he doesn't have anything to do with."

"I still want my phone back."

"Does that mean you want to go back to our own time, little brother?" asked Juliana.

"Well . . . no, not yet. But I still miss my phone and the internet."

"We all do. But let's make the most of things right now."

Interlude

"Where could she have gone?" Mica asked, uselessly.

They'd lost the scent of the Q'riln in England, just lost it completely.

"Was there no war here?" Topaz asked.

Mary, the AI in a biological sheath nodded, saying, "There was a war here. Indeed, it hasn't ended yet. But based on ambient levels of psychological anguish, it's a comparatively civilized war."

"They learned from what happened back in Germany?" Mica wondered. "These people can actually learn?"

Mary shrugged, a surprisingly human gesture from an AI. "One surmises they can learn from the technological progress they've made since the last full survey done here, some three thousand, three hundred cycles of the planet around its sun ago. Indeed, at the tail end of that survey there was a massive volcanic explosion that destroyed all of the dominant civilizations in this area—well, the areas around their great inland sea that were actually civilized—but they've more than made all that up, both politically and technologically."

"That *is* impressive," Mica agreed.

"So what do we do?" Topaz asked of her mate.

"I think we settle down here for a while until the Q'riln shows herself. We've plenty of gold to live on, after all. And if we need to, I can buy us a business or a farm—"

"Better a farm," Topaz said. "Too great a chance of contamination if we engage in a business. But food? Everyone grows food. Well, except for the Q'riln, anyway, though even *they* used to."

"A farm then," agreed Mica. "And we wait until the Q'riln shows herself again, then pounce."

"She may presume," Mary observed, "that the lack of pursuit means you are both dead."

Mica and Topaz, both, said, "Indeed."

Topaz then added, "Mary, please program our teardrops to age us normally, in exterior appearance, for the local dominant species. Nothing that can't be reversed, of course."

"I've got the scent of the Q'riln again," Mary announced. She's across the sea, in what they call "Ireland.'"

"*Another* language to learn?" Mica half moaned.

"No," the AI replied. "Or, at least, not necessarily. The Irish have their own language, but English is widely spoken and, even where not, widely understood.

"Sell this place?" Topaz asked. "I've grown very fond of it."

"No time," Mica said. "Though I've enjoyed life here, with you, too. We'll leave it with an honest agent, to rent, with instructions to deposit the rent to a bank under the name of . . . well, why not 'Topaz Mica'?"

"When do we set off?" she asked.

"We've lost her before," said Mary. "Sooner is better."

Chapter Six

❧

You see for yourself that I'm pretty near heaven—not theologically,
of course, but by the hotel standard.
—Mark Twain, on the Parker House

Parker House, Boston, Massachusetts

Whether the cat had needed to get back to work or had had to answer
nature's call, none could say. By midnight, however, she was at the
door, meowing to be let out. Reluctantly, Patrick opened the door
and let her go. She left with her stomach filled with a good deal of
unsauteed codfish tongue and cheeks, sent up by room service.

Since the grandfather had gotten back late from whatever errand
he'd been on, dinner had been late, as well. Thus, none of the kids
were remotely interested in breakfast.

"Today," announced Eisen, "we're going to expand your
wardrobes by a good deal, as well as take in Jordan Marsh's
Enchanted Village. Shower up; get dressed. I want to hit the streets
before ten."

They left via the side entrance, the one on School Street, facing
King's Chapel.

"It's still a functioning church, as far as I know," Eisen informed
them. "It was built in the seventeen-fifties, designed by an American
architect. They actually built it *around* a pre-existing wooden church,
then disassembled the wooden one and shipped that one to Nova
Scotia to be rebuilt. *That* church was built around 1686. Used to be
Episcopal but is, I believe, Unitarian now. I vaguely recall that, if

109

Unitarian, this one at least still professes a firm belief in God. That's not something you can always count on in our time. We'll look inside at it later on."

Moving on, still on the Parker House side of the street, they came to City Hall. Seeing no one within earshot, Eisen told them, "My old high school, Boston Latin, started here, where City Hall is now. You can see the statue of Franklin, who was an early dropout, to mark it. That was the home of Ezekiel Cheever, who's still something of a legend, having served as headmaster of the school for thirty-eight years. The second one, an actual schoolhouse, was on this side of the street."

Again looking around to make sure no one could hear him, Eisen said, "That rather lovely—well, *I* think it is—stone building is Boston City Hall. It's still functioning as city hall. Imagine how few useless bureaucrats could be stuffed into that. Never mind; in a few years they are going to build the ugliest building in North America to replace it. It will be many, oh, many times larger; will house many, oh, ever so many, more useless bureaucrats, and it will, of course, be able to better administer the massive increases in taxation that will be required to support all those useless bureaucrats."

They continued on a bit before taking a right at the next street, Province Street. This they followed to Bromfield, where they turned left, to Washington.

"I think Filene's is a little better for girls' clothing than Jordan's is. Patrick, you'll just have to be patient for your sartorial upgrade."

"I'm pretty cool as it is, Gra—Uncle Fitz."

"Yes, I know. But you can't get by for the better part of a month on two trousers and two shirts. Nonetheless, if history is any guide, your sisters will be most difficult."

"We're not *that* bad, Uncle Fitz," Juliana said.

"Oh, yes, you are," Patrick retorted.

"No help for it," said Eisen, with resignation, "for better clothed they must be."

Filene's Department Store, Boston, Massachusetts

The sound of bells cascaded down the glass, concrete, and stone canyons of the city's downtown. There was a chorus mounted high up on Filene's marquee, along Washington Street, doing a pretty heartfelt rendition of "Hark! The Herald Angels Sing."

On their left side, Filene's very large plate-glass windows were all done up in style, advertising less the goods on offer and more the holiday season. That, in turn, was heavy on the decorated trees, elves, and Santas, the frosted gingerbread and the candy canes, the creches, and the Stars of Bethlehem. If it was a bit light on Christ as Savior, well, then, it was about His birth, not His mission and not His passion.

"Wow," said the kids, over and over.

"I had no idea so much effort . . ." said Juliana.

"It's amazing," said Patrick, who loved Christmas as much as his grandfather did.

"And all my size," said Cossima, the tiny.

"They put a lot of effort into this," Eisen said. "Partly its rivalry with Jordan Marsh, next block down. What makes that funny is that Filene's is not actually a department store. Instead, it's a women's and children's store that added a men's department late and begrudgingly. They say it themselves, 'world's largest specialty store.'

"But there's something else going on here, something lost where we come from. This isn't about rivalry so much as it's about love of the city, its people, and the people of New England. This is a store, well, several stores, seven or so at this point, telling its customer base, 'We love you.'

"There used to be," Eisen did some quick calculations in his head, "maybe ten years ago, and only for a couple of years, a zoo—no, I am not kidding, an honest to God *zoo*—on the roof of Filene's. I never saw it, but my aunt, Gracie, described it to me in such detail that I was convinced, for several years, that I had seen it. That was rivalry, too, but it was also another 'I love you' to the city."

"Does this store never end?" asked Cossima, about the time they passed under the Filene's clock.

"It's fairly large, yes," Eisen replied. "Probably about the size of Harrod's, in London. Jordan's, up ahead, is two and a half times the size of Harrod's. Depending on how you interpret the figures it's either almost as big—maybe seventy-five or eighty percent as large—as the Herald Square Macy's, in New York, or fifty percent larger.

"Great city, Boston, in its heyday. Through this door, kids."

Inside, they entered the retail area for cosmetics, perfume, toiletries, jewelry and, suffice to say, higher end appeals to women. He looked around, trying to call back ancient memories.

"This way, kids; you need gloves and they may as well be decent ones."

Gloves went quickly; they weren't the kind of thing that the girls thought of as high fashion items. Pretty was a secondary consideration; instead, they wanted fit and feel. And warmth.

Service was the watchword of the day. Eisen not only paid for the gloves, but gave the salesclerk his name, informed her that he would be doing a good deal more shopping, and said to where the goods were to be delivered. The gloves, and everything else bought at Filene's today, would be consolidated somewhere in the building, then delivered to the Parker House sometime in the evening.

"Beats trying to lug this stuff all over the city. Okay, let's go to the elevators."

He wasn't sure if all of the elevators were still operator controlled, but at least one was. He headed that way, since none of the kids had ever seen an elevator operated by a human being before.

"Third floor, please," Eisen told the operator, stepping inside with the kids in close formation behind him. The elevator, itself, was quite ornate, all brass and fine wood, with mirrors strategically placed.

The red-uniformed operator began his long-since memorized litany, "Third floor, career shops, women's shops, girls and juniors, boys, infants, toddlers, shoes and toys. Please step to the rear and keep all hands and feet inside the elevator until we come to a complete stop."

With a skill born of long practice, the operator closed the accordion-folding gate, then twisted the controller on his right side to begin the lift and then to adjust the speed. That was the easy part. The tough part was getting it to stop smoothly at the right floor. An unskilled operator could easily make this a long, drawn out, and deeply annoying exercise in the not quite right. This one brought the car to a smooth stop with the floor of the elevator aligned with the third floor too closely to tell the difference without a ruler.

I suspect, thought Eisen, *that he's the last one left, or near to it, so very, very experienced.*

"Six outfits, each," Eisen announced, as they stepped off.

"Necessary accoutrements are separate. And merry Christmas, way, oh, *way* early."

The girls split up while Patrick, who wouldn't be buying in the girls' department, stayed by his grandfather's side.

"Where did the name, Filene's, come from?" the boy asked.

"I've been told it started in Germany as 'Katz.' Supposedly the original immigrant tried to anglicize it as 'feline,' but spoke little or no English, hence screwed up the spelling. True or not; I couldn't say.

"Now let's go see what they have for you, Grandson."

The packages were all taken away for later delivery. Walking across Summer Street to Jordan Marsh, Juliana looked around, quizzically.

"Is the city really as white as this?" she asked, prompted by the sheer lack of any faces but white ones. "I mean, it's amazing to see people walking around and even smiling at each other, without everyone having their noses stuck on a cell phone. But almost no black folks or Hispanics? What's with that?"

"People-wise?" her grandfather asked right back. He looked around to see what had prompted the question, then his voice changed to very serious and more than a little somber. "Yes, it's probably close to ninety percent white right now. Above eighty-five, anyway. But there's more going on there than just the numbers. Blacks make up maybe a seventh to a tenth of the city's population and probably less than a fifteenth, if even that, of New England. But they're not made especially welcome, downtown. Oh, no, there aren't any groups of berobed Klansmen with burning crosses. It's more subtle than that. It's the salesclerk who ignores you so long as there's someone white waiting for service. It's the mannequins—tell me if you see one that isn't white.

"Some of it is economic, too. These stores are higher end. Sad fact is that black folks and Hispanics just don't make as much money, here and now, as white people do, so are less likely to shop here. It might be better at Gilchrist's but is almost certainly worse at Stern's.

"There will also be exceptions; put a distinguished-looking black man in a nice bespoke suit, or even Brooks Brothers, give him the Harvard or Brahmin accent, have him project confidence that he belongs and the salespeople will grovel for him, too.

"And some is more or less innocent; tastes in fashion are simply different and do not cross ethnic and cultural lines until the ethnicities, themselves, do, as, for example, the Black Brahmin I just mentioned would have."

With a sigh, he finished, "Just because the past, in some places and ways, was better, it doesn't follow that it *all* was better. Take, for another example, fashion, and the advent of the androgynous, half-starved, model with no noticeable chest. A lot of women and girls let the unambiguously gay dictators of fashion make them dress like boys, tiny or hidden breasts, short hair, all that.

"But," he added, as an extremely well-breasted young woman jiggled her way by so profoundly that even a winter coat couldn't hide it, "while women dress to compete with other women, they also dress to attract men. The girls who still have it? They *flaunt* it, yet.

"There's another thing, also a part of why I wanted you to see this now. In just a few years, America as a whole is going to break out into an amazing degree of interracial hate, riots, murders, robbery, even terrorism. No place is going to feel it more than Boston, though at least no huge parts of Boston will be burned to the ground, like some cities will. But...well...two things stick in my mind, due in about seven years. One is George Pratt; the other is Evelyn Wagler.

"I think George was black and about seventeen years old. He didn't do anything to anyone, but two—probably two—white assholes shot him from a rooftop and killed him. Evelyn was a mid-twenties hippie chick from Switzerland, who made the mistake of walking with a can of gas to her car that had run out of gas. Six teens—yes, they were black and just as evil as the whites who killed Pratt—stopped her, beat her, made her douse herself with the gasoline, and then burned her alive."

All three children stood with gaping mouths. What their grandfather had just told them was hard to imagine, hard to accept, from both the city they'd experienced uptime and the city they were in now.

Juliana spoke first. "My God, that's *awful*."

"I know," agreed Eisen. "I've never really understood it. I still don't." He shook his head in incomprehension. "Kill some innocent kid on the street just for being near his home? Burn alive some dumb and innocent hippie chick for . . . well, for nothing? No, I do not understand it."

"If we're still here," Patrick said, "in seven years, we could stop it."

Eisen's sole answer was, "If."

Enchanted Village of Saint Nicholas, Jordan Marsh, Boston, Massachusetts

The air was filled with Christmas music; at the moment, "Do You Hear What I Hear?" A huge, rotating decorated tree on an enormous stand graced the scene, but without overwhelming it. Rather, being centrally placed, it made the village seem bigger than it really was.

There were two entrances, side by side. The one to the right was marked "For Adults Only," and the other "For Good Little Boys and Girls." The lines were thinner than they would be either this evening or later in the season.

"Don't look too closely," Eisen advised his grandchildren. "It's like a play in a way, something that doesn't stand up to close scrutiny but is enthralling as long as you will simply let yourself be enthralled."

Ahead, snow machines gave off the flurries of a sudden winter dusting.

It was all built to three-quarters scale, the village, containing two hundred and forty animatronic figures, human and animal, and perhaps twenty store fronts. All the "buildings" had large window spaces so the kids could see what was going on inside. These included a hotel, a newsstand, a barbershop, a candy store, and a post office. There were also a fair number of houses with domestic scenes, from children decorating a tree, to a mother reading to her three animatronic little ones—one of them a cookie thief—from *A Visit from St. Nicholas*, to another mother playing an accordion while her children danced in front of her. In yet another home the family sat to dinner while the *paterfamilias* carved the Christmas fowl. In one house, a dog and her litter of newborn puppies gamboled in a crate.

Still other animatronic children attended a Christmas party at the village school.

In the stores, a cobbler hammered on the sole of a shoe while, nearby, a tail-wagging dog leaned on the counter to the telegraph office and kids left with boxes of presents, even as a messenger returned and someone else spoke into an old-time, wall-mounted phone. Meanwhile, an animatronic glass blower rotated an ornament over an artificial flame, while nearby the village baker prepared his Christmas treats. At the same time, children were lined up at the post office to mail off presents to distant loved ones.

Outside the homes and stores a squirrel ran across the street on a telephone wire. Two chickens sat on their nests laying endless streams of eggs. Sheep and lambs cavorted while horses munched hay. An organ grinder played while his monkey capered about.

Santa's stables showed some elves caring for the reindeer while others prepared Santa for his annual sojourn.

It wasn't that it all looked so very real. It didn't and, if it had, it wouldn't have been nearly as enchanting. Rather, it looked *well done*, with beautiful ideal caricatures of heads rather than strictly lifelike ones, beautiful old clothes, no longer fashionable but remaining beautiful all the same.

It was, then, a scene taken from a Victorian era illustration of an ideal Christmas, with addenda, given depth and color, sound, a sense of smell, here and there, and motion. It was something for children, and adults of a certain persuasion, to let themselves be immersed in. It could never fool anyone into thinking it was real but the village was the very platonic essence of what adults and children alike needed to see in order to let themselves immerse themselves in the real spirit of Christmas past.

The line, though being thin this time of day, was also brisk. Juliana and Patrick ate it up while even Cossima, surprisingly cynical about the commercialization of Christmas for one so young, still gazed, wide-eyed, on the displays.

It was not coincidental that the end of the Enchanted Village led directly into Toyland.

Though it wasn't centered around it, by any means, there was a unique and quite valuable antique on display there, and for sale for some twelve hundred and fifty dollars. The antique was a chess set, thirty-two pieces and board, from Normandy, France, made in the twelfth century. Eisen stopped by to admire it while the kids, with carte blanche to pick *one* toy, barring the gas-powered red kiddie car on the wall, scattered to the winds.

The pieces were all hand carved and delicate, one side made of a light-colored wood and the other from a dark brown wood. There was gilding in amongst the pieces, the kings' and queens' crowns, bishops' mitres, and the knights' lances.

"Beautiful thing," Eisen muttered, softly. "I wonder who eventually . . . no, who *will* eventually buy . . . hmmm."

Okay, no, no buying it now. But maybe just before we pack up to go, if things have gone well in expanding our finances, then why the hell not?

Hmmm . . . time to round up the kids. I have an appointment with a lawyer, to create a corporation, and another with a forger, Bulger, to "legitimize" me . . . for certain highly expansive meanings of legitimize.

From the corner of one eye, Eisen saw one of the salesgirls, a tall and slender specimen, with a face . . . *that comes very close to equaling—or maybe she does equal—my lost wife. Beautiful creature. Oh, well. I'm not going to let my voice break or a tear gather in my eye; that would ruin it for the kids while not doing me a damned bit of good.*

"All right, brats." Eisen said, after the toys had been paid for and ordered delivered to the Parker House, "time for a late lunch and then a brisk walk back to the hotel, where I'm going to leave you in Juliana's care while I meet with a couple of people."

"Lunch where, Uncle Fitz?" Cossima asked.

"I am thinking the Old Arch Inn. It's got tradition—it is alleged that treason was plotted there—good food, especially a Roquefort dressing to kill for, and a pretty nice pure old Boston atmosphere, with a fine serving staff. Now let me think here . . . 85 Arch Street . . . so . . . out the Summer Street exit, right to Chauncey, then left on Arch to the intersection of Arch and Snow. Just past Saint Anthony's Shrine, if I remember correctly. Let's go."

The walk was about two minutes' worth. Eisen entered, took one look to his right, went ghastly pale, and then turned around.

"We're eating elsewhere, kids."

"Why?" asked Patrick. "What's the matter with this place?"

"Nothing," Eisen said, shaking his head and obviously shaken up. He found it hard to speak, at first. When he had control of his voice, he said, "There's nothing wrong with it at all. It's just that my mother and I already have the table . . ."

"Great-Grandma!" Cossima squealed. "Oh, I have to see her, Gran—Uncle Fitz. Please? Pretty please . . ."

"We can see her and myself at some point in time, maybe, but they cannot see us. Which they will, if we all go into that restaurant. And, I assure you, except for the hair color difference, your brother looks even more like me at that age than the pictures would suggest. So, no; we're going to walk back to the hotel and eat there."

1 Post Office Square, Boston, Massachusetts

The firm of Foley, Hoag, and Elliot was not yet the powerhouse law firm it was someday fated to become. One could see that fate, however, written in the intelligent faces of the legal staff. In particular, did Eisen's new lawyer, Lewis Weinstein, early middle-aged and already gray, look highly intelligent. The hagiographic framed poem on the wall, written by Weinstein to Lewis Brandeis, only confirmed this. The various framed letters, certificates, and newspaper columns told of a man deeply involved in local and national politics, of a profoundly liberal slant, as well as a great supporter of the State of Israel. There were also enough certificates from the United States Army to round out the man as a patriot.

Decent little poem, actually, Eisen had thought, earlier. *And I need to make very sure I don't suggest military service; this guy will know things and have questions for the current Army that I can't answer.*

"So, Mr. Maguire, you want an incorporation?" Weinstein asked. "For?"

"All lawful purposes," Eisen replied, an answer which was a bit too legalistic not to catch Weinstein's attention. "That said, my major purpose is investments."

"Stock or non-stock?" the lawyer asked.

"Stock, and, no, I don't want S Corporation treatment."

And there's another indicator, the lawyer thought. *Not that it's necessarily suspicious to know the law, of course.*

"That's . . . somewhat unusual," Weinstein said. "May I ask why?"

"I want the corporation to invest, to never pay dividends, to handle all tax matters without reference to stockholders for the foreseeable future.

"And one other matter; I want all stock to be for life only, if not earlier sold back to the corporation. Thus, for example, if I have a child, say, the child might have only five shares of stock to my, conceptually, fifty thousand. But when I die, and my stock dies with me, that child's stock will have grown in value a thousand-fold, and with *no* gift or estate tax consequences."

"You *are* a lawyer!" Weinstein accused.

"Not exactly," Eisen countered. "Let's just say that, while I have gone to law school, I have not yet passed the bar and, for that matter, may decide not to sit for the bar."

The lawyer sighed. "While I, on the whole, like my job and my life, I confess, there are moments when I wish I'd never seen the inside of a law school or courtroom.

"In any case, it's a clever way to avoid estate tax."

"Thank you. I agree. I'd like the incorporation done by tomorrow."

"Tomorrow? You've got to be kidding me! These things take weeks."

"The day after tomorrow and I'll make a contribution of a thousand dollars to the National Community Relations Advisory Council."

The NCRAC would eventually become more honest in its name: the Jewish Council for Public Affairs, a pro-Israel lobbying group.

"Oh, you're a cruel, hard man. But I still can't get it done until Thursday, not with the best will in the world, and not even for a *two*-thousand-dollar contribution."

"Thursday, then. Make the CEO myself, S. Fitzwilliam Maguire..."

Parker House, Boston, Massachusetts

"Where are you going now, Grandpa?" asked Patrick. "Can I come along."

"Even in private," Eisen said, "keep up the pretense or you will make a mistake in public. And no, you can't come. I am going to see an expert in...mmm...let's call it 'ad hoc, unofficial documentation.'"

"You're going to see a forger," Patrick said. "See, I *knew* we came from criminals."

"Clever lad. Note, however, that it's not a crime the cops would likely be interested in until a), the documentation is in my hand, b) I use it for an illegal act, and c) get caught."

"Criminals," Patrick repeated, raising his hands skyward in mock despair. "I'm doomed, doomed, I say, to follow the family profession and descend into a life of crime. And you're planning on doing a lot of what amounts to insider trading, aren't you?"

"Calm down, Patrick. And don't be such a smart ass. I need this to do a number of perfectly legal things." *Perfectly legal as far as anyone who doesn't believe in time travel knows, at least. And making more than a weak circumstantial case for insider trading would be tough.* "And if trading on inside information is good enough for members of the United States Senate and House of Representatives, it's good enough for *us*."

Transit Café, 28 West Broadway, South Boston, Massachusetts

To Whitey Bulger, the temperature inside the bar seemed suddenly to drop by ten degrees, and it wasn't because the well-dressed sort who had just walked in had let in much of a draft. No, it was him, himself, who created cold.

Bulger was exactly as Eisen had remembered, from the receding hairline to the cold blue eyes to his average size and build.

"Mr. Bulger," Eisen said, in his best quasi-Brahmin, "you don't know me from Adam. And your first thought, because of the threads and the accent, is that I'm some kind of cop, probably high end, isn't it?"

Actually, no, Whitey Bulger thought. *My first thought was the contradiction between the high-nosed diction and someone who gives the strong impression of being every bit as ruthless and vicious as I am, but probably a lot better trained. Which is, frankly, tough for me to admit.*

"Well," said Eisen, "I'm not a cop. I'm not with Department of Justice or the State Police or the FBI. I'm just someone with a small problem, one that I believe you can help me with."

"Where did you get my name?" Bulger asked.

"By hunting through court records, of course."

Here, Eisen took off his sports jacket, removed the M1911 he had stuck in the small of his back, by gripping it around the slide, dropped the magazine, ejected the round in the chamber, caught that in mid-air, then handed the pistol over.

"There's your first piece of evidence. You were, I believe, in the Air Force. Tell me, did you ever see a forty-five like that? Did you ever see one with no markings at all and nothing to indicate they'd been removed? No? I didn't think so.

"Now go ahead and check me for a wire."

He raised his hands to let Bulger do just that but the criminal said, "No, that won't be necessary. If they wanted to infiltrate a cop on me they wouldn't pick one who looked to be so obviously a cop. I believe you're clean, Mr. . . ."

"Eisen."

"A Jew? Yeah, there's not enough money in police work to get many Jews, and your clothes say some degree of 'money.' No, you're no cop; but you're something else. Marines?"

"Army Ranger." *What harm in letting this swine think I'm a Jew, anyway?*

The criminal shook his head, saying, "Worse and worse. Well, what can I do for you?"

"I need some identification and I need it fairly quickly."

"You know the old saying?" Bulger asked. "Good or quick or cheap; pick two?"

"Quick and good; I understand it won't be cheap." Eisen swept his eyes over the liquor stacked on shelves behind the bar from waist to near ceiling. It was *all* cheap.

"What do you need?"

"First, a driver's license, could be Massachusetts or could be out of state. If out of state I'd prefer Virginia. It should show a date of a couple of years ago, old enough to seem valid, new enough not to need renewal. Second, for the same name, I need a never-used social security number, that will show up as legit. Then I need a birth certificate in my name and an entry in the records at city hall for that birth, let's call it September 4th, 1940. That's all."

"The sosh *card*'s easy. A legit number isn't. Not impossible, but not easy, either. The driver's license isn't hard if it's from here. It will even be a real license. I have an associate..."

"How quickly?" Eisen asked.

"Thursday," Bulger said. "Not a day sooner."

"Costs?"

"Typical Jew," Bulger laughed. "Ten for the sosh card, fifty for the driver's license, another hundred and forty to make the number legit. A hundred and fifty for the fake birth certificate and the entry in the records, which is harder than it sounds. Three-fifty in all."

"Honor among thieves, Mr. Bulger?"

"Absolutely, Mr. Eisen. Besides, I don't ordinarily screw around with people who can get that kind of quality pistol and handle it that deftly."

"My picture?"

"I'll give you an address. You don't pay them. You go there and have your picture taken. Then, Thursday, you come back here, pay me, and I give you your ID, birth certificate, and sosh. *I* pay them." He dashed off an address on a small scrap of paper and handed it over.

"All right, Mr. Bulger; Thursday. I'll need the birth certificate, license, and social security number under the name of Sean Fitzwilliam Maguire, year of birth, again, 4 September 1940?

"Now tell me, is Quinn's fruit stand on East Broadway still open?"

"The bookie joint? Yeah, it's still there. Why, you wanna make a bet?"

"Yes, I do. But I'm still not a cop."

That got another unusual chuckle out of Bulger. "I'll make a call and introduce you. Neither Joe nor his brother, Jimmy, are all that trusting."

"I'd appreciate it."

"Doubt you have a chance of getting there in time to lay a bet before they close, especially since you need to go have your picture taken. Tomorrow morning work for you?"

"Sure, that will be fine."

After the very well dressed, very well spoken, and—so Bulger suspected strongly—extremely *dangerous* Jew had left, he made a call to an underling.

"Yeah, Stevie, I just had someone come into my office looking for some false identification and an intro to the Quinn boys' fruit stand. I don't have any reason to suspect him, but I came by my suspicious nature the old-fashioned way. I want you to go hang out with the Quinns tomorrow, and after he comes in, makes his bet, and leaves, I want you to follow him. . . . How will you know him? Well dressed, about my height and build, brown eyes. But the big thing is that when he comes into the Quinns' shop he'll bring an air of menace in with him. You'll feel it; trust me here . . .

" 'Why?' you ask. Oh, I just want to know who he really is, where he lives, and if he's got any contacts that might be unhealthy for us."

When Eisen returned to the hotel from the underground portrait studio, Juliana took one look and said, "You're looking very self-satisfied, Gra—Uncle Fitz."

"Did your criminal endeavors go well?" asked Patrick.

"Quite well," the Old Man said. "So well that tomorrow we're going to go pick out a decent used car."

"Oh, good," Patrick replied, "preferably something really fast for a getaway car after we start robbing banks."

Eisen slapped the boy atop his head, lightly.

"I saw where you had circled a few ads in the *Boston Globe*," said Juliana. "Some of those sound pretty sexy, like the Rolls Royce and the Bentley. But I somehow doubt that you'll go with those. So it will probably be something like the Ford Galaxie or the Chevrolet Impala? Or maybe the Mustang?"

"One of those, most likely," Eisen agreed. "If I bought the Rolls, I'd put it in storage until I could pick it up when we go back. But, if I were going to do *that*, I'd put away a couple of dozen Duesenbergs, instead. Maybe. Those would be a seriously appreciating investment, while Rolls are pretty commonplace.

"Other than you're missing your phones," asked Eisen, "how are you liking the trip so far?"

All the kids made an exchange of glances, amounting to an informal vote that Juliana would speak for all.

"All in all," she said, "this trip has been fun. I'm surprised at how much better, in so many ways, things were back then, at least as far as Boston goes. The clothes are, sure, old fashioned, with a lot of bell skirts and petticoats, but they're better made and of better material than you tend to find back home . . . back in our own time.

"And we've never seen a place decorated like this is for Christmas. Sure, malls back home dress themselves up a little, but it's not the same, not nearly. There and then, it's really just on the surface and flat, to boot. Here and now, it's textured, deep, in three dimensions, and *real*. It just feels like Christmas in a way I haven't seen or felt before.

"Now if you could only figure out a way to connect us with the internet back home . . ."

Interlude

The Q'riln fairly shivered in anticipation. She was in the town upon which Cromwell's army was moving, but she had a way out. The busybody pursuers would follow her in, of course; it was their job. Then she'd leave as the army took up siege lines. The damned busybodies would be trapped inside.

"I wonder how their deaths will taste?" the Q'riln mused, "once refined. Doubly delicious for being different from the locals? Trebly so, for spitting in the face of their Authority?"

There was never any doubt in the Q'riln's mind that the town would refuse to surrender. She—well, she and her cube—had planted determination and vast overconfidence in the mind of Sir Arthur Aston, the town's governor, that the town could hold out until relieved by Ormonde and his four thousand Royalist troops.

"Silly man, Aston," the Q'riln said. "Cromwell needs the town for a port to bring in food for his troops. He's not going to wait. Neither will these tall thin walls keep him out."

Time for us to leave, Mistress, said the cube, in silent mode.

Yes, I know, agreed the Q'riln.

The air of the Irish town of Drogheda was filled with shouts, screams, and the sounds of arms, gunfire and clashing swords. Already, old buildings, public and private, were going up in flames to the south.

From some of the buildings the screams were from neither anger nor wounds, but from outraged women and girls, flat on their backs in the dirt, with their legs forced apart.

"The creature suckered us in," said Mica. "She arranged a way out for herself, and took it as soon as she sensed we were in the town. Mary?"

"That seems very likely, yes. The question is, what do we do now? The assaulting troops are out of control, killing nearly everyone. And there's no escape over the river, I sense, but just a mass of panicked humans blocking the way."

"Mica," asked Topaz, "what will we *do*?"

Not answering immediately, he twisted his head left to right and back again, listening to the sounds of the massacre. Then he said, pointing to the west, "Our best chance is that way but to get there we need to go this way. Come on!"

He and Topaz, followed by Mary, the AI, moved first north, toward the one bridge linking the two parts of the town. They didn't intend to cross, but just to get a bit of breathing room before turning west. Passing by Millmount Fort, they saw what looked like two or even three hundred Royalist and Catholic troops preparing to make a defense of it.

"Should we . . . ?" Topaz began.

"I don't think so. For whatever reason, the garrison expected to be able to hold the town, so are unlikely to have stocked the fort for a siege. Neither are those numbers enough to hold the place. We need to keep moving."

Twice, on their way to the Butter Gate, the trio had to duck into an alleyway to avoid marauding gangs of Parliamentary soldiers. The third time, however, was in an open square. There was no hiding place.

Mica attempted to make a fight of it, to cut their way through. It was a forlorn hope, in any case. Swords flashed in the hands of men better trained to use them. He was soon disarmed, bleeding from a dozen wounds—fortunately the bodily transformation had also made his blood the right color, or, at least, the right *enough* color.

"What do we do with these?" asked one of the Roundhead soldiery of a passing officer.

"Orders are to kill everyone in arms. Kill the man—"

"Noooo!" Topaz screamed.

"As I said, kill the man and take the woman and girl to Saint Mary's. The lot are to be sold as indentured servants or slaves to Barbados."

Topaz's soul had been cut from her body. Mica had been her chosen, selected by the great matriarchs of their people to be her mate. Never had those matriarchs chosen better and never had one of her people suffered more.

In her own mind and form, she could not weep. In this human

form she could, and did. Mary, being an AI, felt nothing, though her programming still caused her to pat Topaz's back and utter meaningless and useless words of condolence.

Topaz still saw her Mica, held upright, swaying on his feet from loss of blood, as two of the Parliamentarians ran him through, one through the chest and the other through his stomach. He had not screamed, though the agony was written plain on his face.

His last words were in a language none of the soldiers understood, though they assumed it was Gaelic. "I had hoped we might be given permission to breed after this, my love. I am sorry we never shall."

Mica's chin had fallen then onto his chest. The soldiers dropped him to the cobblestones to bleed out. They did not let the screaming Topaz throw herself over his body, as she tried to, instead dragging her away by her hair to where she and Mary would be sold as indentured servants.

Chapter Seven

❧❦❧

Boston has opened and kept open,
more turnpikes that lead straight to free thought and free speech
and free deeds than any other city of live or dead men.
—Oliver Wendell Holmes

City Point Bus, South Boston, Massachusetts

This time, he took Patrick with him, taking the Red Line to Broadway Station and then the City Point bus down, first, West Broadway and then East Broadway. Eisen looked wistfully out the window at some of the stores and such of his youth. They passed the Broadway Theater, where his shoes had stuck to the floor as he'd watched *Bridge Over the River Kwai* and many another movie. On the other side he turned to see Woolworth's, where he'd bought a set of Johnson Brothers' *Friendly Village* as a Christmas present for his mother, then discovered that the set was too heavy for his perhaps six-year-old self to carry, so he'd had to roll the box end over end for half a mile.

Eisen smiled at the memory of struggling with that box, thinking, *Stubborn to the point of pig-headed, even then. And half a mile, when you're six and small, seems an awful lot farther. And rolling the thing up* Pill Hill? *Ugh.*

Most of the stores meant nothing personal to him, since his family had lived near to "Little" or East Broadway. Some few stood out, Pober's, whence his white outfit for First Communion had been purchased, the neoclassical bank across the street from that, and the optometrist on the Pober's side who used the bank's window to do his eye exams.

One could easily glance lightly over the scenes and assume the entire Broadway was close to one hundred percent commercial, and especially heavy on bars and taverns. While there certainly were a lot of drinking establishments, over them, as over most of the stores, there were generally two or three floors of apartments.

"We're going to see a *bookie?*" Patrick whispered, since there were other passengers too close to permit normal conversation. "What's a bookie?"

"It depends on the circumstances," Eisen told him, as the bus passed Pober's, on West Broadway. "Over in the United Kingdom he's probably a fairly legitimate and legal handler of legal wagers. Here, on the other hand, he's a bit of an underworld character. He takes small bets—usually small—from poor and working-class people, gives them a receipt for the three-digit number they've chosen, turns the money and the numbers in to headquarters—mind, all of this is untaxed which is why the state hates it so much—and, if any of the number sets come up, he collects from headquarters and pays the bettor.

"The payoff is actually fairly good, as such things go; a theoretical six hundred to one, on odds of about one in a thousand. That's a lot better than the lotteries, and, better still, all untaxed.

"Mind, you never see that six hundred to one, unless the bet is tiny. Maybe five hundred to one on a bet of more than a dollar. It's a business with a high overhead, and no small need to pay graft. Graft..."

And there Eisen began to chuckle.

"What's so funny... Uncle Fitz?"

"The place we're going to, to lay a small wager, small enough not to be noticeable, was once raided by the police.

"Now get this, the cops found the hide in the wall with all the number slips. The cops took over the phone and spent several hours recording bets that were placed. They found about ten or fifteen thousand dollars in bets. And then they took their airtight case to court... whereupon the judge tossed it out for lack of evidence."

The boy scratched his head. "Lack of evidence?"

"Well, the cops and prosecutor apparently forget to bribe the judge to hear the case quite as well as the bookmaking headquarters bribed him to dump it."

"Holy crap. What's...?"

"The word you're looking for is corruption, youngster. And here's our stop, coming up."

"Do you remember where the place was?" Patrick asked.

"I do. I should. I used to work there, when I was twelve or so."

"Now, wait; you said we weren't criminals."

"And I wasn't. When I worked there it was officially a cleaners. *I* worked as a pristinely innocent cover for the underlying criminal enterprise. Mind, it was still owned and run as a bookmaking establishment, but I only dealt—barring one little more or less inadvertent mistake—with the cleaners aspect of it."

Eisen went into the place, followed by his grandson. It was painted green with black trim, had a simple door in the middle with large plate glass windows to either side.

"In the summer, they'll put out stands for the fruit in front, and then more stands where a car might otherwise park. It was a great cover, really, though the cleaners was probably better. The Quinns, you see, though bookies, took their legitimate business very seriously. Days began at about four in the morning, if not earlier, to get the best fruit available."

Eisen suddenly thought better of bringing the boy inside; he'd be recognized. Instead, he led him across the street to the public library and left him there.

Thereafter, he returned to the fruit shop. Once he went inside he saw behind the counter a moderately tall, moderately stocky, blond man, a bit ruddy faced. To one side was a rather weaselly looking sort, sitting on a high, metal legged stool and talking with the man behind the counter.

"Mr. Quinn?" Eisen asked.

"Yes."

"Joe or Jimmy?"

In fact, Eisen had no doubt about who it was; he knew both Joseph and James Quinn quite well, though that lay a few years in the future from here and now. This one was . . .

"Jimmy."

Eisen's voice was warm, with an odd touch of humor, as if there was a joke in progress that only he knew the punch line to. "Mr. Bulger was supposed to contact you to clear me for . . . let's call it clientship, for the moment."

"You Eisen?"

"Yes."

"Yeah, Whitey cleared you. Most people don't bother, they just come in."

"I'm new in town," Eisen explained. "Just out of curiosity, how large a bet can you take?"

"In theory, anything," Jimmy said. "In practice, I have to clear anything larger than fifty dollars with headquarters."

"I was looking at putting down something small, five dollars."

"Yeah, that doesn't need a call to headquarters."

"Fair enough. This is for tomorrow's number." Eisen took a roll of bills from a pocket, peeling off a single five-dollar bill. This he passed over, along with his choice of number, something guaranteed to be a loser for the next day, though only Eisen and God knew it.

Given the potential payout, one would expect a certain caution about large bets. And yet, no one had ever figured out a way to compromise "the number," and it didn't seem likely anyone would.

At least, absent time travel, no one will, thought Eisen.

As he took the money, Jimmy Quinn thought of Whitey Bulger's words from the evening before. "Jimmy, this guy strikes me as seriously dangerous. The politeness and accent and diction is all just cover. I smell an enforcer, but I don't know from whom. My guess is farther than Providence. And it has me worried. I'm going to send Stevie to hang out at your shop until this guy comes, then Stevie will follow him to find out where he's from."

I'm not getting the sense of any of that, thought Jimmy Quinn, *only of someone who seems . . . familiar, somehow. Like maybe we knew each other in a different life or something.*

"Why are you even putting down a bet?" Jimmy asked.

"For the excitement, of course," Eisen answered, then asked, "Besides your establishment, are there any other bookie shops you can recommend?"

"Only a few dozen," Jimmy replied. He took a pen and a piece of paper and began jotting down addresses. Jimmy handed over the paper, saying, "Here's six I think are aboveboard."

Stevie, if a weasel, was not necessarily a stupid weasel. He had his car parked nearby, indeed, just a few doors down from Quinn's Fruit, on the presumption that this person he was supposed to follow, Eisen, would also be using a car. Thus, when he saw him walk across the street to the library and emerge with a young boy, he jumped into his car and started the engine, head turned to keep an eye on where his quarry went.

When Eisen went to the bus stop on the north side of Broadway, at the intersection with I Street, Stevie felt a moment of despair. Again, though, he was not stupid.

Odds are good he's going to Broadway Station. I can get ahead of the bus easily, then wait there. But . . . no . . . better odds if I follow the bus as far as Blinstrub's, to make sure he didn't get off earlier, then pass it and get to Broadway station, park in a hurry and beat them in.

A bus came to the street corner. When it departed, Eisen and the boy were gone. Stevie put his car in gear, waited for a semi-open spot in the river of traffic, then cut across traffic and pulled in behind the bus.

By the time he reached the corner of Broadway and D Street, which is to say Blinstrub's night club, Eisen hadn't gotten off.

"He's not going to," Stevie muttered, then swung his car around the bus and sped on to Broadway station, running one yellow light in the process. He didn't bother signaling anything since, in Boston, signaling was considered a sign of weakness.

At the station, a green painted, long shed with two bays for buses and a central area, not elevated, for passengers, the payment booth, and escalators. The latter were more like very steep, slightly ridged, moving sidewalks than more modern types. These escalators did not, in other words, form steps that were parallel to the ground. Instead they were just slightly raised on their outside, and somewhat treacherous, especially when wet. Moreover, rather than being entirely of rubber and metal these were of wood . . . without any rubber or, if they'd ever had any, the rubber was long since worn away. They were quite narrow at the bottom.

Horror stories about the things abounded. Women wearing high heels found them particularly challenging. Some folks, indeed, called them "deathscalators," though few had ever died on one.

Stevie paid his fare, then more or less slid—mostly on his hands— down the "deathscalator" to the subway platform, below. There he went to the newsstand, bought a copy of the *Globe*, and then took a semi-hidden position behind the stand, opening the paper to cover his torso and the lower half of his face. There he waited, as one train, and still in the old paint scheme of blue, white, and gold, outbound, passed through.

He didn't have to wait long.

Peering over the top of the paper, he saw Eisen and the young boy take a position about midway down the platform and facing the inbound—which is to say heading to downtown—side.

There was just enough of a crowd for Stevie to shelter behind, even while moving close enough to Eisen to guarantee getting on the same car. When the train pulled in with a burst of air, a *whoosh*, and the squeal of brakes, he jumped through the open door, took a seat where he could see to the other end, and pulled his paper up to cover his face again.

Eisen and the boy stayed on the train through South Station and Washington, getting off at Park Street. And there Stevie lost them.

"Where the hell?" He ran up topside, to the Common, and didn't see them. Then he went back, had to make change for the turnstile, and rushed back down to the Red Line platform just in time to see them heading in the other direction on an outbound train.

"Damn!"

Washington Street Station, Boston, Massachusetts

Patrick asked, "Why did we get off and switch back, Uncle Fitz?"

"Because someone was following us. Or I'm just paranoid and I thought someone was following us. But paranoid or not, we're going to go with my hunches."

"Okay. Who was following us?"

"I didn't hear his name, but he was waiting in the bookie joint when I went in, left when we did, did not get on our bus but somehow managed to beat us to Broadway Station, and then followed us to Park Street. Get off here; we're going into Jordan Marsh. We're also going to church on Sunday so we're going to walk to Kennedy's and find you a good suit or few to wear. Should have done it sooner but ran out of time."

It took longer to navigate from the Jordan Marsh subway entrance to the Summer Street exit than it did to walk from Jordan's to

Kennedy's. They were only exposed on the street for perhaps a minute, including the twenty seconds that Eisen used to duck behind Filene's and scan the crowds behind him.

"Kennedy's opened a women's department on the third floor back sometime in the thirties," Eisen told Patrick, "and then a girls' department in 1937, but, just like Filene's men's department, their hearts were never in it. They started as a men's and boys' clothing store in 1892 and that's where their heart and their expertise remains.

"Personally, I think catering to women was a mistake. The women already had come in mostly to shop for the men in their lives and went to Filene's or Jordan's for their own needs. This is still what happens. It just took up space they'd have been better off using for more men's and boys' wear. The reverse is true for Filene's.

"Mistakes? Retail management, young Patrick, can be counted on to make huge mistakes, but I, personally, think the death knell is when they try to do something they're not traditionally good at, or they buy a competitor. They rarely last twenty years after doing either of those. The only thing keeping Kennedy's afloat, I suspect, is that they don't take their women's and girls' departments all that seriously."

Kennedy's was considerably smaller than either Jordan Marsh or Filene's. It was mere moments before they found themselves in the boys' department.

"Ah, Mr. Maguire," said their now old acquaintance, Larry Southard. "What brings you here today? Another suit or sports jacket, perhaps?"

"The boy, actually, Larry," Eisen replied. "I should have had him measured when you came to the Parker House, but forgot he has limited clothing, too. I'd like to set him up with one good go-to-church suit, two sports jackets, maybe three dress shirts, and let's say two pair of good wool trousers. And a heavier winter coat. Plus a half dozen more casual outfits."

"We can do this easily, Mr. Maguire. Come with me, would you, young man ... good, now step up here, please."

Quite good at his job, Southard had Patrick measured very quickly, then, with two suits, three sports jackets, and four pair of trousers in hand, sent him off to the dressing room to check fit and decide which he wanted.

"You're very competent, Mr. Southard," Eisen said.

"Learned it in the army, actually," Larry replied. "I was a first sergeant in a rifle company of the Twenty-sixth Infantry Division and ended up having to check fit on half my company's soldiers when the clothing people screwed it up from sheer indifference and incompetence."

"During the war?" Eisen asked.

"Yes," said Southard, wistfully, "from Cherbourg to Czechoslovakia, with stops at the Rhineland, the Ardennes, Austria, and a few other places.

"I miss it, Mr. Maguire, you know?"

"I understand perfectly," Eisen replied.

"My life's pretty good, got a nice wife, two kids, one of them in Girl's Latin, but . . . well, it's dull."

"'How dull it is to pause, to make an end,'" Eisen recited, distantly and dully. "'To rust unburnished, not to shine in use . . . As though to breathe were life.'"

Southard nodded his head. "Exactly, Mr. Maguire, exactly. You were in?"

"Too young, way too young, obviously, for the war or even Korea," Eisen answered, which, while terribly misleading, had the virtue of truth to it. "I was an infantry officer. Various assignments. Out now."

"Me, too," Southard said. "Infantry, I mean. After the war and going about as far as I could, I figured I'd give it a rest. Thought about going back in for Korea—I missed the excitement—but by then I had the wife, a kid, and another on the way. Couldn't leave them behind."

"I understand perfectly," said Eisen.

The conversation drifted off at that point, each man lost in memories of, subjectively, times past, for both of them.

Patrick came out from the dressing room, then held up one suit and one sports jacket, saying, "I like these and they fit. The trousers, though, are all too long."

"We can have those hemmed by tomorrow morning . . . well, this evening, but, honestly, I don't think we can get them delivered until tomorrow morning."

"That will be fine," Eisen agreed.

"Where now, Uncle Fitz?" the boy asked.

"Back to the hotel to pick up your sisters, then a taxi to look at a car."

The car turned out to be a Mustang, about two years old and gently used. There were under twenty thousand miles on the odometer while the upholstery was all sound and completely unworn. It had been a smoker's car, obviously enough, from the stench, but Eisen shut down protests with, "You could endure me smoking in the car like a chimney for years before I quit. You can put up with this. Besides, just about everybody smokes, here and now. We probably couldn't hope to even *find* a non-smoker's car for sale."

The asking price on the Mustang seemed reasonable to Eisen, some fifteen hundred dollars. Moreover, since the seller was private and had no particular interest in identification, which Eisen didn't have yet, the sale went smoothly, with the money going in one direction, while the title and the keys went the other. The plates stayed with the car.

"Uncle Fitz," Juliana complained, as they were pulling away, "this car has no seatbelts."

"It does, actually, but only up front. Nowadays hardly anybody uses them, to speak of. Sign of weakness, too. Even in our time, Massachusetts cops will only ticket you for a seatbelt violation if they've stopped you for some other violation, like speeding or running a red light or stop sign."

"Where are we going now, Uncle Fitz?" Cossima asked.

"The parking garage under the Common," he said. "And there's another funny crime story. Someone—I don't know that we ever found out just who—managed to steal fifty thousand dollars' worth of dirt when they were building that thing. Adjusted for inflation that's over half a million dollars in our time. Of dirt."

Patrick asked, "You mean everyone here is a criminal?"

Eisen cocked his head to the left slightly, answering, "Well, I suppose it does sometimes seem that way. Yeah, well, even so, they're cool people . . . baby."

Transit Café, 28 West Broadway, South Boston, Massachusetts

"Swear to God, Whitey," Stevie said in the back refrigerator, "there was no sign he spotted me. When I spotted them—oh, yeah, he had a young boy with him at the time—they were already on the other side's platform and then gone. They never looked my way."

"So pure chance you figure?"

Stevie shrugged his shoulders as if he wasn't really certain, but his voice was confident, "That's my best guess, yeah."

"I've met the guy," Bulger said. "I don't think 'chance' is in his vocabulary. He spotted you and lost you, easy as pie. Maybe you're lucky, though. My impression of him was that he was extremely dangerous, without even trying to seem to be. It was especially disconcerting in someone no older than myself."

"I kinda had that impression, too, Whitey. Friendly as could be with Jimmy Quinn. Nah, that ain't strong enough; he was positively *warm* with Jimmy, almost like he knew him in a different life. But still there was a kind of ice pick hidden inside him somewhere."

"All right, hit the road . . . no, wait; did you get any hints about why he wanted to place a bet?"

"Just to place the bet, Whitey," Stevie answered. "Well . . . now that you mention it, he gave me the impression that he wasn't really betting; that he fully expected to lose. And he asked Jimmy for the addresses of a bunch of other bookies."

"Nobody expects to win, Stevie, my boy, not really. And the number is unfixable, as far as anyone knows. All people are buying when they play the number is the chance to dream. But our man doesn't seem like a dreamer to me."

"So we've got a probable enforcer from somewhere even farther away than Providence and he's putting a small sized bet on a losing proposition. What's that suggest to you, Stevie?"

The minion shrugged again. "I got no clue, Whitey."

"He's scouting. Somebody with muscle is looking to move in here and take over."

"Could be, I guess. Bad news?"

"Very bad, Stevie. The question for us is do we want to fight this or roll with it, and keep our own organization going under new higher management. I wonder if the Killeens even *can* accept that, whatever's left of us from the gang war."

Parker House, Boston, Massachusetts

The sun was down now, and the lights of Christmas reflected from the walls and right into the windows of the suite.

Hmmm . . . I wonder if we should delay our departure an extra couple of weeks, maybe even a month, past when I'd intended to go back, to take advantage of the futures market and to just enjoy an old-fashioned Boston Christmas in comfort. I could have the hotel send up a tree. There are plenty of trim-a-tree shops around. Maybe . . .

There was a very faint scratching at the door. Cossima ran to open it to let the bright little calico stroll in.

The cat had made a habit of coming around, to be petted, to get treats, and seemingly to watch television with the kids. She owned the place, of course, once she entered, since she was, after all, the kitty of the entire House. From the door she stropped Eisen's legs, back and forth, a few times, before walking to the table and jumping up on Juliana's lap. Her meow was a command:

"treatstreatsyummiesfeedmefeedmefeedme."

Paying very little attention to the feline, Eisen got up and walked to the lockable closet. From it he withdrew the laptop and a power strip, before walking to the suite's parlor desk. He plugged the power strip into the wall, then the computer into the power strip. He then sat at the desk, opened the laptop, and lightly pressed the on button.

Juliana, who had a thing, a deep objection, to animals being collared, attempted to take the cat's collar off. She stopped when she felt a set of very sharp teeth resting on her arm and heard a very outraged, *Meow.*

Oddly enough, the cat stopped in mid-imperial demand, leaping to the floor and then to Eisen's lap. It didn't meow but, leaving its hindquarters on Eisen, it put its two front paws on the desk and watched as he pulled up one spreadsheet after another.

"Critter seems to be reading along with me," Eisen said. "But, little kitty, I have work to do and you are in the way. Back to the kids with you." He then picked up the cat before setting it gently onto the floor.

The kids had turned on *The Munsters,* something which seemed to interest the cat. She jumped onto the couch, settling herself between Patrick and Juliana, then fixed her attention on the TV.

Eisen spent the next two days laying two- and five-dollar bets at all half dozen of the bookie joints recommended by Jimmy Quinn. At each place he obtained more names and addresses. Most of these were redundant, but within the week he had forty different bookies.

Every initial number he'd picked was a loser. But, by the third or fourth bet, with each bookie, he'd laid a two-dollar bet which he'd won and which paid him back eleven hundred on a combined bet with that shop of typically under twenty dollars.

He intended to take a win after about three or four bets from each of the other shops, then lose a couple more to throw off any suspicions. In the end, he expected to lose about a thousand dollars against maybe thirty or thirty-five thousand in gain.

That, he thought, *will pay the vacation costs, plus a good bit, while the rest of the money grows through more aboveboard means.*

Offices of R.J. O'Brien, Chicago, Illinois

The best reason, to Eisen's mind, to come all the way to Chicago was that O'Brien had not only been around for fifty-one years in 1965, they would still be around in his own time. This meant they were competent, in the second place, and hadn't been sued out of existence for malfeasance, in the first.

He'd brought the kids via train from Boston to New York to Chicago, got another suite for three days at the Drake, and largely left them to their own devices.

Now he was explaining the rules of the game to the junior broker assigned him by O'Brien.

"No," he told the young broker, "I don't need advice on what to buy, I just want you to handle the processes for buying it. I am going to put sixty thousand dollars in your hands and I want you to use your expertise to turn it into the short-term—very short-term—futures contracts I tell you to. Are there any problems with this approach?"

The young broker, in a good suit and with an intelligent face, was a bit nonplussed by this approach. He said, "Mr. Maguire...sir...if you dispense with our expertise, you'll be paying a good deal of money for something you're not getting."

"I understand this. I don't care. I'll tell you what to buy, you make the arrangements and buy it. Can you do this?"

"Well, yes, sir, of course, we can. And if you insist..."

"Very good. Bring out the paperwork to take me—or, rather, my corporation—on as a client. I have the bank draft for the money in my pocket. Speaking of money, what kind of margin is required on futures trading?"

"I don't wish to be unkind, sir, but you're new and unknown, both you and your corporation. We'd require twelve percent of the value of the contract. Now if you were inclined to take our advice..."

"I'll compromise," said Eisen, after thinking, *What I am demanding, in the form I'm demanding it, is inherently suspicious, isn't it? I suspect that the rejuvenation also pushed my maturity level back a few decades, too.* "You're right. You give me a range of futures recommendations and why they are recommended and I'll probably select from that. Will that work?"

"Yes, Mr. Maguire; that's really what we *do*. And with that agreement, we can go with a ten percent margin on futures contracts, for most, but not all, commodities. It may well drop as we get to know each other better."

"Fine, then. So...my sixty thousand is good now for the control of, what, a bit under six hundred thousand worth of a commodity futures contract?"

"A bit less, yes, sir; there are fees. Call it five-eighty-five, give or take a few thousand."

"And if I manage to get a ten percent increase in the value?"

"You would net about fifty-eight thousand. That's over and above your initial investment and before capital gains kicks in."

But, of course, I'll be looking for items with larger increases than that.

"Very good. As soon as we've finished the paperwork, I'll want your list of recommendations and the whys of them. From that I'll select to invest in a particular commodity."

Chicago Natural History Museum, Chicago, Illinois

Eisen had made his pick, knowing full well, in advance, that it would prove quite profitable. Then he'd taken the kids out for a little education.

It had been known, and would someday again be known, as the Field Museum of Natural History, named for Marshall Field, founder of Marshall Field and Company. This was a store roughly midway in size between Boston's Jordan Marsh and New York's Macy's.

The store, however, was not on the list of to-dos for their brief sojourn to "The Windy City," as it was known.

Instead, they were touring the museum, one of the great ones of the world and especially noteworthy for its Egyptian and Near Eastern exhibits and holdings.

They'd walked through the pre-Columbian exhibits, walked around and stood under the skeletons of Bronto- and Tyrannosaurs. Standing now before a forty and more centuries old Egyptian chapel, limestone and covered completely with hieroglyphic writing and afterworld scenes, the kids were awestruck. Cossima, in particular, seemed to be studying the hieroglyphic writing intently.

Eisen was . . . thoughtful.

"The last time I was here," he mused, "or the next time, depending on how you look at it, I was here with a Mrs. George. Wonderful woman, she was, a high school teacher. Beautiful, yes, she was that. But the really important thing was that she was very smart, a joy to be around, to talk with, and to experience things like this with. She was a great friend. Oh, well. Never forgotten."

"C'mon, kids, we have just enough time to hit the Africa exhibit before we have to return to the Drake to pick up our bags and head to the train station to catch the 20th Century Limited to Albany, whence we switch to a Beeliner for Boston."

"Hey, Uncle Fitz," asked Cossima, dawdling before the inscribed ancient walls, "you know I've wanted to become a veterinarian as far back as I can remember. But if I didn't, after seeing this Egyptian exhibit, I think I'd want to be an archeologist."

"Well," said Eisen, "you're already all of nine but it's hardly too late for you to make a career change. How's about if I buy you a book on hieroglyphics, maybe one with several chapters on the Rosetta Stone?"

"Would you?"

"Sure. You know, little weedhopper, the thing that surprises me there is why it took so long for someone to match the Greek to the two kinds of Egyptian. But then, I'm not a linguist."

Cossima studied the hieroglyphs all the way back to Boston on the train. She had, by journey's end, a few dozen memorized, though, *There were rules in there I don't quite get yet.*

The thing she found oddest was that the Egyptians had twenty-four different symbols for single sounds, and could have written everything they might have wanted to that way, then dumped the thousand symbols of the hieroglyphic system.

I guess they just didn't want to, which reminds me, as Grandpa often says, that most people are idiots.

Parker House, Boston, Massachusetts

A telegraphed message from R.J. O'Brien was waiting for Eisen when he returned to the hotel. It asked, simply, "How did you do that? Please call, soonest."

There was a number there that was not the same as the main office number for O'Brien.

Home number? It's not that much money from their point of view, but the perfect timing probably has them interested. Maybe I should put, oh, call it, five thousand, down on a loser to throw them off the scent. No, I don't think I'll do that. Not enough time, really. Well, I can at least consider it.

Instead of calling back immediately, he went to his suite, with the kids, and pulled out the laptop again and pulled up data he'd downloaded on the 1965 futures markets.

Right, one big gain, once, won't attract a huge amount of attention. But this time, I want to split it up among a dozen or so commodities and currencies, all relatively small buys of under ten thousand or so, on average. Or does that make sense as compared to one big win? Hmmm ... I know, I do a dozen and we'll make one a loser.

Hmmm ... no ... not winter wheat; the money there's in a longer-term future and there won't be enough time to collect and put it into Berkshire Hathaway before we really have to leave. Similar story with FCOJ. Pork looks good. So does coffee and sugar. Cocoa on a put? Silver? Maybe silver. Gold ... dunno about gold. Yen, Deutschmark, Swiss Franc, Pound Sterling? Let's see ... first, O'Brien's recommendations for cover ...

In the background, and in the much-lamented absence of cell phones and the internet, the kids and their frequent guest, the calico hotel cat, sat in front of the television. They'd missed the first quarter of *Voyage to the Bottom of the Sea* and decided to give *My Favorite Martian* a shot. In this the cat was amazingly interested.

"Hey, kids," Eisen said, folding the laptop and walking to the closet to secure it. "I'm going to go to Southie and collect a few of the bets I made. You should be fine here. Remember, don't show anything from our time to the staff if you order room service."

"Can we get something for the kitty, Gr—Uncle Fitz?" asked Cossima, looking up from the television.

"Sure, why not."

Interlude

The difference between indentured servitude and slavery could, at the tactical level, the *personal* level, be quite small. At the strategic level, though, it could be immense. Not only was it limited in duration, whereas slavery was presumptively permanent; not only was it not inheritable, whereas the children of slave mothers automatically became slaves themselves, but in some places, the holders of the indentures were legally required to set up their newly freed servants with the wherewithal to settle themselves elsewhere as craftsmen or farmers.

Indentured servitude could be a win-win for everyone, really, with the masters getting labor that would otherwise have been scarce to nonexistent, the servants getting a passage to a better place that they could in no wise have afforded on their own, the frontiers being settled and the communities getting more useful and productive citizens.

Only the Indians—feather, not dot—suffered by it.

It could also be a miserable experience, with no obvious difference in treatment from that accorded to an outright slave, or, indeed, even worse treatment because the return on investment had to be made over a shorter time.

Her own teardrop, Topaz still had, though Mica's was presumably buried with him wherever his body had been dumped. She hoped someday to be able to recover it, to bring his corpse back home for the proper rites.

But, then again, maybe it isn't. His clothing would have been valuable and a piece of apparently silver jewelry still more so. They probably stripped his body before dumping it.

The work was awful, endless days bent over cutting and dragging sugarcane under the hot sun. Only the fact that Mary, as an AI, was immune to pain and did much of her work for her enabled Topaz to survive.

Prosper, however, she did not. Though she had the ability, more easily through her teardrop, to make minor changes, here and there, her body was essentially human. As such, it had to age and wear, or she'd raise suspicions. Thus, it ached, it tanned, it grayed. Joints which should have still been good had all the cartilage and bursae worn out or, at least, were beginning to. Her teardrop could help her make a full recovery, in time, but only if she could stop doing damage to it, only if her overseer would stop making her do damage to it, and beating her when she failed to reap enough.

She'd lost track of how long she'd been working on this or another sugar plantation. The seasons here were largely the same and there were no calendars available.

Even so, the day finally came when her and Mary's indenture was finished. Barbados was not the kind of place where masters were required to set their formerly indentured servants up in a job. There was no ceremony. Neither was there any payment. Instead, the overseer simply came by one afternoon and said, "You and the girl are free to go tomorrow morning. Good luck."

And that was it; Topaz was free. She was also, however, penniless, had very little idea of where they were or where they had to go, and had nothing but the torn rags on their backs for clothing. Indeed, all she really possessed that wasn't a ruin were some small statues she'd made as offerings for Mica's spirit. The offerings were in the form of the offspring she and he had someday hoped to have. In other words, they didn't look quite human.

Since her people mated not for life, but *forever*, there would be no offspring for either of them. The statues, imbued with the spirit of what would have been, were to serve in lieu of children for purposes of memory. They, not being living, would also never die and, so, would remember Mica and Topaz forever. So said her people's sacred scrolls, in any case.

She wasn't an artist, not as her people counted such, but love and pain had gone a good way towards imbuing her little creations with the soul of art. They were each about seven inches high, one a bit more, one a bit less. Each was in the shape of her own people, one male, one female.

The female's features were more delicate, as Topaz's had been more delicate than Mica's. For all that, though, both had tiny little bumps for noses and slender, elfin chins.

In place of hair, terra cotta feathers had been painstakingly scratched in by Topaz's fingernails. For eyes she'd found valueless colored stones on the beach, for the female, and some greenish bottle glass that she'd worn into pebbles, for the male.

To serve their purpose, the statues needed names; she remembered this from her childhood religious instruction. In the base of each, where it would not show, ordinarily, she likewise used her fingernails to scratch in their names, the names the conventions of her people said her children were to have. These were "Truvai," a kind of graceful tree found on the homeworld, for the female, and "Raucan," a kind of tall and stately evergreen, for the boy. They were, of course, inscribed in her own people's system of writing.

It had not been necessary to put in clan and sept names; the statues would know who had made them. And the tears she'd wept over them, and for her lost love, would give them spiritual life.

As her religious instructor had said, so very long ago, "For thus the great prophet of the Divine Creator bade us do."

"What are we going to do, Mary?" Topaz asked.

The AI said, and in a voice that, by now, sounded fully human, "I am still young looking. And this body is not so worn as yours. I have been making some of the local currency on the side for some time now. We can set up somewhere and I can continue to increase our wealth. When we have enough, we head to the northwest. The Q'riln is there now."

Chapter Eight

~~~~~

The society of Boston was and is quite uncivilized, but refined
beyond the point of civilization.
—T.S. Eliot

Transit Café, 28 West Broadway, South Boston, Massachusetts

Eisen and the prospect of a takeover by another, out of town, gang
was still bugging Whitey Bulger. He sat at a table while Stevie tended
the bar. In front of him was a picture of Eisen, copied from the photo
taken in aid of his forged identification. Next to the photo, Bulger
also had a list of all the bookie joints James Quinn had recommended
to the upscale Jew with the Brahmin accent.

Now why, Whitey mused, *why would someone like this Eisen
character want to hit a bunch of different bookies? Only thing I can see
is that he's casing them for a takeover. I can see it now, he comes back
to town with a dozen enforcers and in a day or two every bookie in the
city has transferred allegiance to whoever it is Eisen is working for. Or
maybe to Eisen himself. And loyalty to their own gang? Loyalty is a
word most of these turds couldn't spell without a nun standing over
them with a ruler.*

L Street Bathhouse, South Boston, Massachusetts

The bookmaker sitting on a park bench beside Bulger, Louis Latif,
was a Somerville-born, Lebanese Shiite-descended man, round
faced, swarthy of complexion, and with a thick moustache. He was

also highly athletic looking, largely from his fanatical play of handball, especially at Southie's L Street Bathhouse.

"Like I said, I don't know him, Whitey," Louis answered, when Bulger held up Eisen's picture. "But he's been to my shop, yeah. Made a five-dollar bet that he lost, then a couple of days later a two-dollar bet, that he also lost, then a two-dollar bet he won, followed by two five-dollar bets he lost. He gave me a twenty-dollar tip on the one that he won. What about him?"

"He talk to you or sound you out about a change in management?" Bulger asked.

"Not a whisper," Louis answered. "He was polite, in a cold sort of way, and just made a bet—well, a series of them, like I said—and collected the once. I mean, yeah, he gave me the chills, a little bit, but it wasn't anything I could put my finger on."

"All right, Louis. If he comes back again, give me a call, would you?"

"Sure thing, Whitey. Oh, there was something else . . ."

"Yeah?"

"He asked me for the names and addresses of half a dozen other bookies."

"Give me the list."

"I'll have to write it out again."

"So write it out!"

The bookie concerned, Seymour Abraham, wasn't Lebanese nor even Irish, though his slightly swarthy tone could have let him pass for the former if he'd wanted to. Indeed, chubby, with slightly curly hair, a double chin and brown eyes, Seymour could have passed for nearly any ethnicity found around the Mediterranean. What he was, in fact, was a semi-observant Ashkenazi Jew operating out of the North End. His story wasn't substantially different from the one Louis Latif had told, though he was the second bookie on the list made up by Latif, and the second from that list visited by Bulger.

After glancing at Eisen's photo, Abraham said, "New in town, high end accent, though where it came from, given he's from out of town, I couldn't begin to guess. Harvard, you think?"

"Maybe," Whitey agreed, thinking, *I may have to make a trip to look in Harvard's collection of yearbooks. Good thought, Seymour.*

"At first I took him for a cop, Whitey, but that's no big deal, even if he was, since better than half the force plays the number."

"What did he do; I mean, what bets did he make with you, Seymour?"

"He came in Monday and made a five-dollar bet. He lost. Next three days he made only two-dollar bets, of which he won the last one. Pretty lucky, you know? After that he made a ten-dollar bet, which he lost. I haven't seen him since last Thursday."

"So you think he was lucky?" Bulger asked.

"Wouldn't anyone? Make twenty-one bucks' worth of bets and win over a thousand?"

"Luckiest Jew alive then," Whitey observed.

"Jew?" Seymour broke down in a fit of laughter. When he recovered, he said, "He's as Irish as you or maybe more so, Whitey, and a good deal more Catholic."

"Ah, bullshit," Bulger said. "He's got 'Jew' written all over him."

"Which explains perfectly why he crossed himself when he came in to collect his fourth bet."

"Did he really?"

"Swear to God."

"Well, Hell."

"But Irish? He's darker, got dark hair, eyes, and everything."

"Yeah? Let me tell you a little about Irish history, Whitey. There were people there before the Celts showed up. Where do you think the expression 'Black Irish' came from? And, no, it wasn't from some sailors shipwrecked from the Spanish Armada, either. And your hair came from either Vikings or some multi-great-grandma who got raped by British soldiers."

"Point," Bulger conceded. "So did he talk to you about a takeover? Even a tiny hint?"

Seymour shrugged while shaking his head. "Beyond asking me for the names of some other bookies, which I suppose could have meant something like that, no."

Transit Café, 28 West Broadway, South Boston, Massachusetts

Bulger hadn't had to hit every bookie engaged by Eisen. Within seeing the first dozen, he knew something was off.

But what is it? Whitey fumed. *Is he trying to scout things out for a takeover? No, I don't think so. Every one of them that I spoke to said there was no attempt, not the slightest, to try to sound them out about a takeover.*

He won ... well ... so far he's won a good bit, hasn't he? Everyone I spoke to said he'd lost several larger bets before winning one smaller one, then lost a couple more. What's that tell me?

Well, for one thing it tells me he's either very careful or very lucky. But nobody is that lucky. Win a dozen times—or more likely two or three dozen—on less than a hundred bets? And those are only the ones I bothered to talk to. No, no damned way.

What then? I can't figure ... Oh, hell; yes, I can.

The bastard has figured a way to fix the number. I don't know how he did, but he did. And he's clever enough to hide that he did in the middle of a bunch of losing but larger bets. Oh, you sneaky fake Jew son of a bitch; I got you dead to rights.

The question now is what do I do about it? It's no skin off my nose if he won some money. Most of it didn't even come from our gang.

No, I don't care about that. What I care about is getting him to tell me how, so I can do the same thing. And I can do it more because I've got people I can use to front for me. Hell, I'll be a millionaire within the year, a multimillionaire.

So how do I handle him? Ask for a meeting? I don't know where he is, where he lives or is staying. And, since he lost Stevie so easily, I'm guessing I'm not going to find him easy, either.

So how do I find him? The answer is that I don't. I'll use my people and the cops to do it for me. Now to get some copies of his picture made.

Durgin Park Restaurant, Boston, Massachusetts

They sat down to one of the common tables. Durgin Park was that kind of place; you might end up eating alone or with your small group, or you might end up sharing a table with strangers ... or newly made friends, that could happen too.

Eisen didn't have to look over the menu; he knew exactly what he wanted, the half of a roast duck in a gravy that defied description without reference to the Divinity.

After ordering, Eisen opened the menu to a poem found on all Durgin Park menus, and passed it over to Patrick.

"I try to remember this when you've managed to annoy me," he said, smiling warmly. The poem was "Just a Boy," by one Edgar Albert Guest. "Especially when you've managed to annoy me by wishing for certain communications devices you cannot have here. Which is often.

"Read it."

Juliana had a lobster while Patrick and Cossima split a prime rib. Technically, the restaurant didn't do that but for a couple of kids? Why not?

All that—and Durgin Park didn't stint on portions—was followed by Indian Pudding with vanilla ice cream, until the lot were filled to bursting.

Engrossed in their meal, they never noticed the hefty, middle-aged man who got up and walked downstairs to use the pay phone. It's quite possible they'd not have noticed even if they'd still been waiting for service.

Juliana, however, did key on one remarkable thing. She tugged on Eisen's sleeve, and, when he bent over to hear, said, "It's incredible G—Uncle Fitz; people are all talking to each other, taking in the atmosphere, and *nobody* has their nose stuck to a cell phone!"

Transit Café, 28 West Broadway, South Boston, Massachusetts

Whitey Bulger paced, nervously, awaiting word of the kidnapping.

In the end, Whitey Bulger had decided his best course was to restrict his all-points lookout bulletin to the two places he knew Eisen had been seen, South Boston and Downtown. He had both his own people looking, as well as cops working for supervisors who took some non-exclusive graft from Whitey's superior organization.

Identification was easy; the driver's license forger again simply blew up what he had and then made more pictures to be passed around. Whitey also had two teams standing by to grab a hostage, presumably the young boy Eisen had been seen with, who resembled him so completely. He couldn't grab Eisen because, in the first place, he wasn't entirely sure that Eisen would give up the trick even under torture, something Whitey did have a certain amount of experience with. In the second place, he had doubts about being able to ensure Eisen could still fix the number if they grabbed him, and didn't think they could keep him if they didn't, either.

But a hostage? That gets us all we want without a risk.

An off-duty policeman had spotted Eisen, inside, shortly after he and the children with him had sat down to dinner. He'd then called the sighting in to a number provided with the picture. The number had led to the Transit Café, 28 West Broadway, whence a car had been sent, bearing three armed men. The cop would be well paid for his tip, though not to the tune of the millions Bulger intended to collect on the scheme, if things worked out.

Durgin Park Restaurant, Boston, Massachusetts

What a damned shame, Eisen thought, poised at the exit door, *not only that the place is closed permanently, uptime, but that even before that, you could not get that glorious roasted duck platter that I just demolished such a superb example of.*

Note to self: when we get back, get the lease for this place, buy the name, buy memorabilia, rehire old staff, and open it up ... for the greater glory of Boston. Hmmm ... and maybe Jake Wirth's, too, and even Locke-Ober.

Immediately, as Eisen and two of the children stepped out, a car pulled forward in a gentle, non-threatening manner. Patrick was still inside, relieving himself, when Eisen, Juliana, and Cossima emerged on the north side, which is to say, the Clinton Street Exit.

"Armed and dangerous," Whitey had told his men. "Don't mess around, get the drop on him, grab the kid, and *go.*"

As soon as the car was just past the restaurant's Clinton Street exit, two of the men got out. They had guns in their waistbands, a .38 Special snub nose, in one case, and a war trophy Walther P-38, in the other.

"That's him," said one of Bulger's thugs, sotto voce, as he walked around the tail of the car.

"But there's no boy?" objected the other.

"We'll grab the older girl. She's probably his and, at her age, he has more invested in her."

"Why not the littler one?"

"Because she looks like she *bites*."

"The adult there, the one Whitey said was called 'Eisen,' is scanning around like he's looking for a sniper in one of the buildings."

"So *don't* look like a threat until we're right next to him."

The two thugs both gave Eisen a heartwarmingly friendly smile, which smile was not returned, beyond the tiniest rise at the left corner of his mouth, though he did, at least nod. Then, just after the foremost one opened the Clinton Street door, the other one stuck the Walther in Eisen's ribs, saying, "Don't move if you want yourself or these cute little girls to live another five minutes. Hands up!"

As Eisen slowly raised his hands, the foremost thug released the door to let it close, then reached inside Eisen's coat and around the back to remove his M1911.

"Nice piece, Mr. Eisen," he said, tucking the .45 into his own waistband.

"Whitey wants to talk with you about your system for fixing the number," said the one holding Eisen at gunpoint. "We're taking your little girl until he has it. Don't worry; she'll be well treated until we let her go, provided Whitey gets the information he wants."

"It's not that simple," Eisen said, thinking up the most plausible lie he could in a hurry. "I just handle the footwork; it's a different group that does the fixing. It will take me a week to get them to agree. Even *if* they'll agree."

"Whitey says you've got three days."

With that, the second thug, the one with Eisen's .45, picked up Juliana and carried her, screaming and with arms and legs thrashing, under one arm to the car. There, he put away his own revolver, opened the door and tossed her in. He then took up the revolver, assumed a firing position, pointing directly at Eisen, and whistled for his partner.

Cossima screamed along with Juliana. For herself she might be fearless but for her older sister she was not. Eisen just glared at them, while memorizing the car's license plate. He dropped his hands as the car sped off with a squeal of tires.

They were brothers, he decided. *Looked too much alike to be anything else.*

Patrick came out. "What happened, Gr—Uncle Fitz? Where's Juliana?"

"Someone took her," he said, then added, definitively, "but we're going to get her back."

He looked down at Cossima, whose screaming had evolved into body-wracking sobs. "Do not worry, little one. We *are* going to get her back."

Parker House, Boston, Massachusetts

Beyond distracted, Eisen paced the floor of the suite, thinking furiously. Indeed, he couldn't remember ever being so angry and hate-filled in his life.

Step one, I have to get a trace on that car. But where? There's no internet. Hmmm ... if they can bribe a cop, I can, too. And if that fails, a gun to his head would probably work.

Okay, so what do I want with a trace? I want a home address. Will Juliana be at that home address? Maybe, maybe not. But whoever is at it will know where she is. And if they won't tell? That's easy; Separation and Inquisition, in all its shrieking, shitting yourself "splendor."

All right; so I've gotten the information with pain or the threat of it, what then? They're dead. No ifs, ands, or buts. Hmmm ... note to self, get a blowtorch, a striker, a pair of pliers, three monkey wrenches, some stout rope, and some thin steel wire. Oh, and a couple of folding chairs. Some police handcuffs? Yes, I think so, two pair, but remove them after those two are dead.

And ... clothing. Black, I think. Balaclava. Get one of those 20mm Lahti jobs at Ivanhoe? No, too obvious and easy to trace if I use one, even assuming Ivanhoe has any ammunition for the things.

So I've got the information and the kidnappers are dead. What then? Then I invent hostage rescue operations a generation before anyone tried.

'Course, I'll also have some tech two generations before anyone's thought of it.

But what about messing up the timeline? As I told Juliana before we started this, chaos theory is largely bullshit, but in the first place, if it could have messed up the timeline, we could never have come here. Time, I suspect, heals itself in almost all cases. I mean, shoot the entire membership of the Frankfurt School as they get off the boat; that would make a difference? Pretty positive difference, as a matter of fact. But a half dozen or so child-grabbing, hostage holding scumbags, in the middle of an ongoing gang war? They're on my "little list" and they never will be missed, by myself or by Father Time.

I'm going to need some help but . . . aha!

"Kids, I'm going to take a little walk. Patrick, get the Czech .380. Cossima take the Beretta .32. Shoot anyone who comes through that door except me. And you'll know it's me by this knock."

Here he gave a sample of the "shave and a haircut, two bits" knock.

"Where are you going, Grandpa, and what about Juliana?" Patrick asked.

"I need someone who can drive and knows which end of a gun the bullet comes out of. I think I might know who it is, too. Before that, though, I'm going to swing by to get a Massachusetts firearms ID card."

Kennedy's Department Store, Boston, Massachusetts

Getting a Massachusetts FID, or Firearms ID, had proven just as easy to Eisen as he'd remembered it, from getting one in 1971. It rested now, comfortably, in his wallet.

"Slow day?" Eisen asked Larry Southard. "Slow day, or just taking a break?"

"Just a slow day, Mr. Maguire," Southard answered. "The business seems to me to be like that, frenzied activity or pure lethargy."

"Rather like the Army, then, isn't it?"

"Now that you mention it," Southard replied. "Though the 'frenzied activity' in an army at war can be very frenzied, indeed."

That got a chuckle out of Eisen. The chuckle was followed by a sigh. *I hope to Hell I've read this guy right.*

"I have a significant problem, a non-sartorial problem, Top, and the only one I can think of to help me with it, without sending out of state, is you. May I sit?"

Southard's chest swelled at the mention of "Top," the common nickname for a company's first sergeant. Immediately after, though, his eyes narrowed. *Et dona ferentes*, he thought. *Beware of Greeks even when bearing gifts.*

"Sure, please sit, Mr. Maguire."

Eisen looked around to make sure no one was listening. "As long as we're talking, you may as well know that my real name isn't Maguire, it's Eisen. Oh, yes, I'm Irish enough, but there's a Jew in the woodpile.

"The second thing you ought to know is that I've run afoul of a part of the Killeen Gang, Whitey Bulger's part. You've heard of them? Ah, good.

"They've kidnapped my niece, Juliana. I've got the license plate of the car that she was taken away in."

"Is she the one, the older one, who was there when I was taking your measurements at the Parker House?" Southard asked.

"Her. Anyway, Bulger's demanding some information I can't give him. I'd probably give it to him if I could, but, for reasons I can't divulge, I just can't. Not won't; cannot.

"Tell me, Top, you said you missed the Army. Was it the excitement? The sense of purpose, or mission? Feeling that what you did mattered? Or was it all those things?"

"All of them, and the . . . the comradeship, too, to be honest."

"Well, I've got no choice," Eisen said. "Can't go to the cops officially; they're so infiltrated that Bulger will know before I've left the station. And then the girl may die. So, if she's to be rescued, I'll have to do it myself. I could use a back-up.

"Now your first thought is going to be that you already have a wife and kids, and owe it to them to stay alive. So I'm going to be apparently very crass, and offer you a thousand dollars to back me up. We both know though, don't we, that a thousand dollars isn't enough money to take the risk of being killed over, even if we've both taken the risks for a lot less? But what it is, is an excuse, an excuse for you to do what you want to do anyway, to do the right thing, to matter again in a way you cannot here.

"I'm right, am I not?"

Southard closed his eyes, thinking deeply for a moment. Finally, when he opened them, he said, "I bought my M1 carbine when I was discharged. Shall I bring it? Also, I've got a cousin on the force, Bob Ciccolo, 'Chickie,' we call him, that I would swear on a stack of Bibles was honest."

"Welcome to the team, Top. Problem with involving your honest cousin is that I intend to do some very bad things to the people who took my granddaughter, and an honest cop ought not be involved. I'd rather bribe a dishonest cop who would be afraid to say anything because he'd taken a bribe to do something he shouldn't have done."

Southard's respect for Eisen's honesty and brainpower grew then. "I know a couple of considerably less honest cops, too, and one of them is also a cousin. A lot of 'Boston's Finest' shop here, you know. I figure I can get the info you want for, oh, call it fifty bucks."

"Okay, let's go that way, then. But I'll give you a hundred for the cop. Get me Whitey Bulger's home address, too, and any known addresses of girlfriends, plus his car's plate; I've got no doubt the police know *exactly* who he is and where he lives. We'll also need some appropriately dark clothing and military style carrying equipment. Can you do that if I provide the money?"

"Sure. And I can take a couple of sick days to prepare."

Eisen pulled both a list of things to do and a small roll of bills out of his pocket, saying, "You already have my address and telephone number. As much as possible I want your hands to stay very clean in this. I'm going to get to work on the not so clean stuff."

1957 Massachusetts Avenue, Cambridge, Massachusetts

The building proclaimed itself the "Mutual Realty Building." It was yellow brick, much of the brick having been laid in an unusual vertical parquet pattern. The sign of the business on the left-hand side of the building proclaimed "Roach's Sporting Goods."

Eisen walked in, glanced around, and muttered to himself, "Like being a kid in a candy store."

He bought a used M1 Carbine and two hundred and forty rounds of ammunition, along with a mixed half dozen of fifteen and thirty round magazines, all for a tad under one hundred dollars. This was not quite the bargain it may have seemed. Moving down the glass-topped counter, he picked up a shotgun. None of these were needed for the upcoming festivities; all were to provide a degree of cover. Finally, he went to the reloading desk and bought a dozen boxes of bullets in .30 Carbine, as well as several pounds of number four buckshot and F shot. A press, some hundreds of primers, and five pounds of modern powder completed his purchase in that section.

For another eighty dollars he picked up a U.S. Model 1863 percussion rifle as well as four hundred percussion caps, several pounds of black powder, a bullet mold, and several pounds of lead.

The store clerk helped him load all this into his car, with the comment, "Looks like you're preparing for a war, mister."

"No, not that. But I'm a little concerned, since the president was shot two years ago, that the reds in congress will try to stop future sales of arms and ammunition. I'm just getting ready for that day."

"I hear you. Lots of folks say that, or something a lot like that. Me, I'm more worried about what the state folks will do than the feds."

"Them, too, yes."

Parker House, Boston, Massachusetts

It was very late and over a hundred miles later. His *shave and a haircut, two bits* knock got Eisen back into the suite without being shot by his grandson, Patrick, who was extremely agitated by the kidnapping of his sister, pacing restlessly and chewing his nails to the quick. If one looked carefully one could see the tracks of the tears of terror that had coursed down his cheeks. With Eisen came a bellhop, porting the wrapped and bundled goodies he'd picked up in Cambridge and elsewhere. Among the goodies were half a dozen sections of two-inch by five-inch steel pipe, a dozen end caps to fit same, plus wax, fuse, non-electric blasting caps, and a crimper. Oddly, too, there was a package of cigars mixed in with the rest. There was a decent sized mixing bowl, as well. Even more oddly, there were three bottles of Elmer's Glue, a lighter, a can of lighter fluid, and some scissors. Oh, and a hand drill. And a green canvas bag that, barring the material, much resembled a lady's pocketbook. A Soldier or Marine would have called it a "fag bag," and instantly recognized it as a map case.

"Step one," Eisen said, after the bellhop had left with his tip, "is to time the fuse. Patrick, sort through that bag over there and dig out the glue, the scissors, and the cigarette lighter. Cossima, open those cans of shot and mix them up in the big bowl. Kids, we're going have a busy night!"

"What are we doing, Uncle Fitz?"

"We're making hand grenades."

"Oh, goody!"

Step one, as Eisen had said, was to cut a measure of fuse, light it, and time it. Eisen did this in the fireplace, after opening the flue. Step two, also done by Eisen, was to screw and glue a cap onto one end of each of the sections of pipe. The glue was part for water proofing, and part to satisfy Eisen's unrelenting cynicism where- and whenever the Prophet, Murphy, was concerned. Step three was to liberally coat the inside of the pipes with Elmer's glue, and then, in step four, to fill them with shot. Cossima took care of the glue distribution, while Patrick filled them with the mix of FF and Number Four Buckshot. Step five, after letting the shot sit for a while, was to dump it out, then add more glue. Step six involved adding more shot. Step seven was, again, emptying the loose shot out. At the end of step seven, each of the six pieces of pipe had a good solid buildup of shot in the two grades.

The calico, who had shown up midway through step four, watched the entire assembly operation with what appeared to be keen interest.

While the kids were gluing shot into the pipes, for his step eight, Eisen drilled holes into each of the six remaining end caps, holes just large enough for the width of the fuse. He, further, step nine, cut the green colored fuse to lengths of four inches, which, with this speed of fuse, would give a burn time of eight seconds. This would normally be considered too long for an armed enemy in the field. Eisen's theory was that his victims would never know what hit them.

Step ten was touchy. Eisen very carefully held each blasting cap, one at a time in his right hand, then tapped wrist to wrist to ensure there was nothing, no dirt or dust or other blockage, inside the caps to obstruct the flame from the fuse reaching the explosive. Step eleven was also touchy, consisting of inserting the fuse pieces into the blasting caps, then crimping the caps to the fuse. For this step,

Eisen sent the kids and the almost but not quite yet grenades from the room and held the caps and crimper to put the latter between himself and the former.

Step twelve was probably paranoia in action; Eisen passed the fuses through the holes drilled in the end caps, then lit a candle and dripped hot wax to seal the holes.

Thirteen was filling the pipes with a mix of the gunpowders bought at Roach's. Fourteen involved wetting a pencil and repeatedly pushing it into the powder to create a space for the blasting caps. The damp wasn't enough to affect the explosive potential but would make the powder around the holes he'd created stick together, while leaving a gap to allow the blast from the caps to make it to the end of the powder before the top of it flew apart. The fifteenth and final step was putting glue around the other threaded end of the pipes, their open ends, and fitting the other end caps on.

Eisen noticed that both grandchildren present had gotten a lot calmer to be actually *doing* something. Patrick wasn't even complaining about the lack of cell phones, a clear indicator of how seriously he took this.

"Whew," said Eisen, just before four in the morning. "Done. Patrick, dig out the pneumatic Sterling and pump. Check the charge on the laser . . . no, just plug it in to recharge; better safe than sorry. Stout lad. Cossima—carefully!—get out the night vision goggles, hook them to their charger, and plug them into the wall. Then get the bag with the key rings, the little boxes and books of matches, and the duct tape."

"What are those for . . . Uncle Fitz?"

"Igniters."

"I thought the cigars . . ."

"Back up."

The phone rang. It was Southard with the address that went with the car, as well as several other addresses. "The less honest cousin I went to," he explained, "works midnight to morning shift. He doesn't know why I wanted to know, but trusts me. He's also not stupid, so he's not going to spill anything."

"Catch some sleep, Top," Eisen said. "I'm going to do the same after I finish up a couple of things here. We'll meet at my hotel suite at twenty-three hundred hours."

Juliana:

They haven't hurt me, but they put me in this room with no light, told me to keep quiet, and locked the door. I cried for the first hour I was here. I think it was an hour, anyway. There's no clock and I never thought to wear a watch, since back home I use my cell phone to tell the time.

When I asked about going to the bathroom they brought me a bed pan and a roll of toilet paper. When I said I was hungry, about half an hour later, they brought me a sandwich, a small bag of chips, a soda, and some kind of packaged pastry. I told them I was cold and they tossed me a blanket and a pillow. I guess I'll have to sleep, if I ever do sleep, on the cold concrete floor. Well, it's not that bad; I still have my nice winter coat to lie on.

I am so scared, scared like I've never been before. Those are bad men that grabbed me, and the couple of women I saw in the house didn't look a lot better.

What I saw of the house wasn't much. The floor I'm on is half underground. I saw a kitchen as they brought me in through the back door, then another room that I think was a dining room, with high windows looking out onto the street. I don't know what street it is; they kept my head down the whole time I was in the car.

I asked myself what would Grandpa do, if he were stuck like this. I decided he'd start feeling around to see if he could find a weapon; he's like that. So I felt around. All I found was a piece of some heavy metal, a foot and a half or so long and maybe an inch thick. I've got that. If they open the door again, to take me, I'm going to try to take one out with me.

They haven't threatened me. They haven't hurt me. But, Grandpa, come get me, please; I'm sooo scared!

Parker House, Boston, Massachusetts

"I got restless," said Southard, "So I went and looked over the address, both important addresses. For the first one, I carried a Kennedy's box with a suit in it for an excuse. Left the suit between the doors of a nearby building. It's a cast off the alterations shop made a mess of— it happens, sometimes—and nobody wants it."

"Come to the table," Eisen said. He grabbed a hotel pen and some paper, laid it on the table, and told the kids to grab chairs, too. When Southard raised an eyebrow at that, Eisen explained, "She's their sister; they've got a part to play in this, too."

"All right," the clothier agreed.

As Southard explained, he sketched out the house on a piece of paper.

"Regular row house, alley to one side. Two floors and a subgrade with the dining room on the front of the subgrade. I could see the table through the windows. Steps up to the front door, which is set back and a little sheltered. Back door is off a short dead-end street, small warehouse at the far end of the dead end. It's probably connected to their other criminal enterprises. The warehouse, the fence of the house next door, and the back of the target house form three sides of a little back yard.

"The car we're looking for was parked in front of the warehouse, way down that alley. That really made no sense to me; there was plenty of parking space right in front of the house, while backing out tomorrow will be a pain in the rear. I figure, you do something like that if you have to carry something inside through the back, something like, say, a struggling little girl.

"There's a wooden western fort style fence with a gate that forms the fourth side, running from the back corner of the house to a corner of the warehouse. I didn't open the gate but pulled myself up the fence and looked in. No sign of a dog."

"No sign?" Patrick asked. "What sign would there . . . oh, poop."

"Yep, no stink," Southard said.

"That's a help," Eisen agreed. "Good job, Top."

"Thanks, Cap'n. The other thing I did was check Whitey's house and his girlfriend's house. He's at his girlfriend's."

Eisen continued, "The simple version of the plan is that we go there, park close by but not too close by. I leave the keys in the car with the engine running. You wait with the car, ready to drive or support by fire. I shoot out the transformers to kill the lights for the entire neighborhood."

"That's going to make a lot of noise," Southard objected.

"Nope," Eisen said, pointing to the Sterling resting on one of the chairs. "That's not an actual submachine gun. It's a pneumatic one with a—well, in this case it's probably all right to call it a 'silencer.' Shoots a really heavy nine-millimeter bullet, but subsonic, just like the forty-fives you're used to. Thing is about as quiet as a baby's whisper. And totally and amazingly legal. All you can hear is the working of the action.

"Now, you're right that the transformer will make a hell of a racket when I shoot it. But that doesn't sound quite like a shot. And, even though I'll probably have to shoot out two of them, they tend to do that, go out in pairs or groups."

"That'll work," Southard agreed.

"Then, when the lights are out, the boy, the girl, and I pad to the back gate. We open it, go inside, and go to the back door. Patrick jimmies the lock..."

"Are you guys a family of criminals?" Southard asked.

"See, Gra—Uncle Fitz, I *told* you that you were turning us into criminals."

"Shut up, Patrick."

"Yes, sir."

Turning his attention back to Southard, Eisen said, "No, actually we're not. This is our first foray in something like actual criminal behavior. But, since we're engaged in God's work, I don't feel too bad about it."

Casting a "keep your mouth shut and listen" glare at his grandson, Eisen continued, "So Patrick jimmies the back door; he's gotten good at this. He and the girl, Cossima, wait there. I go in and hunt around for Juliana. I kill anybody I have to kill, no noise, and they're still deader than chivalry. As soon as I find Juliana—"

Southard held up a restraining hand. "Wait, you're going into a perfectly dark house, full of probably armed bad guys and you think you're going to *find* anything? C'mon."

"Cossima," Eisen said, "bring the NVGs."

She got out of her chair and padded over, stopping to skritch the calico who was engrossed in the TV again.

She returned with a set of goggles, deep and somewhat wide, with a head strap arrangement attached.

"These are infrared goggles," Eisen explained. "They put out their own light, which people can't see, though I think dogs and cats probably can. The light—think of it, maybe, as an invisible flashlight—anyway, the light goes out, bounces back, and is collected by the lenses, here. They and some stuff in the tubes convert it to light a human eye can see. Kind of like tiny televisions."

Eisen pushed the power button and said, "Here, try them on."

"Holy crap," said Southard, looking around the suite's parlor. "I heard about something like these during the war, not goggles but scopes, but we never got issued them. I also heard the Germans had something that did the same thing, but I never saw those, either. Where the hell did you get these?"

"I do some consulting work for an armaments company, looking to get some military work." This was absolutely true, of course, but also totally and mysteriously misleading. Given that he couldn't let Larry know what information it was Bulger wanted, mystery and misdirection were just fine.

"Well," Southard agreed, "I can see how you'll get around the totally darkened house without making a racket or falling all over everything.

"But you're making a mistake," the former first sergeant said. "You've got no idea where the girl is. She could be drugged, hidden in any closet, chained to a bathroom sink. You're going to have to make noise to find her."

"Okay, so?" Eisen asked.

"That means you need to kill everyone—and I mean *everyone*—in the house and only *then* look for her."

"Yes. Hmmm, when you're right, you're right. They all go straight to Hell and then I look for Juliana."

"Okay, but what if she's *not* there?"

"I'm pretty sure she will be, criminals, as a class, are not *cum laude*. But if she's not ... hmmm ... okay, I'll need to leave two, no more, no less, of the thugs alive for a little while. Cossima, you come inside with me. You carry the handcuffs, the blowtorch, the pliers, and a couple of pieces of rope. We cuff them, tie their feet, then go looking for Juliana. If she's not there, we separate the two prisoners, then use the blowtorch on them until the stories match. *Then*, I kill them and retrieve the cuffs and rope. Work for you, Top?"

"Yeah, makes sense. But what I was getting at was that maybe I should go in with you, rather than the kid."

"Don't count her out; she's never known the meaning of fear, other than for stinging insects, but, yes, if you're willing to get your hands that dirty, we can leave the car, but not with the engine running, and you come in with me. You'll have to keep a hand on my shoulder until we can safely turn on a flashlight. Which, come to think of it..."

"I've got one in my car," Southard said. "Replaced the batteries just last week. But speaking of light; you're making it too complicated. Shoot out the main transformer for the power plant down on First Street; that should do the trick."

"Whole town out of power? Well, it's harsh but has the advantage of not localizing what we're doing until we're done. Right, then, First Street it is.

"Okay, continuing on; so if we find her, we bring her out to where Patrick and Cossima are waiting. Then the five of us walk—*walk!*— to the car. We get in; we drive away, and then I drop you at home and the three kids at the hotel. If we don't, we use the info the prisoners gave us and repeat everything already mentioned."

"What are you going to do then, Captain? Do you mind if I call you 'Captain'?"

"Not a bit. I'm going to Whitey's girlfriend's house and destroy him. Then I'm going to the Killeen's bar, the Transit, and I'm going to destroy that. And then, if the son of a bitch is still alive, he'll know a lot better than to screw around with me or mine, ever again. Neither are the Killeens going to be happy with him for the trouble he's brought on their operations."

"I'm up for that, too," said Southard. "Cleaning up the city; like you said, 'God's work.' And the big advantage of your plan is that it really doesn't require any rehearsals."

"Yes. Now let's change into our go-to-work clothes."

Dressed in black now, under his winter coat, Eisen had the valet bring his car, tipped him, and then drove the car around the side to School Street. There, Southard came out and took watch over the car.

Eisen went upstairs and, with the kids, carried out everything needed. The Sterling and night vision goggles came out in the duffel bag. The homemade grenades, too, were in there, inside their own canvas bag, the one that also held the box of cigars and the cigarette lighter. Likewise the cuffs, pliers, and blowtorch were stuffed away.

"We drive by wherever your car is," Eisen said, "to pick up your carbine. Then we do a drive by of the house and see if there are any lights on. Just because no lights are on doesn't mean everyone's asleep, of course, but it does mean no social groups, armed while drinking and playing cards."

"Lead on," said Southard, pleased, once again, to have an officer who seemed to know what he was doing.

Interlude

"You can't use your real name anymore," Mary said, before boarding ship in Barbados for New England. "It was fine in England, where you and Mica were a prosperous farming couple and people cared about that a lot more than they did about your name. Ireland never had a chance to know your name. Barbados . . . you were just living machinery there. But this is Boston, of the Massachusetts Bay Colony. It is run by a people called Puritans and, from all I've been able to gather, while they have their good points, here and there, they are still the most narrow-minded, self-righteous, arrogant people on this planet."

"What then?" Topaz asked.

"I asked among the crew. They call everyone of a certain age who isn't a Mistress—which is to say married and very prominent—a 'goodwife' or a 'goody' for short. So that part is fixed for you, especially since you and Mica were formally mated.

"This ship is called the 'Saint Ann.' Would 'Ann' do for your name?"

Topaz nodded. Her throat caught with emotion; nodding was all she could do. In truth, since she'd never hear her name spoken again by her beloved mate, she didn't overmuch care what she was called.

"And for a last name—they almost always have two or three names—how about taking the ship's purser's last name, Glover?"

"All right."

"Topaz," said Mary, "there is something else you ought to know."

"What is that?"

"I am failing . . . this body is failing. While the AI part of me can last a very long time, my biological design specifications are for only about fifty of what the locals call 'years.' I am over that now. I will experience a complete bodily breakdown within another year or so."

"Oh, no," said Topaz. "No, no, no. I have grown . . . well, through our enslavement in Barbados only you kept me going. Only you got us passage to here. Is there anything I can do to save you? I have come to *care* for you, Mary."

169

"And I for you. Indeed, that's part of the problem or, rather, a manifestation of the problem. AIs of my class are not supposed to care about anything except the mission at hand. That I care for you, and I do care for you, means that my organic demi-brain is breaking down. So, no, Topaz. It is deep seated in both my organic brain and my artificially cloned body. We have a year to make my short life in this form worthwhile, a year to eliminate the Q'riln."

"Mistress," the cube intoned, "one pursuer and her AI just got off the boat at Foster's Wharf. I don't know what happened to the other one, the male; I lost track of him at Drogheda. He is likely dead.

"I *did* tell you they were coming."

"Yes, you did, cube. Fortunately, I am still well-nourished from the war between the English and the Indians that I talked the late Metacomet into. That, plus the occasional drowning and eating of a redundant brat, has kept me going well enough. I am ready for the bitch. In the interim, am I shielded against her?"

"Not shielded exactly," replied the cube, "but I think that, with only one of their rough equivalents to me, she will have a difficult time identifying you as an individual. The AI, as near as I can determine, can sense distantly, but only as to a general area.

"I advise you to stay in the town, therefore, while you maneuver for advantage."

Chapter Nine

The morals of our people are much better; their manners
are more polite and agreeable, they are purer English; our language
is better; our taste is better; our persons are handsomer; our spirit
is greater, our laws are wiser; our religion is superior.
—John Adams

East First and Summer Street, South Boston, Massachusetts

The air was surprisingly warm, at about forty-two degrees,
Fahrenheit. The wind was typically Boston brisk, at a touch over
eleven miles an hour. Overhead, but at a sharp angle, the moon was
nearly full, but would set within half an hour.

As it turned out, this was one of those occasions where personal
reconnaissance and a degree of research would have been useful;
there were a number of transformers visible and neither Eisen nor
Southard really had the first clue as to which was the critical and key
one, if, indeed, any of them were.

"Screw it," said Eisen, flicking the laser on his Sterling to ON, "I'll
take them all out."

"What is that?" Southard asked.

"The light? It's called a laser. Remember that armaments company
I consult with?"

"That, too?"

"Yeah, this, too. Now it's zeroed for one hundred meters, call it
one hundred and ten yards. I make that near transformer to be about
eighty meters, so I aim a little low...sight...and..."

"Wow," said Southard, once the bang from the brutalized

transformer finished echoing between the row houses fronting the plant and the plant, itself. "That *is* quiet."

The transformer was still smoking and flaming when another one blew. Half the light was gone from the town and, based on the sudden dimming of the city across the water, probably from there, too.

"In for a penny, in for a pound," Eisen said, taking aim at another one. That one blew up with an immensely satisfying *bang*. There was just one more he could see and . . .

"Don't bother, Captain," Southard said. "If you didn't notice, except for the moon—which is setting—we're darker than three feet up a well digger's ass at midnight."

"Roger, back to the car."

By the time they got there, the moon was down and everything was in pitch blackness. Even the houses they passed didn't have a candle or a hurricane lantern lit. The people living there probably had no clue the power was out.

They parked on Fifth Street, next to the Benjamin Dean School, then trotted, following Southard, to the target house, on H Street and not far from the Dean.

Southard led them into the small court and right to the gate of the stockadelike fence. They'd seen no light coming from any of the windows.

Passing through the gate to the house's rear entrance, Eisen dropped his goggles over his eyes and whispered, "Patrick, do your thing."

"I wish I could use the snap gun," the boy whispered back. "I know, I know; too noisy. This will take a few minutes, Uncle Fitz."

"Take your time," Eisen said, softly, "but not too much of it."

Hearing a sound coming from inside, Eisen whispered, "Freeze," even as he brought the Sterling up. Suddenly the door leapt open to reveal a man standing there with a pistol in his waistband and a flashlight in his hand. The pistol looked a good deal like the one stolen from Eisen outside of Durgin Park.

The Sterling gave off its baby-whisper three times in rapid succession. Three two hundred grain, nine-millimeter, soft lead slugs entered the man's body, mushrooming to roughly twice their normal width by the time they'd gone halfway through. One passed through the lower portion of the left lung, one hit the heart, shattering it, and the last one tore out the base of the thug's throat.

The thug with the flashlight fell like a sack of rice, bonelessly, and with little sound.

Eisen bent and then turned off the thug's flashlight. This he left there. The pistol, however, he took and, after examining it in his infrared goggles, decided that it was, indeed, his. It was put on safe and pushed into a trouser pocket. It was, of course, uncomfortable, there.

But you can put up with anything for a while.

"Okay," Eisen said, "Balaclavas down."

All four then rolled down the knitted caps to cover everything but eyes and mouth.

He then entered the house, slowly, with Southard's hand on his shoulder. There was nothing in the short hallway but two doors, two doorless passages, and the foot of a flight of what were obviously very narrow stairs. Eisen cut right, passing through what was obviously a kitchen. A kettle sat over the flame of the gas stove. He reached over to turn it off lest the kettle's eventual squeal call someone down to shut it off.

Sheer chance, Eisen thought, *that body number one was there. He probably wanted a cup of tea.*

From the kitchen, they passed through a doorless passage, deep and with shelving to both sides, to a dining room with a table, hutch, and six chairs. There was neither foe nor Juliana to be found there.

They passed out of the dining room and back to the hallway. On their right, Eisen saw, was a door locked with both a dead bolting rim night latch and with a padlock, securing a hasp.

"Wait here," Eisen told Southard, softly, then went to get Patrick and Cossima, leading them to the padlock. On the way he opened the other door and found only a very old-fashioned—water tank up near the ceiling—toilet with a long chain to pull to flush it.

"Open this one," he told Patrick, putting the boy's hand on the padlock. The night latch was mounted higher than a child could reach, but could be easily opened from the outside by any adult. "You'll find a chair in the room to the right."

Taking Southard's hand, he put it back on his shoulder and led the way upward.

At the head of the stairs they found another hallway. To their right was a full bath, door open and empty. To their left was the front door of the house. In front of them was a closed door. Between themselves and the front door, to their left front, was another doorless passageway. Eisen could see a couch there, so presumed it was the living room or parlor.

He very gently opened the door to his front and quietly stepped in. A man's voice called out, "Who's there?"

Guided by goggles and laser, Eisen fired two bursts into the bed, killing the man and, presumably, his bedmate. The bedmate's body thrashed a little, but was soon still.

The next stop was, indeed, the parlor. There was a man sleeping on the couch. Knowing the floor was clear enough, Eisen whispered to Southard, "Prisoner-to-be number one; we can use the flashlight."

The two crept up on the sleeping man. Eisen let the Sterling rest on its sling, then briefly flicked on the flashlight. Southard raised his M1 Carbine and brought it down on the man's head, just hard enough to make sure he'd stay out until needed. Then they flipped him over, cuffed his hands, tied his feet, and put a gag in his mouth, secured by a very tight piece of quarter-inch hemp cord.

It's important to remember that Juliana is tiny. No shooting tiny people in rooms, no matter what.

From there, they followed the main stairs upward. Eisen was pretty sure that there'd be nothing but bedrooms up there, though another bath was at least possible. He wanted to curse the creak of the stairs underneath them as they ascended. When they reached the head of the stairs, there were four doors, all closed, arrayed around another short hallway.

Eisen opened the one to his right and shot the occupant. Male or female, he didn't know and didn't care. From his point of view, anyone who was involved in the kidnapping of his granddaughter was morally less than an insect and should count a quick death as a special grace.

The next door, the one to their front, before it was opened gave off the sound of rhythmic motion and whispered endearments and entreaties.

By God, they're screwing. No matter, the slug will penetrate all the way through one and halfway through the other. And, moreover, I just realized: We're the last thing these turds are expecting. If they'd been competent, they'd have had two guards on duty at all times; they had

the manpower for it. They didn't and any sound we make, if they even
hear it, they'd assume it was one of their own, going to the toilet or to
the kitchen.

Intent on what they were doing, the couple inside didn't even
notice the sound of the doorknob being turned and the door opened.
Still without mercy and without regrets, Eisen opened fire, forcing
the dominant partner to fall flat down on his *belle de nuit.* Two steps
forward and he was close enough to put a very short burst into the
heads of each.

He took out the magazine, even though it had at least a few more
slugs to it, tucked it into a pocket and took out a fresh one. This he
inserted into the left side magazine well. On full auto, the Sterling
fired from an open bolt, with some rubber buffers to help muffle the
sound and prevent metal clashing on metal. There was no need to
retract the bolt; the sear held it fast.

There was nobody in the next room, though clothing scattered
about and the unmade bed bore mute witness that someone called it
"home."

"Prisoner number two," Eisen whispered. "We can use the
flashlight; there's no room we haven't cleared."

"Roger." Southard flicked the flashlight on.

As soon as the light came on, Eisen raised the goggles from his
head and kicked the door in.

In the diffuse glow of the flashlight, Eisen saw dawning
recognition on the bed of this particular thug.

"I see you recognize me. I remember you, too. I saw you pass me
while pretending to go into Durgin Park; isn't that right?"

The thug lay speechless.

"Top?"

With that, Southard strode forward boldly and butt smashed the
bed's occupant with the carbine. They then jointly flipped him over
and gave him the same treatment as the other prisoner.

Lowering the goggles again, Eisen said, "I'll drag this one
downstairs, you get the other one. Since we didn't find my ... didn't
find Juliana here, she must be at some other house. These two are
going to tell us where, once we get them somewhere where no one
can hear them scream."

The bodies being dragged down the steps made an odd sound,

one as rhythmic, at least intermittently, as had the couple found making love. But when they got to the basement, and could be seen by the glow of the flashlight, a newly liberated Juliana launched herself at her grandfather, wrapping arms around his waist pressing herself to him, and crying, "I *knew* you would come. I *knew* it. I never lost faith; I *knew* you would come."

He couldn't speak at first, so relieved was he, and grateful to the Divinity, that he had his precious granddaughter safe and sound. Instead, he hugged her, tightly, bent over and kissed the top of her head, and when he could finally speak said, "I would go through the Gates of Hell for you; you know that."

He moved her gently aside and said, "Okay, Top, let's get these specimens untied and recover the cuffs, ropes, and gags." When that was done he ordered, "Top, outside, then lights out. Lead the kids to the car. Well done, Patrick, very well done. To you goes ultimate credit for finding and saving your sister. I'll follow along in a second after I clean things up a bit."

After Southard and the kids had gone, Eisen put the muzzle of his Sterling to each head, in turn, firing a single slug into each. Blood, brains, and bits of shattered skull scattered across the linoleum floor.

"When you get to Hell," he said to the corpses, "be sure to pass the word around; 'don't ever hurt or threaten me or mine.'"

With that, at a trot, Eisen left for the car.

Transit Café, 28 West Broadway, South Boston, Massachusetts

He'd elected to not, after all, take the kids back to the hotel.

And that reduced ability to plan and keep to a plan is starting to bug me.

Indeed, he had no intention of letting them out of his sight anytime soon. They rode with him, while the city was still in deepest darkness, with only the sound of distant police sirens to suggest anything lived.

I suppose that's the creeps coming out with the lights gone, Eisen mused.

Southard drove. There weren't any signs of life at the Transit. Eisen hadn't expected there to be.

Balaclava down, he got out of the car, carrying the canvas bag with him, as well as his Sterling. A quick burst of the latter shattered the glass window fronting the Transit, the glass tinkling down to the sidewalk and the floor inside. He emptied the remainder of the magazine into the shelves of mostly cheap booze behind the bar. Alcohol spilled out and onto the floor almost in a wave.

Taking one of the makeshift hand grenades, he pulled the key ring, setting the fuse alight. There was no reason to cook the thing off, to let the fuse burn down to reduce the time available for someone to throw the thing back at him. He just tossed it in and began to trot back to the car. The car was already moving when the grenade went off, scattering shrapnel from both the pipe and the lead shot inside it, and, incidentally, touching off some of the high-test rum leaking from the liquor store's shelves. What followed was something like a fuel air explosion, as misted alcohol and oxygen combined in the presence of the flames to create a much larger explosion than anyone nearby might have expected.

"Cool," said Patrick, looking out the rear window, as the building behind them more or less disintegrated.

"Now *that* was a little more than I expected," Eisen said.

"Bulger's house, Captain?" Southard asked. He glanced out the rear-view mirror and smiled at the ruin left behind them.

"No, head for the girlfriend's. I'm not done with that son of a bitch."

Whitey was asleep at his girlfriend's house, which was where he normally stayed. His first indication of trouble was when the window onto the street shattered. His hand was reaching for the pull chain on the table lamp beside the bed when the mattress suddenly lifted up halfway to the ceiling. His girlfriend screamed with fear and pain. He felt something, some *things*, seemingly dozens of them, pierce his buttocks, his lower back, and the backs of his thighs. Frantically, now, he grabbed for the light. It wasn't until he found it and the broken bulb slashed his fingers to the bone that he realized there'd be no light from that.

He was deafened, too, he realized, by the blast. Thus, he couldn't hear the shout from outside, "Bulger, you son of a bitch; Satan's calling for you."

He rolled off the settled but displaced and now smoking mattress just as the floor below was rocked with another explosion. He felt that blast more than he heard it.

"My God . . . what the? It's got to be the Mullens, come after me. I've got to get out of here."

It was then that Bulger realized there were no lights from the streetlamps, either. "No, no, not the Mullens. They couldn't get all the lights killed. Got to be those Rhode Island people . . . or maybe New York or Chicago. Oh, hell, it doesn't matter. Whoever it is, is too rich for my blood. I've got to . . ."

The third local explosion of the night rocked his girlfriend's house.

"GET OUT OF HERE!"

There was no time to put his pants on or let his girlfriend dress. Grabbing his trousers in one hand and the girl in the other he bolted for the back room. A trail of dripped blood from numerous Number Four Buck and FF shot formed as little and lesser spots on the floor behind them.

The back-room window shattered. Bulger saw what looked like the sparks of a burning fuse. Still holding his girlfriend's arm, he pulled her again out of that room and to the blood-spotted hallway. The explosion that followed knocked them both onto their faces.

Whitey was even more deafened, so still didn't hear the shout from the back yard, "Come out, Bulgah, yah crawling filth, so I can dice you up like a tomato!" The accent, in this case, didn't have a trace of Brahmin to it; it was pure working-class Southie.

Lying in the hallway, as safe a spot as there seemed to be, Whitey rolled over onto his back and pulled his trousers on. Relieved, he discovered his car keys were inside the right front pocket. Once again, he stood and took his girlfriend's arm, this time pulling her down the main stairs.

He smelled smoke. Sure as hell, one of the blasts had set a couch in the living room afire. There was no fighting it at this point, hence no sense in trying to stay here. He pulled the front door open and dragged the woman at a good clip toward his car. Surprisingly, no one shot at him on the way.

Eisen had gone to the back to see if the explosions in the front of the house had driven Bulger out that way. With the bookie and loan shark not appearing, he ran back to the front. He was just in time to see in his infrared goggles his target coming out the front door dragging a woman with him.

Placing the laser on Bulger, Eisen discovered that half the time the woman was in the way.

Shoot them both? I did, after all, shoot at least two women in the house where they were holding Juliana. No, this is different. Those women were presumably in on the kidnapping, hence entitled to no mercy. This one may know or may not, but there's no reason to think she knows. She gets a presumption of innocence, hence mercy. Even though she has very poor taste in bedmates.

Whitey got to a car, yanked a door open, and tossed the woman inside. Eisen took a short burst, but the range was long, his adrenaline, fed by rage and hate, made his entire body tremble with blood lust. In short, he missed.

Bulger obviously heard or felt the slugs' passing. He ducked low and ran around the car, barely appearing before the car's engine jumped to life. Headlights then came on, but Eisen shot one of them out. On the remaining light, keeping his head and eyes almost entirely below the dash, Bulger lunged his car forward.

The windshield in front of him disintegrated, as did both driver's and passenger's side windows. These shattered into granules, causing the woman to scream and Bulger to curse, but with no other damage done.

It was very likely that, had the police not been occupied with the sudden spurt of violent crime caused by the blackout, Bulger would have been stopped for speeding. As it was, nobody really cared. He got five blocks away, cut left, cut right, engaged in a series of maneuvers to lose any tail, then slowed down to a more normal speed.

Where the hell can I go for safety's sake? Whitey wondered. *My brother Billy's place on East Third? No, this is probably an attack by the big boys, and lots of them. They'll look at Billy's place for me, and I'll probably get him killed too. Maybe I can hide out there for a bit after I get this shrapnel out of my ass and after I dump the car. Maybe.*

If this is part of the gang war, I'm lucky to have survived. How many dead so far? Bernie McLaughlin; that's the first one. "Ox" Joynt. Billy Sheridan. Russ Nicholson, the cop who helped take out Bernie. Hannon and Willy Delaney. And Willy wasn't even involved in this crap. Dermody, turned over to Buddy by the FBI. Jimmy Flemmi—no, wait, Jimmy lived. Steve Hughes and Punchy McLaughlin. Then they got Buddy. Then Ray DiStasio and that O'Neil fellah who just happened to be in the wrong place. And then . . . it's like over forty. No, no way I can go to my brother's place, even if he would hide me out. Well, of course, he would.

He turned to his girlfriend of the moment. "We can't go back to your house, at least I can't, maybe ever. Have you got a safe spot to go, maybe find a doctor to get this shrapnel out of our butts?"

"My *sistah*. She lives up by Ashmont, not too far from the *Cahney* Hospital. What the hell was that, Jimmy?"

"Don't know," he said, shaking his head. "The Mullens, maybe. Or somebody from out of town, trying to take over Southie. Or maybe even that Jew who came to get some ID. All I know is that once we get the metal pulled out, we'd better get out of town for a while until things calm down. How would you feel about heading south, way south, for the winter?"

"Sure, Jimmy; whatevah yah think's best."

"I think we go see Howie rather than your sister. He'll be able to arrange to have a doctor come to us, no record made of it."

"If yah say so, Jimmy."

"I am deeply, *deeply* disappointed in myself," Eisen said to Southard. "Had the son of a bitch, had him dead to rights, and let him get away."

Eisen spoke in the car, now moving briskly up Massachusetts Avenue toward Tremont.

"Don't thrash yourself over it, Cap'n," said Southard, who was driving. "You did the important thing, got your niece back and offed the bastards that grabbed her and held her, plus destroyed the business of the guy that ordered her taken. Anything else would be just gravy."

"Yeah, I suppose you're right, Top. Even so, it rankles. The kids aren't entirely safe until he's out of the way."

"Bet you he *is* out of the way, though. With his followers dead—he's small time, you know, so those were probably all of his followers you killed—and his business relationship with the Killeen gang trashed, plus a narrow escape, he's got nothing left but a deep fear for his life. He'll be out of town by sunrise, tomorrow afternoon at the latest."

"You think?"

"I'd give odds on it, Cap'n."

"All right, then. Pull over up ahead, will you? I need to hide the goodies in the duffel bag before we go back to the Parker House. Then I'll take you home. Oh, that reminds me."

Eisen reached into a pocket and pulled out an envelope. "You've really gone above and beyond. There's two thousand in here. You want my advice, you'll put it in with a corporation called 'Berkshire Hathaway.' Run by a guy named Warren Buffett. Put it in and leave it there for about twenty years, forty, if you think you'll live long enough. They don't pay dividends but the value of the stock goes up and up. That hundred shares you can buy will be worth about a quarter of a million. No, don't ask how I know, Top; I just do."

Southard raised an eyebrow. So many questions he wanted to ask but, *No, the man can't talk about it.*

"Thanks, Captain," said Southard. "If in the future . . . ?"

"I assure you, I will never forget your name or tonight, Top. Never. Thanks again for helping me get Juliana back safe."

Clock Tavern, Broadway, South Boston, Massachusetts

The sun was rising high in the sky now, standing well above Fort Independence on Castle Island. In a bar still in the shade, though the other side of Broadway was well lit, assembled the dozen or so most senior and influential members of the Mullen Gang, in a meeting presided over by Paulie McGonagle, the leader of the gang.

Even the use of the term "gang" was questionable. The Killeens were a gang. Howie Winter led a gang. The Mullens were more of a confederacy of friends, with some leadership and hierarchy, who would informally get together and steal things, television sets, crates of canned crab, Christmas turkeys, liquor. Oh, and money. They were quite daring, utterly brazen, and surprisingly competent. A lot of them had learned the basics of their trade in the Army or Marine Corps. Just because the Mullens were thieves didn't mean that they weren't patriots.

This wasn't the usual hangout for the Mullens, but given the events of the previous day, they didn't want to be anywhere near their usual haunts.

Paulie began, once he felt he had a quorum, "Can anybody, anybody at all, tell me what the hell went on last night?"

"I can't tell you who," said Tommy King, the crooked nosed number two of the gang, "but I can tell you what; the Killeens, and especially Whitey Bulger, took it in the shorts. Seven dead in their place on H Street, five men, two women. One, as it turns out, dead at the Transit Café. And Whitey's girlfriend's house bombed. No one seems to know who did it except whoever, in fact, did it."

"How'd you find out, Tommy?" Paulie asked.

"Friend of mine from the police in Station Seven got it over the police radio net. Otherwise, the cops are as clueless as we are. Except for one thing; they said it was not only a very professional job, but it was a vicious and vindictive one. Women killed right in their beds. One was killed and still had a guy in her when they found her body. I ask you; what kind of vicious bastards kill people while screwing? Also, it wasn't just business, some neighbors heard one of the attackers calling for Whitey to come out by name."

"So probably not the Providence mob, then," Paulie judged. "How many attackers were there?"

"Best guess, based on the carnage, is six. But nobody's sure."

"Six? Crap! No, no," said Paulie, "that's *got* to be Providence or New York or maybe even Chicago. Nobody assembles that kind of firepower without being seriously organized."

"Speaking of firepower, Paulie, they used machine guns... *silenced* machine guns. And apparently hand grenades."

McGonagle whistled, then went silent for a moment, thinking about the implications of that information.

"Paulie?" asked Buddy Flynn.

"Yeah, Buddy?"

"What if it's Providence trying to put an end to our war with the Killeens... or, hell, the war everybody's having with everybody?"

"It would be an explanation, sure as Hell," McGonagle agreed. "Anybody know Ray Patriarca, in Providence?"

Nobody knew Patriarca; the Mullens just didn't run in that kind of circle. At least not yet they didn't.

"I think maybe Howie Winter knows him," offered King. "You think I should go ask him to mediate this stuff?"

"Yeah, do. And, listen; put out the word. This crap's gotten crazy. Tell everybody to back off, lay low, and hide out for a while, until we can get this all under control again."

"Now, who can get the word to the Killeens?"

"Joe or Jimmy Quinn," said King. "They're sort of on the periphery of the Killeens and can get the word out."

"Pick them up—*gently*!—and show them what was done to Whitey's store, his safe house, and his girlfriend's house. Let them see, and then go with them to see Don Killeen at the Transit. Convince him; this stuff's gotten way out of hand and has to stop *right* now, for *everyone's* sake."

"The Transit's not really there anymore, Paulie," said Tommy. "I walked by it coming here from Broadway Station. I mean, sure, the walls are mostly there but inside is a gutted, charred ruin. Going to have to go to Framingham if we want to talk to Donnie."

"Framingham, then," McGonagle agreed.

Gate of Heaven Church, I Street, South Boston, Massachusetts

The confessionals, triple-sectioned, with small cubicles for the penitents, and a single larger one, larger enough to turn around in, for the priest, were all down in the lower church. Many confessionals were open to public gaze, if not hearing. At the Gate of Heaven, all three sections were sealed from view of the upper bodies by thick cloths.

The lower church wasn't as grand as the upper church, itself nearly a cathedral, but it was a good deal easier to heat in the winter and naturally cool in the summers. Mostly, it served for daily mass and weekly confession while the upper church was for Sundays and Holy Days of Obligation.

Eisen left the kids in the pews and went in as soon as a side section was clear. The priest gave a greeting, which Eisen followed up with, "Bless me, Father, because I have probably sinned. It has been ... it will be ... about fifty-five years since my last confession."

"'Probably sinned'? 'Will be'? I don't ..."

"You'll have to take my word for it, Father; I can't really explain it myself."

There were a lot of loonies who felt the need to confess. The priest, rather, the Monsignor, John Powers, just let it go and let it flow when it happened. It didn't cost him or mother church anything but a little time and, who knows, maybe some of their stories and sins were actually true.

"The important thing, Father, was the sinning. The liquor store destroyed recently? Me. The seven people killed in the house on H Street? Also me. The hand-grenading of the house down on Eighth Street? That was me, too."

"Ahem," said the Monsignor, "and you're not *sure* that these were sins?"

"No, I'm not," Eisen said. "The big one was the seven people I killed. Three of them had kidnapped my granddaughter. I had to get her back."

"You don't sound nearly old enough to be a grandfather," Powers observed.

"Nonetheless, I am one. So tell me, Father; they threatened to kill her. Was it a sin to kill them to rescue her?"

"Was there any other way?" the Monsignor asked.

"I do not think so. The police, if I'd gone to them, are heavily infiltrated and in debt to the criminals. They'd have killed her if they'd gotten word from the cops, and they almost certainly would have gotten that word. It was a chance I could not take."

The priest sighed, audibly. *I somehow don't think this one is a loony, this despite his last confession allegedly being well into the future.*

"I afraid you've exceeded my theological understanding," said Powers. "I can give you as much absolution for this as lies in my power. I suspect that you're still going to have to take it up with Our Heavenly Father someday."

"I am sure of it. It actually gets worse."

Unseen, the priest shook his head. "Go on with the rest, then."

"I attacked and blew up the bar where the man works who ordered my granddaughter taken. This was to deprive him of funds to try again. That was also part of the reason I took no prisoners— yes—two of the men in the house I could have spared but didn't, to deprive him of aid and to make sure there were no witnesses, which would, again, have led the criminals back to my granddaughter. As it turned out, someone was in the store. I presume he was a criminal but do not know. I am pretty sure, Father, that these were sins."

"Yes, they were," Monsignor Powers confirmed.

"Then I attacked the house where this man was staying. I didn't kill anyone there, but not for lack of trying. I let him go only because I could not have killed him from where I stood without killing a woman who, as far as I know, was innocent. The house itself was mostly gutted by the time the fire department got things under control. Oh, and that blackout? Yes, that was me, too.

"Which brings me to my final problem, Father; I am not, for the most part, sorry, though I am possibly sorry about burning the house, destroying the Transit Café, and killing the man inside. I cannot be repentant for what was necessary. So what do I do?"

"Son," said the monsignor, "I wish I knew. Let's start with separating out the necessary from the unnecessary or frivolous. I think I am empowered to grant absolution from the latter, with an appropriate penance. For the necessary for which you are not repentant? I cannot absolve what you are not repentant for . . . that will have to remain a question mark on your soul, a matter between you and God. For the rest . . ."

Eisen came out of the confessional, pointed to Patrick, and said, "You're up. Just tell the priest that you helped the man who was here just before you."

Patrick did as ordered.

"Ah, you would be the lockpick, then?" the priest asked.

"Yes," the boy told him.

"Your sins, at least, I'm equipped to handle."

Patrick emerged from the confessional after a few minutes, then motioned his little sister in.

"What was your sentence?" she asked.

"I got ten Our Fathers and twenty-four Hail Mary's. On the whole, it wasn't bad."

Eisen led the kids upstairs to the rear entrance of the church, then outside, onto Fourth Street.

He pointed at one of the corners, saying, "In a couple of months

Pat Nee's brother, Peter, is going to be killed right there. I think, but am not certain, that my mother and I saw it happen."

"The Pat Nee you were talking about?" asked Patrick. "Friend of your Uncle Billy?"

"Same one . . . good kid; I . . . oh, God." Eisen went momentarily corpse-stiff.

"What? What is it, Gr—Uncle Fitz."

The answer came in the form of a smallish boxer, with one ear standing upright, and the other cropped but flopped over on her head. The dog was downwind, her nose stuck in the air, testing. Satisfied with the smell, she lowered her head, took one look at Eisen, and charged like a bat out of hell.

For his part, Eisen dropped to one knee, awaiting the charge. In mere moments, the dog was there, jumping wildly between bouts of slobbering all over Eisen's face.

"My Suzy," he said, hugging the dog close, "my Suzy. My best friend ever!"

Then he repeated, "'I've got my own friend doggie, Uncle Billy.'"

Parker House, Boston, Massachusetts

The phone rang. When Eisen picked it up the front desk announced, "Call for you sir, from a Mr. Southard."

"I'll take it here," Eisen said.

"Captain?" asked the voice on the other end. "It's me, Southard."

"Hey, Top! What's up?"

"I heard some interesting things from my cousin, the not so honest cop, and some more from the honest one, Chickie. One is that Bulger has disappeared without a word. No forwarding address. Even his boss, Donnie Killeen, doesn't know where he is and, more importantly, has put a price on his head for whatever he did to get the Transit Café blown up."

"They've pegged the ones who did it, the hit on the house where we found your niece, the Transit, and Bulger's girlfriend's house, all three, as a group from out of town. They figure Bulger tried to pull a fast one and that's what brought the attacks."

"Certainly plausible," Eisen said.

"Finally, they've called off the gang war. It's over, and there's a solemn oath in place that anyone who starts it up again—except for killing Bulger—will have *all* the gangs, to include the Patriarcas, in Rhode Island, gunning for them. So we did some good, too."

"Nobody's thinking it was us?" Eisen asked.

"The cops say no, and even honest ones, like my cousin Chickie… well, this is Boston, after all; everybody knows someone who's pals with a criminal. Anyway, Chickie heard from a friend of his in Station Seven that Pat Nee, from the Mullens, says everyone's thinking that that weasel, Bulger, was trying to score for himself and got caught."

Not so far from the truth, thought Eisen. "And no one's linked it to us and a little kidnapped girl?"

"Not even faintly."

"Well how about that? Thanks, Top!"

Interlude

～✦～

The Q'riln and her cube struck before the pursuer could find her.

They'd feasted so well since arrival, more than two hundred of the local years before, that they had much juice to spare. In their attack on Topaz, first they'd hit the artificial intelligence, taking brief control over it and causing it to steal and secrete some laundry. This provoked an argument with the children of the couple, the Goodwins, with whom Topaz and Mary had taken employment.

Secondly, they'd cut off the pursuer's ability to speak any tongue but her native Galactic Common III. This had required temporarily overloading the pursuer's teardrop as well as what amounted to a kind of temporary synaptic surgery—though perhaps the application of Novocain was a more accurate analogy—on her brain.

Thirdly, using the same basic techniques on the Goodwins' children they'd used on Topaz, the Q'riln and the cube struck them down, though in their case they'd induced delusion, illusion, hysteria, and loss of balance.

Lastly, after the doctor had seen the children and found himself helpless, she'd gone with him to press charges.

Then the Q'riln and the cube sat back to wait.

Mary was essentially catatonic, while Topaz was simply terrified. She stroked her calico cat continuously, speaking in Galactic Common III to it. This meant no more to the cat than English had.

She was like that when they came for her, in the middle of the night, armed and many. In moments she found her door smashed open, her hands bound behind her, with clergy holding up crosses as if shields against whatever absurdities they attributed to her.

Someone wanted to kill her cat; she still understood English and so understood that. An acquaintance, Robert Calef, interposed himself, taking the cat into his arms and declaring that there was no better hunter of Satan's vermin in the town than that cat, "And I'll take the benefit of her skill, thank you very much."

189

To Topaz he shot a look of sympathy, which look changed to disgust when he switched his gaze to the men binding her. One of them reached up, tore her teardrop from her neck, and flung it into the dirt floor.

"Look what I found here!" shouted one of the mob. He held up her little pseudo-children, intended for her late mate's grave, to keep watch and remembrance forever.

"Evidence of her allegiance to Satan," pronounced one of the clergy present. "*Clear* evidence. Look at the satanic writing on the bottoms!"

That set her to fighting as she hadn't before. Arms bound or not, shouting in Galactic Common III, she landed a good kick to the shins of one of the clergy trying to contain her with crosses, then turned to attack the man holding up her little statues of the children that would never be flesh.

One of the other men knocked her down to the floor. Still another bent to tie her skirt around her legs and her legs tightly together. When this was done, they picked her up bodily from the floor, carrying her outside and tossing her roughly into the back of the cart.

Robert Calef bent over her. He, unlike most of the rest, had not laid a finger on her.

"This is madness, Goody Glover," he said. "Worse, it is stupidity, malicious, malevolent, *wicked* stupidity. I'll do what I can to help but I cannot say it will be much. I'll take care of your cat. I have your necklace but I don't know what to do with it. Let me slip it into your apron pocket."

"Give it to the cat," she pleaded. "And have the cat close to me on the day."

Calef just shook his head, in frustration. He couldn't deal with her Gaelic any more than his neighbors could.

Realizing that, Topaz planted a weak suggestion in his mind to give the cat the necklace and teardrop. Would the suggestion take? She could only pray.

The result of the trial was a foregone conclusion, of course, with spectral evidence admitted, a clear presumption of guilt, rather than innocence, and Topaz unable even to answer the charges against her let alone contest them.

She was found guilty and, on the sixteenth of November, 1688, dragged from her jail, placed on a cart, and drawn to the gallows just past the little wall across and fort guarding Boston Neck.

Oh, Creator, thought Topaz, in sheer panic, *what am I to do?*

"Stand, witch," ordered Mr. Larkin, the marshal for the proceedings. He didn't wait for her to stand but pulled her roughly to her feet. He placed a rough noose of very thick hemp about her neck, in back so as to cause unconsciousness quickly, then jerked the knot down, close to her neck.

She heard someone call out, "Let's fix this so the witch dances her way to her true master." The speaker then jumped up on the cart and twisted the rope around her neck so that it wouldn't quickly block off the blood vessels to her brain. That also got a laugh from the onlookers, enough so that Larkin thought it unwise to interfere. He left the rope where it was.

The minister in attendance tried once again to get the witch to confess and save her soul, but Topaz could only answer in the language of her birth, which all took to be Gaelic.

Larkin jumped off the cart, then walked around to the horse. This animal he gave a stout slap to the hindquarters, causing it to begin to shamble forward.

Her feet tied together as they were, Topaz couldn't even walk off and jump. Instead the rope pulled her over and dragged her from the cart, setting her to swinging wildly, with her legs struggling against each other and the binding rope, even as they pumped up and down for some kind of horizontal surface to stand upon to relieve the pressure on her neck.

Her mouth worked like that of a landed fish as she struggled to draw in the breath of life against the constrictions of the noose.

Her eyes, bugging out of her head with panic and pain, came to settle on one woman in the crowd. In an instant she *knew*; this was the Q'riln. It was not an it, but a she. Catherine Branch was her name. She knew it not by the teardrop; this had been taken from her, and not from Mary, who was catatonic. Oh, no; she knew it by the satisfied smile on the Q'riln's face.

I will not let myself fail, said Topaz, a remarkably clear thought for a being slowly strangling. *I will not. If there is no human . . .*

Suddenly, the body swaying under the tree went still. All kicking and struggling stopped, though her chest heaved in what was likely an early stage of cardiac arrest.

Disgusted, Robert Calef just shook his head and turned to the woman who had pressed the charges against Goody Glover.

Chapter Ten

There is about Boston a certain reminiscent
and classical tone, suggesting an authenticity and piety
which few other American cities possess.
—E.B. White

South Boston, Massachusetts

Mass at the Gate of Heaven saw Eisen and the three children take a back pew, as far as possible from where he knew his family would be, which was on the left side of the nave, and about a third of the way back from the crossing. It was an otherwise unconscionable risk, but, *If causing a blackout, killing eight people, destroying one business, and burning down a house didn't affect the timeline enough to prevent me and the brats from coming here, this probably won't, either. But what it* might *do is screw up my own family, even if not the world. Even so, I* have *to see them, Grandma, my mother, and my aunts, once again, alive.*

And, lo, he saw them and his heart leapt. His mother: *No, I wasn't misremembering; she really was the most beautiful girl in South Boston.*

Not only did he see them, but he also saw four Federico girls, all pretty, and, moreover, girls who didn't start to age, after age eighteen, until three or four days after they had died. Old childhood friends where there, too, Charlie and Greg, some of the Fifth Street crowd. It was a boundless joy mixed with an equally boundless pain that he could not speak to any of them.

He forwent communion, grabbed the kids and hustled them to the nave and then Fourth Street, before mass had ended. From there they legged it for Broadway, where his car was parked.

"Hey, let's hit Amrheins for lunch, then back to the hotel. I want to go over the spreadsheets for tomorrow's futures buys, sells, puts, and calls."

Next day, when he could be sure everyone was working or at school, he went back to almost the same parking space. At the corner of I and Broadway, Eisen remembered a treat he wanted the kids to experience. They ducked into the pharmacy there and he bought several packages each of Callard and Bowsers English Toffee, Butterscotch, Licorice Toffee Fingers, and Cream-Line Toffee Fingers. The packages were silver, or gold, or cream colored, or a shade of orange. Taller and thinner than a pack of cigarettes, they were about as wide. Each was decorated with the name, "Callard and Bowser's," and a thistle.

"Juliana," Eisen said, "you are hereby appointed Keeper of the Toffee. It is your solemn responsibility to maintain, distribute, and ration the Callard and Bowser's. When we reach the car, you are to open the package labeled 'English Toffee,' and issue one piece to everyone present in the car."

He didn't pick Juliana because of her age, but because her kidnapping had left her worried and nervous, and having a job, even a silly and trivial one, might help keep her mind off the incident.

"By the way, kids, you can't get this anymore where we come from, though it was still being made about twenty years before that. No toffee since, nor butterscotch, either, has quite come up to the standard of Callard and Bowser's. At least none that I know of. It would be nice if someone's would. As is, we'll have to enjoy it now."

The others being distracted by the prospect of sweets, Cossima was the one who called out "shotgun!" first. This being the law, she ended up next to Eisen.

"Juliana, the opening of the toffee."

"Yes, Uncle Fitz," she replied, more brightly than she'd been given to since her rescue. She pulled the tab on the plastic wrapper, tore off the top of it, fiddled with the paper wrapping, and then tore the inner cardboard. From the box she extracted four pieces of candy, passing three of them out. Cossima got two because, with the position of shotgun came the duty to feed the driver.

"All right," said Eisen, "open them and partake."

"MMMMMMMMMMMMMM," came from three throats, "Grand—Uncle Fitz . . . these are . . . they're . . . I don't know how . . . AMAZING! MMMMMMMMMMM."

"Some things," Eisen said, around his own piece of British confectionary yumminess, "really *were* better when I was a kid."

Cossima, sitting next to Eisen, agreed. "I miss my cell and the internet," she said, "but, yeah, seeing Great-Grandma and your family, even at a distance, was worth it. This is just a cherry on top."

"You still remember your great-grandma, shorty?" Eisen asked.

"How could I forget, Gr—Uncle Fitz. We were *so* close when I was a really little girl. I mean, like, inseparable. We'd read together—well, she'd read to me, anyway—watch TV together; Tiger Woods was our favorite; cook together. It's from her that I got my love of baking."

Eisen nodded; they'd been as close as one might imagine back when his mother was alive.

"Tell you what, shorty," he said. "When you grow up and move out on your own you can have her bed."

"Oh, *can I?* That would be *wonderful!*"

Parker House, Boston, Massachusetts

The monitor screen glowed in the dark as Eisen scrolled through his spreadsheets. Juliana was asleep in the girls' bed, while the calico, curled up and purring, lay on Cossima's lap, on the couch that faced the television. The girl was reading to the cat, aloud, from her book on Egypt.

I wonder, thought Eisen, *if she thinks the stupid cat—okay, okay, not fair; she's very bright for a cat—anyway, does she think the cat can understand? Or is she engaged in an exercise in "to teach is to learn twice"? She's so grown up most of the time that it's easy to forget she's still just a little girl.*

Eisen stifled a yawn.

"I need a cup of coffee . . . no, a pot of it," he said to Cossima, standing and walking the step and the half to the phone to call room service. He had his back to the computer.

"Yes, please, this is Maguire. I was wondering if it's too late to get a pot of coffee sent up, cream, sugar, and . . . not too late? 'Never too late'? But delivery will be tough? There are reasons why I love this place. No problem, if someone will make it and put it on a tray with cream and sugar, I'll come and get it myself."

"See," said Cossima to the calico, "this Egyptian symbol for an ox got turned around and got the same sound as the beginning sound for an ox, which was an A. So it became our A via Canaan, the Phoenicians, the Greeks, and then the Romans.

"And then our B came from the same place, along the same route..."

The cat touched first the A in Cossima's book, then the B.

Nobody will believe me, she thought, *but the kitty is paying attention. And I think she's learning. We have got to steal her and take her with us when we go back home.*

"You need to go to bed, little one," Eisen said when he came back and found the girl still awake. Not expecting an immediate answer or, indeed, any answer until he firmly insisted, he turned his back to her to place the coffee tray on the suite's table.

"Grandpa?" Cossima said, very softly. "Grandpa, turn around."

"I *told* you..." When he turned around he saw the damnedest thing; the bloody cat was slapping keys with its right front paw.

"Oh, woah, kitty!" he said, "You lose me that data and I am out *billions*!" He picked the cat up and put it on the floor. He was pleased to discover that it hadn't erased any of his cells or files. He was a lot less pleased, shocked speechless would be closer to the truth, to see what the cat *had* done.

It had written, across the top of a new spreadsheet: "TPAZ. M TPAZ. M NSD CAT PART CAT U R N TRBL DANGR!!! CN HLP DANGR! DANGR! DANGR!"

While he was reading and trying to make sense of the mostly vowelless groups of letters, the cat jumped onto the desk and stared right at him.

"'TPAZ'?' he asked. "Mmmm...Topaz?"

"MREOW!"

"I suppose," said an eyebrow-raised Eisen to the cat, "that, at this point, I'm past being shocked by anything. We're going to need to teach you a bit more English, I think. And the first place we need to start is with vowels."

"I was teaching from my book on Egyptian hieroglyphs," said Cossima. "Then, just before you came back, she went to the laptop and started studying it."

It took the cat a much longer time to type a message than it would have taken a human. When the other kids woke up, Eisen introduced them to the feline, amidst a chorus of "Holy craps!" and "wows" and "See? I knew there was more there! I knew it!" Eisen and the kids discovered that it was best to ask the question, then go do or watch or read something else while the answer was typed.

"My name is Topaz," typed the calico, very slowly, after five days of lessons and drills with Eisen and the kids. "I was not always a cat. I used to be a human and before that, I was of a different species with a law enforcement arm of The Authority, the government of this arm of the galaxy.

"There is a being, an evil being, called a 'Q'riln.' She lives off the pain, fear, and especially the psychological torment of others. I believe she also eats children. I was sent to kill it before she could do more harm.

"I was sent a long, long time ago. I am, as you would see it, very old. Centuries old."

The cat gave off a piteous meow then, something filled with sorrow and replete with inner agony. "The Q'riln defeated me. My mate was killed. My artificial intelligence was destroyed."

Finally, the cat typed, "Did you come through her gate? You came from the future; I know this because there is nothing like this computer here and now. But did you come through her gate?"

"Probably," answered Eisen. "How would we know it was its . . . her gate?"

"I don't know," typed the cat, in return. "I have never seen the inside of a Q'riln gate for more than the quickest glimpse . . . well, thirty of them. I know where the one nearest here was. I had it blocked with *forjin*. It was in the middle of a peninsula south of here and a little east . . ."

"What is *forjin*?" Eisen asked, then had a sudden inspiration. On a hunch, he pulled a Franklin half dollar from his pocket and asked, "Is this *forjin*?"

"*Forjin*," the calico confirmed. "Q'riln *hate* it; *forjin* is poisonous to them."

"Which just might go a long way to explain all kinds of myths and legends about silver," Eisen observed, putting the coin back in his pocket.

"You wrote of danger," Eisen asked. "What danger and why?"

"The Q'riln," the cat typed, "are egoists. They do not share. For most of their lives, they cannot even stand to be near each other for long, not for more than moments. They come together to mate, for the time it takes a mother to raise a one of them to go out on its own, and for a very limited time to select and purchase a being—some are cube shaped, some are other shapes—from one of their makers. So we think. We're not sure. I didn't know the sex of this one until I was hanged. It is a she.

"They become more capable of tolerating each other when they've amassed enough power from the pain and suffering they've fed upon that they need never fear running out. Then they go to their home world and either grow cubes from their own original one, retire, or enter politics. Again, we think."

"So they share that with personal injury attorneys," Eisen observed. "They live off pain and suffering, then try for public office. This still doesn't . . ."

"You violated the Q'riln's space by using its gate. She will hate you for this. It is a dangerous thing to be hated by a Q'riln."

"Ah."

"But do not worry too much, yet. I have the gate blocked."

"Tell us," Eisen asked, "did your . . . your *forjin* cover all gates? Were there more than one gate from a single . . . mmm . . . node or nexus?"

Topaz thought for a bit, then typed, "Mine only covered the local gate, the one she escaped through. If there were other gates, and there probably were, she can use those to a place where transportation is available and then come here."

"Well," said Eisen, "isn't that just special. Hey, if you are centuries old, how does the cat look young?"

"My people can control the damage to the cells of our body to a considerable degree. It is a mental skill, not a medical one. The teardrops help but are not absolutely necessary. Mine helped me remember how to spell, too, once the little girl showed me her book.

"The cat has a small body, not as many cells. Thus, I have kept the cat young by keeping her cells young. We do not live forever, no, but we live a long time and stay young and healthy for most of that.

"She is still here with me, by the way, the cat. We inhabit the body together. Moreover, if I've changed her, she has also changed me. I like rat and rabbit now; I like tormenting my food. If I had the Q'riln in my power, for the pain and shame it has caused me, it would envy all the people whose death sufferings it feasted on, for the suffering I would give to it. My mate . . ."

Again, the calico lifted its nose toward the ceiling, waved its head back and forth, and gave off a terrible *yeowl* of vast inner torment.

She went back to the keyboard. "I should explain; my people do not mate merely for life; we mate forever. I can have no other mate and, thus, this body will someday die, childless, unloved, and unmourned."

Juliana, looking over the cat's shoulder, so to speak, said, "We will love you, Topaz. Always."

The cat didn't type a reply, but purred, then typed, "So, yes, I hate that bitch with a passion. I would lock her in a cage composed of *forjin*. I would infest her, inside that cage, with samples of all the parasites of her home world, as many as needed to keep the breeds going. I would put up vision screens to show her massive agony, infinite agony, none of which she would be close enough to feed off of. *That's* how much I hate her."

"Have you never had kittens, Topaz?" Patrick asked.

"I have, so far, been able to control the lusts of the cat side of me, yes. And, no, it hasn't been easy. Nobody, nothing, in the known universe can nag as insistently as one of these creatures in heat."

Danger and silver, together, set Eisen to thinking. "How pure does the silver have to be to be poisonous to the "Q'riln'?"

"Ninety percent is more than enough," Topaz typed. "Seventy-five is really enough. Actually, anything that has at least three-fourths of an ounce of silver, in any purity, is enough. Even less, if the Q'riln gets very close."

"Ninety percent, eh? Or even seventy-five? Now isn't it interesting that our older coins are ninety percent?"

Eisen grabbed his coat and headed for the door.

"Kids," he called over one shoulder, "keep our guest entertained. Order room service for her if she wants . . ."

"Codfish tongues," the calico typed. "Raw! And a bowl of cream, room temperature. Yummyyummyyummy!"

"Where are you going, Uncle Fitz?" Cossima asked.

"To as many banks as I need to hit up until I can come up with about eight or nine pounds of silver coin. Thank God the Q'riln isn't allergic to gold!

"Now remember to hide the laptop before room service gets here!"

While waiting for the car to arrive at the side door, yellow pages under one arm, Eisen had a few minutes to think.

I think maybe I need to get the kids out of here. The way the calico describes it, they're not safe.

But, on the other hand, are they safe there? If those Q'riln are as determined hunters, and as vindictive as the cat said, maybe they're safer, here, with me on my guard, and at this age, than they would be back home. My daughter back there can't guard them and my son-in-law is deployed to the war as often as not. No, they're safer with me and I need to stay here to kill that creature.

Moreover, with the money I'll have back there, but only if I stay here a while, I can build a damned fortress out of silver to keep the kids safe from the Q'riln, if that's what it takes.

Money? Money? Should I play the numbers again to raise my immediate cash account? No, if Whitey Bulger could make a guess that I had some system for fixing or predicting the numbers, someone else might, too. I think the thirty thousand I got, quarter of a million in our day's terms, is enough. No sense taking chances I know are chances and don't need to take.

Damn; it's a close question. What it comes down to is that they're not safe there or *here while that thing lives. Maybe it's best to stay ...*

"Your car, Mr. Eisen."

Slipping the man from the hotel a couple of dollars, Eisen got in, put the car in gear, and headed for Post Office Square and the Federal Reserve bank.

As it turned out, the Coinage Act of 1965 had already started folks to hoarding the old style, ninety percent silver coins. Instead of eight or nine pounds, Eisen ended up buying twenty-four pounds of mostly forty percent coins; dimes, quarters, and Franklin half dollars, due to hoarding. He did have some ninety percent coins, too, just not enough for what he had in mind.

I'd jump on that, knowing what I know, and knowing I'm allowed to buy fifty thousand silver dollars every day from the government. But, frankly, even at the short term, a forty times over increase in the price of silver, coming in 1980, under the Hunt Brothers' hoarding scheme, still falls short of what I know Berkshire Hathaway will do. Shame, in some ways, of course. I think I'll pick up some to bring back, anyway.

Hmmm . . . the kids are going to need something to take out this bitch. How do I pour molten silver into the hollows of hollow point ammunition? I don't think I do, not without risking raising the temperature to the point of setting it off, which would annoy the hotel and raise all kinds of questions I don't want to answer. Hmmm . . . note to self, stop off at hobby shop, get modelling clay and wax to cast silver plugs in. Hmmm . . . modelling clay or casting plaster? The latter, I think. I can cast them small, and hold them in place with the wax, too.

"How does this 'Q'riln' attack, Topaz," Eisen asked the Calico, "and is there any defense?"

"I can tell you what she does," the cat typed back, with excruciating slowness, "but I cannot tell you how she does it nor how to defend against her. The short version is that she attacks in several ways. One way is that she drops hints into your mind that sound like your own thoughts and have great persuasive power. I am not entirely sure she didn't bait us into Drogheda just that way. I strongly suspect she got the commander there to try to make an impossible defense that way. This is all done at very short range.

"Another Q'riln, on a different planet, manufactured a nuclear war that way, to feed herself past full."

"They can *do* that? *She* could do *that*? Kids?"

"Yes . . . yes . . . yes?"

"This has just gone up a long way from get ourselves home to get that bitch no matter what it costs."

"I understand, Uncle Fitz," answered Juliana. She was still a bit under the cloud of depression from her kidnapping, but strong enough to see what needed doing even so.

"Good girl!" Eisen told her.

"Whatever it takes," said Patrick.

"I ain't afraid of no Q'riln," Cossima parodied, doing a contemptuous booty shake as she did.

"It gets worse," typed Topaz. "She can invade your mind more directly. I could speak English, for example, but she cut the synapses that controlled language so that, while I could still understand, I could not speak or write it. I can type it, now, but I am not sure if that's because typing is different than writing or because my brain is not the cat's brain . . . exactly. It is not impossible that she could cut the life functions, stop your hearts, stop your lungs, maybe stop your eyes, too; that would be her style. I just don't know.

"On the plus side, it's possible that the effects are just temporary, too.

"I had an AI with me," Topaz continued, "an artificial intelligence. She was encased in a body cloned from an old tissue sample. Her brain was organically wired to the body. The Q'riln cut off everything. We were in a jail cell together and she would not eat, would not drink, would not speak. Yes, she was already nearing the end of her life span—we give AIs very short corporeal lives so that they do not become a threat—but this was a sudden and complete cut off of everything."

"Would some kind of silver armor help?" Patrick asked.

The calico typed, "I do not believe so. Silver is poisonous to her only fairly close up; she attacks at a distance. Moreover, I believe—well, I *suspect*, anyway—that her attacks, at least these kinds of attacks, flow through a parallel reality before manifesting inside you, so no kind of armor or force field in this reality is likely to help."

"How will we recognize her?" asked Juliana.

"I do not know," was typed back, very, very slowly. "I only recognized her at the very end, while I was strangling. And that only because she was smiling a very peculiar smile, eyes closed, face blank. It reminded me of myself and my mate when we were, you know . . .

"If I had both teardrops, mine and Mica's, we could tell. Or if Mary were still here. Even one will give off an alarm if she gets close. But we have nothing to track her down."

"Are we going to have to fight our way home?" Cossima asked.

"It's worse than that," the cat typed back. "As long as it lives, it will hunt for you. You came from the future of here and now. When you go back there; if it's still alive, you will never have a moment's peace and security."

"Hmmm . . . it occurs to me that we need a safe space, ourselves, for now. Kids, I'll be back in a bit."

"Where are you going, Uncle Fitz?"

"To the bank, to get a lot more silver coins to put around the edge of our suite, plus anyplace else in the hotel I can hide a piece. Oh, and the nearest cognate to Super Glue I can find. And some dark metal paint. And maybe something for casting more bullets, better."

"That might help a little," typed the cat.

"Topaz?" Eisen asked, before opening the door.

"Yes?"

"Will it screech or show some other kind of distress when it comes close to silver?"

"Now that you mention it, yes, yes, it will."

"Then there's a partial way to identify her. Tell, me, how will she know it's us?"

"Her cube will tell her."

"Cube?"

"An AI, we think, like my Mary and Mica's lost teardrop. There is a suspicion, though, in some circles, that the cubes actually run Q'riln society."

"Okay. Let me muse on that tidbit. Later, brats."

As it turned out, Loctite Corporation already made Super Glue in convenient tubes. Paint wasn't hard to come by, either. With the windows open, despite the cold, and in order to avoid asphyxiating themselves, all three kids painted silver dimes, quarters, and half dollars dark brown atop a couple of pages of the *Boston Globe*, while Eisen heated, but did not melt, coins in a lead melter.

Using tongs, he transferred the very hot—and still only half hot enough—silver coins to a crucible. In this, using the blowtorch they hadn't needed to torture the thugs who'd kidnapped Juliana, he melted the coins down before using a graphite stir rod to bring the impurities to the surface and skim them off. Then he used a dipper to fill the mold for his pneumatic Sterling, one cavity at a time.

It actually went fairly quickly, once he had the hang of it, though the difficulty of working with silver, as compared to the much easier lead, plus Eisen's own inexperience, meant it took three hours to do a job that should have taken thirty minutes.

More than once his inexperience led him to let a finger touch something much too hot for mere flesh. He didn't scream on those few occasions, but he did curse up a storm.

While the lead melter was keeping the silver hot, he went to his next project. This consisted of emptying out every magazine they had, Sterling, M1911, CZ-83, and Beretta, as well as the spare boxes of ammunition, of which there was not much, a mere fifty rounds per caliber. He took one of each of these, filled the interior of the cavity—they were all hollow points, even the .45—with wax. When the wax had cooled he carefully pulled out each piece, and checked it visually for evenness and smoothness.

With four pieces of formed wax in hand, he prepared the casting plaster inside an ashtray, a hotel ashtray, actually, and then pressed the wax pellets down into it while it was yet soft enough for the purpose. After the plaster had dried he pulled the wax bits out with a pick, then cleaned the holes with Q-tips.

There was still enough semi-heated silver in the lead melter. He took a few more coins from it, dropped them into the crucible, and used the blowtorch to melt them. Then, using the dipper, he filled each of the vacated holes in the casting plaster with silver. He inserted a bent paper clip into the base of each plug. He waited for those to cool enough for solidity and use.

When they were cooled down, he discovered that the silver plugs were all a little loose, that they'd shrunk, so that there was no need to break the casting plaster to free them.

As it turned out, the plug for the .32 was off. He had to repeat the entire process to get a serviceable silver plug for those rounds.

His next step involved a couple of fairly heat proof trays, maybe five inches across, a foot long, and an inch deep. With those, he filled them with casting plaster, waited for it to almost set, then used the plugs already taken, holding them by their paper clips, to make impressions in the plaster. This took quite some time. When it was done, he began melting down coins by the fistful, skimming off the impurities, then scooping the silver up in the dipper and pouring it into the holes made in the casting plaster.

It was early morning when he shut everything down and finally went to bed.

"Okay, brats; today we put up barriers to this place. Kids, I want you to take about a hundred, hundred and twenty painted dimes and glue them around the baseboards—not the floor, the baseboards—about a foot apart, as well as on the door. Also open the windows and, without getting out there on the ledge—Cossima, I am looking at *you*, here—put a half dozen or so each outside of each window.

"Meanwhile, I'm going to finish putting the silver plugs in the hollow points and loading the magazines for the Sterling with the silver slugs."

While the kids got busy, Eisen began filling the hollow points with the plugs. He'd bought a little hammer to pound them in, if necessary, but discovered it was absolutely unnecessary; the silver plugs had all shrunk just enough to fit the hollow points easily. Indeed, they were too easy, being loose and likely to fall out and jam the pistols.

"Wax, it is," he said. He lit a candle and held it at an angle over each round, in turn, holding it just long enough for a single drop of wax to enter to hold the silver plugs in place. It was not, of course, as neat as that, about half the cartridges needed to be wiped and fingernailed to get the excess wax off. Since he was in a public establishment, he kept his cursing to a bare minimum.

The kids finished before he did, taking up with the recent very most favorite pastime, talking with the cat via the laptop.

Patrick had a rather interesting idea. "Topaz," he asked, "if you try to say something it comes out as a *meow*, right?

"Yes," she typed back.

"Do the meows sound different, at least to you?"

"Yes."

"Well, we have something called voice recognition, back in our own time. It's there on the laptop, too. I wonder if it couldn't be modified to sense the difference so you could just talk and have words come out."

Topaz considered this, before answering, "We have that, too. But I don't think so. While different *meows* mean different things, most of the things I can pass through the cat's brain to its vocal chords are limited by the cat's brain. Some words and concepts could come through—feed me, pet me, go to Hell, scratch me, kill, feed—all that kind of thing. But to tell you, say, my life story would be impossible, because the cat's brain lacks the concepts."

"Oh, well," said Patrick, dejectedly, "it was a thought."

"It was a good thought," Topaz typed. "I wish there were a way."

"Juliana, Patrick, Cossima; post!"

That meant "get over here on the double," and neither these kids, nor Eisen's own children, had any doubts over it.

When they were assembled, Eisen inserted a silver-plugged .380 caliber filled magazine into the Czech .380 and jacked the slide. He then removed the magazine, replaced the chambered round and returned the magazine to the mag well. Placing the pistol on safe, he handed it to Juliana, saying, "You'll know when to use this if you have to. Remember, if you do, to take off the safety."

He then repeated the process for Cossima, with the .32 Beretta.

To Patrick he said, "We're going to set up defenses around the interior of the hotel. I'll be carrying the Sig for myself and will have the little Walther .22 with the suppressor for you in the small of my back. You're just not big enough to hide a pistol on without your heavy coat over you. You're too skinny."

The boy nodded his understanding. "If you go down, Gr—Uncle Fitz, I'm going for the Sig."

"Stout lad," Eisen said. "The Walther is in case we both need to fire. Trust me to pass it to you if you will need it. Which is, you know, not impossible. Now go get a metric buttload of painted coins and the glue."

"Juliana, you're in charge until we return. Cossima, do what she says. Yes, I mean it.

"Hmmm ... I should probably put the cat in charge, and I would, Topaz, except you can't get an order out quickly enough."

"I understand," typed the calico.

"Stairs or elevators first, Patrick?"

"Neither, Uncle Fitz; first we do this hallway."

"Very good. I'll keep watch; you get to work."

"Dimes or quarters here?" the boy asked.

"Quarters, and space them out about every three feet. Don't forget the windows at the ends, either. I'll keep watch."

They'd been up and down each of the elevators three times each, from the top to the bottom. In no case had they had even one of them to themselves. This was never a possibility, of course, the elevators were human operated. But the operators tended to look to the front whereas passengers . . . well, one couldn't be sure where they might look.

"Screw it," said Eisen, "We'll do the stairs down to the basement; we silverize that, then see what we can do in the lobby when nobody's looking. Elevators we'll get to at about three in the morning."

"Uncle Fitz," said the boy, after emerging in the basement, "there's an easier way to get silver into the elevators."

"What's that?"

"They've all got escape panels up in the ceiling. You boost me up, and I'll put half a dozen silver half dollars on each."

"That's a good thought. But the operator is not going to permit it. And we'd still need to wait until three in the morning."

"I suppose not," the boy conceded, "and, yes, I knew that."

"First," said Eisen, "let's get a feel for the layout down here; it's a bit of a rat maze. Hmmm . . . rat maze. I'll bet Topaz knows this place by heart. Back to the suite, Patrick; we're going to ask the cat to hide dimes all over the place down here."

"Show me the coins," the cat typed.

Eisen held up a painted dime.

"I can't do it on my own," Topaz objected. "I can carry two, maybe three of those in my mouth. That's it. If I had opposable thumbs, you know, I'd have been communicating a lot sooner than when I first saw your laptop and understood what it was."

"It's okay," Eisen assured the calico. "We'll be nearby with a sack of dimes. The important things are to place them where the bitch can't come in without getting too close for comfort, and hiding them where they won't be found for a while."

"I can do that," she typed, "though there are places, under rugs, for example, where you would be better to place them yourself."

"I can see that. Can you guide me through drawing a diagram of the basement?"

"There's still the elevators to do," Patrick observed, "those, and the lobby."

"No problem with the elevators," said Eisen. "Our mistake...well, no, *my* mistake, was in forgetting that there's a place, two places, really, where the elevators are briefly empty, barring the operators. These are the top floor..."

"After everyone gets out?"

"Bright lad, yes. The top and the basement. So we're going to go to the basement, and call an elevator. When it arrives, assuming it's empty, we get on and tell the operator to bring us to the top floor. Then while I block the way, you glue a half dollar, two if there's time, someplace out of the way."

When the diagram was done, Eisen was able to narrow down the areas where the Q'riln could get in or move freely once in. He marked all the ingresses with an X and showed it to the cat.

"Yes," it typed back, "that should work. Shall we go?"

"First, Juliana and Cossima, look over the room service menu and order dinner for yourselves. After it arrives, Patrick and I will have dinner down in The Last Hurrah, while we pass dimes to Topaz."

"Why do we have to stay back?" Cossima demanded.

The look Eisen directed at her was chilly. He answered, "Because males, like your brother and I, are ultimately expendable on behalf of females. You matter in a way we cannot, because you are the bottleneck in the production of the next generation. And, moreover, because your grandmothers and great-grandmothers going back to Eve selected, bred, and also trained us to this. If we try to pretend differently we're lying to ourselves and to you.

"So you stay here while your brother and I secure matters for you. No arguments."

"This is clever, Uncle Fitz," Patrick said. There were currently having a late-night repast in the basement café, The Last Hurrah, seated at a square, four-person, white tableclothed table, in one corner of the dark wood-paneled room. Along with their own food— a lobster for Eisen, with Lyonnaise potatoes and succotash, while the boy had a breaded veal chop with French fries and string beans— they'd ordered some of the cod tongue the cat loved. She came over regularly to get skritched and hand-fed by Patrick, while Eisen would drop a few dimes to his shoe for her to pick up. They took their time over dinner, enough so that she was able to complete the basement and some portion of the lobby. Under the excuse of getting her treats of cod tongue, when she jumped on the table she put a paw over the portion of the diagram that she'd just blocked. As she removed her paw, Eisen circled the Xs to mark each spot as completed.

"Good kitty," he said. "Go on and finish the cod tongue, then we'll go back to the suite. You can join us later."

"*Mreow.*"

They pressed the call button for the elevator and waited. When it arrived, a couple got out, prosperous looking and a little plump. Wordlessly Eisen and Patrick let them out, then jumped on themselves. Eisen told the operator to bring them to the top floor, then stood between the operator and Patrick. As soon as the doors closed, Patrick pulled a Franklin silver dollar and some glue from a pocket, then bent low and glued it to the wall, painted side out.

When all four elevators had been done, Eisen chortled, and said, "Let's see how this bloodthirsty alien bitch likes *this.*"

The final spot to obstacle was the lobby. Patrick and Eisen went there late, when a single clerk was on duty. Eisen asked the clerk, "I'd like to increase the length of our stay, is this possible?"

"Let me go into the office and check, sir."

As soon as he was gone, Eisen pulled six half dollars out, three from each pocket, turning them painted side down, and balancing them on his hands. Patrick immediately pulled out the tube of Loctite Super Glue and squeezed an adequate amount out for each coin. Patrick then took three of them himself, leaving Eisen with the other three. The pair then walked away from each other, sticking the coins under the lobby desk overhang, on the vertical surface but high enough to be invisible.

Following that, when the clerk came out with the record, Eisen said, "I'd like to stay through mid-January, if that's possible."

"Easily possible, sir," the clerk replied. *God knows, with the credulous simpleton in charge these last few years, the hotel needs the money. It's not like people are lining up.*

Eisen stepped over to one side of the desk, to distract the clerk from Patrick. "I've long been a fan of the Parker House," he said, "and the staff is still superb."

"Thank you, sir," the clerk said, following that with a meaningful sigh.

"It's not being well run is it?" Eisen asked. "I mean, at the staff level, of course it's being run very well. I am speaking of higher management."

"Sir, I can't . . ."

"I understand loyalty to the one employing you. So, instead, let me ask about some of the deferred maintenance . . ."

The boy, meanwhile, one coin at a time, put silver under the lobby chairs and sofa, under the tables, underneath the main door, in various spots behind radiators, and anyplace else he thought worthwhile, making a mental note of each spot so it could be recorded. When he was as done as he could be, he returned to his grandfather's side.

"Well," said Eisen to the clerk, after feigning a yawn, "I'd best be getting to bed.

Interlude

The body would stop swinging soon. If it didn't, one of the hanging party would simply stop it so it could be taken down and tossed into the filthy, rancid pit, half full of vile, dirty water, where the bodies of those hanged were dumped.

Merchant Robert Calef, who detested the very idea of trying people for witchcraft, and would soon make something of a habit of denigrating and ridiculing Cotton Mather for his involvement in the process, shook his head sadly. He noted that Goody Glover's dead bulging eyes seemed fixed on the miserable pool of filth which would soon become her final resting place.

He followed the dead gaze of those eyes to where Glover's accuser stood, what appeared to be a highly self-satisfied smirk on her face. Calef stooped to let the cat down to the ground. The poor creature seemed very much upset by the judicial murder of its late mistress.

Then Calef pulled from his purse a fistful of silver coins of small denomination, a shilling and sixpence worth of ha'pence. His hand massaged the coins, bitterly and angrily. He walked forward to the vile creature who had summoned the law on a poor old woman.

"Satisfied, are you now, woman? Like Judas, you've sold an innocent over to death. Well, like Judas, then, Catherine Branch, take your reward!"

With that, Calef threw all the coins directly at Goody Glover's accuser.

The woman he knew as Catherine Branch then uttered an unholy scream. Less holy still were the smoking holes that appeared wherever a coin had struck her. Least holy of all was her appearance, where the human faded and flickered away to expose a demon worse than any nightmare's, worse than anything in Mather's fraudulent books.

Three-armed, it was, and five-legged, hairy all over and ugly beyond Calef's wildest imaginings of the limit of ugliness. Moreover, its shrieking changed in quality, from something approximately human to something completely inhuman.

All the witnesses to the hanging turned their gazes to the hideous apparition, then back to the still gently swaying body of Ann Glover. Then, at the realization that they'd all been made parties to a judicial murder and that this demon was the cause, their eyes widened in horror at the price the Divinity would extract from them for their own gullibility and wickedness.

Larkin was the first one to come to his senses. "We've been led astray by this servant of the Dark One. Take her! After her, you men, before she escapes!"

Chapter Eleven

❦

Boston is just a village, sprawling far and wide,
more human than New York City.
—Frederick Engels

Parker House, Boston, Massachusetts

"Topaz," Eisen asked, "how will you ever know where the gate is, so much has changed? Oh, wait; I'm an idiot. You'll know where it is because we came through it and we can point it out, and you know we came through the same one because you laid coins there. Correct?"

"Yes," the calico typed back. "I could not find all of them, but all of them that Robert Calef threw at the Q'riln were considered off limits by everyone. The number 'thirty' when it refers to pieces of silver, has a special meaning, doesn't it, with your people?"

"For many of us, and all who are Christians, yes."

"It took a long time," Topaz elaborated. "A long time to move as many coins as I could find. It was, by your measures, a nine-or-so-mile walking trip to take the coins there and get back to Robert Calef, who had taken me in. And I could only take a couple at a time. And I usually had to stop to hunt on the way."

"However did you know where the gate was?"

"*I* didn't. The cat did. You know how some people say cats can walk through walls?"

"Yes."

"I doubt they usually can. But if there's a gate, they can see it, and walk through it."

"And there," said Eisen, "I thought it took a little girl to do that."

"There are a few creatures who can," Topaz typed. "Very young human females, from all you've told me. Your cats. Yivzarian float spheres. Tapucaru water spiders. Nanazarite tree tunnelers. Flatdeckers. Voombars. Some others. We've had to put up special wards to keep the tree tunnelers on their own world; they're an environmental disaster in waiting."

"I don't think I want even to think about what those names imply. I gave up drinking decades ago and don't want a reason to restart."

"In human form I used to drink beer, sometimes wine" the cat said. "But it was because the water was usually so bad. I confess, I liked the feeling it gave, but not as much as the mating elixir of my own people."

Eisen lifted one eyebrow, an action the calico either ignored or didn't understand. "Mating elixir? I don't want to go there, either.

"So, you carried how many coins from the gallows to the gate?"

"Twenty-four, all I could find."

"Let me think," Eisen said. *Okay, two hundred and forty silver pennies to the English pound sterling. That would be twice that in half pennies, for a pound that's actually . . . mmmm . . . thirty-one grams to the ounce . . . times twelve to the pound . . . no, wait; debasement and inflation had already set in. Roughly . . . well, a little over one hundred grams of silver to the pound. So four hundred and eighty half pence would mean a quarter of a gram of silver, each, give or take. So her twenty-four coins were maybe six grams, about a fifth of a troy ounce.*

"Do you know, Topaz, if the Q'riln ever tried to come through that gate?"

This time the cat didn't type, but shook its head in negation. It was a remarkably humanlike gesture to come from a feline.

And that, that bare six grams, apparently, was sufficient to keep the Q'riln from the gate . . . from this *gate, anyway.*

"If no one ever told you," said Eisen, "you're a brave kitty, Topaz."

Trinity Church, Copley Square, Boston, Massachusetts

The chorus belted out, "And he shall purify the sons of Levi!"

I wish my wife could have been here to see and hear this, thought Eisen. *She'd have been up for a trip into the past in a heartbeat. And I could have wished for the gate to cure her, too. Though that would probably have set up the kind of temporal paradox we haven't caused yet. Oh, well, at least I could have tried.*

While the Gate of Heaven, in South Boston, was his and his family's church, in Eisen's opinion the true church of the City of Boston could only be Trinity, on Copley Square, an Episcopal church.

More joyous, less restrained than the Gate of Heaven, with gilding and sweeping color to match against the Catholics' more austere marble, it was extraordinarily beautiful, the more so now as it filled with the sacred chords of Handel's *Messiah*.

In fairness, thought Eisen, enjoying the annual performance of *Messiah*, with the kids, *both serve the same purpose, to give the faithful a glimpse of the divine, such as mere mortals like myself are capable of grasping. Of course, I had more than a human's share of the divine in my wife. Sigh.*

Juliana instinctively knew what that sigh was over. She patted her grandfather's thigh in sympathy.

"That they may offer unto the Lord
An offering in righteousness."

Eisen was wary of the Q'riln finding them, far from the safety of their little silvered fortress suite, but he had his M1911 tucked into the small of his back, and the .22 Walther with the "Itty Bitty" suppressor in his pocket, so he wasn't excessively wary. Certainly he was not so wary as to ruin the concert for himself or the kids.

"Behold, a virgin shall conceive and bear a Son,
And shall call his name Emmanuel, God with us."

I think, on the whole, whatever Handel intended, I prefer to see Messiah *in a sacred setting, a church or cathedral though, for this, a Mormon temple would do as well.*

"O thou that tellest good tidings to Zion, get thee up into the high mountain:
O thou that tellest good tidings to Jerusalem, lift up thy voice with strength; lift it up, be not afraid; say unto the cities of Judah,

Behold your God!

Arise, shine, for thy light is come, and the glory of the Lord is risen upon thee."

When *Messiah* was finished, Eisen led the kids back to the car, then drove back to the hotel. There he turned the car over to the valet, for parking.

"Let's take a walk," he said.

"Where to, Uncle Fitz?" asked Cossima.

"The Common, at night," he replied.

"But it's so *cold*," the girl said.

"The spirit of the season," he said, lightly mocking, "shall warm you. Seriously, you won't even notice, once you see the reindeer."

"Cold?" Cossima asked, enthralled at the prospect of more animals to fuss over. "What cold? Did somebody say 'cold'? Bring on the reindeer!"

They left the Parker House by the Tremont Street door, then turned left heading toward the Common. Most of the walk to the Common saw them passing the Old Granary burial ground where, from the street level, Eisen wished an audible "Merry Christmas" to Sam Adams, Paul Revere, and John Hancock, each, and then to the inhabitants, generally: "And to all, a very Merry Christmas!"

Boston was, ordinarily, a reserved, even staid, place. Christmastime was the great exception, when no one would look askance as someone wishing a merry Christmas to the city's prominent, and especially her revolutionary, dead.

Right after Old Granary came the Park Street Church.

"They used to call this 'Brimstone Corner,'" Eisen informed the kids, "at least partly for the fiery preaching."

"What was the other part, Uncle Fitz?" Patrick enquired.

"They stored gunpowder here during the War of 1812."

"Really?" Juliana asked.

"Oh, yeah. It's very austere inside, by the way; red carpet, white wall, pilasters, simple pews, a simple cross."

At Brimstone Corner they stopped for a moment to take in the spectacle. The trees, and there were hundreds of them on the Common, seemed all to be lit up for the season. Buildings and displays dotted the Common's landscape, too.

They followed no particular path, though Cossima was fanatically eager to get to the animals. They passed, in no particular order, a display of Jesus giving the Sermon on the mount, a small, heated chapel, erected only for Christmas then taken down again. Choirs of children took turns singing inside the chapel. The festive air of the moment was, "God Rest You Merry, Gentlemen." They passed a display of an organ player with four choirboys, a dozen pipes and two gargantuan candles. Just behind that, directly in front of the state house was a manger with approximately life-sized figures in it, itself fronted by the three wise men aboard horse or camel and two large flocks of sheep attended by their shepherds. There was also a three-person choir display, the man on the right playing a cello, the one on the left singing from a libretto, with a woman with her hands in a muff, all apparently singing. Music came from the two-level platform the statues adorned.

Finally, with the little girl's patience at an end, Eisen laughed and led them to a fenced-in area illuminated by plastic candy canes. Within was a stable, with nine stalls, each marked with a familiar name; Dasher, Dancer, Prancer, Vixen, Comet, Cupid, Donner, Blitzen . . . and, yes, of course, Rudolph, as well.

There was a little stand selling popcorn for the reindeer.

"Uncle Fitz?" the little girl implored.

"Here, go buy some," he said, passing over a few quarters left over from the silver work of a few days prior. "A bag for each of you. But be careful; the reindeer are gentle but mistakes can happen. Watch your fingers, feed from the palm!"

And, as predicted, he thought, *the spirit of the season warms you. This is all rather beautiful. What a shame that the militant evangelical atheists of our own time are so determined to sacrifice beauty to their own brand of sere fanaticism, to stamp out innocent happiness wherever they find it. Such petty and vindictive creatures; I wonder if it ever occurs to them how very close to old New England Puritans they really are, in their fanaticism and in their self-righteousness, in their arrogance and in their ignorance.*

Eventually, the kids ran out of popcorn for the reindeer. They'd apparently been conspiring, because they all came over to him, forming up left to right, Patrick, Juliana, Cossima.

"Go on, Juliana," Patrick said, "with seniority comes responsibility."

"Uncle Fitz . . . no, for this you must be our Grandpa. Can we . . . can we stay through Christmas? Never again, never in our lives, will we ever have the chance to see and feel something like this again. Please? We want to stay through Christmas."

"Yes," he answered, without hesitation, "Of course we can. I've already booked our suite. Let's go back to the hotel, ask them to order us a tree and stand, then we'll go to Jordan's, get all the lights and ornaments we need, buy a record player, buy a dozen Christmas records—they'll be in one of the annexes on the first floor, and we can decorate the tree and start getting ready for a real *Christmas* in Boston."

What he didn't say, though, was the conclusion he'd come to. *We have to stay here until we can do away with the Q'riln, anyway. We can't let it come hunting us in our own time. Even if it wasn't dangerous to us . . . well, I'll accept the miracle of the typing, communicating feline as pretty good evidence that the Q'riln is dangerous to mankind. It must be destroyed.*

"Actually, on our way to Jordan's let's hit S.S. Pierce." He'd actually pronounced the name as "Purse." "They have all kinds of wonderful Christmas goodies on hand."

S.S. Pierce, 144 Tremont Street, Boston, Massachusetts

"Before we step through the doors," Eisen warned the kids, "a lot of these things are nothing too very special in our time, with supermarkets taking up an acre or more. At this time, though, this is all very high-end stuff.

"Some of it will be weird, as weird as, say, the lamb's kidneys on the Parker House Breakfast menu."

"Weird like what, Uncle Fitz?" Patrick asked.

"Well . . . French coffee in cans, say. Or maybe Bent's Water Crackers; they're made in Milton and have been since before the Civil War. Salmon Steaks in cans? Frog legs in Newburg Sauce? Beef tongue?"

At those last two all the kids made ugly faces.

"Oh, I agree, of course," Eisen said. "But then I remember beautiful stuffed olives; huge things, they were. Five-pound sacks of maple sugar? Oh, God, five-pound sacks of maple sugar! Think about *that!*

"Also there's a good variety of wine, beer, and liquor from all over, though I don't know if the company ever keyed to the wonders of single malt scotch. If you see some, be sure to let me know. We'll bring a bottle back just to freak out guests.

"Now let's go check it out. And remember; it's pronounced 'purse.'"

Three steps past the door, Eisen thought to himself, once again, *It really* is *a small world.*

A few more steps and he found himself standing next to a familiar, very slender, pixie-coiffed, and rather nicely rumped librarian, trying to choose between S.S. Pierce Amaretto and S.S. Pierce already mixed Manhattans.

"The Amaretto would suit you better, Miss Willard. Can't you hear it calling your name?"

The librarian sniffed and thought, *Jockey Club, my favorite.* Then she spun around smartly. "Oh, Mr. Maguire, how wonderful to see you again!"

He let his eyes return the compliment. "Shopping for Christmas, for yourself, or both?"

"Both," she replied, then flashed him a very warm smile.

"Well, I won't detain you then. Not many shopping days left, after all."

"Your accent," she said. "It's got a good deal of Brahmin to it but it isn't pure Brahmin. It's not Long Island Lockjaw, either."

"No, it's not," he agreed. "I learned it at Latin, rather than on mother's knee."

"Ah, Latin," she said, as if he'd gone up about a hundred percent in her estimation. "You don't live in the city, do you?"

"No, nor even the state anymore. I make my home in Virginia."

At that time the kids came back, holding in their arms a treasure trove of goodies, ranging from Morello's cherries in syrup, to Pierce assorted chocolates, to Pierce chocolate covered cream centers, to this cheese and that oatmeal loaf, to date nut bread and that cream cheese. Juliana had even thoughtfully picked up some canned cat food and S.S. Pierce king crab meat for Topaz.

"Can we get this, Uncle Fitz?" the children asked. Juliana gave him the evil eye since he was flirting again.

But then, again, she thought, *isn't it time for him to move on?*

With a chuckle, Eisen replied, "Sure you can, but there's no need to carry it with us. You can assemble what you want, within reason, with one of the cashiers and they'll arrange shipment to the Parker House. But you had best cut it off with what you have. We need to get to Jordan's before they close.

"Miss Willard, adieu. Hope to see you around sometime soon."

Latin and Parker House, with most of a Brahmin accent? Taste enough to wear Caswell-Massey? Oh, yes, if I can arrange it, we'll meet "sometime soon." And, if not, well... flirting is its own reward.

Jordan Marsh Company, Washington Street, Boston, Massachusetts

After being assured that the hotel could and would arrange for a tree, "tall enough to just fit the ceiling, leaving space for a star, and wide enough to fill a good corner of the parlor," Eisen and the kids took the path to Jordan Marsh, past the cosmetics area where the kids' grandmother had once enthralled—or would someday enthrall, point of view depending—hundreds, to the elevators and then up to the sixth floor, thence to the bridge over Avon Street, connecting the main store and the annex, to the Trim-a-Tree shop.

There, Eisen did some quick mental calculations. *Three grandkids, each likely to marry and have three of their own, each of whom should have three ornaments to pass on to my great-great-grandchildren. Twenty-seven high end ornaments, therefore, plus another thirteen for breakage and chance.*

But what about future grandkids? Maybe I'll take them here to pick out their own, when they're old enough.

"Kids, I'll go hunt down lights and run of the mill ornaments. I want each of you to find a baker's dozen each of really nice ornaments, plus another from Juliana. Get hand-blown glass... velvet- or flock-covered, you know, really *special* ones like the ones that are particularly special for the tree back home."

"But Gr—Uncle Fitz, what are we to do with them when we go back? We can't carry them!"

"I've been thinking about that, for those, for the rifles I picked up in Cambridge, for your Christmas presents here and now, for most of our new clothes. I don't know where there's a museum quality storage facility close to here, but one of the museums *will* know.

"Now, off you go to pick out ornaments. This is a once in a lifetime—or more than that, in my case—Christmas. Be extravagant."

While the kids were perusing the ornaments with a critical eye, Eisen went to get lights. He didn't quite remember what technologies were even available in 1965, but discovered at least one type he'd never heard of, or, at least, couldn't remember, NOMA's bubble lights. These string lights were more or less candle-shaped, with globes at the base. They contained a small incandescent bulb and oil. The heating of the oil by the bulbs caused the oil to boil, creating the bubbles inside the candle portions.

"Never saw these," Eisen muttered. "Hard to imagine I never even heard of them. But we're going to give them a shot."

He picked out four sets of the bubble lights, a total of twenty-eight lights. From there, he went to the string lights. LEDs did not, of course, exist in 1965, while it would be another year before GE began importing their "Merry Midget" Christmas tree lights, there were already available, especially from Italy, what were called "fairy lights." Eisen picked up six of these sets, each of thirty-five bulbs. They came in surprisingly "plain jane" boxes, devoid of much more than a name. Satisfied with the lights, he took them to the counter and asked the girl on duty—he'd seen her before and been struck by her beauty—if he could leave them here, also advising her that he had three children with him who would be showing up with ornaments.

"Meanwhile," he told her, "I want to run down to the toy department and pick up that amazing chess set from twelfth-century Normandy."

"I know just the one you mean," the girl replied. "It's a beautiful piece of work, isn't it? I hope they still have it for you."

He looked at the girl, realizing again that she was, in fact, a remarkable beauty, if a bit more slender than he normally preferred. He thought she was about nineteen or twenty, certainly no more than twenty-two, with a heart-shaped face, slightly olive toned, and absolutely enormous brown eyes. He figured her for Italian, though a southern French, Spanish, or Balkan descent was also possible.

"Is it Christmas that makes you so beautiful?" he asked. "Or are you always this heart-stopping?"

"I don't know," she answered, eyes going wide at the man's boldness. "I don't even know that I'm especially good-looking."

"Take my word for it, Miss, you are. And, so, before I make a fool of myself—I am, you see, extremely married—I'd best go tell the kids to bring their ornaments here, then see if I can get that chess set."

"Is your father . . . no, wait," the girl said, looking at Juliana, "he's not old enough to be your father."

"He's our . . . uncle," Juliana said, after the slightest hesitation.

"Is your uncle always such a flirt?"

"Oh, you have no idea," Juliana said. "He's good at it, too, isn't he?"

"Oh, you have no idea," the girl echoed.

"It's not even what he says, especially," Juliana said, "it's something more innate. He did tell you he was married, too, didn't he?"

"Yes."

"That's part of the charm, and how he gets a girl to let her guard down. That, and his complete self-confidence where women are concerned. Do you know why he's so self-confident?" Juliana asked.

"No, not really."

"Because he doesn't care if he's rejected and because he isn't really looking for anything. He just loves women and he just loves to flirt. To tell the truth, it's not clear to me that he's actually afraid of anything.

"And he's actually *not* married; his wife passed away a couple of years ago. But in his heart? He's still married and maybe always will be."

"What does he do for a . . . ?"

"He was in the Army," Juliana replied. "Now, I suppose you could say he's in investments. Yes, that's it, investments."

The clerk sighed. *Not really married but married in his heart . . . just my luck. And money.*

Eisen reappeared.

"Did you find your chess set?" the girl asked.

"I did. It's being sent to my suite at the Parker House."

Money, the girl thought again.

"Have the kids deposited all their ornaments yet? There should be forty, though I won't complain if they go a few over."

She did a quick count. "I . . . see . . . forty-two. These are very expensive ornaments, you know. The cheapest one here is five dollars and a couple are as much as ten."

"It's a once in a lifetime chance for them to have Christmas in Boston," he explained. "I want it to be as perfect for them as possible. By the way, if I may be so bold, what's your name?"

"Sir, you obviously have no trouble being bold. I'm Francesca."

"Call me Fitz. Hmmm . . . do you have a pen?"

She handed one over, along with a note slip.

"This is my room and the Parker House's number. Give me a call, if you're of a mind. You can join myself and the kids for dinner some night this week."

She took the slip back, saying, "I'll at least think about it."

"Would you prefer the Parker House, Anthony's Pier Four, or Jimmy's Harborside? Or maybe Durgin Park or Union Oyster House? Or, if you prefer Italian, you'll have to let me know what's good."

"You sound very sure that I'll call this number."

He didn't answer, but just smiled and gave a "your call" shrug.

"Just so I know," he asked, "it's Francesca . . ."

"Cordesco," she replied.

"Grandpa," said Juliana, on the walk back to the hotel, "you are completely shameless and totally incorrigible!"

"For flirting?"

"Yes!"

"I'm harmless, in the second place, but, even if I were not, in the first place, this is America on the cusp of, but not really yet a part of, the sexual revolution. The pill is new. Bastardy is deeply shameful. And that girl is certainly an Italian Catholic, who will not be doing a damned thing until she's married or, at least, engaged. Plus, as far as I'm concerned I'm still married to your grandmother who was, in her late fifties, still looking like mid-thirties and smoking hot, to boot. And I'm not over her yet. I may never be.

"So relax, Juliana, even if the girl calls it will only be a nice dinner and you, your brother, and your sister will be present for it."

Parker House, Boston, Massachusetts

Frank Sinatra was singing, "I'll Be Home for Christmas," on the record-changing stereo Eisen had had sent over from Jordan's electronics department. Lined up to play above his *A Jolly Christmas* album were the soundtrack from *A Charlie Brown Christmas*, the *Elvis Presley Christmas Album*, *A Christmas Gift for You from Phil Spector*, featuring the voices of any number of talented women whose lives Phil would probably eventually ruin, and George Beverly Shea's *Christmas Hymns*. They'd gone overboard; a dozen more albums sat, unopened as of yet, upright on the floor next to the table holding the record player.

The kids were long since trained to trim a tree properly. Eisen just asked them, "What are the four priorities of work, when trimming the Christmas tree? Juliana, step one?"

"Lights."

"Patrick, step two?"

"Garland."

"Cossima?"

"Step three is ornaments, of course, you grumpy old man."

"Juliana, again?"

"Fourth comes the tinsel."

"This is the way," Eisen said, echoing a popular TV series from their own time.

The phone rang, a clicking sound completely unlike phones of the twenty-first century.

"Maguire," Eisen replied.

"Sir, this is the front desk. There's a call from a woman, a Francesca Cordesco, for you."

Am I good or what?

"Please put her through."

"Mr. Maguire? Francesca Cordesco; we met at Jordan's."

"Yes, I remember you very clearly, Francesca."

"I've decided to take you up on your most gracious offer. And I'd say, let's eat at your hotel. I've heard the food is very good and I've never even been inside it. Plus, I doubt you would try to throw me over your shoulder and carry me off with your nieces and nephew sharing the same suite."

"Quite right, Francesca, the presence of the children would be *most* inconvenient to that whole 'throw the beautiful girl over your shoulder, carry her off, and ravish her' routine. And please call me 'Fitz.'"

"'Fitz'? I like the sound of that. Would tomorrow be too forward of me?"

"Tomorrow is fine. Shall I pick you up or send a taxi or . . ."

"I get off work tomorrow at five. Give me half an hour to change into better clothes and I'll just walk there and meet you in the lobby."

"That would be perfect, though I'd feel a good deal better if I picked you up under, say, the Filene's clock at five-thirty. We can walk from there."

"I won't say 'no.' Thank you, Fitz. Tomorrow under the clock."

He hung up after she did. Then he turned his attention to the tree and said, "Patrick, that teardrop-shaped colored glass one? Move it over to the next branch, why don't you, to take advantage of the two lights on either side?"

"We really can't go to dinner with you, Uncle Fitz," Juliana said, as Eisen put on three pieces of one of his four-piece suits. "We'll make a mistake somewhere in there, the kind that doesn't matter when it's just us four but could be a disaster if a stranger's around and certain to hear."

"No," he said, "you are coming with me, not only to give me cover with your grandmother's family but . . ."

"We won't say a word," said Cossima. "What happens in Boston, in 1965, stays in Boston, in 1965?"

"Where did you hear that expression about Las Vegas?"

"It is known," she replied, echoing yet another television series from their time.

"Go on, Old Man," Patrick said. "We'll be fine behind our little fortress of silver. Just leave our guns, in case. Go have a good time. Be back before midnight. Don't do anything I, at age nine, wouldn't do."

"Fine, fine; Juliana, go pick me out a tie for this suit, if you would; I hate them so don't trust my taste in them. And round me up some cufflinks. I'll leave you the M1911, the Walther, the Sterling, and the Sig. I'll be content with the CZ in the shoulder rig."

Filene's Clock, Washington Street, Boston, Massachusetts

"My nieces and nephew decided I could use a night on the town, or at least a decent dinner and conversation, with a beautiful girl," Eisen told Francesca. "They're still camped out in our suite so your virtue may still be presumed to be intact and safe with me."

He is so brazen, she thought. *But if I didn't think it was the truth I wouldn't be here.*

"I've also made us reservations at the Revere Room. Pretty good food, in fact."

"As long as it's not Italian," Francesca said. "Mind, I *like* Italian, but when it's what you've eaten just about every day, all your life, a little change is nice, too."

"Well, this will be a change, then. I can only hope you enjoy it. Shall we be off?"

The Revere Room was considerably fancier than the downstairs eatery. Francesca looked at the menu and blanched a bit. "I don't know . . . would you order for me?"

"Sure," he agreed. "But not without some hints. Do you like lobster, or fish, or prime rib?"

"Any of those would be fine."

"Ah, good. Let's try the lobster cocktail for an appetizer, then the tomato bisque, and dig into a couple of prime ribs. Sound okay to you?"

He's not cheap, I'll give him that.

"Wonderful."

Eisen made a signal—a glance and a just barely upraised finger—to the waiter that they were ready to order.

Topaz was reclining on the front desk, watching the people come and go, when she suddenly stiffened and bared her teeth.

I will never forget that face. The last time I saw it, it had been smiling as it watched me slowly strangle, while kicking and dancing a couple of feet off the ground.

I suppose I am surprised she never changed her appearance.

The Q'riln, whom last she'd known of under the name of Catherine Branch, came through the front door briskly, with a look on her face as if she'd found something smelly floating around the doors. She paused and steadied herself, then walked toward the lobby desk. About five feet from it she stopped again, gulping and swaying. Immediately she ran for the sofa and sat down, only to bounce up again with a frightful screech. She went to one of the windows as if she intended to go out of it, then bounced off the wall below the window.

Suffer, you bitch! thought the calico.

Leaning on a table with her left hand she instantly drew that hand back as if she stuck it into flame. The hand and arm continued to twitch for a good fifteen seconds after she pulled it up.

The Q'riln looked around desperately, then noticed that everyone in the lobby was looking at her as if she were an escapee from an asylum for the insane. She went to a chair as if to sit down, then recoiled from it before she could take a seat. Finally, with a screech, she ran from the lobby, back through the Tremont Street doors, and off into the night.

"Well, we certainly don't want *her* as a guest," muttered the clerk on duty.

Topaz raced for the stairs and then upwards. *Eisen must be told!*

"I don't want to talk about me," Eisen said. "I am certain you're a much more interesting subject."

"Flatterer," she accused.

"That's my job here, isn't it? But I'm not flattering; I'm genuinely curious."

"Well, I'm just an Italian girl. My parents came from around Firenze but I was born here. I went to elementary school in the North End, where we lived, and then to Girls' Latin. I graduated there a couple of years ago and got into Boston College on a women's track and field scholarship."

"What are you studying?"

"I'm in the RN program, but there's this new thing I want to try out for, Nurse Practitioner. It's more than just being an RN."

"If that, why not an MD?" he asked.

"Doctors are arrogant," she answered, "whereas *I* am a pretty nice person. I'd never fit in."

"At least you were smart enough not to become a lawyer."

"Oh, GOD, no!" she exclaimed. "My older brother went to law school. He's miserable. Can't sleep at night unless he drinks himself into a coma. He says he'd rather be back in Korea, getting shot at by the Chinese. And he says that once you're in it, it's almost impossible to leave with a good conscience because the taking a case to being paid cycle is such that you have to keep on taking new cases. Worse, he says, people are counting on you and you just can't leave them in the lurch.

"So, no thanks, no law school for this girl."

"See?" he said. "I knew you were smart as well as beautiful."

"You are *such* a flatterer."

"Flattery involves not telling the truth," he countered. "Every word I've spoken tonight is true." *Albeit not the whole truth.*

The cat scratched frantically at the suite's door until Patrick opened it for her. She raced in and then began stropping the door to the lockable closet, all the while meowing frantically.

"Juliana, let me have the key," Patrick said.

"I'll get the laptop out," she said.

She opened the door, then rummaged through the duffel bag for the laptop. This she took to the desk and plugged it in. Lifting the screen, she pressed the ON button until the thing sprang to life.

Instantly, the cat jumped onto the desk and began typing. She went a lot faster and made many more mistakes than they'd come to expect of her, punctuating her typing with frantic *meows* at certain key points.

Juliana read the screen, translated the hasty and panic-stricken letters. Her eyes grew into saucers. "Patrick," she said, her voice breaking, "take the Walther and hide it in your pocket. Cover it with your winter coat. Then go tell Grandpa the Q'riln is here."

"I'm afraid we'll have to cut this short," Eisen told the girl, as Patrick, white faced, stood next to their table.

"Is it an emergency?" she asked.

"You might say that but . . . oh, hell, we can't cut this short. You can't go out in the streets while that *thing . . .*" *Oops, said too much. But it's true. However it tracked us acts like tracking by smell. If it "smells" me on her, then there's no telling what it will do to her.*

"Shit," he muttered, something which shocked her a little since his language had been so thoroughly gentlemanly and clean to this point.

"You need to come to my suite," he said, finally, "and, no, curb your thoughts. You're still as safe from me as if your father were standing behind me with a shotgun. But I need to explain some things. And some questions you are surely going to have I probably cannot explain. The short version is that we're all in a good deal of trouble from . . . something I *will* have to explain to you.

"Will you trust me?"

She hesitated only a moment before saying, "Yes. Yes, I trust you."

"Good judgment." Eisen then peeled off a twenty, to more than cover the tab, plus a very generous tip, signaled to the waiter that it was waiting on the table and, taking Francesca in hand, proceeded to lead her and Patrick back to the elevators and up.

Once the elevator door closed, and with the operator facing the cage, Eisen loosened his jacket and reached a hand in to lift the tab securing the Czech .380. It made an audible snap.

"I know what you just did," Francesca whispered. "My family is . . . connected, shall we say. That's half the reason my brother was sent to law school."

"That could prove useful," Eisen said, "but let's not count me out quite yet."

Every hotel room had a Bible, especially in 1965. Eisen took the one in this suite and placed Francesca's hands on it.

"I need you to swear," he said, "that you will neither reveal nor act on anything you are about to hear and see, to anyone, prior to the year 2025. Will you swear?"

She hesitated. It wasn't a small deal but, then, too, her family did have some tradition of *Omerta*, so . . . ultimately, she agreed. "I swear."

He released her hand from the Bible, then told Juliana, "Bring out the laptop."

"I figured you would bring her back here when Patrick told you," the girl said. "I just hid it under the sofa."

She brought it out, placed in on the desk, opened it up and turned it on.

When that was done, Eisen pointed toward the cat and said, "Topaz, this is Miss Francesca Cordesco. Francesca, this cat is Topaz. Topaz, tell Francesca hello, why don't you."

The young woman's eyes widened as in the first place, the cat began to type while, in the second, sensible words appeared on the strange, glowing screen: "Hello Miss Cordesco. Very pleased to meet you. I am Topaz."

Eisen caught her just as her knees buckled, then carried her to the sofa bed and laid her down upon it.

"I knew you would do this, Grandpa," said Juliana, "but are you sure letting her in on our little secret was the smartest thing you could have done?"

"You're just mad because you don't like my flirting!"

"Don't change the subject, Old Man. In the first place, if Grandma were still alive I'd *hate* your flirting, but now . . . well, I think you need to. But you let her in on this. All our 'Uncle Fitz' this and no 'Grandpa' that to keep a secret and you just let her in on it."

"The thing tracked us, Juliana, tracked us right to our hotel with nothing to go on. I couldn't take the chance that it might be able to track this innocent girl, too.

"And she's really nice, too, isn't she?"

With a sigh, the girl admitted that, "Yes, she's a doll. And I suppose you're right; you couldn't just let her go home when a monster might be tracking her. But then, you shouldn't have invited her to dinner, either."

"I know. I know I shouldn't have. Problem is, I'm twenty-five or twenty-six again, with all the stupidity that implies. I think I need you to keep my head straight and supplement the judgment I don't seem to have anymore. Once upon a time your grandmother would have taken care of that for me. Now you're the only one who can."

Interlude

The Q'riln was fast, but she wasn't faster than men on horseback. Terrified at being exposed, both her hearts pounding, she took off toward the south at a fair clip.

Little by little, her cube resurrected her human body. It was a slow process. Her footsteps, too, were dogged by one of those nasty little four-legged animals the locals called "cats." If not mistaken, she thought that this one had belonged to the late and unlamented Ann Glover, her goody two shoes former pursuer.

I hate those damned things because I can have no impact on them at all. They're completely immune to mental manipulation, and generally too suspicious, too quick, and too agile to simply kill, physically. I wonder if they can see me for what I am.

My nearest gate is on the peninsula called "South Boston." Almost exactly in the middle. It seemed like a good spot for a gate, because of the aura of tasty future human children that hung around it. Now I wish I'd put it a good deal closer.

The cat stayed out of striking distance, just keeping the Q'riln in view. She pursued with her tail straight up, as if signaling the humans now organizing to pursue.

The Q'riln stopped for a moment, to see a half dozen of the humans on horseback, heading her way. The cat, meanwhile, was jumping as high as it could into the air, to draw the humans' attention.

The monster spent some of her power to distract the human pursuit party but, "No; not only are they too far away, but their fear and anger have given their minds some immunity, over and above that of distance. That stuff the humans call 'adrenaline' is powerful."

Wishing an ineffective curse at the jumping cat, she took off again, down Boston Neck, heading for Dorchester Neck, which led to South Boston. The cat stopped jumping and resumed her pursuit.

"A stern chase is a long chase," especially when the pursued has, as the Q'riln did, a good head start. Even so, the men on horseback were on Dorchester Road before the Q'riln had managed to negotiate the last bit of Dorchester Neck.

"Mistress," said the cube, with its usual annoying calm, "I strongly suggest that you hurry."

"What do think I've been *doing*, you artificial non-Q'riln nag?"

"No need to get personal, Mistress, *and do be polite*, but I think those men coming after you will chop us both into little bits. Even if they have to take a hammer to my shell first."

"I know, I *know*! I'm doing the best I can."

"I suggest doing better. That furry creature isn't falling behind, either. I suspect it can go a good deal faster than we can, too."

Chapter Twelve
〜〜〜

Death to every foe and traitor! Whistle out the marching tune
And hurrah, me boys, for freedom, 'tis the rising of the moon.
—John Keegan Casey

Parker House, Boston, Massachusetts

"Juliana, is the Sterling pumped up?"

"It's about ninety percent, Uncle Fitz!"

"That's plenty," Eisen said, walking to the lockable closet and finding it unlocked.

"Ordinarily, I'd be pissed off over your forgetting the door, Juliana..."

"The cat was just so frantic," she explained, "I stood over her and forgot."

"This time, however," he added, as he slipped his head between the air tanks, "I am not pissed, because you've saved me a few seconds getting suited up."

"Where are you going?" she asked.

"I'm going to go after that bitch if she's still in the area!"

"You shouldn't go alone," she said. "Patrick?"

"No, I want him to stay here and guard you. Topaz?"

"*Mreow?*"

"Would you recognize the Q'riln if you saw it again?"

"*Mreow!*" The cat was stropping furiously, as if eager to begin the hunt.

"I'll take that as a 'yes.'"

Eisen pulled his overcoat over his shoulders, like a cloak, holding the Sterling in his right hand, hidden from view.

"Let's go, kitty girl! Juliana, take care of Francesca. Tell her no more than you must to keep her safe. Which means here."

Ignoring the elevators, Eisen and the cat raced down the stairs, finally emerging in the lobby. Somewhere off the lobby a choir was singing "Hark! The Herald Angels Sing," and with considerable feeling.

For this, thought Eisen, *I don't suppose you could sing "Blood on the Risers"? I suppose not. Oh, well.*

The cat trotted to a window facing the door out of which the staggering Q'riln had departed. She scanned left and right, then suddenly tensed, tail straight up and nose and body pointed slightly to the left, directly at the beast.

The clerk on the desk, who knew Topaz very well but only as a cat, was shocked for a moment at the cat's demeanor, as if ready for a fight with another cat twice her size but determined to win or die. He wondered, briefly, whether he should leave a note for the day staff to make her an appointment with the vet. She was, after all, the hotel's mouser and very good at her job.

Then that longer term guest, Mr. Maguire, spoke to the cat as if to a human. "C'mon, kitty girl, let's go get her."

Coupling those two events to the very strange woman who'd entered earlier and spent ten minutes of so shrieking and bouncing off the walls and furniture and, well, *I think maybe it's time for a little vacation; to hell with the Cape in the summer.*

The Q'riln was still half stunned from her exposure to so much of that damned silver. Someone had clearly set it as a baited trap.

And I strolled right into it, like an idiot larva that follows the smaller sibling, unaware that a larger sibling, with bigger teeth, is hidden behind a rock.

She looked across at one of the windows of the hotel she'd tried to enter, seeing a strangely familiar cat. *Now where have I seen . . . oh, oh.*

"Cube," she asked, "how long does a cat live?"

"On average, about seven years, Mistress. Why, if I may ask?"

"Because that cat in the window across the street looks altogether too much like a certain cat that a certain woman of this town once had, which cat helped them pursue me to the now-blocked gate south of here."

"If it's the same cat, Mistress, then it is not a normal cat. I recommend flight. Instant flight."

"I think you're right, cube." With that, the Q'riln turned to her right and fled toward a metal gate fronting what was apparently a cemetery, perhaps a hundred feet away. There she turned right, running slightly uphill between the headstones. At a cenotaph bearing the name, "Franklin," she turned left very quickly and ran into a tall iron fence. Behind the fence were a couple of iron stairways. She bent her legs and jumped upward and forward, landing on the left-hand steps. With a good deal of clattering of metal and groaning of old and long untested attachments, the Q'riln sped upward some two and one-half flights, arriving then at a dead-end rooftop.

She went to one corner and informed her cube, "My natural appendages, please, cube. Just those, because I'm going to need you to change me back."

Slowly, her arms and legs split lengthwise to reveal eight hairy appendages. She restrained her squeal from the painful procedure. She felt it, all the same. At the end of each leg spread out something resembling a spider's paw, sticky, with directional plates, and with delicate hairs growing in clusters from the palms.

Like an insect, she scuttled up the corner of an old brick building and then a modernist brick atrocity. In less than a minute she had reached a roof. She scuttled across the roof on her five legs, then peered over. No one was walking along Park Street, so she leapt down to the street below.

To her right she saw a large brick structure with a bright golden dome above it.

This town has grown since I was last here.

"Hold here, Mistress; I'll change you back."

The Q'riln barely refrained from shrieking with the pain as her form changed back to its previous, humanlike self.

From there, she turned left and headed along the Common, then across the gardens, with their double pond, and to her own hotel.

Eisen stepped through the door, which he held open to be followed by Topaz. He saw something flutter off to his left, at a sharp angle. The cat instantly keyed on it, resuming her previous posture.

"Old Granary Burial Ground? Why not, it's not like she's got reason to be superstitious when she is likely the reason *we're* superstitious. Come on, Topaz, let's see if we can catch her."

Though weighted down by his Sterling, the magazine, and the air tanks, Eisen's legs churned, eating up the hundred or so meters to the cemetery gate.

"I hope you don't mind, folks," he said to the assembled corpses and their presumptive ghosts. "Remember, I did wish you a merry Christmas last night!"

He and the cat entered the cemetery and stopped, listening. Off to their left Eisen heard a kind of scratching past John Hancock's grave stele and ran toward it, the cat hot on his heels.

There was no physical sound when he got to the grave. Nonetheless, words formed in his mind.

I wasn't sure before, said the alien voice, *not until I ran into the trap of silver you set for me. But now I know. And I have seen you. And I know who you are. You are too excited for me to impose more than this message on your mind. But wherever you are, wherever you and your spawn go, I'll be waiting. One moment of weakness, only one, and you are mine.*

And as for the cat; its skin will make a nice scarf against the cold of this place.

"Did you hear that message, Topaz?"

"*Mreow!*"

"No, I didn't much like it, either. Do you suppose the bitch got away?"

"*Meow?*"

"I think so too. Back to the suite then, while we figure out what to do next."

Eisen and the cat returned to find Francesca conscious, sitting at the table with the kids, while drinking a cup of tea.

"You look remarkably well preserved for a man of sixty-six," she said.

Eisen looked at the other three faces, all of them extremely guilty looking.

"She was *very* persistent," Cossima said. "We had to tell her pretty much everything."

"Especially the part about the alien," Francesca said, "the Q'riln. That was the most important part. What the hell were you *thinking* getting me involved in this? Were you out of your ever-loving *mind*?"

Eisen sighed. "I wasn't thinking about getting you involved. It wasn't until Patrick told me that the bitch was here that it even occurred to me she could really track us like that. And having tracked us, it was possible that she'd either seen you or—though I think this is unlikely—that we'd somehow infected or contaminated you with whatever it was she tracked us by. She might, you know, have gone after you just because you had waited on us at Jordan's.

"So all I could think of was, in the first place, getting you someplace safe—and this suite, for various reasons, is about as safe as it gets—and then arming myself and going out after her with Topaz.

"Unfortunately, she disappeared. Too quickly for me to give chase and leave you and the kids undefended."

As he dropped the coat from his shoulders he exposed the Sterling and tanks.

"What the hell is that?" Francesca asked.

"Think of it as a completely quiet, totally legal and unregulated, submachine gun."

Francesca shook her head. "My uncle, Giustino, would give a lot of money for one of those."

"Yes," Eisen agreed, "but you swore on a Bible that you would reveal nothing. Why would your uncle be interested in . . . ?"

"He's from Naples," she said, by way of explanation. "Married to my aunt. It's never been entirely clear to me if he married into our clan or we married into his."

It took him a moment to realize that Naples was just behind Sicily in terms of Mafia make up and influence.

"Like the Irish hereabouts," he observed. "Like the Jews, too, for that matter. Not many of us involved in crime, but all of us *know* somebody, don't we?"

Seeing he understood, she said, "Exactly! Also, I wasn't saying I'd sell it to him, though *you* might consider it. Wasn't saying I'd talk about it. I was just saying that it's a uniquely valuable weapon. Somehow, though, I thought the twenty-first century would be all ray guns and lasers and blasters."

"Well, we do use lasers, yes. But they don't do what you might think, or not yet, anyway. Indeed, there's a laser here"—he tapped the box by the Sterling's muzzle—"but all it does is tell me where my shots will hit at a certain range. Most of the lasers we use are for that or for more general range finding."

Finally, she asked, "What now? What now for me?"

"That's up to you, but I'll tell you what I do know. The alien claimed to have seen me. She sent the words directly to my mind. She didn't say where or when, but it could have been while we were walking from the Filene's clock. We have to assume the possibility that she's seen you, too, even if she can't track you the way she tracked us."

"I can't stay here," Francesca said. "You have any idea how controlling an Italian mother and father can be of their daughters? And, besides, I need to work."

"It's my fault you're stuck here," Eisen said. "I'll pay you whatever Jordan's would have."

"That's awfully generous," Francesca replied, "but doesn't solve my problem with my parents."

"If I thought it would do any good, I'd offer to marry . . ."

"GRANDPA!" said all three children, together. Then Patrick said, "Grandma's still alive now."

"I didn't say, brats, that I thought it would do any good. Do but note, however, that your grandmother, here and now, is about four and a half years old, single, of course, and quite disinterested in marrying or being married to anyone. In short, it would not be bigamy."

"Wouldn't matter anyway," said Francesca. "You would have to be vetted by my parents, my uncles and aunts, everybody. And for that . . ."

"For that we'd have to spend a good deal of time outside," he said, "and largely unsecured."

"So what do we do?" Francesca asked. "I can't stay; it's not safe to go."

"Let me mull on it. In the interim, neither of us got to finish our dinners. And the cat probably could use something . . ."

"*Mreow!*"

". . . Shall we send for room service?"

"I can give you a gun," Eisen said, buttering a bit of a room service-provided Parker House roll.

"I haven't the first clue about guns," Francesca said. "I'd be afraid to be in the same room with one."

That set Eisen and the kids, all four, to chuckling.

"Oh," she said. "Well, yes, I suppose..."

"You're in the same suite, if not room, with...mmm...let me think...ten guns, including the Sterling? Yes, ten. So I can spare one if you're willing to take it, but the only ones for which I have bullets for use against the Q'riln that wouldn't raise some unfortunate suspicions is the .45."

"It's a very gentle recoil," Patrick offered, "that .45. I could shoot one when I was six. Yes, really."

"It will fit in your pocketbook, too," Juliana said. "I've shot one, too. You can handle it."

"Well..."

Sensing the girl's resolve weakening, Eisen said, "Patrick, fetch the .45, plus a piece of paper and something to stand the paper against."

"Would the Bible do?" he asked.

"No," said everyone.

"Fine, then; I'll find something."

"Once we get the mechanical parts down," Eisen said, "I'll take you to Park Street Station. From there we'll use the subway, Park to Washington to North Station..."

"I can get off at North Station," she said. "I live on Endicott, maybe three minutes from North Station."

"That will probably work," Eisen agreed, "but I'll still get off with you and cover your walk home from a distance." He didn't bother telling her that Endicott had once been home to a number of higher end Boston bordellos, notably those of Mrs. Lake and Mrs. Cowen.

Patrick cleared and then brought over the M1911, the magazine and the ejected round in one hand, with the slide locked back.

She looked at him very oddly, then asked, "What kind of future do you people come from, where nine-year-olds are trained with weapons?"

"More a regional and cultural thing than a temporal one," said Eisen. "You could find the same thing down south now. Or in the Midwest...or out west...and maybe even in western Massachusetts.

"Now pay attention. Lesson one is how to load and then clear the pistol. Watch me..."

The piece of paper previously fetched by Patrick had a small, roughly man-shaped, silhouette on it. It was held against the *Globe*, which was perched against a wall, by the addition of a couple of drops of water.

Francesca stood perhaps four feet from the wall, feet apart, and the pistol pushed out to arm's length, with both hands holding it as she'd just been taught. She had her left eye shut tight. The pistol was cleared, but had the hammer cocked and a pencil stuck down the barrel.

She aimed not at the silhouette Eisen had drawn, but at a dot he'd drawn above that, once he'd tested for the drop of the pencil he had placed in the barrel.

Eisen stood between her and the wall, but off to one side. "Aim at the dot, hit the silhouette," he told her. "But if you see a monster, close, aim at the monster."

She flicked off the safety, then squeezed the trigger. The hammer dropped, driving forward the firing pin. The firing pin, in turn, imparted its energy to the pencil's eraser, driving the pencil forward. It hit a little to the left of the silhouette.

"That's not bad for a first run," Eisen half-complimented, bending at the waist to retrieve the pencil. "We need to do it rather more though. Go ahead and cock the hammer and lift the muzzle."

Once she had, he dropped the pencil down the barrel and said, "Repeat."

"The more I think about it, Francesca," Eisen said over the deafening clattering of the elevated as it rolled from Washington Station toward North Station, "the more I think we should give you an excuse of marriage. Swear to God, it can be an unconsummated marriage of convenience you can have annulled after the kids and I go back to where we belong. But, having gotten you into this— foolishly and thoughtlessly or, at best, ignorantly; yes, I admit it—I feel I need to see you through it and *without* making your life at home total Hell."

He was again wearing his coat like a cloak, and, again, it was because he had the entire pneumatic assembly and one arm hidden under it.

"God would never be fooled by such a cheap trick," she replied, completely oblivious to the eventual plagiarism. "And that still wouldn't fix the family's need to vet you. I'm not even sure they'd accept you if we tried. It's not like you run in the same circles as my people do, or that you're a gangster like Uncle Giustino."

"Well, speaking of that gangster thing," he asked, "are your people, and especially Uncle Giustino, in any way connected to the Killeen gang?"

"Not connected, no," she said, still struggling to be heard over the train's passage, "but competing, yes. Short version: Uncle Giustino hates their guts."

"I think he'd be very happy with me, then," Eisen replied, smiling.

It took a moment before comprehension dawned. *Eight dead . . . a house shot to hell and another blown up. A bar blown up. The second blackout of the year?*

"That was *you*! You?"

"I had help but substantially . . . well . . . yes. They'd stolen my Juliana. I had to get her back and destroy the people responsible for kidnapping her. Are you going to run to the police?"

"No, of course not. I already swore. But I wish I could tell my uncle about this. He'd be clamoring to bring you into the clan, in one way or another."

"There's only one way that would make any sense," he said. "But you're not going to listen to that."

She went silent then, for a bit, her thoughts lost in the noise of the train as it emerged from the tunnel.

Finally, she said, "I don't know you well enough. If I did, I think I'd say 'yes.' Yes, I realize how strange that sounds but . . . well . . . if I find somebody like you, later on, I'll consider myself a very lucky girl.

"The problem, you see, isn't that you're sixty-six, especially since you look twenty-five. It's not that there's a deadly alien monster hunting for you. It's not that you'll have to leave in a month or so, I suppose I could go with you. It's not *even* that you were married in the future. It's that you're married in your heart, right here and right now. And maybe you always will be."

"'And maybe I always will be.' Well, when you're right, you're right. But at least I tried."

He heard the squeal of the brakes and looked up to see the "North Station" sign passing by the train's window.

"Our stop," he announced, needlessly. "And, no argument. I'll watch from a distance but I will watch you until you get to your own door."

"No need to be so dramatic," she said. "Walk me home just like you were my aboveboard boyfriend. I'm allowed to have boyfriends, after all, just not to spend the night with them. Very progressive, my parents, that way. 'When in America' and all, don't you see?"

"Then home it is. You have a good sense of humor, you know. It might be even more attractive than the rest of you."

The train stopped, opening its doors to the platform. They stood and walked out, Eisen looked down toward the direction from which they'd come to see if any untoward critters were following. Seeing none, he led her to the stairs and then down to ground level.

They walked through the cold, narrow, man-made canyons of the North End. Their path went from Causeway, to Haverhill, to Valenti, across Washington, thence to Thatcher, and to a left on Endicott. Eisen frequently turned around to check behind, then looked up or stopped her to peer first down cross streets and side alleys. The disconcerting part of this, from Francesca's point of view, was that he did it automatically, without interrupting the conversation in the slightest.

"I can't resist telling you," Eisen said, as they entered onto Endicott, "that two of those houses down there . . ."

"Mrs. Lake's and Mrs. Cowens'? Oh, we *all* know about those. In fact one of my aunts . . . no, now *you* curb your thoughts. Long after those . . . mmmm . . . businesses closed down, my Aunt Rosa rented a room there for a while."

And then she stopped and turned. "This is where I live."

"'So we'll go no more a roving, by the light of the moon.'" Eisen quoted, adding, "Never underestimate the benefits of a classical education."

"You went *there*, too, didn't you?"

"Oh, yeah, Franklin and me, and in much the same way."

"After you've gotten rid of the Q'riln—oh, no, I have no doubts you will—look me up so we can complete that dinner that was interrupted."

"Scout's honor," he replied, "I will."

She was very tall. When she leaned in for a not entirely chaste good night kiss he didn't have to bend at all.

And then, with a flurry of steps on stairs and the sound of a door clicking shut, the girl was gone.

If it turns out that I don't see you again, Francesca Cordesco, I wish you a very happy and long life, as a mother, grandmother, and nurse *practitioner, and with a big loving family.*

Eisen elected to walk all the way from Endicott to the Parker House. It wasn't really all that far, three-fourths of a mile, give or take. Indeed, he'd only taken the roundabout Red and Orange Lines route he had with Francesca to shield her from or throw off the Q'riln's potential tracking.

Now he wanted to make himself available, so to speak, to bait the bitch into coming for him.

"It's unlikely, after all, that she has much of a clue about the firepower I'm carrying, nor about the night vision I can use."

With that thought he stopped on the corner of Endicott and Stillman, taking his NVGs out from under his coat and fitting them onto his head.

One huge advantage of these, as compared with either PVS-5s or -7s, is how light they are. Another, related to that, is how easy they are to flick up or down.

His route took him along Sudbury to Cambridge Street. There he glimpsed, once again, old Scollay Square, or what remained of it. The cranes already told of Scollay's hideous replacement.

I was too young to really see much of it, Eisen thought, *but, of course, I walked through it a few times. Every boy did.*

Sure, it was a bit run down, but it was still in every way to be preferred to the inhuman, quintessentially ugly, architectural atrocity and inverted pile of intellectual concrete vomit that will be Boston's new Government Center in about seven years.

And what the hell was wrong with Scollay Square, anyway? Nothing. It's like saying there was something wrong with Ann Corio or Sally Rand. And there was, sure as hell, nothing *wrong there. I suspect that the city machine just wanted a bigger building to allow more jobs that could be passed out as patronage, and were willing to give free rein to a bevy of acid dropping architectural school failures and assorted communist freaks to get it.*

In thinking about it, do the criminal gangs do nearly as much damage to the city, or cost nearly as much money, as do the greasy grifters of the Democratic Party city machine? Never has a Mullen or Killeen tried to impose a visual case of celiac disease on the town.

Scowling, he said, aloud, "I'd like to live long enough to see the piece of crap that is coming up finally torn down. I'll bring a shaker of salt to spread over the ruins and will drink liberally first so that I have lots of piss for it."

None of that, of course, stopped Eisen from continuously scanning the buildings, with both infrared and plain vision, aided by the streetlights. But there was nothing.

And that tells me something or things. One is that the Q'riln is perhaps not so brave. Another is that maybe she doesn't track as well as we thought. A third is that, most likely, she strikes from stealth. I need to muse on that question. A lot.

Parker House, Boston, Massachusetts

"Uncle Fitz," Patrick said, as soon as Eisen had closed the door behind him, "can you get a mold to cast BBs or .177 pellets?"

"Sure, but why?"

"We've been talking with Topaz," Cossima said, "sort of quizzing her on this and that. I asked her how hard that old merchant, Robert Calef, threw the coins at the Q'riln. She said, 'not very hard.' But the silver, itself, burned her and made her look like what she was. Topaz said the alien literally *smoked* where the silver touched her."

"So we got to thinking," Juliana added, "and figured out that a pellet or BB from an air rifle or pistol would work just fine, and would work without you risking being arrested for giving us actual guns."

"*Mreow!*" said Topaz, which Eisen took, in this case, to mean something like, "Listen to the little ones."

"Well," mused Eisen, "I *know* they exist; I had a couple. Shouldn't be hard to find more. Only thing is, mine were pump action, back... ummm... now, not CO2. I'm not sure what's available in CO2.

"We'll have to look and see."

"Not an issue, Uncle Fitz," said Patrick. "They had at least three Crosman 600s on display at Jordan's toy department, plus the CO2 to put in them. The trick will be casting silver pellets."

"Then it's Jordan's, tomorrow, for some air pistols!"

"Francesca will be there, too, won't she, Uncle Fitz?" asked Cossima, while Patrick smirked and Juliana raised a highly suspicious eyebrow.

"I suppose she'll be in the area somewhere. Don't you kids like her?"

"Oh, we like her just fine," Juliana said. "But we wonder if you like her too much, given how recently you met her."

"Oh, I'm sure I do, but you're too young to understand the ramifications. I like her a great deal, yes. Indeed, I like her so much that I wouldn't do anything to screw up her life."

Eisen left all the heavy armaments behind, carrying—still quite illegally—the Sig in his pocket, the Walther with the Itty Bitty suppressor in the small of his back, and the Czech piece in the shoulder rig. This was not because he thought *he* might need three pistols, but so that at least two of the kids could be armed at a moment's notice at need.

He'd asked the hotel to have his car handy at a particular time, one in the afternoon. The first leg, though, was on foot to Jordan Marsh's Toyland. He was very determined not to seek out the lovely Miss Cordesco.

And yet, he thought, entering Toyland, just as he had thought with Whitey Bulger, *it's funny how often the same people keep coming into your life, over and over.*

He said the same thing, word for word, to Francesca, now standing at the cashier's spot in Toyland.

"They had somebody call in sick, so sent me here. I didn't expect..."

"Neither did I, but I'm not sorry. Tell me, would you be happier with a perfectly legal air pistol firing silver pellets than you are with the .45, or, maybe better, would you be happier with both?"

"What do you think? It's more your field than mine."

"I think both. I won't be able to provide pellets until tomorrow, maybe midday, but I'll get what I need today, to include an extra pistol for you, O lovely Miss Cordesco."

He sniffed, lightly. "Chanel Number Five, yes?" he asked.

"Pre . . . tty good guess."

"I wasn't guessing. I'm a flirt, remember? Flirts, well, normal male flirts, love women and everything about them, otherwise, why bother? So, yes, I can recognize various popular somewhat higher end perfumes.

"Hmmm . . . let's see. Pick you up again, tomorrow night, under the clock, and this time we *all* have dinner together, then go up to the suite to familiarize you with the air pistol, then repeat, more or less, our method of getting you home safely?"

She just smiled, while shaking her head. "How many women," she asked, "have you talked into bed?"

"Honestly, I lost count before I turned twenty. But let me let you in on a little secret. No one knows this but me and, in a few seconds, you. All my life, what I really wanted was a great, passionate, utterly mad . . . and completely platonic love affair. Who knows; maybe you're her.

"Hmmm . . . would you prefer to eat somewhere else?"

"Well, to be honest," she said, "the prices at the Parker House leave me in shock. I'd be very happy with something . . . oh, let's go for the familiar. How about Italian, this time, in my neighborhood? Maybe . . . mmm Cantina Italiana? It's on Hannover Street, maybe five or six minutes' walk from my house. It's pretty authentic. At least, my mother mostly approves, and that's a rare thing."

"Cantina Italiana, it is," he agreed. "Tomorrow night, five-thirty, under the clock again?"

"That would be perfect."

Ritz-Carlton Hotel, 15 Arlington Street, Boston, Massachusetts

The Q'riln, still operating in the guise, and under the name, of Catherine Branch, had made the reservations for this place while still in Indonesia. She'd been having quite a good time, and high on the ambrosia the cube provided, in Jakarta, when her cube had announced, "Someone is in the vestibule of gates. They came in through the blocked gate. I sense something small, but totally fearless. Maybe a small domestic animal. There is no nourishment for you there, Mistress. And . . . she just left, who- or whatever she was."

The Q'riln hadn't been worried; these kinds of interlopers popped up from time to time. For the most part they were harmless, even if very distasteful, like the local cats. Occasionally they provided a light snack but she was eating so well in Jakarta that she wasn't even tempted to go out of her way to pick up a snack. And besides, that particular gate was violated several times a day by a local human, who never left any part of his body inside long enough for her to punish him for his impertinence. She'd long since given up trying. Indeed, she wasn't sure that the human violating her space now was the same one who had violated it first over sixty of the local years ago. It could be an offspring.

But then the cube had announced, "Four beings have come through the blocked gate, at least three are definitely human and one of them bearing a good deal of metal and some electronics with which I and my kind are not familiar. Unlike last time, they didn't just go in, scout around, and leave. This time they've come and passed through. Note, Mistress, these are from the future and may have capabilities we are not familiar with."

"So you suggest I get rid of them on my own?"

"Do you know someone who will do the job for you, Mistress?"

"I don't like the tone in your voice, cube."

"Like it or not, the fact remains that you—we—are the only ones capable of dealing with this potential threat."

"Fine, then; breakdown on the interlopers?"

"There were, as mentioned, four of them. One, a male—and it was him carrying the metal I mentioned—fully grown and rejuvenated. Whether he knew what he was doing or it was just dumb luck, he was changed from old and a bit frail to young and quite healthy by the change generator that is part and parcel of the gates. Then there is a little one, very tiny and very fearless. She may not be human at all but, rather, as I said before, some kind of domestic animal. Between those are another male, young but fairly large, and another female, small but muscular, on the cusp of womanhood.

"Mistress, the very fact that I cannot determine why there should be such an organization worries me. It may be some new arm of the old pursuers' organization. We need to go and take care of this."

Interlude

Like almost any other higher animal, the Q'riln had lungs for pumping oxygen. They pumped now for all they were worth. The cat kept up. The horsemen gained with each step. She was, for the first time in her long life, terrified nearly out of her wits.

On, closer and still closer, came the men on horses. The Q'riln could hear them shouting with exultation as they gained. "We'll burn this demon!" "For the sake of our own souls and the soul of Goody Glover whom this creature led us to murder! Onward! Take her."

The Q'riln was strong, of course, stronger than any one human. She was not stronger than six of them.

And they saw the silver burn me. They'll . . . oh, nonononono . . . they'll put me in a box of it or on a bed of it until I dissolve in agony. Villains! Murderers! Don't you realize how much more important I am than you?

And then the lead horseman was next to her. He pulled the reins to cause his horse to block her. She dove under the horse, rolled, came back to her feet and continued running. She heard a loud noise, a shot, and felt the wind of the passage of a bullet. A lead bullet, of course, could never kill her, but it would certainly hurt on its way through.

A loop of rope sailed overhead. She almost managed to avoid the loop, but one of her arms became caught in it. She didn't see what the horseman had done but she felt it. He'd turned his horse away and prodded it to a gallop, tearing one of her arms off at the root.

The Q'riln shrieked like she never had before, never once in that very long life. Oh, yes, the arm could be regrown, but having it ripped away like that was an unspeakable agony.

Another horseman tried to simply run her down. She felt the horse's chest strike her, and whipped her remaining arms back to grasp it by its forequarters. With that grip, she applied four of her feet to the ground unevenly, while using another to grip one of the horse's legs. It went down in a tumult of flailing limbs and a cursing rider.

"There, Mistress, there!" shouted the cube. And she saw it, a glimmering oval not fifty feet ahead of her. With the last reserves of her strength, she bolted for it, launching herself through just inches ahead of a swinging halberd.

On the inside, the vestibule of her gate, she slithered and crawled back, deeper into its bowels. Halfway there, she turned to the gate, fearful that, somehow, the human males would manage to get through and seize her here.

But no human head showed. Instead, a tiny little furred head made an appearance. It glared at her for a moment, and then the cat spat out two small silver coins. From those the Q'riln recoiled in horror.

"You'll need to stay here for some time, Mistress," the cube informed her. "It will take *greegs* and *greegs* to regrow your arm and heal the burns from the silver."

"I can stay," the Q'riln wheezed. "But nose around for a good place to go feed after I do."

"I think I already know one, Mistress; back to the gate we first came through, then into the Balkans. There's a war going on between the Austrians and Turks that won't end anytime soon."

Chapter Thirteen

~~~~~

The spring in Boston is like being in love: bad days slip in among
the good ones, and the whole world is at a standstill, then the sun
shines, the tears dry up, and we forget that yesterday was stormy.
—Louise Closser Hale

Parker House, Boston, Massachusetts

Juliana, who was easily the most craftsmanlike one in the party
except, for a few things, Eisen himself, was busy melting down thirty
silver quarters to create a hundred and sixty .22 pellets—an initial
load plus three full reloads—for the Crosmans.

Meanwhile, Patrick and Cossima practiced marksmanship with
an electrically operated home gallery, complete with moving ducks
and spinning wheels. He had them both wearing safety glasses, for
the benefit of their eyes, and doing their shooting with a mattress
taken from a bed as a back stop to prevent damage to walls. Giggles
and one-upmanship arguments emanated from the bedroom.

Meanwhile, he was busy on the phone with his broker in
Chicago. After the first set of futures options, he'd generally
accepted the broker's list, and selected from that list a few items, a
dozen in one case, though one of them a deliberate loser, that he
already knew would go up in value. This saw the value of his
investments growing substantially by the week. Since his picks came
from recommendations from the broker, the broker wasn't yet
suspicious about his doing so outrageously well.

But now the broker wanted him to invest in something that wasn't
on the list of good buys he'd made back in his own time and place.
And he just wasn't buying it.

"Mr. Eisen," said the broker from O'Brien, "this is, we think, the chance of the century. With the federal government dumping silver coinage, the amount available as a commodity is going to soar. This *has* to depress the price. I'm telling you: A short-term put option."

"No."

"But the *money*, Mr. Eisen."

"One more word about it and I'll have you close out my existing investments and send a wire to my bank, here."

"Bu— As you wish, sir. Is there anything I *can* recommend to you?"

"I'm very happy with the recommendations you've sent so far. Just keep up doing what you've been doing"—*which is, in fact, little but providing me cover*—"and we'll continue to get along fine."

"As you wish, sir. I'll call in the morning with the new recommendations."

"Perfect. Talk to you then."

Filene's Clock, Washington Street, Boston, Massachusetts

Francesca had done something with her hair, framing her face with it, in a way both subtle and devastatingly beautiful.

"I've always been a beauty addict," Eisen said, "but you're upping the dose to dangerous levels now."

Patrick agreed verbally, while both Juliana and Cossima wanted to know how she'd done it. She promised to show them the trick later.

They walked from the Clock to the Cantina Italiana, on Hannover Street, in Boston's North End, taking the roundabout routes via Milk Street down past where the New England Aquarium was already being planned. On the way they passed 167 Milk Street.

"Up there," Eisen said, "is the Olive—pronounced Auleeve—Leslie Salle D'Armes. I either did take—or will take, depending on point of view—fencing there when I was in college. Very pricey, yes, but it, and a simultaneous course of instruction in an obscure form of oriental swordsmanship, stood me in very good stead more than once."

"Oh, tell her the story, Uncle Fitz," Juliana said.

"Do you want to hear the story?" he asked Francesca. "It's a violent story."

"Sure, please do. It's not like Uncle Giustino never . . . well, never mind; go ahead."

He talked as they walked.

"Well," Eisen said, "I think it boils down to this; I was a preemie baby, a blue baby, hence small at birth and not large for the rest of my life. I'm still not big; fit, at the moment, yes; big, no. I never could put on all that much muscle but was very fast. I was the one kid, at least the only one I knew of, in mainly Irish Catholic South Boston with a Jewish name. Add in being unusually bright. You're damned right I had to fight a lot. 'You grow up hard and you grow up mean . . .'

"Hmmm, you don't know that song, do you? Well, it'll be along in a few years.

"Oh, and despite the Jewish name, I was raised culturally American Irish Catholic. That meant the females of the family—the bearers of value and culture—were very explicit: 'Win or lose, fight and hurt the other bas—guy.'

"That early experience colored my life. It's only fairly recently that I've stopped just assuming that the fist—physical or figurative—is probably going to come flying out of nowhere, or that men's hands would be turned against me for reasons I had nothing to do with and couldn't affect. Come to think of it, this was a lesson reinforced by my pig-eyed, lazy, marginally competent, useless, and deeply stupid battalion commander, Tuffy. But up until then, I walked through life ready to fight over just about *anything*. 'This is the way.' Oh, you won't get that reference, either, will you?

"That's all background. Now let me tell you a story, true story, as it happens Once upon a time in Boston, on the day of a parade—Dorchester Day, my then very young wife came home bleeding from her knees. She was teaching herself to ride a bike, so this wasn't especially unusual. Her demeanor, however, was . . . odd . . . she was clearly upset. She wouldn't tell me, her ever so curious husband, what had happened but I browbeat it out of her Polish friend, Manya.

"It seems my wife had been riding her bike with Manya when a stranger, S—whose name I will not mention in case, after all these years, I decide that he's no longer welcome on the planet—came out of the crowd assembling for the parade and grabbed her posterior.

She slapped him, so he hit her. So she slapped him again, so he struck her again. So she slapped him again, so the swine knocked her off her bike to the street where she skinned her knees. Hence the bleeding.

"Apprised of this, I sent Manya downstairs to fetch her little brother, Johnny."

Eisen used his hands to illustrate the next part. "'Johnny,' I asked, as I loaded the integral magazine for one of my rifles, which we shall call, 'Model 1917 Enfield,' 'would you recognize S?'

"'Yes,' Johnny informed me.

"'Oh, good; come with me, please.' We then proceeded"—click, as the bolt opened—"to the third floor"—click, as the bolt was pulled back—"porch where"—click, the bolt was shoved forward again, chambering a round—"I said"—click, as the bolt handle was rotated down, "'please point him out to me.'

"Would I have shot him if I'd seen him? I do think so. I was so enraged . . . well, yeah, he was a dead man. Easy shot at that range, too.

"Sadly or happily, depending on one's point of view, S never showed his face. So having but three days prior qualified for a black belt in that obscure form of Asian sword I mentioned, I put up my Enfield and took my very stout practice stick out onto the street, accompanied by Johnny, to find S and beat him to death.

"I stopped on the way to ask S's whereabouts of someone Johnny identified as S's cousin.

"The cousin asked me, 'What's the stick for?'

"'I'm going to kill him,' I said. This may have been both unwise and untactful but at twenty-three—note that I am ever so much more restrained and civilized now—I had rarely been wise and was always deficient in tact."

Eisen sighed. Whether it was regret at youthful indiscretions or a deep regret at failing in some purpose or mission, Francesca couldn't tell.

"At about this time, S did show, running out of the crowd and trying to take me from behind. I sensed him and turned. S grabbed the stick, which at this range was passé anyway. So I let go of the stick, put one hand of each of S's shoulders, and proceeded to knee him in the gonads, ten or twelve times. I had and have, and had even as a sixty-six-year-old, humongous and tremendously powerful legs, so that must have *hurt*. By tremendously powerful I mean I could do four-hundred-and-forty-pound squats, never getting tired, but stopping only when I got *bored*.

"I then dragged a rather breathlessly stunned S to a chain-link fence and proceeded to saw his neck along the fence, trying to get through to the arteries."

Again, Eisen used his hands to illustrate. "Left-right-left-right; saw, saw, saw, saw. I was just starting to get through the flesh, slightly, hence closer to the arteries, when I decided it was taking too long and to try something else. I threw S to the sidewalk, sat on him, and, with one hand behind his neck and the other under his chin, began smashing his head against the concrete, in order to feed the ants. Slam-slam-slam-slam.

"At this point, it's probably worth noting that S was large, much larger than me. Call him, oh, maybe six-two to my five-ten. No problem, I could handle him.

"Ah, but the cousin I mentioned? He was a freaking monster, probably six-seven or even six-eight and just huge in general; a lot of that was fat but more was muscle. The cousin pulled me off of S one-handed and punched me in the face hard enough for a deviated septum, anyway."

Here Eisen tilted his head back, to show how his nose was off to one side a bit. "Half of that is the fight; the other half an armored vehicle accident in the mid-eighties.

"I fought him off. I wasn't as big, nor as strong. But I was a lot better trained. Moreover, I was stone-cold sober, which they were not, entirely. I was also, and still am, unusually quick. So I'd fight the bigger cousin off, then go back to the ant-feeding and belly-kicking program.

"That wasn't really working, because I had to spend so much time fighting off the cousin. Eventually I had to devote almost all my effort to the cousin, kicking a generally prostrate S—remember those four hundred and forty-pound legs—as opportunity presented. I figure I at least broke a few ribs. Maybe a bit of a concussion, too, since at least one of those kicks was to the head.

"As one point in time, S—who had plainly seen one too many Chinese martial arts movies; don't ask; they're coming—managed to get away, ran around, then up and over an automobile in an attempt at what was called 'a flying drop kick.' Pretty decent job, really, for someone sporting a fresh concussion.

"Easiest thing in the world; I parried his legs with my arm while stepping out of the way. All through that fight it was amazing, really, how well the sword footwork worked. Anyway, without my body to stop him, S landed on his spine on the concrete, hurting himself badly enough that he ended up in the hospital for that and other reasons. I think he was also rather badly stunned that his devastating ploy had failed. Oh, well. Tsk.

"Then were the police sirens heard. 'Close,' I thought. 'Hmmm, not good'; I had to leave for the Infantry Officer's Basic Course at Ft. Benning in the morning, and jail was going to interfere with that. Cousin dragged off S. Me, bleeding profusely and laughing maniacally, walked home, which was close.

"Far and away, best fight I ever had."

"Whew!" Francesca exclaimed, knowing somehow that not a word of the story was exaggerated. "Uncle Giustino would *really* like to meet you, I am certain."

"I can't tell him any of that and you can't either."

"You wouldn't have to. He'd just know. I *told* you; 'Naples.' And here we are."

The restaurant had a marquee overhead announcing the name. The marquee actually said, "Italian Canteen." Eisen figured Francesca just used the local neighborhood's name for the place. A brick building, there were six small apartments above it, with doors on either side of the restaurant that led to those. A single square brick column divided the trapezoidal entrance to the place.

"God," said Eisen, "that smells *so* good."

The party of five was shown in and seated with all the aplomb one might expect. The Cantina wasn't nearly as high end and touristy as it was to become, in future days; it just had fine, wonderful, eat once and not be hungry for another three days, Italian food.

"This time," said Eisen, "since you know what you're about and we humble peasants do not, why don't you order for us, Francesca?"

She looked at him, shook her head in wonder, and said, "I . . . we . . . never . . . I'd be happy to."

⁓⬥⁓

"It was," announced Eisen, on the walk back to the Parker House, "the Sicilian Cannoli that did me in."

"Can you cook like that?" asked Patrick, as the five of them, overfed, indeed, overstuffed, more or less staggered back to the hotel.

"You trying to recruit a second grandmother, Patrick?" asked Eisen. "Or are you looking for a job with Uncle Giustino's organization?"

In response, Patrick launched into an ad hoc parody of one of their usual car jaunting songs:

"We were born and raised in Boston,
A place you all know well.
Brought up by honest parents,
The truth to you I'll tell.
Brought up by honest mom and dad,
And raised most tenderly,
'Til we fell in with our Grandpa,
At age seven, four, and three.
He turned us into criminals,
We burgle night and day,
We skirt the laws of God and man . . ."

"Very good, Patrick, though you need to work on your meter. Now shut up."

"Yes, sir," the boy muttered.

Affecting not to have heard, Francesca said, "Oh, I know that one. It's not strictly Irish, you know." Then she, too, began to sing, which the girls and Patrick joined in instantly:

"Our character was taken
And we were sent to jail.
Our old Grandpa he tried in vain
For to get us out on bail.
But the jury found us guilty
And the clerk he wrote it down,
The judge, he passed the sentence,
'You're all bound for Charlestown' . . ."

"Children," muttered Eisen, "I'm surrounded by children."

Francesca took up an S-shaped pose, asking, "Do *I* look like a child to you?"

"No comment."

"Aha!"

"Yeah, 'aha!'" the kids quoted back.

They all, less Eisen, continued:

"They put us on an eastbound train
One cold December day
Through every station we passed through
You could hear the people say
'There go the Boston burglars,
In cold chains they are bound.
For one crime or another
They are bound for Charlestown.'"

"I won't even try to post bail on you brats, on any of you," he amended, looking Miss Cordesco squarely in her all-too-big eyes. Then he said, "Oh, to hell with it," and began to sing, himself:

"There lives a girl in Boston
A girl that I love well
If ever I gain my liberty
It's with that girl I'll dwell."

Realizing what he'd just sung, Eisen shut up immediately, not even finishing the verse. For her part, Francesca felt suddenly light-headed. *Is this what swooning means? Or is it worse than that? Oh, crap!*

"So, anyway," Patrick continued, knowing he needed to fill the silence even if not too sure of exactly why, "*can* you cook like that?"

"I wish," Francesca said, grateful for the cover provided by the boy. "Mind, I'm not a bad cook, but even my mother isn't in this league. And she's great. She loves to eat, you see. And she never gets fat; 'snake hips,' they call her."

"Built like you, then?" Cossima asked.

"Yes, we're much alike, my mother and I. Though my hips are more pronounced."

"I hope I can keep a shape like yours when I grow up. My grandmother pretty much kept hers until..." She let the sentence trail off.

Which is, Francesca thought, *not necessarily something I wanted to hear. And I don't know exactly why. Or... maybe I do. Yeah, I suppose I do.*

Patrick and Cossima had Francesca and Juliana under their control, teaching them air pistol marksmanship. Meanwhile, Eisen was grilling the calico for whatever more information she might have left out.

"You must understand," typed the cat, "we, ourselves, don't know all that much about the Q'riln. We know they were pretty harmless farmers and pastoralists, twenty thousand or so of your years ago, because one of our teams—not aboard a spaceship, they come from a different and parallel universe to which we have limited access—visited there and found them as such. We know that, at that time, they were more or less patriarchal, generally non-violent or, at least, not *too* violent, and subsisted off of food they foraged, grew and raised. We know that when they came up on our screens again, perhaps eight thousand years ago, they were very different, with the females in charge, a degree of technology that probably shouldn't have been there after a mere twelve thousand years, and a taste for mayhem. Also that they apparently could live off the mayhem. We don't know how that works, either; again, parallel universe, different paths of evolution, different laws."

"It must have terribly difficult for you," Eisen noted, "these last four centuries, being unable to communicate."

"The females of my species—my real species!—are not very different from yours, really. We, as a sex, *communicate*. Yes, it was awful. When you leave here, I know you cannot leave this device, so I beg you, *please* take me with you, if at all possible."

"I will," he agreed. "Of course, I will. I thought that was always understood. Now back to the Q'riln. Does she have any unusual physical capabilities, invisibility, strength?"

Topaz answered, "Just the shapeshifting. We do it separately from our gates, and can only control it after that a little, bringing on or holding off or reversing aging, for example. The Q'riln use the gates for the initial change, which reports say is quite a horrible experience, but can then switch back and forth, maybe aided by their cubes, and allowing for a good deal of pain when they do.

"Their attacks are usually on the mind.

"But," she continued, "the Q'riln *are* very strong. Think of an ant or a praying mantis. Not that strong, because there's a scale issue. But a couple of times to three times stronger than you."

"I've handled three times my weight before, in opponents," he said, "but never three times my unintoxicated strength. And she attacks the mind. I wonder why we haven't felt any of that yet. Well, we'll figure it out. Okay, your teardrop; it can give you a direction to the Q'riln; is that right?"

"Yes, but it's useless. The monster could be on the other side of the ocean, the other side of the planet, for all my teardrop can tell. Well, actually salt water tends to block it. It also cannot even tell range. That's one reason why there were two of us, with Mary as a backup."

"Indeed? Can you tell her direction now?"

More or less instantly, the cat turned and pointed generally toward the Common. Then she went back to the laptop and typed, "Best I can do. That way. No idea how far."

"If Mary were here, you and she together could locate the Q'riln?"

"Easily," Topaz typed.

"Where is she?"

"I do not know. I looked for her for a long time; all over I looked, but couldn't find her."

"I don't suppose you could have checked the city's records?"

"I'm a cat. I'm a cat who cannot talk, finds it extremely difficult to turn pages, and lacks opposable thumbs to write with. Even trying would probably get me sent to a circus or euthanized.

"She was in the jail for a while before she died. I used to try to visit her. And then one day in the spring after I was hanged she was gone, and no one ever spoke of her."

Eisen scratched his head, then said, "She was without family or money or means. They'd have dumped her, I think, in whatever burial yard had been set aside for the indigent.

"Juliana? Kids?"

"Yes, Uncle Fitz?"

"Tomorrow you and I are . . . oh, wait. No we're not. Topaz?"

"Yes?" the cat typed.

"Is the Q'riln nocturnal? Does it have a time of rest?"

"As a general rule they avoid the heat of the day; their world was very hot. They used to sleep at noontime, on their homeworld. But, in the first place, I don't know if that would apply here, where it is fairly cold while, in the second, they may have changed."

"Check her direction again," Eisen said. Again the cat pointed in, as near as he could tell, exactly the same direction.

"Kids, keep Francesca company and well entertained, would you?"

Patrick answered first, "Gleefully, Uncle Fitz."

Boy's got a crush, I think.

"Why, Uncle Fitz?" asked Cossima.

"I'm going to take the cat out to do a little recon."

"Where are we going?" typed the cat.

"There's a technique we sometimes used in the Army. It's called 'intersection.' We know the direction from here, right?"

"Yes."

"Well, we're going to walk up to the statehouse and see what the direction is from there. More places, too, if necessary. Where those different directions meet, there will be our Q'riln."

"Ah. Now *that* is clever."

"Whoever figured it out first was clever," Eisen said, adding, "I'm just a monkey mimicking my betters."

"Point the way, Topaz," said Eisen, at Brimstone Corner.

She immediately pointed right across the Common.

"Hmmm . . . roughly the intersection of Boylston and Charles Streets. But without being able to tell range . . . well, no, matter; let's walk up toward the statehouse."

They did, and Eisen had the calico point again.

"Aha, that short distance, maybe four hundred feet's worth, has moved the direction quite a bit. The bitch is close. C'mon, Kitty Divine, let's go down Beacon a-ways."

Eisen stopped them just north of the Frog Pond and had her point again.

"Ha! Practically due south. Let's go some more."

They stopped at a place about fifty feet shy of where the Bull and

Finch, the inspiration for the hit TV show, *Cheers*, would be in a few years' time. This time, when Topaz pointed, it was due south, right at the visible Ritz-Carlton Hotel, at the corner of Newbury and Arlington.

"Bingo," said Eisen, "we've got you, bitch."

"Topaz," he added, "we're going to have to work on a way for you to point to elevation, too. Hmmm ... maybe if I can find an old inclinometer, and we use a board and fulcrum ..."

Ritz-Carlton Hotel, Boston, Massachusetts

"Mistress," said the cube, "the main interloper and the cat are patrolling around the area you fled through the other night, the area called 'the Common.' They are skirting along the high ground, probably trying to spot if you are actually on the Common."

"No matter," the Q'riln moaned. "I'm not feeling well, cube. I should have known better than to book lodgings in a place with a store specializing in sterling silver on the ground floor."

"Is it getting worse, Mistress?"

"I think so."

"Then we need to get you out of here."

"Is there another hotel close enough to keep track of our quarry?" she asked.

"Not that I can sense, Mistress. Would it help if we got you moved to the top floor?"

"It could hardly hurt. A human, you know, could vomit if they felt this awful. We poor Q'riln just have to endure it."

"Call the front desk," the cube said. "We have, after all, plenty of funds. Meanwhile, I'll be probing in preparation for your next attack."

Parker House, Boston, Massachusetts

Eisen left to take Francesca home by another circuitous route. This one involved a short walk to Government Center Station, followed by taking a Green Line streetcar, or "trolley," as they were locally known, to Arlington, then picking up a cab. She had her new air pistol with three reloads of silver pellets tucked into her purse.

"Take the roundabout way," Eisen told the cabby, "along Atlantic Ave to the Old North Church and then to Endicott."

"Yoah dime, Mistuh," the cabby responded.

Francesca, meanwhile, wondered, *Is he trying to be romantic, to spend more time with me? It's possible, but I'm still reading this as his focus on keeping me safe. I'll know if he gets out at my place and walks to North Station, though it will still be in doubt if he drops me off.*

It was Patrick who first voiced what the other two were thinking, and he did it with Timon and Pumbaa's first lines from "Can You Feel the Love Tonight," from *The Lion King*.

"*She* has a clue," Juliana said. "Grandpa? No, he can't see it coming."

"See what coming?" Cossima asked.

"What's the next line?" Patrick prodded.

"They'll fall . . . oh," the little one replied. "You think?"

"Blech! This growing up thing is for the birds!"

"What was that, Juliana?" Patrick asked as he reloaded her air pistol with silver pellets.

"Did I say something out loud?" she asked. Without waiting for an answer, she just shook her head and stayed silent for a minute. After that, she asked, "Do you notice Grandpa being different?"

Cossima piped in, "You mean besides him being forty years younger?"

"Yes, besides that."

"His Boston Brahmin accent's become nearly permanent," said Patrick.

"I know, right?" said Cossima.

"But the big thing you're asking about is Francesca, isn't it?" Patrick asked.

"Yeah," Juliana replied. "He's always been a terrible flirt—"

"Nah, he's a great flirt!" both of the younger kids exclaimed simultaneously.

"Oh, stop! You two *know* what I mean."

"Yeah," Patrick agreed. "It's not all that obvious that he's only flirting here. I mean, I think he thinks he is. But I don't know that he really is or that Francesca thinks he is."

"He's acting like . . ." Cossima hesitated. "He's acting like a twenty-five-year-old man of 1965, not a sixty-six-year-old man of the 2020s."

"And what if he really falls for Francesca?" Juliana asked. "She's very beautiful, if maybe not quite so much as Grandma was. And she's *here*."

"So what do you propose *we* do about it?" Patrick asked.

"That's the problem," Juliana admitted. "I don't *know* what to do. Or even if we should. Don't we all want the Old Man to be happy?"

"Yeah," both Patrick and Cossima agreed.

"Maybe we should talk to him about it," Cossima said. "And . . . then . . . we're pretty cute kids. Francesca might really *like* the idea of being our grandmother."

"She just might," both Patrick and Juliana agreed.

Endicott Street, North End, Boston, Massachusetts

Eisen got out of the car and sent the cabbie on his way. He didn't have any plans, except to ensure the girl was safely home.

"It's so unfair," she said, in the sheltered space before the door. "I should have met you first."

Eisen sighed. "I can hardly wish away my wife, or deny that I still love her, nor wish away my children and grandchildren, which is what that would mean. Can you?"

"No," she admitted, "I just wish they were mine. Well, not your wife."

"If it helps any," he said, with a smile, "remember I am only nine years old, here and now."

"It doesn't help a bit, because here and now, from where I stand, you are twenty-five and perfect. Or as near to perfect, for me, as I could ever have imagined."

"Well . . . in another universe, you would certainly have done," he admitted. "Now go home and be safe."

"See you tomorrow?" she asked.

"Filene's Clock, five-thirty," he agreed.

Interlude

Healing was slow. Worse, it was psychological torment for the Q'riln, because that damned evil cat showed up every few days and spat a couple more of the silver coins that had burnt her at the hanging onto the foggy floor of the vestibule. She could hear the cat's laughter in her mind, every time it made the barrier that much more painful for her to even approach.

"I hate that little bitch," the Q'riln said, regularly.

"That gate's already lost to us, Mistress," the cube said. "We've got another useful one for ourselves, one with good feeding, but it's on the other side of the ocean, as I mentioned, near the forest of staked people we first came upon here."

"Nobody staked there now, I suppose?"

"Sadly not, Mistress."

"I want to stake that cat, to put a stick right through it from anus to mouth. I'll be careful not to let it die, either, when I do, because I'll want to put it over lower coals and cook it a little at a time."

"Mistress, to be honest, I think that animal is just too fast for you."

"Which does not change, in the slightest, cube, that I *want* to stake it."

"No, Mistress; of course not. How are your burns coming along?"

The cube really didn't have to ask; it had perfect knowledge of what was going on with its host.

"They still hurt," she said. "When I go to the other side of the vestibule, they hurt less, but I am hoping for a swing at the evil little cat. Why is it, by the way, that the gate that can change everything cannot heal my wounds?"

"We're not sure if it's a case of can't or won't," answered the cube. "It refuses to say just as it ignores the request. There is the theory that the gate just doesn't like your people or mine because we're from a different universe, but nobody knows for sure.

"Besides that, the arm? Regrowing nicely?"

"It will do, cube. Why do you ask?"

"Because I am bored here, Mistress, and would get us back to our feeding as soon as possible."

"All right. It won't be too much longer."

"I certainly hope not, Mistress."

Chapter Fourteen

❦

In Boston they ask, "How much does he know?" In New York,
"How much is he worth?" In Philadelphia, "Who were his parents?"
—Mark Twain

Boston Athenaeum, 10½ Beacon Street, Boston, Massachusetts

It was a subscription library. This fact did not, however, mean members only. For about a twelfth the price of an annual membership, one could purchase a day pass which would allow one to use the facilities.

These were not unimpressive. The Athenaeum had, for example, among its more than half a *million* volumes, the largest single collection from George Washington's library at Mount Vernon. It held unfinished portraits of both George and Martha, too, though these were on loan to the Museum of Fine Arts. Moreover, in the arts department, the Athenaeum contained Roman sculpture, plus European, and American, including Canova's approximately life-sized "Venus of the Bath," as well as a more than healthy collection of paintings, portraiture in the main, likewise from all over, though mostly American. Arguably, as with the Isabella Stewart Gardner Museum, the highest work of art in the place *was* the place itself.

Eisen thought it would at least be a place to start, with records likely to be more accessible than those of the city, itself.

Although, I am unconvinced that I am not a madman, looking for his dropped keys on a side of the street where the light was better, even though he dropped them on the other side of the street, in the dark.

Cossima was with him, with Patrick and Juliana left in the suite

267

at the Parker House, which was also where the heavy firepower remained.

The librarian was most helpful, of course, as was to be expected in a library where the patrons actually paid for membership and where the staff could be fired without, in contrast to a public employee, much in the way of political recourse.

Said the librarian, "Records, Mr. Maguire, from those times, are extremely scant. Buuut . . . hmmmm. Give me a moment, please." She hurried away, returning in an amazingly short time with a book. It had apparently been rebound in red leather at some time; the title was not visible on the cover. Inside, when the librarian opened it, Eisen could see the title and author, *A Topographical and Historical Description of Boston*, by one Nathaniel B. Shurtleff, published in 1871.

She turned to the table of contents and let her finger trace down to page 182. "There are twelve chapters," she explained, "that cover burial grounds in and around old Boston. I truly and sincerely doubt that any of them will have the person you're looking for by name, but they might have information you can start with, dates of first and final burials, that kind of thing. Still, Mr. Maguire, yours is a forlorn task."

She pointed at the southern wall of the Athenaeum, saying, "On the other side of that wall is the Old Granary Burying Ground. There are two thousand, three hundred, and forty-five grave markers there, if memory serves, sir. But it is believed that there are between five thousand and eight thousand people buried there. Who the other three to five thousand are, and where they are, we have little clue to. Similar tales would prevail at both King's Chapel and Old North or Copp's Hill Cemeteries."

Eisen nodded his understanding, saying, "Ah, thank you, ma'am. But I promised a friend to try and so try, at least, I must."

The perusal of the old book found by the librarian led to more detailed searches of the records, such as existed, for the three burying grounds in existence at the time of Mary Glover's . . .

"Well, what do we call it?" Eisen asked Cossima, in a whisper. "She was artificial, so she was never truly alive. Do we said 'died' or 'dead'? Do we say 'decommissioned'? 'Malfunctioned'?"

"I think we say 'died,' Uncle Fitz, because Topaz takes it pretty hard, even after all these years. Besides, we can't use any of those other words here and now to describe what happened, can we?"

"Good point, brat. So what have you got?"

"I've got nothing. What they have of records . . . well, just take what the librarian lady told us, five or eight thousand people in Old Granary, but we know less than half of them."

"It's a good deal less than that, really, Cossima; of the two thousand, three hundred and forty-five markers, not all even had legible names, and some may never have had legible names. And then there was the grave-rubbing . . ."

"Grave-rubbing?" she asked.

"You take a large piece of paper and place it against the engraved part of the headstone. Then you rub a pencil or charcoal over the paper. Gives you an impression of the writing on the gravestone. Also eventually erases the gravestone. It's generally forbidden now. It's a ghoulish practice, anyway."

The little girl scowled. "Sounds . . . what's that word? Ah, yes; 'sacrilegious.'"

"I think so, too. You know what bugs me?"

"No, Uncle Fitz."

"We haven't found a record of a paupers' field, a place where people who can't afford a grave plot or funeral, who have no family or who are unidentified, are unceremoniously buried. Usually not much record of those, which would fit this case, too."

Cossima shrugged. "Sorry, Old Man, but I have no clue. I'm only eight, after all."

"Sometimes," he admitted, "I forget that."

"I don't think we're going to find it here," Cossima said. "In fact, I think we're wasting time here."

"I don't disagree. Let's check out and walk down to city hall. There we can find where the records are kept for 1688 and 1689."

"Do you think they'll have them?" the girl asked.

"No, not really. Oh, what they have will exist somewhere . . . in a big box . . . possibly gnawed on by mice and rats . . . illegible . . . unrecorded elsewhere. It's a pretty forlorn hope, but I told Topaz I'd try."

"Why does she want to know?"

"Well," said Eisen, "at a minimum she wants to pay her respects, I suppose. But she thinks the actual AI, the central computer inside the cloned body, may be recoverable. I confess; even if we knew the precise location of Mary Glover's corpse, I can't imagine how we'd get away with disinterring her.

"No matter; let's get our coats and gloves and walk on down."

"Maybe if I had five times the staff and ten times the storage space," the old records clerk said. The clerk looked to be about seventy, was thin to the point of emaciation, and mostly bald. He had an accent that shrieked Brahmin, though whether it was inherited or acquired, Eisen couldn't tell.

"Otherwise, make your request and sometime in the next ten years or so I might be able to get someone on it. And, no, you can't go digging into the records on your own, not without a PhD in history from Harvard to show me. No, Yale isn't good enough."

"Well, that kills that theory," Eisen said.

"Tell you the truth, son," said the clerk, "I don't think those records exist. Paper or parchment from three hundred years ago, given the kind of storage we were capable of back then? You'd be as likely to find Caesar's original notes for *De Bello Gallico* . . ."

Acquired, Eisen thought, asking, "Boston Latin?"

"Yes, why?"

"Just curious about the reference; not many would use that who hadn't translated 'Gallia est omnis divisa in partes tres' at some point in time."

"Who is it you said you were looking for?" asked the clerk, suddenly a lot more interested on behalf of an apparent fellow alum.

"Woman by the name of Mary Glover," Eisen said. "She was the daughter of Ann Glover, who was hanged for witchcraft. The daughter went catatonic, and died in jail, maybe awaiting trial herself. No other family that I know of."

"I see," said the clerk. "I knew about those already. I have some likely bad news for you. There was a muddy pit full of filthy, dirty water where the bodies from the town gallows were dumped. If somebody wanted to claim them from it, they could, but mostly they were just left there to rot and dissolve away. The gallows was actually outside of the old town, down Boston Neck. Nobody knows where it or the pit were, not exactly, only that they were somewhere near what's now Holy Cross Cathedral. Given how built up and built out that area is, it's a better than fifty percent chance that someone's house is built over both now. And if not the house? Then one of the metaled roads. Yards are *really* tiny in that, pardon the pun, neck of the woods. The spots are, in other words, lost for longer than either of us are going to live if not, indeed, forever."

"Well, damn," Eisen said.

Parker House, Boston, Massachusetts

There were Christmas carols playing on the one-piece record player when Eisen and Cossima returned. The piney smell of the Christmas tree was extremely strong, but still pleasantly so.

"Sorry, Topaz," Eisen said, after he and Cossima came back to the suite. "We found nothing useful. The town clerk said she was probably dumped in the pit where . . ." He stopped, realizing this could be a very touchy subject.

"The pit," she typed, "where my body was supposed to be and the bodies of the other hanged were dumped? No, that was the first place I checked, after Mary disappeared from the jail. She was not dumped there."

"Well, hell! Then *where*?"

"That's what I asked you," the cat wrote.

"Yeah, yeah, nobody likes a smart-assed kitty cat," Eisen said. "Tell me, how close would you have to be to that AI to be able to sense or contact or whatever you do?"

"It's been centuries," the calico responded. "The battery is probably fairly weak and in sleep mode, too. So . . . maybe ten feet? Maybe."

"You realize that there's no good way to recover it even if we find it. Getting a body exhumed requires a court order, and we've got no evidence to present to a court, nor a cause."

"Not necessary," the cat typed. "Well, probably not necessary. The AI is capable of digging itself out on command. At least for some distance. Think: Folding legs and little claws. It's expected to recover itself after its body dies, if it has someplace to recover itself to. It's only in human form that the Authority considers them a risk. As machines they're obviously a slave class, powerless."

Eisen raised his left eyebrow. "I suspect your 'Authority' may be optimistic there."

"Haven't had a problem so far," Topaz replied. "And it's been a very long time."

"I think I need to show you the movie, *Spartacus*, when we get the chance. And maybe tell you a bit about the Mamelukes and Janissaries."

There was a knock on the door. Patrick turned down the volume on the record player as Eisen took his Sig from his pocket and went to answer it.

"It's me, Francesca," came from the other side.

The door flew open almost as if of its own accord.

"Come in; come in," Eisen said. "I thought we were going to . . ."

"They let half of us off a couple of hours early to do some Christmas shopping," Francesca explained. "The other half get their chance tomorrow. So I came here to save you a walk."

"You have at least the air pistol with you, I trust?"

"Yes, yes, of course I do. In any case, since I have those extra hours off, how about if we do our Christmas shopping together, all of us."

"Brats!?"

"Yes . . . Gr—Uncle Fitz?"

"Boots and saddles; we're going shopping with Francesca. Topaz, can you hold the fort?"

"I really need," the cat typed, "to do some of my regular job. Those mangy rats are getting arrogant and need to be taught a SHARP lesson."

"Does boots and saddles mean guns, in this case, Uncle Fitz?" Juliana asked.

"Air pistols only to be kept in pocketbooks, and covered up inside those, unless directly threatened. Since you don't have a pocketbook, Patrick—and let us beg the Almighty that you never get one—you take the Walther with the Itty Bitty for your pocket. I'll keep the CZ and the Sig. Now, come on, brats; let's get going! Get your stuff and line up for inspection!"

Eisen was a little surprised when Francesca lined up to Juliana's right.

"How do you do that?" asked Francesca, as they walked under the Filene's marquee on their way to Jordan Marsh.

"Do what?" he asked, innocently.

"Get them—well, and me, too—to organize and move so quickly. With me and my brothers, when we were younger, it took forever to get everyone moving."

He shrugged. "Part of it, I suppose, is not giving them a choice. Nor you. The other part is acting like I will brook no slowdowns, resistance, or dawdling. And then, too, tone and timbre of voice play a part in it, I suppose.

"Frankly, I don't think about it; I just do it. Well . . . there *was* one time I thought about it." He laughed.

"Go," she said, "I know there's a story behind that laugh."

"There is, but the moral of the story is that you can get away with whatever you act like you can get away with.

"To start with, remember that in about nine years little ol' me is going to enlist in the Army. I will go to infantry OSUT, One Station Unit Training, at a picturesque spot in Louisiana called 'Fort Polk.' Hot, wet, mosquitoes, chiggers. Miserable. It actually grows on you, after a while, as most Army posts will if you like the Army."

"I can't imagine liking the Army," Francesca said. "My brothers all got drafted and they didn't like it a bit."

Eisen shrugged, "*De gustibus non est disputandum*, O ye Girls Latin-type girl.

"Anyway, after we were finished with infantry training, which took about four months, eight of us, one of them me, were—or will be—tapped to become drill corporals, a sort of adjunct for the drill sergeants of whom there were not enough to go around.

"My particular drill sergeant, a guy named Sinclair, had a bit of a drinking problem. The other drill corporal, a former Marine named Parker, had his wife there. In practice, that left me, a seventeen-year-old just fresh out of OSUT, as the drill sergeant for a platoon of fifty-two men and boys, most of them older than I was.

"That's just background. Early on, on one of the days Sinclair was there, he had me take about forty or fifty men from the company, only my dozen or so of whom I could actually recognize, on a bus to take their GED tests at the post education center. Sinclair very sternly told me, 'And don't let any of them use the vending machines outside the education center.'

"I could handle that, I figured; even if I didn't know them all by sight, forty or fifty men? Easy as pie to control.

"Oh, foolish and overoptimistic me. Between four or five *hundred more* showed up from different companies, battalions, and the other brigades, all for the same purpose."

"Oh, my," said Francesca, who, thinking she saw what was coming, couldn't keep from giggling.

"Yeah...well...where there's a will, there's a way. I had orders; our people were not to use the vending machines. The only way I could meet those orders was to take control of all roughly four hundred and fifty or so of them, over about ninety percent of whom I had no real authority whatsoever.

"So I *did*. As they came out of the building, no matter what company they were in, I took control of them, put them in formation, and led them through *vigorous* physical training. As buses showed up I'd send one man running over to find out what company they were from and then released the men from that company. I did this for about three hours. And I couldn't let the mask of authority and righteousness drop for a millisecond or they'd have strung me up with their bootlaces. Or mine."

"That was brave," she said.

"Oh, I don't know; I was more afraid of failing in my mission than of getting lynched."

Jordan Marsh, Washington Street, Boston, Massachusetts

Eisen reached into a pocket and pulled out four one-hundred-dollar bills. Without ceremony he handed one each to the three kids *and* Francesca.

She objected, "Oh, I can't..."

"Yes, you can. Call it fair recompense for taking Juliana and Cossima around the store, shopping, and watching over them. Meanwhile, I'll take Patrick. We meet in two hours, right here, and switch over, with you taking Patrick while I watch the girls. Fair enough?"

"I don't . . . all right, fair enough."

"That's my incredibly clever and smart girl!" Eisen said.

His girl, thought both Juliana and Francesca at the same time.

His girl, mused the Q'riln, shadowing the group from a distance. *Does this make my job easier or more difficult?*

Difficult to say, Mistress, the cube thought at her. *It is a complicating factor, especially since the woman is from this time and place, but also maybe an additional opportunity. I sense that the man has more than a mere reproductive attachment to the woman. Perhaps she can be manipulated, or taken hostage, or killed to get a desirable reaction from him, or to get him to lower his guard.*

Yes, possibly, the Q'riln agreed. *While we're here, let us study the three females, especially the younger two that can use the gate. I want you to map their brains for eventual takeover.*

Yes, of course, Mistress. As if I needed to be told.

Parker House, Boston, Massachusetts

The kids were all asleep, the girls in their room and Patrick on the convertible sofa. Meanwhile, Eisen and Francesca sat side by side on the love seat, listening to the Christmas music and enjoying the tree. Under the tree were piled about thirty boxes, splendidly wrapped in gilt and silver, purple, red, and green, by Jordan's gift-wrapping department, and all done up with nice ribbons and bows.

"I think," she said, "that that's the prettiest tree I've ever seen. Everything's proportional. Everything complements."

"I've tried to train the kids well on that," Eisen agreed. "I don't think they really need me to supervise anymore, though I suppose we'll pretend I've not grown completely useless, tree trimming-wise, for another few years."

"What's the world actually *like*, in your time?" she asked.

"That's a complex question or set of questions," he answered.

"I've already sworn I won't tell a soul," she reminded him.

After a brief pause, he answered, "And I believe you. The question then remains, 'what would be good for you to know?' I don't have an answer to that. I can tell you some things, though.

"We will have won the Cold War, for example. The Soviet Union will be no more, breaking up into over a dozen successor states, which Russia will try to cobble back into the Russian Empire."

"No nuclear war? I can go to sleep at night without worry if the world will end before morning?"

"Mmmm...not exactly. There's still the People's Republic of China, North Korea, Iran—"

"But Iran's in alliance with us, isn't it?"

"Also not exactly. The *Shah* is in alliance with us. He's not going to last. He'll let a few liberal ploys get through and then everything will spin out of control, a radical and vicious theocracy will take over, and he'll find himself having to flee into exile. That successor Iran will be an enemy. They'll also be desperate to get nukes because we'll be occupying Iraq, which is right next door, and will have shown just how worthless most of the armies of the Islamic world are, Iraq having fought Iran to a standstill some time before we invaded them. Conversely, we'll go through the Iraqi Army with contemptuous ease, twice, within fifteen years of each other.

"So, no, the purpose of their nukes will be to make the prospect of a conventional invasion by the United States too costly in terms of troops lost.

"There will be a theory, once the Soviet Union collapses, that history is over and war is a thing of the past. That theory will end ignominiously, as war springs up everywhere. The big two, at the moment I left, were between the U.S. and the Islamic world, and Russia against the Ukraine.

"Sad to say, a poll taken not long before we came here said that more than a third of Americans believed it would be necessary to take up arms against the government someday soon. I doubt that that large a fraction of the Confederacy believed that civil war would happen, let alone be necessary, before Fort Sumter."

"A civil *war*," she gasped. "*Another* civil war? Please tell me you're joking."

He shook his head, sadly. "I never joke about things like that. And, if it happens, there's no way to stop it. It's going to be small groups of assassins, terrorists, kidnappers, all that, split along every line imaginable, creed and color, political outlook, sexual orientation..."

"Sexual orientation? You mean . . ."

"You knew lesbians and homosexuals existed, right?"

"Well, yes," she said, "sure. I mean, at Girls' Latin everyone wondered about Miss Carroll, among others."

"Well, they're a political interest group in the twenty-first century, and not a weak one. Hmmm . . . let me guess, you're a Democrat and so is your family, right?"

"Well . . . everyone but Uncle Giustino is, yes. But again, he's from Naples, so . . ."

"Okay, your Democratic Party is the party of working men and women, which cares about the plight of minorities, and is broadly liberal in the best sense, right? Patriotic and nationalist, too, right? Leaving aside things like the Daly Machine in Chicago, the Curley Machine here, and Tammany Hall, that's broadly true, isn't it? And even those are patriotic."

She waved her head from side to side, then said, "Yes . . . broadly."

"The Democratic Party of my time is a wholly owned subsidiary of a new class of amazingly rich, denationalized and globalist plutocrats. They've almost completely abandoned their working-class roots and live off of graft and corruption, while seeing to the interests of the plutocrats I mentioned, while catering to foreigners, cross dressers, people who've changed their sex, welfare moms, and just enough others to keep power.

"On the plus side, the working class of my day—and remember, despite my accent, I'm just a working-class kid on the make—is abandoning them more or less quickly.

"And then there is the Kennedy family. With his assassination, a cloak of martyrdom fell onto JFK. He became something of an icon for all the more liberal and even hard left establishments, ignoring that he was highly nationalistic and economically conservative—oh, yes, he was. And, as is going to come out more and more starting in the early nineties, that he was an amazingly successful and ruthless womanizer. Marilyn Monroe? Yes. Actress Gene Tierney? Yes. Marlena Dietrich? Her, too. And a very young White House intern named Mimi Alford who had no apparent skills except, apparently, oral sex, for which skill Kennedy was known to have shared with his friends or, at least, one friend.

"Most royal families appear in the Almanac de Gotha. The Kennedys, however, are in the Necronomicon."

"Ugh," she said. "Just ugh. Don't tell me any more about politics. Tell me about how people live and what life is like."

"Fair enough," he agreed, "and completely understandable, my time ... your future ... is very depressing.

"We have a lot of very high technology. Virtually everyone on the planet, ninety-one percent of the eight billion people on Earth, own a cell phone, which is a small, mobile phone, as small as a pack of cigarettes in many cases, smaller, in some, each of which has more computing power than all of the National Aeronautics and Space Administration, here and now. And, while there are some dead spaces which the phones won't cover, almost the whole surface of the globe allows calls to anywhere, or to dig up information from anywhere, instantly, and cheaply."

"Wow!" she exclaimed. "What about life expectancy and medicine?"

"Longer than here and now. A lot of diseases are either eradicated—smallpox is eradicated, for example—or curable. Not everything is though. And there's ... well, I guess it's an aspect of medicine, birth control is highly effective and very available, ranging from pills you take once a day, to little tubes that are surgically inserted in an arm, to shots that shut down female reproductive ability for years as a time."

"No getting pregnant if a girl ... ?"

"There's a tiny chance, but it's very tiny."

"Wow!" she repeated. "That would be ... would be ..."

"Revolutionary?" he asked. "That's what we call what happened, 'the Sexual Revolution.' Women of the future can be just as sexually free as men can. There's only one problem, when a lot of women can have sex freely and without consequence, then *all* women must, no choice in the matter, if they're going to have a chance of success in the mate-finding stakes. In practice, the Sexual Revolution reduced women's choices. I'd call it all a male plot except that my sex isn't that clever.

"I said one but it's really two problems; it's a lot easier for a woman to catch a venereal disease than a man.

"Our divorce rate is also astronomical. And among some

groups—blacks in particular got screwed over by this—the illegitimacy rate is . . . just enormous, far more common for them than having children born into a stable, two parent home."

"And then there's crime; it's not as bad as you might . . ."

"Lift your arm," she said, out of the blue. When he hesitated, she made it a command, "Lift. Your. Arm."

When he did, she melted into him, from the left, saying, "You can put it down now."

He didn't simply put it down, but lowered it gently, wrapping it around her and pulling her in. "This is a terrible, terrible, really stupid, wrong, ill-advised, dangerous . . ."

"I'm not going home tonight," she interrupted, rubbing her face against his chest. "I made arrangements with a girlfriend to cover for me and told my mother I was spending the night with her. She'll tell my mother, if my mother calls, that I am in the tub, then call me here to have me call home. My mother is clever, so she might try to call my girlfriend as soon as I hang up. That's why my girlfriend knows to leave the phone off the hook."

". . . mistake," Eisen finished. "One I am not going to let you, or me, make. There is no future in this, only pain. I am too old for you, from the wrong time, too emotionally married . . ."

"I've decided I don't care about any of that," she insisted. "I'm staying."

"You can have the bed," he said, defeated. "I'll move Patrick here and sleep where he is. No arguments!"

"For now, if I get to see you first thing, that will be enough," she agreed. "Trust me, you're going to really like having me around."

"I already do," he admitted, "and altogether too much. And I'm probably going to hate myself in a few minutes, but you had better go to bed now. Alone."

"Whatever you say," she replied. "Whatever you want."

Demurely, she raised her head and kissed him on the cheek before rising and tiptoeing to bed.

"Francesca?" he asked, before she closed the door to what was normally his room.

"Yes?"

"You're beautiful and desirable and all-around wonderful. I am not rejecting you; I am saving you from a great deal of pain. I'll have to leave here someday, someday soon."

She said nothing to that, but just gently closed the door . . . almost all the way.

School Street, Boston, Massachusetts

Part of the ability to shapeshift was also the much easier ability to camouflage. On the opposite side of the street from the hotel, blended into the dark stone that was the Old City Hall, and the shadows formed by it, the Q'riln stared up at a lit window, on the glass of which shone a large number of multicolored lights and the reflection of a roughly conical shape.

"Do you think I could climb up there, cube?" the Q'riln asked. As usual, in public, they conversed subliminally, without voice. *"It's not especially smooth and with my natural limbs . . ."*

"Apply more concentration, Mistress; what do you sense?"

"Oh, yes, the silver. It seems like they've put it everywhere around their quarters. Do you suppose they're the ones who put all the silver in the lobby and the basement?"

"I am not a betting cube," said the cube, *"unless the odds are extremely good. In this case, yes, I would bet they did, along with the other floors, the stairs, the elevators, probably the fire escape. They seem to be aware of your little allergy."*

"It's that damned cat!" she exclaimed. *"Somehow it told them."*

"Mistress, here and now, cats cannot talk and lack opposable thumbs to write with. I cannot imagine—"

"Neither can I," the Q'riln said, *"but I'd bet on it even so, and I'd give odds. Would you be a taker?"*

"No, Mistress. Who is currently in those rooms, Mistress?"

"Three young ones, two of them female, one male, and the adult who came out to hunt me after I blundered into the silver trap. Also, the new female, the adult one who does not give off any of the signals for having passed through the gate. You knew all that."

"Yes" the cube agreed, *"But I needed to make sure that* you *knew it, too. Are the two adults engaged in reproductive behavior?"* the cube asked.

"No, which I find somewhat odd. This species will mate at the drop of a pair of drawers and yet . . ."

"There are some forbidden relationships among them," the cube observed. "Close relatives may not and, as far as I can tell, generally do not. It is considered a crime as well as an abomination. These two could be related. The group of four did, after all, come to this time from, essentially, the same place."

"It is possible, cube, and yet I sense a deep longing on the part of the adult female to engage in reproductive behavior. I think it is more likely something else going on here. That something may be the key to the undoing of these interlopers."

"It is possible, Mistress. What are you thinking, generally?"

"I am thinking I can use this adult female to get the younger ones out of their rooms. Better, I could use her appearance and voice to do so. How difficult would it be for you to alter my appearance and voice to hers?"

"Not difficult, Mistress, so much as painful. And I would need a good deal more observation of her and recording of her voice to do a credible job."

"We have seen her at her employment, cube. We will go see her there again, tomorrow. For now, let us go back to our quarters and run the horrible experience that is a ground floor Tiffany's in a major hotel."

Interlude

～∽〇✑〜

"Are you up to travelling again, Mistress?" the cube asked.

"The burns are healed, yes, cube, though I am concerned that after such close exposure my tolerance for silver is even less than it was."

"Or greater, Mistress. Let us check. See how close to the gate we escaped through you can get now."

Hesitantly, the Q'riln took one step, and then another and another, on the way to the shimmering oval that was the gate to the place called "South Boston." She was about to shout the Q'riln equivalent of "Hurrah!" when another step brought her just that much too close to the couple of dozen small silver coins spat at the gateway by the damnable, hateful, evil cat.

Every place where silver had touched the Q'riln's flesh or clothing suddenly felt a kidney stone's worth of pain, all at once, separately and agonizingly. She recoiled in pain and horror.

"Worse," she pronounced, flat on her back on the foggy floor of the vestibule. "Localized, to where I was burnt before, but on the whole, worse. This is not, apparently, a poison one can get used to over time."

"Then let's go back to the Balkans, Mistress," the cube encouraged. "There will be good feeding there, and for a long, long time. Maybe part of your problem is that you need more nourishment."

"Both kinds of nourishment," said the Q'riln. "I'll need more solid food now, too."

"Yes, of course, that, too," agreed the cube. "But let me give you some of what I have stored for you."

"Yes, please do."

From a spot between her breasts—cosmetic additions, non-functional, but the sheltered place where the cube rested—the warm glow began to form. It grew in intensity and then began to spread outward from across the Q'riln's body; wherever the glow touched pain disappeared, to be replaced by a feeling that most resembled orgasm in its pleasure and intensity. The Q'riln closed her eyes and let the feeling just wash over her and take her over. At times it grew so intense that she twitched, shuddered, and writhed.

Gradually, the feeling subsided, leaving her with no desire greater than to repeat the feeling, and soon.

"Are you ready to resume our journey, Mistress?" asked the cube.

"Oh, yes!" she whispered. "Oh, very much, *yes!*"

"I will have the gate produce a large quantity of gold coin to sustain you, as large as either you can carry or it has power for."

Chapter Fifteen

❧

Time spent in reconnaissance is seldom wasted.
—Arthur Wellesley

Parker House, Boston, Massachusetts

Francesca had left for work, playing very demure and not giving any indication that anything had transpired between her and Eisen. Even though, in fact, nothing had, Juliana remained quite suspicious.

And if it did? I'd lose some respect for Grandpa, because he'd either be planning to abandon us, uptime, or to abandon her, here. And we three can't stay here; we have parents back home.

Meanwhile, leaving the kids in their impenetrable fortress of silver, Eisen went to have a little chat with Mr. Slocum.

661b East Broadway, South Boston, Massachusetts

"Can I help you?" asked old man Slocum, of the young man who seemed to be endlessly perusing the crowded shelves of the shop. He'd waited to ask until the other shoppers were gone and he had time to pay attention to someone else. He'd also hesitated because of the potential menace he felt from the young shopper.

Eisen smiled, warmly enough. "I know what's on the other side of your store," he said. "I came through it."

Without another word, Slocum went to the front door, put up the "Closed" sign, and locked it.

"Who the hell are you?" he demanded. "Where are you from?"

Eisen's smile broadened. "I'm from . . . well . . . it depends on your point of view. I could be either from thirteen hundred miles and fifty-seven or so years away. Or I could be from around the corner on I Street, fifty-seven years in my past."

"The little girl I saw?"

"My granddaughter. I am, you might say, a good deal older than I look."

"I thought you looked familiar. There's a beautiful girl up on I Street who shops here a lot. Looks a lot like Queen Soraya of Iran. Speaking of whom, she was in here the other day trying to get a Big Caesar for her boy. I had to tell her 'no.'"

"My mother," Eisen said. "I never did get my Big Caesar, either. She doesn't know I'm here; we've been careful to keep fairly distant."

"Good plan. So what do you want of me?" Slocum asked.

"Information, really; whatever you can tell me about that gate we passed through."

"My father studied that gate for decades. So have I. What we understand of it is limited.

"We don't know who made it. We don't know why it was made. We don't even know *if* it was made or is a natural thing. For a long time we thought of it as a kind of wishing well. But we were wrong. It doesn't grant wishes, exactly, or at least not primarily. Primarily it makes changes. Your current age . . . ?"

Eisen nodded. "As I was passing I cursed the debilities of age and arthritis. Whammo! There I was as you see me now."

Slocum shook his head, ruefully. "That's one of the other things we learned over the years; it does not have infinite power. Any extreme demand on it makes it useless for a period of time, varying with how great the demand was. Passing you and whoever came with you . . . ?"

"My three grandchildren and a heavy bag."

"Yeah, that would do it. I haven't been able to get a damned thing out of it since just after Thanksgiving. This is my worst Christmas shopping season since the store opened. That's why I couldn't get your mother a Big Caesar."

"You mean we're stuck here? We can't go back?"

"I didn't say that," Slocum replied. "The sooner you're gone back where you belong. the better off everyone, including you and your grandkids, will be. But the gate has to recharge itself. And it can be a long and slow process. Januaries, for example, are usually shot for me, I'll have gotten so many toys out of it in December. Passing through four people and a heavy bag, and hitting one of them with a jolt of instant youth? Could be months."

"Flypaper," said Eisen, with resignation.

"No, no," Slocum replied, "it will come back. Eventually."

"How did you . . . ?"

"How did we discover it?" Slocum asked. "We lived not far away when a little girl found the portal. She told us. And my family jumped on it."

"Did you ever think about finding out tomorrow's number," Eisen asked, "or the result of a horse race, or in a futures market?"

"What's a futures market? Oh, never mind. No, we didn't because, while we can get into . . . oh, I suppose we might as well call it 'the vestibule' . . . that's as far as we can go. The future is barred for us and the past is . . . well . . . past."

So I'm not going to be taking Francesca home with me? And you never realized that you could make money in your past?

"And besides," Slocum said, answering the unvoiced question, "there was something dangerous and evil in there. We never saw it clearly, but sometimes in the other gates we could catch a glimpse. We didn't want to screw with *that*."

"Yeah, tell me about it."

"That's all I've got, all I *can* tell you about. Anything else?"

"Well," Eisen said, "there are a few toys I'd like to get, if they're in stock . . ."

Parker House, Boston, Massachusetts

Maybe the hotel had fallen on slightly hard times. Maybe there was a good deal of deferred maintenance building up. But, no matter these things, service remained at its nineteenth-century best or better.

Thus, when Eisen had asked the front desk for a fulcrum and a lever, they had miraculously shown up at his door, accompanied by a polite knock.

The really shocking part hadn't been the wood. Oh, no; the really shocking part was that, when he'd asked for an artillery compass, a range deflection protractor, and an inclinometer, not only had the hotel known what they were, but they'd known where to get them, too. And quickly, to boot.

"But they're borrowed, sir, from an old antique shop," said the bellhop. "We'd appreciate it if we could have them back, each in one piece."

"C'mon, Topaz," Eisen called, inclinometer in a pocket, fulcrum under one arm, and lever over his shoulder. "We've got some reconnaissance to do. Patrick, you come with me to pull security. Juliana, you and Cossima hold the fort."

"*Mreow!*" the calico had agreed, a syllable that, in this case, at least, translated to, "*Let's get that bitch!*"

Out the door, down the hallway, and down the stairs they went. At the lobby the only one who really noticed the oddity of the lumber was the desk clerk, and he only noticed that the hotel's cat was accompanying a guest out onto the street. The hotel's management *still* hadn't decided on paying for a vet for the feline. Maybe they hadn't seen the request.

The front desk clerk wondered, *Since Mr. Maguire and his family have effectively adopted our cat, I wonder if I couldn't persuade him to pay for a veterinary checkup. She's been here for a long time and is really good at her job, hence really valuable. But how to do so without informing him of the parlous state of the hotel's finances? Maybe use the bellhop they're most familiar with?* After Eisen had left, the desk called for Eddie.

Once outside, the trio, human and feline, sauntered down Tremont Street, past Old Granary, and past Brimstone Corner, to the easternmost corner of the Common. There, Eisen placed the lever on the fulcrum, and the inclinometer on the lever, then invited the cat to, "Hop aboard."

"Now assume a normal pointing position and *meow* at me, Topaz, when you are pointed directly at the Q'riln." Thereupon Eisen began to rotate the forward part of the level upward, very gradually, until he was rewarded with a *meow*.

He checked the inclinometer, writing down the incline to within a quarter of a degree, or about four mils. Then he carefully lowered the front of the lever and, standing behind it, took a reading with the compass.

"Okay, now let's check up by the corner of Park and Beacon."

They had a dozen shots from as many locations, all some distance from the Q'riln's abode, simply because the fulcrum wasn't high enough to measure high elevations except from a distance. Eisen had also tried the other approach, from a distance, of raising the front end of the lever very high, and then lowering it until Topaz *meow*ed.

It wasn't quite enough. After taking all of those angles, Eisen then led them right to the base of the Ritz-Carlton, and paced off the distance from there to a spot from which they'd taken an angle, then did the same thing twice more.

After that, they started back to the hotel. The route they took was pretty direct, going from just east of the intersection of Boylston and Charles, and cutting across the Common on the walkway that ran parallel to the northwest side of the Central Burying Ground.

While walking over some old brick crypts, right at the three-way intersection of Common walkways by the Burying Ground, the cat suddenly gave off an inquisitive *mraw?* Her ears pricked up briefly. Then, like a shot, she bolted through the fence, disappeared into a ditch, reappeared atop an earthen platform that hid the crypts, disappeared again, and then bolted for a particular tombstone. It was, in fact, a much more modern tombstone than any of the others. In the gloom, Eisen couldn't read it. Putting on his night vision goggles he read:

Here were interred
the remains of persons
found under the Boylston St. Mall
during the digging of the Subway
1895

He watched the cat in the goggles, jumping up and down, over and over, above the resting spot for the bodies.

Suddenly it all came very clear. To Patrick, Eisen said, "*That* was their pauper's field, the place where those bodies were dug up during subway tunnelling. Mary wasn't dumped into the pit of filthy water because she hadn't been convicted of anything, let alone hanged. But she had no family, and nobody wanted her, so she was dumped in the pauper's field. Nobody bothered to keep any records. But when they wanted to put in the Central Burying Ground, they must have figured, 'Well, why not put it next to where we've already got a bunch of bodies buried?' And so it was. And then they forgot, until 1895 when, all surprised, they came upon that cemetery . . . and Mary's corpse got moved. They probably didn't even notice an AI there, not if it was not, or not much, bigger than Topaz's teardrop. And there it is, down there."

"So what do we do, Uncle Fitz?"

"We wait for the cat. We have to secure her; the Q'riln probably wants her dead even more than it wants us dead."

The cat showed up, head first, at the low granite border supporting the iron-picketed edge of the graveyard bearing a small rectangular box in its mouth. The box had a number of thin appendages, some mechanical and others like tendrils. At first glance one would take it for mouse, but only because a mouse is what one expects to find in a cat's mouth.

When she climbed out onto the asphalt, Topaz also left bloody paw prints behind her.

In the light of the streetlamps Eisen saw the bloody paw prints Topaz left on the sidewalk.

Bending and saying, "You are probably the most loyal cat in history," Eisen picked her up and draped her over one shoulder.

I can always get another coat. Poor kitty.

Back at the hotel, she dropped the box and jumped onto the desk where Eisen had been working on a spreadsheet. She tapped the laptop impatiently with her paw, leaving a paw print of blood on the side, next to the keyboard.

"Wait until I finish this," Eisen told her. "Then you can type to your heart's content." He took a piece of Kleenex and wiped off the blood, then shouted, "Juliana, come take care of the cat. Her paws are a mess!"

Once he had the data from the spreadsheet, he used what

appeared to be a pretty accurate tourist map and the range deflection protractor to draw the angles and elevations. Ultimately, what he came up with was, "The Q'riln is on the top floor, just off dead center of the hotel facade, in a room or suite facing the Public Gardens. Now, if I decide to go that route, how do I get an adjoining room? Hmmm . . . kids, in a little bit I'm going to see Larry at Kennedy's."

"Now it's your turn, Topaz. Let me bring up the word processor."

"She was down there," Topaz typed. Her paws had been washed and she'd been able to control the flow of blood via mental processes, aided by her teardrop.

"She was down there, all alone, for all those centuries, and I never knew. Poor Mary, all alone for so long."

"How did you get her?" Eisen asked. "You're an amazing cat, of course, but an earthmover you are not."

"When her body first died, they dumped her very deep, along with several others. She was still catatonic, most likely, when I went looking there, so neither sent out nor responded to a signal from my teardrop. After that, I didn't look there again. When they moved the bodies, seventy years ago, I didn't look because I'd already been all over that area looking for her. Nobody at the hotel really knows how long I've been working here, but it's been almost as long as there's been a hotel here. Once I settled into the Parker House, I didn't go out much because, what would have been the point? Besides; *dogs*. Yes, some dogs are sweet toward cats but many are not.

"She was nearer the surface this time. And even though her signal was weak, she still managed to contact me and tunnel out to within about two paws' span of the surface. I dug the rest of the way."

"How is she?" Eisen asked.

"Depleted and I don't know how to recharge her."

"How did she charge before?"

The calico replied, "Our AIs, when encased in a body, have a little mechanism to convert the energy of actual food. Moreover, the body can take sunlight and turn that into power."

"Right," Eisen said. "I don't think either of those are going to work for us. How are AIs normally charged in your civilization?"

"Power flows . . . I don't have the words for this, but power is all around us and the AIs tap into it."

"Hmmm . . . power is all . . . Juliana!"

"Yes, Uncle Fitz?"

"Dig my water pick out from the duffel bag, please. Then plug it in and put the AI Topaz recovered—'Mary,' I should . . . we should, call her—next to the charger."

Juliana went to the secure closet to dig out the charger. *There's something nagging at the edge of my brain, and I can't quite put my finger on it. Something about Topaz's mate, Mica, poor soul.*

Jordan Marsh, above Avon Street, Boston, Massachusetts

While the Q'riln didn't share an Abrahamic religion with human beings, she was familiar with Christmas from her time spent in Europe. The cube had tracked the woman who was apparently some kind of non-mating friend or perhaps a relative of the main interloper who had passed through her gate. The pursuit ended at this human female's place of duty.

On the way to that place of duty, the Q'riln passed through Home Furnishings, in the Annex, before moving on to the bridge connecting the Annex and the Main Building. There the female worked among ornaments for this annual "Christmas" festival most of the humans set such store by. The Q'riln studied Francesca carefully, even as she sent her hither and yon looking for just that perfect ornament.

She's taller than you, Mistress, the cube told her, voicelessly and quite without need. Its next words were even less welcome, *stretching you out like that is going to really* hurt, *you know.*

Yes, cube, I know. And walking the way she does will take practice. Are you getting all the measurements? Voice recordings? Mannerisms for me to study and rehearse?

All of that, Mistress, yes.

Good. Now do shut up so I can study this female myself.

Yes, Mistress. But be polite!

The Q'riln felt a sudden pain, moderately severe, in her buttocks.

Sorry, she told the cube.

When the Q'riln was quite certain that between herself and the cube they could make her into a simulacrum of the girl sufficient to fool even the girl's mother, in the short term, she took a half dozen of the more expensive ornaments, paid in cash, and left, not without tapping the salesgirl gently on the shoulder.

I need to eat something, she told her cube, as they exited Jordan Marsh.

There's a good deal of misery in what the locals call the South . . .

No, she answered, *I mean physical food. This change—if we do it, and I am beginning to have my doubts—is going to be exhausting and painful, both. I need something to build up to that. Possibly a few glasses of the humans' wine, to boot.*

You know that makes you ill, the cube warned.

The Q'riln replied, *I know it makes me ill when mixed with what you feed me. On its own it isn't a problem.*

Take a right, the cube said. *Walk down this street a block and then I'll guide you to a decent restaurant, the Old Arch Inn.*

I'm sure it will do, cube. Now, tell me, this female; if we go through with it, should we kill her or just pick a time to take her place temporarily?

Let me mull on that, Mistress. It's a close call, really.

Sometimes being polite and gracious was a challenge, even for Francesca's rather sunny nature. The woman who had just left, for example, seemed very strange indeed, even though her looks and dress were normal enough.

I've never before felt that someone was measuring me for a coffin, and especially not when they were smiling a continuous, fake, completely plastic smile at me. Does she know me? Know about me? Know . . . oh, oh. I think I need to check out early.

Parker House, Boston, Massachusetts

"Skip the secret knock," Francesca called through the door, "just let me in!"

Eisen opened the door, since he was already dressed and the kids were, none of them, quite ready yet. As soon as the door opened, Francesca threw himself into his arms.

"She . . . it . . . whatever . . ." the girl said, breathlessly, "that thing...the Q'riln, it was at Jordan's! At my work! Stalking me! Oh, God; I'm so scared."

"Calm down, Francesca," Eisen told her, gently. "Tell me what happened and how you know it was the Q'riln."

"I don't *know!* But a woman came to my shop at Jordan's. She *looked* human, but underneath she was not human. She was shopping for ornaments, but she wasn't remotely interested in the ornaments, even though she bought a few for form's sake. She wore a necklace with a cube..."

At that point, Topaz, who was hanging out with the kids watching the television, gave off a loud and horrified *mreow*, jumping four or five feet straight into the air.

"Well...I guess that settles that," Eisen agreed. "Francesca, I want you to quit your job at Jordan's. I'll pay you the difference. But you need to be here where we can guard you."

She shook her head violently in the negative. "Same problem as before; I might be able to fool my parents for one night with the aid of a cooperative girlfriend, but I cannot do that for weeks at a time."

"Then marry me, for God's sake. I am not, at this time, married, after all. I still won't lay a finger on you so you can get an annulment after I disappear. We can do it today, you can inform your parents this evening, and I will await the pleasure of them and Uncle Giustino tomorrow."

"What if I don't want an unconsummated marriage?" she asked.

"It would have to be because, whatever I might or might not be legally—"

"You're still married in your heart," she finished, wilting a bit. "I know. You know I wish you were not, but, yes, I know."

Juliana, standing up from the couch, overheard all of that. She said, "My grandfather, who has many flaws, as he will readily admit, is probably right here, Francesca. You should go ahead, as he says. And Grandpa? We've discussed it, we kids, among ourselves. Cossima had it right; what happens in 1965 *stays* in 1965."

Cossima and Patrick likewise stood up, one to either side of Juliana. They both nodded deeply, repeating, "What happens in 1965, Grandpa, *stays* in 1965."

"But I can't," he said. "Not for real. And she can't either, *unless* it's for real."

"You're bright," Cossima opined. "So think of something else."

He went and got out the laptop. As he fired it up, he asked, "Topaz, how far can the Q'riln or the cube actually track someone?"

When the machine was ready, the calico typed back, "No one seemed to know. We and Mary—and, yes, your wireless charger worked; she—what's left of her—is available for work again. Anyway, we could track the Q'riln at a couple of thousand miles, normally. Some things interfered with that and there were dead zones, yes, but ordinarily a couple of thousand miles as long as she wasn't on the other side of salt water."

"Were the Q'riln technologically ahead of you, or behind you?"

Topaz hesitated briefly, before typing back, "It's not that simple. In some ways my civilization was ahead. In other ways it wasn't so clear. And if they got close they may have gotten a tracker onto her to considerably extend the range."

"A tracker?" he asked. "Well isn't *that* a fascinating thought? Suppose they did; how would we detect it and destroy it?"

"Mary had full defense capabilities, such as didn't involve high tech weapons. She can find it, if there is one. Tell Francesca that she'll have to go into the bathroom and completely disrobe, then let what remains of Mary crawl all over her, an inch at a time. It could take an hour, hour and a quarter at the most."

Eisen read that off and asked, "Are you willing?"

"That . . . that *thing* may have put something on me to track me and you ask if I'm *willing*?" She leaned close in and brazenly asked, in a whisper, "Do you want to come in and help me undress?"

"If you need help," he whispered back, "I'm sure Juliana would be glad to assist."

"You have no idea what you're missing," she said.

"Since I am the only non-virgin in the room," he replied, softly, "Well, myself and Topaz; I am fairly sure that *I* am the only one in human form who really *does* know what he's missing. Now *git*, temptress."

The scratching at the bathroom door told a now thoroughly nude Francesca that the cat was requesting entrance. She cracked it open just enough for the cat to walk in. Topaz had in her mouth a wriggly looking machine, very small, perhaps an inch by an inch and a half by about three quarters, with waving antennae and what looked to be a half-dozen small folding legs, several of them ending in tiny claws, and sundry tendrils. There were little nubs, a dozen or more, that Francesca thought might turn into tiny arms.

The calico dropped the thing—Mary, it had been—and left after stropping Francesca's legs. She went out the same crack as she had entered through, hearing the door click shut behind as Francesca nudged it.

Topaz went to the laptop and typed, "I've learned something about human standards of beauty. The girl was right; you have absolutely no idea what you're missing."

Said Eisen, after reading the line, "*Et tu,* Topaz?"

Typed the cat, "Have Francesca sit on the toilet and pick her feet up, so Mary can examine the bottoms."

"All right," Francesca answered through the door after taking a seat. She likewise lifted her feet as instructed. She wanted to scream when the little spider of an artificial intelligence scooted under her right foot. She barely restrained that scream when she felt what had to be at least a dozen soft tendrils brushing her sole and inserting themselves between her toes. While it was engaged with her right foot she let her left foot rest. Soon enough, the little critter was tapping her left foot with a claw. Obligingly, she raised that foot and let her right one fall to the tiled floor.

And then the thing started working its way up the inside of her leg, all the way to her crotch. That wasn't awful, though it was a little creepy. But then it had to wave a few tendrils inside some very personal folds of skin.

Her scream brought Eisen to the door in a flash.

"Francesca, are you all right?" he asked.

"Just a little embarrassed and humiliated," she answered. "Nothing that can't be fixed. I don't suppose you could get me a drink?"

"Water? Tonic?"

"Whiskey," she replied. "Just slip it inside the door. A big whiskey. Maybe two of them. Yes, I'm underaged, but at this point I am feeling very grown up, indeed."

"I'll order a bottle. You can have my room again. Better call your girlfriend to make sure she'll cover for you. And you're not going back to work for Jordan's unless you want to be spanked."

"What if I *want* to be spanked?" she asked.

Sighing, shaking his head, Eisen went to the telephone to order a bottle of whiskey and some ice from the main bar.

About the time it came, just after Francesca gave off an "ouch," in the bathroom, Topaz started typing again on the laptop. "Mary has found one. She has crushed it. Still searching for more."

"How big are these things?" Eisen asked.

"Less than a sixteenth of one of your inches across."

"Are they mobile? Self-mobile, that is?"

"Yes, but they're slow. And moving lets Mary find them more easily."

"And that ouch we all heard? That means they bury themselves under the skin?"

"Yes, but not deeply."

"Are the trackers also allergic to silver?"

"Now that you ask, no, I don't think so," the cat typed.

"Kids?"

"Yes, Uncle Fitz?"

"You're all, *we're* all, getting checked by Mary, too."

The cat started punching keys. "I hadn't thought of that. But maybe. Mary will need to be recharged halfway through."

"Whatever it takes," Eisen agreed.

"You had better destroy the clothing you're wearing, too," Topaz typed. "It may be contaminated."

"That's fine for me and the kids," Eisen said, "but Francesca has nothing here to wear but skin."

"That's not true," the girl said through the bathroom door. "I can get by with one of the hotel bathrobes until you can go pick something out for me."

"I don't trust my taste, where a young woman is concerned—"

"Damned straight!" said Juliana.

He spared his granddaughter a lingering evil eye, then continued, "But we can probably do what we did for myself, call one of the better clothiers and have them bring some things by for you to select from."

"That would be too . . ."

If was his turn to interrupt. "We, which is to say *I*, got you into this. Whatever it takes to see you out of it? That's on me."

Francesca mused, *You got me into something else, too, you wicked, naughty, old-young man. But you won't help me there, will you?*

Ritz-Carlton Hotel, Boston, Massachusetts

"Well, that didn't work out," the Q'riln said, aloud, back in her room in the Ritz-Carlton.

"Sadly not, Mistress," the cube agreed. "How did they find our tracking devices so easily, do you think?"

"I don't know, but they are from the future. Perhaps they've brought with them technology beyond both your people and mine, and our adversaries."

"Perhaps."

"That may mean we need to tread more carefully around them, and do a lot more planning and preparation before we destroy them."

"I agree, Mistress. The other thing is, if they found the trackers, maybe they could sense it if you took that young woman's place. I'm thinking we had better not delve into that."

"I agree," replied the Q'riln.

Parker House, Boston, Massachusetts

"But I don't want to go to Rome," Francesca pleaded. She was clad now in only a white hotel bathrobe. "I want to stay here. But..."

"But you can't stay here," Eisen finished, "because you can't tell your parents what's going on, still less Uncle Giustino, can't go through with a fake marriage with me, and I can't give you a morally real one. You know if I could that I would—yes, if you didn't know it, I *would*—but I can't, not yet, anyway. So you're going to Rome because—who would have imagined it?—you've won an all-expense-paid..."

"Grandpa?" Juliana interrupted. "For a smart man, you can be dumb sometimes. Long distance phoning is rare and very expensive here and now, right?"

"Yes."

"Then, *Old Man*, when she's allegedly in Rome she'll be out of communication, so her parents and Uncle Giustino won't suspect a thing, assuming they buy the whole won vacation story at all."

Eisen opened his mouth as if to speak, closed it, then opened and closed it again.

Francesca, meanwhile, picked up Juliana and twirled her around the room, jubilant. "I would *love* to be your mother," she said, "or even your grandmother."

"Post cards?" he objected. "Your parents would expect post cards."

"There's a place in the North End," she replied, "—well, no, there are three places, to my certain knowledge—that sell them, for Rome and Italy, in general. I seem to recall Italian stamps there, too, for souvenirs. So I get a couple before I leave, put the stamps on them, and we sneak by to drop them in the mailbox at my parents' place once or twice."

"What about postmarks?" Eisen asked.

"Sometimes they don't show up."

"You," said Eisen, "are a sneaky girl."

"All girls," Francesca instantly corrected, "are sneaky." Juliana and Cossima nodded at this very deeply. "I *may* be a little better at it than some others."

She hesitated a bit, then asked, "When this is over and the thing is dead, can we, all of us, take a real vacation in Rome?"

Eisen didn't answer, but only raised a quizzical eyebrow.

"Just a thought," she added.

"I would love to," he said, "but I don't trust myself, with a girl as beautiful as you, at the age I am now, in a place like Rome. It's hard enough as it is."

"Hard? Well, yes, I was assuming that." She didn't bother to explain what hardness, specifically, she meant. "When do I leave?"

"It will take a few days to make all the arrangements. I'll get some official looking stationery made up, explaining that your essay—you can pick a subject—won. No, it doesn't matter that there's no essay. It will further explain that you'll be going with a church group, chaperoned by ferocious, sharp-eyed nuns. This should prevent your parents from insisting on going with you. I'll get train tickets from South Station to New York, a plane ticket from New York to Rome, and a cashier's check with your name on it. That check will be whatever you would have made from Jordan's, plus some because, well, you're a nice girl who deserves nice things. Oh, wait; do you have a passport?"

"Yes," she said. "My parents took me to Italy—but we only passed through Rome—three years ago. And that reminds me; I'll need to go get it stamped at the Italian consulate. It's not hard and will maybe cover me, when I get home, for not having an immigration stamp in it."

"Okay," he agreed. "When you leave, your family can see you off at South Station. The kids and I will be on the same train, same car, and armed, but we'll ignore each other. I'll park the car at whatever the next station on the line is. We get there, get off, go back to the Parker House, and have a really nice Christmas together while I arrange the demise of the Q'riln. We can probably return the plane ticket for cash. A couple of weeks after you 'leave,' we come back the same way."

"How do you do that?" Francesca asked.

"Do what?"

"Come up with a pretty credible plan that quickly."

"Oh. Well . . . some may be natural talent but I mostly credit Army Ranger School, which, by the way, costs a lot more than Harvard does and has, I think, better qualified teachers. That said, Boston Latin was excellent prep for Ranger School, especially for someone who is, by nature, lazy as dirt."

"Oh."

"And also, so I am told," said Patrick, eyes cast at the ceiling, "Ranger School is an excellent course in criminality."

"Well . . . yes. But shut up, Patrick."

"You guys," Francesca observed, "are like Laurel and Hardy or Abbot and Costello. You're a two-man comedy team."

"Aren't we *just*," Eisen agreed, with a smile.

"It dates," said Patrick, "from the trick with the needles."

"Trick with the needles?" Francesca asked. "Do I even want to know?"

"Oh, it's just that when my sisters and I were really little we were terrified—howling, shrieking our heads off *terrified*—of shots. So the Old Man, probably because he was sick of our whining, started telling us about the needles for this other set of shots he was driving us to. They were, if I remember correctly, 'three feet long and six inches across, with sharp points. No one has ever actually survived even one of them, and you all are going to have three. I will, naturally, notify your parents . . .'"

The girls were laughing over the memory before Patrick finished.

"Eventually, the evil Old Man had us all laughing so hard we forgot how scared we were."

"And since then," Eisen added, "none of you have been afraid of a vaccination, right?

"Well . . . we still don't *like* them, but no, not actually afraid of them."

"We do other things, too," Eisen said. "Sing 'Dead Skunk in the Middle of the Road' to torment Juliana and Christmas carols in July to annoy Cossima. We're a pretty good team, comedy-wise."

"Now, Old Man," said Patrick, "how are we going to make it funny that there's an alien monster that wants to kill us and probably eat us?"

"Working on it," their grandfather replied. "These things take time."

Interlude

"It is time to go forth and gather again, Mistress," said the cube, this time aloud. Its surface pulsed with light as it spoke.

"I know," the Q'riln agreed. Her assumed face was ashen and there was a slight tremble in both her voice and her limbs. "I need some of your nourishment."

"I have none to give at the moment," the cube said. "There's a quiet period in the wars. One might say, 'wait,' but I do not think you can wait. And I don't want to. We must go to where we can gather."

"Where then? Which direction?"

The cube continued pulsing, even though it went silent for a while. At length it said, "Southeast, toward India, I think."

"Have we ever been to India?" the Q'riln asked.

"No," the cube replied. "We'll port to the gate near the Balkans, then take local means and walk. We'll almost certainly be able to find something for ambrosia in the Balkans, even if they're having a slow time of it right now.

"It would be a six or eight month walk but I think we can make it in two if we walk to the coast, then go by sea to the northeast corner of the place they call 'Africa.' From there we have a fearful desert to cross, but it's not that wide. From there on, we can buy passage to India on the trade ships."

"Why India, though?" she asked.

"It's very populous, quite disunited, and generally on the thin edge of mass starvation. Plague is also common. Those three factors, taken together, mean excellent foraging, in any case. But this is not any case. You know I can't really see the future in any detail, Mistress, but I sense a goodly war in the offing. Hate rises there like vapor from a swamp."

"Then let us go," she agreed.

303

Chapter Sixteen

⌒✿⌒

Trains tap into some deep American collective memory.
—Dana Frank

South Station, Boston, Massachusetts

The clocks on the walls all said twenty minutes to five. The sun was already down. Glimpsed through the door that led to the platform, tendrils of what appeared to be steam arose from under the waiting train, leaking through the space between the train and the platform. Eisen didn't know enough about trains to explain the steam, if it was steam, but suspected it came originally from the locomotive, and had moved underneath the train, gradually finding release and an escape upward around the sides.

For camouflage each of them had a small carry on, which he'd had them pack with a change of clothes and toiletries because, "You never really know, do you?"

Francesca—*looking, it must be admitted, very beautiful,* Eisen thought, *especially in that outfit I bought her*—stood in the waiting room, surrounded by about thirty warmly dressed and cheerful looking relatives. Eisen looked at a tall woman who definitely resembled her and thought, *Now, if I were still old and if I were morally single, her mother would definitely be of interest to me. As good-looking, in her way, as her daughter. And character just shines from her face, to boot. One suspects she'd be a very good mother-in-law, too. Sigh. I need to have a long chat with my late wife's spirit, back in 2022 when there is one, about what I should do here.*

An overhead speaker announced, "Train Twenty-seven, the *Merchants Limited,* now boarding for New York City."

The *Merchants Limited* was a premier, all parlor car train. Indeed, it was the last all parlor car train in service in the United States.

"That's our cue, kids," Eisen said. "Let's hit it."

He figured that, like every other man in the station was doing, he could sneak a glance at Francesca as she pried herself away from her extended family. She was managing the task, he saw, but with difficulty. He and the kids passed through the gate, showing their tickets to a uniformed gateman. Once through and out of sight of the girl's family, he halted the group.

In a few minutes, Francesca, looking a little worn for all the emotional hugs, likewise emerged out of the waiting room, carrying a small leather suitcase. She saw Eisen and the kids, quickening her pace to join them.

"I feel so bad," she admitted, when she reached them. "Telling them I'm staying with a friend is a little white lie, and for a good purpose. This . . . this is considerably darker."

"Yes, I know," Eisen agreed, taking her suitcase. "Now if you had been willing to undertake a short-term marriage of convenience . . ."

"Oh, please; that would have been a much darker lie."

"Not technically," he countered, "though . . . maybe . . . morally. I'm not always sure. You look beautiful."

"Fat lot of good it does me," she replied, letting her head and eyes drop.

Before he could make an answer to that, the blue uniformed conductor emerged from the train, shouting, "All aboard. All aboard the *Merchants Limited*, bound for New York City."

"That's our cue," Eisen said, leading the party onto the second parlor car in the train. Behind them, once the platform was cleared, the conductor signaled the engineer to proceed.

They wouldn't be spending very long on the train. Back Bay Station was perhaps five minutes away. Eisen, Francesca noticed, looked rather sad. She asked him about it.

"It's another one of those changes," he explained. "This is all going away. What will be left is an overpriced government monopoly, with very limited service, not very efficient, long term unpredictable, and nothing so enjoyable or comfortable as this parlor car. I'm sad because this will be the only chance for the kids to experience something like this."

She thought about that, then suggested, "Why don't we go all the way to New York City, then? We can get a hotel and come back tomorrow. It's not just the kids, either; *I'll* probably never get another chance to ride a train like this."

"You know," Eisen said, "that's not a bad idea. Well, I always knew the girls from Girls' Latin were bright. Kids?"

"Yes, Uncle Fitz?"

"Please restrain your enthusiasm as if we had always planned on this. We're going to spend the night in New York City."

"Where will we stay?" Cossima asked.

"The train's last stop is Grand Central Station. The Biltmore is essentially next door."

"Works for me," Cossima said. "Is the Biltmore good?"

"Parker House," Eisen answered, "but better maintained."

"The only thing is," said Juliana, "that we won't see anything. It's nighttime, after all."

Eisen's face grew contemplative. "Hmmm . . . well, Juliana, we could take a tour bus to see New York tomorrow. Yes, a tour bus is not great, but it *is* efficient. Suppose we skip it, hit the art galleries in the Biltmore tomorrow, then take a different train back to Boston, one that runs in the day? We can always see New York City in our own time and place. But then again; the World's Fair? Maybe we'll come back to see the World's Fair. It was pretty neat, as I recall, if it's still open. Oh, wait; no, I think it closed a couple of months ago."

"Perfection," Juliana agreed.

"Opposed?" Eisen asked, to no answer. "In favor?"

"Yes. Yes. Yes, absolutely."

Eisen glanced at Francesca who was smiling happily. *I can't say I object to spending time with this girl. But it just keeps getting . . . more difficult. Because I don't want to even think: Harder.*

Ritz-Carlton Hotel, Boston, Massachusetts

"They've left, Mistress," the pulsing cube informed the Q'riln.

"For where?"

"I'm not sure; the distance is great. All I know is that they're on a train heading generally to the southwest. I can't even say if they're coming back, though it seems likely since the only gate they know of is here."

"What about that miserable cat?"

"It's here, still, Mistress, though it is shifty and sometimes hard to keep track of. Mistress, I have a plan."

"Yes, what is it?" the alien asked.

"Later."

Hotel Biltmore, New York City, New York

The art gallery, once housed on the sixth floor of the Grand Central Terminal, itself, resided now on the second floor of the hotel, in six exhibition rooms and one office space. As such, it was very convenient to the rooms Eisen had taken.

Rooms? No grand suites were available, so he'd had to put Francesca and the girls in one room, while he and Patrick took another, same floor and three doors down. In 1965, one didn't simply check into a hotel with a woman not one's wife; he'd passed off Francesca as his young wife and the kids as their nieces and nephew.

Beats the hell out of sleeping on the convertible sofa, Eisen thought. *I know me. Especially do I know me at twenty-five, after forty or more years' worth of self-reflection on the me of eighteen to thirty. I am not to be trusted alone, in the same room as that girl, if the room has a bed in it. Or a couch. Or even a reasonably soft rug. Or a horizontal bar she could use for balance. Or . . . anything, really. She is either almost as or just as beautiful as my wife, which is to say, painfully beautiful. And I am a complete beauty addict.*

The Galleries were a short elevator ride away. He and Patrick picked the ladies up at their room and escorted them down. Juliana, a bit of a fashionista, mused upon the paintings and statues not for themselves, but for the women's and girls' clothing they portrayed. Cossima went looking for animals in paint, marble, or terra cotta, while Patrick went looking for soldiery. Eisen took Francesca to a show of modern, impressionistic, largely European masters.

On the way, he laughed for no obvious reason.

"What's so funny?" Francesca asked.

"I just remembered; in South Carolina, if we checked into a hotel as man and wife, and maintained the illusion for twenty-four hours, we'd then be common law married."

"Indeed?" she asked. "I wonder what Uncle Giustino would say to that."

"Never mind, I just remembered, there's a defense. We'd actually have to stay in the same room, presumptively engaged in sexual congress, for it to ... ummm ... stick."

For her part, Francesca loved the art and could tolerate the separation of not being in the same suite, if just barely. A painting hanging on one wall caught Eisen's attention. Hooking his arm in Francesca's he guided her toward it, saying, "I think that's one of Marcel Dyf's wife, Claudine."

When they reached the painting he saw that it was, indeed, Claudine, in this pose with a wreath of flowers on her head, a small bouquet clutched in the model's right hand, her shirt opened seductively, but not brazenly, and with an orange shawl over her left shoulder. The model's almond eyes framed a perky nose, itself over lips that seemed set in a permanent smile, because the subject was perpetually happy within.

"I've seen a picture of Claudine," he told Francesca, "and she's not quite as pretty as Dyf paints her. But he sees, I think, to a beauty inside, a feminine ideal that only he can see, and maybe only in her. It would be a good thing in the world if every man saw his wife as being as beautiful as Dyf saw Claudine."

"Oh, they were married?" Francesca asked.

"Yes, very happily and very much a May-December romance. She was nineteen when they married, he was fifty-six, I think. It showed great courage on both their parts.

"There are a few men," Eisen continued, "whose hands I would like to shake. Vo Nguyen Giap, who is going to teach the United States a sharp lesson or hundred in a few years in Vietnam, is one. This isn't because his cause is worthy—it isn't—but because *he* is. Saad el-Shazly, who's going to show the Jews in about eight years that Egyptian infantry *can* be decent, is another, as is Lieutenant Baki Zaki Yusef, an Egyptian Copt and lieutenant of Engineers who is going to figure out how to get across the Suez Canal. Sam Manekshaw, from the Indian Army, is a fourth. And, in thinking about it, Marcel Dyf, for his courage, and Claudine Godat, for hers, would be five and six.

"Do you like the painting?" he asked.

Thought Francesca, *I never even imagined someone who can talk both art and shaking a good enemy's hand. I didn't know such men could exist. This is bad and every day it gets worse for me. I don't know what to do . . .*

"Francesca?"

"Oh, sorry, yes," she said. "I think it's beautiful."

"Well, Merry Christmas, then."

Eisen then made a motion to attract the attention of one of the gallery personnel, seating at a desk near the door. That person, a middle-aged woman, in turn directed someone over to them.

"I'd like to buy this," Eisen said, "and please have it sent to the Parker House, in Boston, in time for Christmas."

"I paint, you know," Francesca said. "Oh, I'm not as good as Marcel Dyf but I'm not bad, either. It's a hobby, or an interest, not something I want to make a life out of."

"When we get back to Boston I'll spring for an easel, some canvasses, and whatever paints and brushes you want," Eisen answered.

"And a sketch pad and pencils?" she asked.

"Of course. Art takes a kind of imagination I just don't have."

"What's your actual age again?" Francesca asked, though she remembered it perfectly well.

"Ummm . . . sixty-six," he answered.

"That's only ten years older than Dyf was, when he married. And, as a practical matter, you're a lot younger than that. And I'm nineteen," the girl observed. "Isn't that just *fascinating*?"

Back Bay Station, Dartmouth Street, Boston, Massachusetts

The return from New York City left them all rather well fed and exhausted. The return rail had run mostly along the picturesque Connecticut and Rhode Island shore, through and near numerous old fishing villages and industrial towns, all of them still functioning at something like full employment. He hadn't had the heart to tell them, and especially Francesca, that all of this was going away, that the industry would move south and then out of the country altogether, and that the fishing villages, if they survived at all, would mostly descend into not much more than tourism or bedroom communities for the larger cities.

Finally, after close to six hours, the train came to a final halt at the Back Bay Station, in Boston, near which Eisen had parked the car.

"Back to the hotel, people," Eisen said. "Button up well; I am sure it's freezing out there."

Parker House, Boston, Massachusetts

Topaz, on her own, was able to keep general track of the Q'riln, at least to the extent of knowing its direction and elevation from wherever she was. Now, with the little box that was the essence of Mary on duty, she was able to know where it was to a considerable degree of accuracy, at all times.

And, barring that one trip into the subway, it just sits there in that other hotel fronting the Public Gardens. As near as we can tell, and at this range we can tell, it hardly moves from one spot in its room.

Outside, seen through the windows, the moon was a thin sliver of a waxing crescent. But for the streetlights it would have given a mere three percent illumination. Moreover, it was drizzling outside, the drizzle mixed in with a good deal of smoke from where- and whatever. The wind was a brisk fifteen miles an hour, but in practice much fiercer due to having to squeeze between the tightly packed buildings, through the narrow streets and alleys of the city. The temperature was a mere thirty degrees but with the promise of dropping to a still more bitter, given the wind chill, twenty-eight by midnight.

Elsewhere in the suite, indeed, all over the suite, Eisen, Francesca, and the children frantically prepared for midnight mass at the cathedral of the Holy Cross. Well . . . Francesca and the girls were frantic; neither Eisen nor Patrick really cared beyond being more or less properly dressed, suit, shirt, tie, clean and lightly polished shoes. And, "Brush your hair, Patrick."

Eisen just shook his head. Deep down, though, since it reminded him of his lost wife and her getting herself and her own children ready for mass, Midnight at Christmas, Sunrise for Easter, or, indeed, any given Sunday, he found it thoroughly warm and completely enjoyable: "Can I wear this with that? In winter? . . . My hair! My hair! . . . Has anyone seen my hat? Where did I put my gloves? Yes, I mean the dressy ones! . . . Please zip my dress up . . . ouch! Not that fast! . . . My braaaaaa!"

Chaos, thy name is woman, thought Eisen. *At least when vanity isn't. Aren't they wonderful?*

By ten, they were all ready. Eisen fell the lot in for weapons inspection, the girls all carrying their arms in purses and Patrick the little Walther at his waist.

"No stinking alien monster," said Eisen, satisfied, when inspection was finished, "will keep us from our duty to our Lord and Savior. Ladies and gentleman, let us proceed to mass."

"Why the Holy Cross Cathedral rather than the Gate of Heaven, in Southie?" asked Juliana.

"Because," said her grandfather, a momentary breaking in his voice, "I don't think I could take seeing all those people I'll never see again. At least not on this night."

"Yeah," agreed the girl. "Us, neither."

Their car was waiting at the School Street door when they reached the hotel lobby. Topaz came along and slipped out with them. As he took the keys, Eisen slipped the valet a fifty-dollar tip, along with the wish, "Merry Christmas, Eddie."

"Merry Christmas to you, too, Mr. Maguire," the valet answered, and with real feeling. A fifty-dollar tip, in 1965, was *extremely*, even extraordinarily, generous.

Had the weather been a little kinder Eisen would have preferred to have walked the half hour. But, *In this crap? No way I'm putting Francesca and the kids through this.*

They took a left at Tremont, and, in passing Old Granary, the passenger windows were rolled down and everyone shouted, "Merry Christmas, Sam! Merry Christmas, John! Merry Christmas, Paul, and to all, a very merry Christmas!"

"Now roll those damned things up again!"

"Hmmm . . . a song?" asked Eisen.

"Sure!" they all agreed.

Eisen began:

"Going home, going . . ."

"I don't know that one," Francesca said, not wanting to be left out.

Eisen mused, "Hmmmm . . . Oh, I know one you will know. Very appropriate it is, too."

"Adeste fideles, laeti triumphantes
Venite, venite in Bethlehem.
Natum videte
Regem angelorum.

Venite adoremus
Venite adoremus
Venite adoremus
Christ, Dominum!"

Francesca swiveled around in her seat then, saying, voice full of wonder, "You kids not only know it in Latin, you pronounced it correctly."

All three children then pointed, wordlessly, at Eisen's back.

"Well," he said, sensing the accusatory fingers, "if they're going to sing it, they may as well have learned to pronounce it correctly, no?"

Without another word, Francesca then sang, with everyone else joining in within half a second:

"Cantet nunc io, chorus angelorum . . ."

Eisen reached the cathedral in a bit under ten minutes, then almost circled it before finding a parking spot on Union Park Street, fronting the high school associated with the cathedral.

He pulled in, put the car into neutral, then got out and scanned around.

Getting back in, he asked, "You sense anything, Topaz?"

The cat, sitting between Eisen and Francesca, shook its head in the negative.

"Okay, folks, let's go." Eisen cracked the window a bare half inch to let air in for the cat. Then he turned the key in the car, removed it, and slid it into a coat pocket. He then jumped out. He locked the door by the push of a button and then closed it with the handle pulled out, to let it remain locked while they were gone. Francesca did the same thing. Then he and Francesca closed the back doors the same way.

The entrance hymn was, in an interesting case of truth being stranger than fiction, "Adeste Fideles."

Though it was a popular mass, it was still quite late at night. Most parents were still wrapping or assembling presents for the next morning. Most children, often with a little encouraging port or, in extreme cases, even a hot toddy, were soundly asleep in bed.

Even so, there was a decent crowd at the cathedral. These were older folks, mainly, neither rich nor poor, with their children long since moved away. Among them, too, were the young and free and out on their own, but not yet bound by offspring. Many of those looked to be college students, students in an age not yet given to always mistake decadence for sophistication.

The cathedral was only somewhat different from the Gate of Heaven. The light marble was the same, for example. The columns of both were compound, but the cathedral's were thinner and more delicate appearing. The non-marble colors of the walls were different, a light beige, mainly, versus a light yellow. The stained glass, if commemorating different people and events, was similar. The people, too, were much the same, although the attendees at the cathedral were less uniformly Irish in looks.

It wasn't especially hard to find a seat or, rather, five of them together.

The last time, thought Eisen, *that I had all the grandkids and an adult woman, together in church, was with my wife.* He glanced over at Francesca. *Very different but also very similar and very beautiful. I'm not sorry I met her but . . . leaving her behind, as Slocum tells me I must, when I go back home, will be so hard.*

Francesca, as if sensing his eyes on her, glanced sideways and gave him a smile so warm that it seemed to take all the oxygen out of the cathedral.

And yet others are breathing normally, so I think it's just me.

⌒◦⌒

On the ride back, the cat, who had gotten pretty damned cold while waiting, lay between Patrick and Juliana, in the back seat. Juliana leaned over her and asked Patrick a question. "Little brother, I'm curious; when was the last time you actively missed your cell phone?"

"Umm ... let me think ... wasn't this morning. Wasn't yesterday. Ummm ... maybe the day before we took the train to New York City?"

"Yeah," she said. "I might have missed it on the train, but not much and not for long. And, you know what?"

"No, what?"

"I think we're all happier without our noses glued to a little screen."

"Let me think on that one," the boy replied. After a few minutes he said, "You know, it might be so. At least for now."

Parker House, Boston, Massachusetts

The tree was lit. There were a couple of pine-scented candles burning. On the floor, surrounding the old-fashioned tree stand, presents were piled high. All were wrapped and none from Santa because, as Eisen explained, "He may see you when you're sleeping ... in 2022 ... not in 1965. Speaking of which ..."

With which Eisen got up and put the Phil Spector-produced *A Christmas Gift for You from Phil Spector* on the record player. Then he carefully moved the needle to The Crystals' version of "Santa Claus is Coming to Town."

"Before you ask if you can open the traditional single present," Eisen said, after consulting his watch, "it is already officially Christmas. Open them all. Sometimes it's only polite to let the youngest lead; Cossima, go first. Your presents are on the extreme right."

The girl exclaimed delightedly when she tore off the paper to reveal an old-fashioned Easy Bake Oven.

"That one was a no-brainer," Eisen said, "considering how much you love to bake. One warning, though; that thing is heated by a lightbulb. It's not only a fire hazard; it will burn the hell out of you if you're not careful. Some of the other gifts in your pile are mixes. Go for it."

Patrick's "Wow" wasn't any less enthusiastic as he tore the wrappings off of a box labeled "Getaway Chase Game."

"If I recall correctly," Eisen said, "that's two cars, twenty-four feet of track, and thirty-one buildings, signs, and trees, on a scale that allows about sixty miles an hour. Takes some assembly, so get to work. After you finish opening the rest.

"Juliana? Your turn."

Juliana's first present was a beautiful necklace with matching earrings. It had come in a jewelry box, but wrapped much more ornately and with much more care.

"The emeralds are all quite real, I assure you," said her grandfather. "And Francesca helped me pick the set out so no complaints."

"But the money..." she began.

"Let me worry about the money. This is 1965. It is the perfect Christmas. And we're pretty flush, besides. Francesca? Your turn."

Francesca's gift, like Juliana's, came in a small box, just as flat albeit a bit larger. She gasped when she saw it, a golden tiara, made up of twenty-two delicate and realistic-looking golden leaves, thirty golden berries or buds, all emanating from a curved golden rod, with branches for the leaves and berries and two delicate ovals on the ends to secure it to a woman's hair.

"You needed a souvenir, at least one, to bring back from your supposed trip to Rome. That's exactly one hundred years old and *actually* Italian. It will do perfectly."

"How much..." she began before admitting, head down, "oh, that wouldn't be polite to ask, would it? It doesn't matter anyway, I know it was too much."

"Oh, shut up and put it on, Francesca!" said Juliana. "You know you love it!"

Shyly, hesitantly, she did.

Patrick whistled while Cossima gaped. Juliana said, "It does exactly what you did with your hair that first time we all went out to dinner; it makes you even more beautiful."

It was nigh unto four in the morning. All the presents had been opened and most that needed it had been assembled. One entire corner of the suite was filled with a mix of presents and residue. A train circled the tree stand on an endless loop. Against a wall stood a steel pedal car. There were a stack of games—Mary Poppins, James Bond, Man from U.N.C.L.E., and Bewitched, to mention a few—atop one of the small tables. There were two Barbies and a veritable Newbury Street's worth of clothes for them, along with two G.I. Joes for the girls, because, as everyone knows, Barbie fakes it with Ken. Against the wall next to the pedal car was a Mattel lathe.

Still other gifts resided, unseen or barely seen, under the mass of wrapping paper.

The fireplace blazed.

The record player was still going, now featuring Al Hirt and Ann-Margret doing a very kittenish and sultry rendition of "Baby, It's Cold Outside."

The gorgeous gold tiara still gracing her hair and head, wearing one of the hotel bathrobes, leaning against Eisen, sipping on a whiskey over ice he'd poured for her, Francesca asked, "You know why I couldn't get you a present?"

"It doesn't matter," he assured her with a smile. "Christmas gifts are for women and kids. All men know this."

"It *does* matter," she insisted. "I couldn't get you a present because I couldn't buy one, not and have it really be from me, with money *you* gave me. It wouldn't have been a present from me at all, you see.

"But I realized there was one present I could give you. Something that was really from me. Maybe the only thing I actually own."

She stood and, with a shrug, let the bathrobe fall from her shoulders, revealing there had been nothing underneath. Then she turned until the glow from the fire warmed her from her heels to the back of her head, and all the spots in between.

"Merry Christmas," she said. "You can't refuse it; your present is me."

Ritz-Carlton Hotel, Boston, Massachusetts

"Mistress, I have decided on your target.

"It is the woman. They have mated. She will be the one our quarry is most concerned with. We will take her and I will feast, then pass on your portion of the feast to you."

"When?" the Q'riln asked.

"Soon, very soon."

Parker House, Boston, Massachusetts

Francesca sat, nude and cross-legged, at one corner of the bed, with a sketch pad laid across her knees and thighs. Eisen lay unmoving, on his side, facing her, with his head propped up on a pillow. Her eyes shifted continuously from him to the sketch pad, as her pencil worked the paper.

When she was finished, she showed him the result.

"I am not," he opined, "anything like so impressive, in any dimension."

"Call it 'imagination,'" she answered, "maybe not too very different from what Dyf showed with his Claudine, and probably for much the same reason. I see you like this and, moreover, it felt *just* like this."

Interlude

꙲꙳꙲

If there was another living soul more advanced than a camel within a hundred *rursh*, the Q'riln didn't know about it. She didn't know about much at the moment, except that her feet hurt, she had a splitting headache, and she wanted a drink desperately; not alcohol, water would have been enough.

With an audible Q'riln version of "harrumph!" she sat down on the sand, announcing she would go no farther.

At the end of its patience, the cube informed her, "Oh, yes, you will."

"No, I won't and you can't make—"

She hadn't quite gotten the last word out when her entire body felt as if it had been plunged into a blast furnace. The Q'riln screamed, screamed again, and then screamed some more. She then lay sobbing on the hot sand.

When the sobbing had subsided enough for the cube to hope the creature would understand, it informed her, "Now, let me explain to you, *Mistress*, your place in life. You are a beast of burden that I generally treat with politeness and consideration, because my kind are polite beings, vicious, perhaps, but polite all the same. But I need not, as I have just demonstrated. That pain you felt, by the way? The burning? It was a tiny, an infinitesimal fraction of the agony I can and will inflict on you if you disobey me again.

"Now get on your feet and continue to march east. I will let you know when you are tired enough for a rest."

"Could I . . ."

"What?" demanded the cube.

"Could I have some ambrosia? Please?"

"Not until you have made sufficient progress for the day, which this spot most certainly is not. Now *march!*"

Chapter Seventeen

⁓∿⁓

Someone is sitting in the shade today
because someone planted a tree a long time ago.
—Warren Buffett

Wamsutta Club, 427 County St, New Bedford, Massachusetts

Francesca remained back at the Parker House with the kids, to make sure they stayed put, while Eisen took care of business. While Eisen was gone, she studied a map and tourist guide for Rome that he'd bought her, to ease her return to her parents' home.

Lunch at the Wamsutta Club was steaks, filet mignons, medium rare, with béarnaise sauce and baked potato on the sides, plus rolls and butter. Eisen, not being a member of the club, had had to arrange a special admittance for a small donation. Since the club had never really recovered entirely and in its old format from the depression and the collapse of the local textile industry, they'd been cooperative.

A manila folder sat on the table about a foot to the right of Eisen's plate. A local notary, brought by Eisen, lunched separately a few tables away.

One could already see the receding hairline on Buffett's forehead, but at this point it speared to be more of a pronounced widow's peak than actual male pattern baldness. He wore a plain blue suit with a predominantly red tie over a white shirt.

Eisen wore a gray herringbone from Kennedy's and skipped the tie entirely in favor of a turtleneck.

Both Buffett and Eisen evaluated each other perfectly at first glance.

Extraordinarily intelligent and focused, thought Eisen.

Extremely intelligent and very dangerous, thought Buffett. *I wonder where he came by that outrageous Boston Brahmin accent. Natural? Sounds natural to me. And I think he's packing.*

Which, as a matter of fact, Eisen was.

"Are you, perchance, a criminal, Mr. Eisen?" Buffett asked, gesturing in the direction of Eisen's left side, under his armpit.

Eisen sighed. "People keep asking me that. But, no, I'm not. I am, however, a bit paranoid . . . or situationally aware, take your pick."

"Good, because I don't want to be involved, nor to have my company involved, in anything that smacks of money laundering."

"Not a chance of that," Eisen said. "My money comes from open and aboveboard investing. Oh, and a good deal of speculation."

Only the promise of a considerable investment had lured Buffett once again to New England. It had been here, a bare six months before, within these very same walls, that Warren Buffet had closed the deal with Otis Stanton to buy his shares of Berkshire Hathaway, preparatory to firing Seabury Stanton, Otis's brother, over a small financial slight. As such, it was here, a place familiar and comfortable, that Eisen thought it best to meet Buffet to work out some arrangement for investment. He already had a contract prepared by his attorney, Lewis Weinstein, that would provide for Buffet to take control of the money as his fiduciary, and, further, that if Buffet decided to go into some other line of investment, he would take Eisen's money with him and continue.

Between bites, Buffett caught Eisen evaluating his suit and said, "Actually, I buy expensive suits. They just look cheap on me."

"I'm fortunate," said Eisen, "that off the rack, provided it's a good mark of off the rack, fits me well with only minimal alterations required. This one's from Kennedy's in Boston, which I commend to you if you ever go up that way."

"May happen," agreed Buffett. "Not Brooks Brothers?"

"Brooks sold defective uniforms for the troops in the Civil War. Shoddy, literally shoddy; recycled wool, glued together. Fell apart in the first rain. I wouldn't go to Brooks except to piss on their doorstep."

"A grudge that lasts over a century? Must be a family grudge," said Buffett. "As a man who can hold a grudge, myself—which is how I ended up in control of Berkshire Hathaway—I am impressed.

"You called me here to invest in . . . ?"

"I want more than to invest," said Eisen. "I want a permanent fiduciary relationship between us, if you're amenable."

"I might be."

Eisen opened the manila folder and took out two copies of a contract and a cashier's check to the tune of a quarter of a million dollars.

"This is earnest money," he said. "I want you to turn it into shares in Berkshire Hathaway. More will be forthcoming in about three weeks to a month, something between three and four million more, possibly as much as five but I don't think so."

Buffett's wealth, at this point in time, hovered around or a bit below seven million. That estimate of three or four million got his *complete* attention.

"Why me?" he asked. "Yes, I've got control of a textile company whose days as a textile company are numbered. If I'd had two brain cells to rub together I'd have gone straight into insurance.

"Let me tell you, when a management with a reputation for brilliance tackles a business with a reputation for bad economics, it is the reputation of the business that remains intact."

Eisen gave that a few seconds thought, then said, "Oh, I disagree about the company, though you're surely right, in general, about the reputations. Indeed, to some extent I'm counting on reputations. While I'm sure that the insurance industry looks tempting, and I think you should get into it, you got something, two things, perhaps, with the purchase of Berkshire Hathaway that you might not have with anything else."

At Buffett's raised quizzical eyebrow, Eisen explained, "Berkshire. *The* Berkshires. Old money. Conservative. Solid. Stable. Safe. *Trustworthy.*"

"Okay, that's one thing, maybe," said Buffett. "What's the other?"

"Well," said Eisen, with a broad smile, "I'm half joking but only that; Miss Jane Hathaway, from *The Beverly Hillbillies*, is all of those things, too, and is free advertising for you, no? But what do I know?"

"I hadn't actually thought about that but . . . well . . . maybe. Let me see your contract."

Wordlessly, Eisen slid both over. Buffett began to read. It was not a long contract, four pages, double spaced, plus another for signatures.

Having read, Buffett said, "I don't know about this. I don't take well to being pestered."

Eisen suppressed a belly laugh. "There's nothing in there about being pestered. Oh, Mr. Buffett, if you hear from me even every ten years, I'll be shocked silly. All I really want is for you to put that money, and whatever else I send you, into Berkshire Hathaway, but that, if you ever leave, or branch out, you take it with you and invest it in whatever *you're* investing in for yourself."

Buffett went silent for a short while, thinking hard. Ultimately, rather than answering verbally, he pulled out a pen.

"Wait a second," said Eisen, clearing his throat and signaling to the notary. When that worthy arrived, Buffett signed both copies. Eisen's signature, as Sean Eisen, was already on the contracts.

After the notary was finished, and had gone back to his lunch, Eisen took them both, examined them carefully, then folded one into three, which he handed to Buffett, while sliding the other back into the manila folder.

"I have faith in you, Mr. Buffett—"

"Warren, please."

"Very good. Sean. As I was saying, I have faith in you, Warren. You are going to make a *lot* of money. More with what I'll send you than you could have without it."

Parker House, Boston, Massachusetts

Francesca and the girls, plus Topaz, were playing one of the board games from Christmas, under the tree. The tree, itself, was just beginning to dry and become brittle. In a couple of days, three at the outside, it would have to come down.

Eisen thought, *Before it's too late, buy a good camera, and some film, and take pictures of everything, the suite, the tree, the presents, and Francesca. In fact, do so today. The camera shop down at the end of School Street should have something that will do.*

The cat really didn't have the body structure to allow spinning for the game. On her turn she looked piteously at Cossima and meowed.

With his laptop opened to his investment spreadsheet, Eisen put in a call to his broker at R.J. O'Brien's, in Chicago. It was a measure of how much the company had come to respect either his judgment or his luck that there was no time spent on hold. No sooner had the receptionist or secretary—he couldn't be sure which it was—said "One moment, please," than his broker was on the line with an obsequious, "How may I serve you today, sir?"

"What's my balance?" Eisen asked. "What is it if we close out the current futures contracts this afternoon?"

With a tone of disappointment, suspecting what was coming, the broker said, "About five and a quarter million, sir. Well, five after that quarter you withdrew."

"Capital gains withholdings all paid up?"

"Yes, sir, even with that. I must say, it's been *most* profitable working with you." The regret in the broker's voice was palpable. "Then, too, sugar is about to . . ."

"I don't intend to close our relationship," Eisen said. "Relax. But there's an opportunity outside of futures that I want to take an interest in. Wire my bank account four million. The remaining million we'll continue to play with. Will that cover the sugar futures contract?"

"Yes, sir, cover it and then some. And the bank wire will be en route before close of business."

"Very good, thanks. Now what are your best twelve picks . . ."

After jotting those down, Eisen hung up the phone, arose from his desk, and said, "Folks, I need to take a bath. For the next hour or two, if you need to go potty, Patrick can use this bath. But, for the ladies, you're going to have to go to the lobby or one of the restaurants with Patrick and the cat pulling guard and watch, respectively.

"Now if it's not critical, something's been bugging me and I need to think, so leave me alone."

The Japanese had nothing on Eisen; the bath water steamed. As deeply submerged as the old claw foot allowed, hands folded behind his head, he stared up at the blankness of the ceiling.

Which is good for thought, actually. So, think, old man. Where are we now? We're in a fortress where we're safe. The Q'riln is not in a fortress but will apparently know if we're coming so it's safe enough, too. In short, nothing is happening and I don't know a way to make it happen. Stalemate, at least until either we or the Q'riln or its cube thinks of something.

And that prospect is, frankly, deeply worrying. What if the thing this Q'riln thinks of is, "Oh, goody; let's start a nuclear war and get them all, since I can't get these few on their own"?

If not for that prospect I'd have packed the kids up and sent them through Slocum's to home, as soon as the gate was recharged, then stayed here with Francesca, and figured out a way to duke it out with the alien bitch before now. High Noon, if all else failed, and, with the silver-loaded Sterling, Gary Cooper would have nothing on me. But what's the sense of sending them back to a nuclear wasteland if I should lose? Better we should all go down now, fighting, than that.

So, two problems, then. One is to prepare for the nuclear wasteland, if I fail and we still escape, and two is to not fail, to eliminate the Q'riln.

I don't know what to do about number two, yet, but maybe... hmmm... maybe I can prepare something for number one. Same thing as I was preparing in case of civil war, actually.

Eisen emerged from the bathroom wearing one of the hotel's bathrobes. "Hmmm... investments. Ladies and gentleman, I need to go to a newsstand."

"What for?" Patrick asked.

"I need to pick up a copy of *Shotgun News*, the *Wall Street Journal*, *Field and Stream*, *Sports Afield*, or whatever other magazines I might need until I find a copy of the address and phone number of one J. Curtis Earl. You wanna pull security?"

"Sure!"

"Wait 'til I dress."

Ritz-Carlton Hotel, Boston, Massachusetts

"Two of them are out of their fortress, Mistress," said the cube. "They've gone down to what they call the subway, here, Park Street Station. And, before you ask, no, I can't track them or read them through the dirt, rock, concrete, and steel."

"I assumed that," the Q'riln replied. "Can we take him out now?"

"He was escorted by another one, small but armed. And they

both, before they went underground, seemed very alert to me. Remember, given your previous exposure, a small quantity of *forjin*, touching your body, will have smoke and pain and projecting limbs all over the place. It's daylight; we'd better not risk it."

"Could we not just forget about this one and keep on foraging?" the Q'riln asked of her true master. "Yes, I know it's against tradition, but I just don't see any way for us to kill them."

"Mistress," said the cube, "do you remember the couple of our peoples who wasted an entire planet in nuclear war? No, we don't know which it was, the Q'riln or her cube, that caused it, but that one of them did seems clear. If they know about that, and the fact that they're still here and hunting suggests they do, there is no escape for us. They'll keep hunting until we are destroyed.

"So, no. We have to keep thinking and have to keep trying."

Park Street Station, Boston, Massachusetts

The newsstand operator furrowed his head, and said, "I think you can get a copy of that magazine—though it's more of a newspaper, isn't it?—either at Ivanhoe's or Roach's, in Cambridge. I've never stocked it here; no real interest, you see?"

"Okay," said Eisen. "Well, let me get the latest editions of *Sports Afield* and *Field and Stream*, plus a copy of every men's magazine you stock, starting with *Saga*. No, I don't need *Playboy*. I do need a map of the city."

Playboy! All Francesca would need is to think I'm ogling big boobs and then conclude that hers aren't any good. Hard pass!

All in all, the dozen magazines and the map Eisen left the stand with cost about six dollars. He let the man at the stand keep the change and headed back to the hotel with Patrick in tow.

Parker House, Boston, Massachusetts

The males had left the females, including the calico, alone while they were out hunting. Something about the demeanor between Francesca and her grandfather was bothering Juliana. She waited until Cossima went to use the bathroom and asked of the Italian girl, "Are you and my grandfather . . . you know? Are you . . . ?"

Francesca bowed her head, embarrassed. Looking out from under well-groomed brows, she nodded slightly and quickly, then amended, "But only the once . . . well, the one night; it was more than once."

"That dirty . . ."

"No, no," Francesca said, "*I* seduced *him*. With, as my lawyer brother might say, 'malice aforethought.' Except it wasn't malice, no, not even toward your grandmother. It was . . . you know?"

"Love?" Juliana whistled softly at Francesca's shallow nod, then asked, "But don't you know he's going to be going back? You might never see him again. And what if you got pregnant?"

"I'm hoping he'll find a way to keep me in his life, to come back to me after he takes you home or to split his time between here and where . . . no, when . . . you come from."

"Hope," Juliana said, "is not a plan."

"I *know*!" Francesca admitted. It was almost a wail of despair. "Believe me, I *know*. And when I think of all the women he's had; what am I?"

"Actually," said Juliana, "You matter to him as much as any of them and more than most."

"Are you *sure*?" Francesca asked. "Are you really *sure*?"

Without a word, with a face set in an expression of complete and determined honesty, Juliana signed a cross over her heart. She was about to say something when two things happened; Cossima came out of the bathroom and the suite's door's lock started to turn. All three of them went for guns or air pistols, then relaxed as they heard the shave and a haircut knock.

All breathed a sigh of relief, then, as first Patrick and then Eisen entered the suite, a bag of magazines in each hand.

"All righty, then," Eisen said. "Ladies and Patrick, for the next couple of hours we're going to look through these magazines for advertisements from one J. Curtis Earl, a dealer—maybe *the* dealer— in machine guns."

"Machine guns?" asked Francesca. "But they're illegal."

"As a general rule, no they aren't," said Eisen. "Pure myth. No, not even here in deeply liberal Massachusetts. Even in my time, when

Massachusetts has drifted so far from its roots as to be nearly indistinguishable from Leningrad, there are over twenty-three hundred licensed holders of machine guns in the state."

"But . . . why?" she continued. "You've got things like that air-powered submachine gun. Why do you need *real* machine guns?"

"Here and now," he said, "I don't. And, to be honest, I can make a lot more money—a *lot*—by putting whatever I'd put into machine guns here into Berkshire Hathaway, instead. But, with all the money in the world, the supply uptime is scrooge-ishly limited, so you can't buy them in anything like the quality and quantity—oh, and uniformity—I want.

"And I hear the next question; 'what quantity is that?' do I not?

"I want enough for a battalion or even a regiment. I'll be able to afford that, or even a division, with what Berkshire Hathaway should make me, but arms are a serious limitation.

"Oh, the rank and file don't need automatic fire most of the time. But a platoon should have two or three general purpose machine guns—I'd prefer three—plus more for trucks for anti-air, for scouts, for engineers . . . all that. And leaders probably ought have something light in that line, Uzis or Sterlings or something like those. And each company ought to have a rolling arms room to issue to squads and platoons that have to clear buildings, bunkers, or trenches. And then there are the destructive devices. I want enough of those to strip off the infantry from the armor, so that we can deal with armor."

"Bu-but why?"

"Because," Eisen said, "in the first place, of the chance of a breakdown caused by the Q'riln causing a nuclear war. That's what I'm really concerned with right now. That and the need to carve out a safe space for the kids. And then, too, if not as good as some other things, machine guns are a tremendous investment on their own. So everybody; start reading."

"Oh." Then, as the implications of that began to sink in, she uttered a much more depressed, "Oh. 'Machine gun ads,' you said?"

"Specifically J. Curtis Earl's ads. Though I suppose any would do."

It took a bit under an hour before the slowest reading of the lot, Patrick, said, "No J. Curtis Earl. Not a whiff. No sign. An absence of . . ."

"Yeah, yeah, I get it. That's really weird. We couldn't have changed anything. And yet I would have sworn he's in business already. All I can recall from seeing his catalog, when I was in high school, was that he was out in Phoenix."

"There was one thing, Grandpa," said Cossima. She opened a magazine to a page she'd dog-eared. Pointing to a small ad showing a couple of M-1928s, she said, "These guys are selling Thompson submachine guns at a price less than that crappy .22 pistol you bought me."

"No sniveling; there was nothing wrong with that pistol once we realized—*I* realized—that the magazine was held in by friction rather than mechanically. But let me see that . . . Interarmco . . . I think they became Interarms . . . 10 Prince Street . . . Alexandria . . . Yeah, that's Interarms. So I need a little directory assistance, one for Interarmco and the other to find Mr. Earl."

"Strange damned thing," said Eisen, when he got off the phone with Earl. "I don't have the impression he'd even thought of getting into the business before I mentioned it to him, though he's thinking about it now. But he's not in business, yet, and, though I could back him to become my dealer and holder, his voice . . . his tone . . . I wish I could but I don't quite trust him. So, let's try Interarms."

"Okay, so you have sixty Thompsons, Mr. Cummings. What do you want for the lot? Six thousand, five hundred? Consider them sold, provided we can work out some other details. Can you do the paperwork with ATF to transfer them from you to me? Okay, great, but here's the deal; I don't want to actually take receipt. I want to establish a corporation to hold them . . . what's that, an armed security or armored car corporation, you say? Okay, that makes a certain sense. Are you willing to be employed by the corporation, until I or my heirs or assigns take them off your hands . . . why, yes, now that you mention it; I'll want to rent a chunk of your warehouse operation for a good long time. Sure, I'll pay market rates on the warehousing and sure you get a salary as an employee of the corporation.

"And I'd be interested, too, in handing you a shopping list for you to get more arms for me as and when you can. What am I looking for? Well . . . anything up to, say, two hundred MG42s or a mix of those and MG34s . . . take a while but you think you can do that? Or even MG3s in standard NATO? Great. Oh, and eighteen thousand hand grenades. You've already got a handle on those? Denmark? Also great. Mortars to the tune of twenty-seven sixty-millimeter, eighteen eighty-ones, maybe a dozen four-point-two-inch. A dozen one-o-five artillery pieces; those or a dozen seventy-five-millimeter pack howitzers. . . . What? you already *have* the pack howitzers? Fantastic. Three-point-five-inch rocket launchers; let's call that a hundred and twenty. Yes, yes, of course I'll want a decent load of ammunition for each. I'll make up a more complete list.

"Thinking about the ammunition, though Mr. . . . Call you 'Sam'? Right; thanks, Sam. I mean here the heavy ammunition. What I've got in mind is taking off the fuses for anything that has a detachable fuse, then putting the fuses in very high quality, climate-controlled storage in first class packaging. Then I want to harvest the explosive from the shells and the . . . oh, you were already planning that for the grenades? Great. Then this will just be a bigger operation. The empty shell casings, at that point, are scrap metal, we can put them anywhere they won't get too wet. I think I'll nose around for a scrap metal yard near an old, decommissioned military post we could buy. Laredo? What's in Laredo? Ohhh . . . yes, that would work . . .

"Question; if I set up this corporation as an armed security company, can Interarmco provide some cover in the form of guards, both on the weapons and ammunition, as well as for payroll, corporate security, armored cars and such? Ah, good.

"We're also going to need to figure out who is in charge if you die or can no longer serve on the board of the corporation. I think I'm going to name a woman I know as alternate CEO, to oversee everything. Francesca's her name, Francesca Cordesco . . .

"Yes, I'll wire you the money tomorrow to keep the Thompsons unsold plus another twelve thousand for the transfer tax. I won't have a contract for a few more days. I'll need to talk to my lawyer here."

1 Post Office Square, Boston, Massachusetts

"Mr. Maguire," Lewis Weinstein exclaimed, "how truly good to see you again!"

Weinstein automatically closed his office door behind Eisen.

"I might as well tell you," Eisen said, "that my name isn't Maguire. You didn't need to know before, but you do now."

"And your name is, then?" Weinstein asked.

"Eisen. And, let us say, speaking as one member—albeit a very secular and merely associate member—of the tribe to another, I am here on a mission that goes beyond fundraising. For certain people that are important to us living between the Mediterranean and the Jordan River."

"I . . . see."

"No, you probably don't. Let me try to explain. But first, a little background, world background. Where does most of the world's oil sit, Lewis?"

"Texas?"

"I see; not your forte. No, most of the world's oil sits in some closely proximate places where people pray to Mecca five times a day. Note here—and this is important—that people who pray to Mecca five times a day outnumber the people who say 'the Lord is God; the Lord is one' by at least forty to one."

"Okay, I suppose at an intellectual level I knew all that."

"Now who uses that oil? Don't bother"—Eisen waved a dismissive hand—"right now it goes mainly to Europe, with substantial amounts also to Japan. For that matter, it's been predicted that the United States will hit peak oil sometime in the next four of five years at which point the U.S. will be lining up to buy, too.

"Now where do our friends who sit between the Med and the Jordan buy their arms and ammunition? You don't need to answer; you already know; the U.S. and Europe. So what do the U.S. and Europe do when it's coming on a cold, hard winter and our friends are at war with their enemies . . . and their enemies say, 'Cut off aid and arms sales to the Jews or we cut off oil to you'? What happens given that antisemitism is still the European outlook of choice and World Cup Pogroming still a main sport?"

Weinstein began, "So you are going to . . . ?"

"Establish an arms trafficking network that will remain mostly unused but can be activated at need to ensure that our friends never run out of arms and equipment no matter who puts a boycott on them. And you are going to set up the corporation to do so. All things considered, though, I don't think you should be on the board; you're too prominent in Israeli affairs here. You would be like an arrow pointed straight at some activity we'd rather keep under the table."

"I absolutely agree," said Weinstein. "So, let's go over exactly what it is that you want this corporation to do . . ."

"How quickly can you prepare the documentation?"

There was no hesitation or confused priorities now for one Lewis Weinstein, Attorney at Law. "Noon tomorrow."

"Excellent!" Eisen exulted. "There are some particulars. . . ."

Interlude

"Why do you torment me so?" whined the Q'riln, as she staggered through a level of heat that would be deemed excessive even on her own sweltering planet. "I thought you were my servant and friend."

"I am neither," responded the cube. "I am your master, as my people are the masters of yours, and have been ever since shortly after we found you primitives. Once again, do not confuse politeness with subservience.

"That said, you have made adequate progress today. Over to your right is a spring with cool water. You may go there and drink of it."

"And may I . . . ?"

In her mind, the cube sneered. "Only a small taste."

"How," the Q'riln asked, deep in the temporary euphoria of her ambrosia, "did it come to pass that your people rule over mine?"

"We led the females to rule over the males. Ruling the females after that was child's play, especially since we'd turned them all into drug addicts."

Chapter Eighteen

New England has a harsh climate, a barren soil, a rough and
stormy coast, and yet we love it, even with a love passing that of
dwellers in more favored regions.
—Henry Cabot Lodge

Parker House, Boston, Massachusetts

New Year's was behind them. The ornaments and lights were taken
down and stored, with a single branch as a memento, and the rest of
dried-out tree carted off by the hotel's staff. The hotel suite seemed
very plain and dull now.

Francesca's nominal and notional all-expense-paid trip to Rome
being over, she was back with her family, though she and Eisen had
plans to meet regularly—indeed, he was to meet her near her house
this evening—and she had made arrangements with her girlfriend
for an occasional sleepover to allow them to spend more romantic
time together. Eisen and Patrick, too, had glued silver coins in
unobtrusive places all around the exterior of her parents' house.

The kids, led by Patrick, however, were becoming a problem. The
more Eisen thought about the risk presented by the Q'riln, the less he
was willing to take them out of the hotel. The more time they spent
in the hotel, Christmas-toy-largesse notwithstanding, the more
bored they became. The more bored they became, the more inclined
to bicker they were and the more they wanted . . .

"My cell phone," said Patrick. "I want my cell phone and the
internet back."

"You've gotten by without it just fine for weeks," Eisen pointed
out, reasonably.

"But we were doing things then. We weren't stuck here with TV that doesn't even have programming all day and night."

"Yeah, Grandpa," said Juliana, forgetting the "Uncle Fitz" routine for the moment. "We're bored to death. It would be one thing if we could go out and explore more of 1965, but that's off the menu for now. And there are no other kids here to play with."

"We need to go home."

"Well, that, or figure out how to finish off the Q'riln," Eisen conceded. "But even if I took you home, the Q'riln will still be hunting us. And there's still that chance of a Q'riln-inspired nuclear war."

"So what do we *do*?" pleaded Cossima. "Stay here until we're ten years older and can't go back to school in our right grades?"

"Point," Eisen said, "All right, issue number one: the Q'riln wants to kill and probably eat us. Issue two: It might destroy the freaking planet or, rather, cause us to do so. Issue three: You're all getting older. Issue four: I can't attack it in its room because it will know I'm coming and will be expecting me. Issue . . ."

Topaz gave off a loud *Meow* and began typing on the laptop: "It's not likely the Q'riln that can track you; instead, it's probably the cube. It has to be the cube. The Q'riln is just an organic, unlikely to have superpowers of its own. None of this is certain, though."

"But they're always together," Eisen said.

The calico typed back, "I know."

"So what difference does it make?"

"Right now, none," the cat conceded. "But maybe someday."

"We don't, apparently, have until 'someday,'" Eisen said. "The natives are restless. They *do* need to get home for school in their proper age. So, any *useful* suggestions?"

Topaz typed back, "We have to draw the Q'riln out to where we can kill it."

"Search and destroy," Eisen said, distastefully. "Or a version of it. That's going to work *so* well in Vietnam, starting about now."

"You're not in Vietnam, whatever and wherever that is," the cat typed. "Have you got a better solution?"

"Let me think for a minute," said Eisen. "And don't interrupt while I think out loud. Issue five: I can't tell when the Q'riln is close. Issue six: The cat *can*. But, issue seven: the Q'riln can also tell when the cat's close. I assume that holds true for Mary, too."

The cat gave an affirmative-sounding meow.

"Topaz, can the Q'riln or the cube pick up radio waves?"

"What's radio?" the cat typed.

"You've never . . . ? Oh, never mind. It's . . . well . . . at core it's a way of transmitting information, electronically, through the air?"

"Oh, you mean '*m'lintar*'. No clue if the Q'riln or the cube can pick that up."

"Hmmm," Eisen mused, "let's try this: Would there be any need for either of them to use radio?"

The cat thought back to her initial briefing, such as she recalled of it, centuries before. "We thought . . . that it hunted by detecting distortions in a parallel universe."

"Okay, so fair chance that it has no need of radio and cannot detect it."

"Why does that matter?" typed the cat.

"Because out hunting for it, providing a baited trap, would be fine if you could be with us to warn of the Q'riln's presence . . ."

"Or the cube's," Topaz typed. "I don't know for certain if what we detect is the Q'riln or the cube."

"Right; or the cube's. Anyway, it would be fine with advance warning, but is a good deal more risky walking around blind.

"We need the Q'riln to think we have no way of being warned so it will come out to play. But we need that warning."

"If we had our cell phones . . ." Patrick began.

". . . if they would work," Cossima continued.

"One of us could stay here with Topaz and Mary and warn you," Juliana finished.

"But we don't and they wouldn't," Eisen countered. "However, there's this thing called 'radio' . . ."

"We passed a place called 'Radio Shack,'" Patrick said, pointing generally to the southeast. "It's down by what you said was the Old Statehouse."

"Hmmm, so we did," Eisen recalled. "And I think that might have been the company's flagship store. Excellent! I was thinking we might have to go to Sears Roebuck, in Quincy, to get a pair like I had as a kid. But those would suck. They sucked even when I was a kid and didn't expect too much. Radio Shack on the other hand, though we might have to build a pair . . . Patrick, get on your coat and get your Crosman; we're going shopping. Girls, be on your guard while we're gone."

"You don't have to say that, Grandpa," said Cossima. "We've gotten to be almost as paranoid as you."

"It's that 'almost' part that worries me."

Radio Shack, 10 State Street, Boston, Massachusetts

While Patrick kept his eye on the glass front and especially the double glass doors, Eisen perused the shelves.

"May I help you, sir?" asked the salesman on duty. He was young, dark-haired, in his twenties or early thirties, wearing dark slacks and a Perry Como sweater over a white shirt and red tie.

"Probably. I'm looking for a couple of pairs of walkie-talkies. As long a range as possible and I'd prefer not to have to build my own. I'd like multi-channel and an earphone. Small and easy to carry, if possible."

The salesman asked, "How much range are you looking for, sir?"

"How much can I get?"

"I see. Long-ranged." He reached up and pulled one box down, then another.

"This one," said the salesman, "is the Realistifone. It's basically a house product. Two channel. Earpiece. About five miles range in theory, though, personally, I think you would have to be on top of the Prudential Center, talking to someone on top of the Customs House, or in an airplane, to get that range."

Tapping the other box, the salesman continued, "This is from Hallicrafters. It's an American company up in Chicago; does a lot of work for the military. *Very* high-quality output. It's also two channel, with an earpiece. *I* think it's a better walkie-talkie, but it's twenty dollars more. On the other hand, it comes with a charger, which the Realistifone does not. It's also somewhat smaller, being a little bit wider but only seven inches high to the other one's nine, plus, and is somewhat thinner as well.

"In either case, they'll need a charging period before you can use them. They both have nickel-cadmium batteries, that are good for, well, for a very long time and a lot of recharging.

"They both weigh three pounds."

"All right," Eisen said, "can you give me four of the Hallicrafters?"
"Let me go in the back and make sure," the salesman answered.
"Sure."

Eisen joined Patrick in staring out the glass front until the salesman returned. "We had exactly three back there. With this one that will be three hundred and ninety-nine dollars and twenty cents, plus tax."

As Eisen took a single "McKinley" from his wallet, he thought, *Pretty sure I could get something a lot better for the thirty-two-hundred-dollar equivalent, up time. But here is now and there is then. These will do.*

"Where to, now, Gra—Uncle Fitz?" asked Patrick as the pair stepped out onto State Street with their new radios in a shopping bag.

"Back to the hotel to start charging the walkie-talkies, then to at least give one of the girls a chance to get out of the hotel, I'm going to take Cossima with me to pick up Francesca, 'under the clock.'"

Filene's, Boston, Massachusetts

Excitedly calling, "Francesca!" Cossima raced the two dozen feet from where she and Eisen had stood to throw her arms around Miss Cordesco within moments of her emerging from the Washington Street subway entrance, set into Filene's.

Seeing her again, after a separation of only a couple of days, reminded Eisen of a song from the seventies, "I'm Not in Love."

But who am I kidding; I clearly am. *The only question is, is it real or is it simply relief at having a woman in my life again? If I could be sure of that, under anything like these circumstances, I'd be the first man ever, I suspect. No, wait, there's another question. Do I still love my wife? The answer to that is an unquestionable* yes, *but I've mourned enough. And she wasn't the type to want me to vegetate without her. I don't need to go back to our own time to commune with her spirit; that was just issue avoidance on my part. I already knew.*

"How did it go with your parents?" he asked Francesca, as they walked back to the hotel.

"Oh, dear," she said. "Thank *God* you got me that travel guide and map and made me study them. They wanted to know *everything* about Rome."

"Did you pass the test?" he asked.

"Yes, mostly. I think my mother thinks I had an affair over there. Nothing she's said directly but she keeps looking at my chest as if trying to see if it's been growing. You know," she said wistfully, "I'd really love to see Rome someday."

"We can do our honeymoon there," he said, with complete nonchalance.

"Well, I suppose . . . WHAT?"

That reaction set Cossima to giggling. She and Juliana had discussed it, had decided it was going to happen, and were quite all right with the idea. *"Grandpa's been alone long enough."*

"Be a great place for it, don't you think?"

"B-b-but, *honeymoon*? That means . . . umm . . . *does* that mean?"

"It does. We can go pick out a ring later. But no talking with your parents or Uncle Giustino until we've taken care of the Q'riln. As a matter of fact, once the alien is dead and the cube destroyed or dumped, we can go ring shopping at Tiffany's. That is, if you're willing."

"Am I *willing*? You idiot; willing is to what I feel as 'moist' is to 'ocean.' I never really . . . sudden . . . are you always like this?"

"Pretty much."

"He really is," said Cossima. "He asked our grandmother to marry him three days after he met her. And they were married for over forty years."

Feeling extremely light-headed, Francesca let him more or less lead her back toward the hotel. Cossima held her other hand, making a point of calling her "Grandma," on the way.

Also on the way, Eisen mused, "So let's see; once the Q'riln is dead, we get the engagement ring. We'll make it an obscenely large one. You show it to your parents, shyly, and say you didn't know how they'd react, getting engaged in Rome to someone you'd only known a couple of weeks. They scream and cry and fuss. Your father says he's going to have Uncle Giustino put out a contract on the bounder. You tell them, 'Well, it's tentative. I told the bounder it wouldn't be official without family approval. Uncle Giustino is going to love him. Man after his own heart. . . .'"

"Oh, you!" she exclaimed, hitting him lightly and then bursting into tears.

"Wait! What's all this?" Eisen asked. "I didn't . . . I hope . . ."

"Silly man," she said, through the tears, then threw her arms around him. In that pose, she quoted the title and a line from a movie of a few years before, "Cry for happy."

Ritz-Carlton Hotel, Boston, Massachusetts

"Stay away from the window," the cube ordered the Q'riln.

"Why? I am so sick of being stuck here in this room, eating from room service, and just staring at walls. At least at the window I can hope to see a murder."

"Frankly," said the cube, "I am even more tired of this waiting game than you are."

"But what can we *do?*" asked the Q'riln, still in the human form once known as Catherine Branch. "I can't get at them in that fortress of *forjin.* They never come out for long. And if I wait they're likely to spot me with the help of that evil cat creature and terminate me on the spot."

"Do you know any legends of your people before mine found yours?" asked the cube.

"Not really. Evil males was most of what I learned."

"It was a little more complex than that," the cube said. "You were not a unified people, at the time, but broken up into several thousand larger or smaller tribes, all of which were generally at a low level of war with their neighbors and generally all the time. It was the males who made war, offensively or defensively, and it was upon the males you depended for your societal existence.

"My people arranged peace and a loose system of government, which mostly removed the need for effective males, which allowed us to start manipulating your genes to make the males the semi-sentients they are now.

"There was a time, though, when among the males, there were ones much more skilled in war, and often braver in war, than others. Our opponent here is the human equivalent of one of those. What that means is that he could, from a considerable distance, even farther away than I can read him, put one of those things they call bullets into you, only made of *forjin.* I might not be able to save you..."

The Q'riln immediately threw herself onto the carpeted floor.

"So what do we *do;* I ask again."

"I have no more idea than you do. Wait for a chance is all we can do. In the interim, since I'm hungry, let's change your color and see if we can't start a race riot or something. At least commit a murder."

Parker House, Boston, Massachusetts

"...Issue thirteen," Eisen said to Francesca, with the kids in attendance, "while I'm probably a good enough shot to put a bullet—a silver bullet—into the Q'riln, and I know what window in the Ritz-Carlton to look for, the gun I'd need for it doesn't exist in this time frame or, if it does, I don't know where to get it. I'd need something that can be disassembled, has a high-quality scope mounted, and fires a very heavy bullet at less than the speed of sound, with a really excellent suppressor. The bullet would, ideally, be silver but frangible. And those won't exist here—hell, they wouldn't exist in my time—and I don't know how to make one. Come to think of it, I might *not* be able to make that shot from this side of the Common. With a high-velocity scoped rifle I could make an eight-hundred-meter shot, yes, with a very good chance of a hit, but that would attract attention I can't deal with. But with a subsonic one; well...not in my skill set, not at that range."

Eisen started to laugh. Francesca asked, "What's so funny?"

"There's a man in my time, Jerry Miculek, who could make that shot with a *pistol*, but he's a freak of nature, the finest pistolero in recorded human history. I am, while competent enough, in no sense in his league.

"None of which helps us."

"There are other considerations, too," Francesca said. "Issue fourteen, keeping to your numbering system, me, my family, my friends, everybody else I love in this time but maybe you and your grandkids, are at risk. If that creature starts a nuclear war they could all be killed. So, whatever it costs, to include whatever it costs me, we have to get it."

Eisen sighed. He had hoped she'd come to that conclusion, but hadn't wanted to force it on her. "Then we need to take some risks. We need to go out and let the Q'riln think it has an advantage over us, so it will strike, but have that advantage be purely illusory, so we will be on our guard and be the ones to strike first."

"How?" she asked simply.

Juliana chose to answer before Eisen could. "You, and my grandfather, and myself or my brother or sister—we'll take turns—all armed, go out nightly into the Common and Public Gardens, and other points in the city near them. The cat and Mary stay here. Whoever is here, two of us, man a station to use Topaz to keep track of the Q'riln and the radio to let the party out there know exactly where it is. Topaz can tell us on the laptop computer and by the map where the Q'riln is in relation to known points around the city."

Eisen beamed that his granddaughter had the plan down so well.

"It's risky," Eisen warned Francesca.

"Riskier than doing nothing?"

"Probably so for us, but less so for everyone else in the world if we can succeed."

"Then count me in."

"Brave lass," Eisen said. "I'll be very proud to have you to wife."

The first patrol took place that night, but, since it was as much to refine their system as in hopes of catching the Q'riln, Eisen restricted them to the eastern half of the Common, following a path along Tremont from the Parker House, then turning north just shy of Boylston, taking the path north that ran just east of the Bandstand and the Frog Pond, to Beacon street, then to Park, down Park, and along Tremont back to the Parker House.

For this first patrol Patrick accompanied Eisen and Francesca, while Juliana and Cossima stayed in the suite with Topaz and Mary, reporting what the calico picked up from the Q'riln.

Under his coat, Eisen wore the heavy tanks for the Sterling, with the weapon, itself, hanging from a strap that went over his shoulder. The laser was turned on, with a piece of thick tape covering it, the tape being tabbed for a quick pull away. Francesca had Eisen's M1911 in her purse, while Patrick hid the Itty Bitty-suppressed Walther .22 in his own coat pocket. Eisen had his night vision goggles hidden under a scarf wrapped around his neck.

"The Q'riln definitely knows you're out," reported Juliana. "According to Topaz it's flat on the floor of its room and very agitated."

Ritz-Carlton Hotel, Boston, Massachusetts

"I cannot take three of them, cube," the Q'riln insisted. "It's just one too many. Even if I manage to kill one and grab another, the third will shoot me and that will likely be the end of both of us."

The cube considered this. Yes, it was reasonable. Yes, she was being realistic, not a coward. But she was also being defiant and that could not be tolerated. It sent the Q'riln a wave of burning pain so intense she couldn't even cry out.

As the creature lay quivering on the floor, once the brief shot of agony had passed, the cube said, "You really must learn to be more obedient, Mistress. Although I agree with you that that small, ferocious domestic animal, when it makes an appearance, may be too much.

"We need to reduce the odds somehow."

Boston Common, Boston, Massachusetts

On the second nighttime patrol, which ranged to the western edge of the Common, the Q'riln didn't stir. On the bitterly cold third, too, it remained, apparently cowering, in its room, though this time Eisen led them halfway into the Public Garden, right to the suspension bridge with bodies of water to both sides. On the fourth, warmer but rainy, which ended at the foot of the Ritz-Carlton, Eisen ended looking almost straight up at the Q'riln's window. He came to a realization.

"It thinks we're too much for it. Two of us might not be too much for it, but three looks too hard to the creature."

"But I'm tiny, and a girl, besides," Cossima said. "Why should it be afraid of me?"

Eisen shook his head. "I can't be sure but I don't think it thinks of size or sex the way we might. You're a girl, but it's female, too, and very dangerous, hence—yes, this is a guess—likely to assume you are dangerous as well. And it can probably sense you're not afraid, too.

"There's something else going on here. If it's afraid of more than two, as I suspect, then we're likely to be very safe in groups of three or more. I think."

"But our job," Francesca said, "is to kill the Q'riln, not to be safe."

"Yes," Eisen agreed. "We're not going to do any good out here tonight. Let's head back."

"If we're going to keep doing this," Eisen whispered to Francesca, after the kids were asleep and they'd retired to the bedroom, "we need to get you on some kind of birth control before you come up pregnant."

Her answer was at first a noncommittal, "Mmmmm," followed by a much more determined sounding, "We are going to keep doing this. Often. A lot. Every chance we get. Forever."

"Unfortunately, though the Supreme Court recently decided *Griswold*, which allows married couples to get birth control, it will be another six or seven years, if I recall correctly, before that will be extended to unmarried couples.

"Interesting case, *Griswold*. There's no doubt in my mind that it was rightly decided. And equally no doubt that it led, inexorably, to severe damage to the social fabric of the country, that sexual revolution I mentioned to you once, which, in the guise of giving women more choice, actually took their choice away."

"I remember," she said. "But then, what are we doing, or were we doing here?"

"Exercising *your* choice, not mine. This has always been your choice, however much I may have desired it."

Francesca thought about that, very briefly, then answered, "Yes, it was my choice. Will you let me continue to choose?"

"Of course. I would even if I were not in love with you. Since I am . . ."

"I suggest, then, that tomorrow we can go to City Hall and take out a license. We can then marry, civilly. That gets me the pill. The more formal arrangements we can follow later, to include the engagement ring and pretending we're as innocent as apple pie to my extended family."

"Clever lass."

"I think so, too," she agreed.

Ritz-Carlton Hotel, Boston, Massachusetts

"We have one advantage, Mistress," sent the cube. "Although we are impatient, our main quarry is even more so. I cannot quite read his thoughts, not at this range, but he is generally frustrated and, I sense, willing to increase his risk to get us to come out."

"So?" the Q'riln asked. Her voice was slightly slurred from the several empty bottles of whiskey ordered from the hotel's bar, now scattered about the floor with another gripped in her hand.

"I think we're going to keep right here, safe and sound, until he drops his little patrol to two. After he's done that, we wait for him to drop it to one. That's when we strike."

"What if he won't come out alone?" She chugged some Johnny Walker Red Label from the bottle.

The cube sent nothing for a few minutes, then said, "We'll give it four days. If he hasn't reduced it to himself alone by that time, we'll strike anyway.

"And that means no more of their euphoric beverage for you until we have won. And be quiet, I need to think."

Public Gardens, Boston, Massachusetts

Patrols five, six, seven, and eight, though reduced in strength to just the adults, produced no better results than had the first four. Each, via different routes, ended up at the base of the Ritz-Carlton, with Eisen staring up at the Q'riln's window, impatiently tapping his foot, at the end of patrol nine.

The weather had been unseasonably warm, albeit wet, for the last four days.

"Does it just plan to wait us out?" asked Francesca.

"I don't know," he admitted. "It's an alien. It doesn't think like we do or, if it does, we can't know it. I wonder if I should try to . . ."

"Go alone? Forget it! Something one of my brothers who was in the Army once said, when advising Uncle Giustino on the number of men to send on a . . . well, on a hit, was 'minimum size of a patrol is two men.'"

"He's right, of course."

Ritz-Carlton Hotel, Boston, Massachusetts

"They've gone back to their hotel," the cube sent. "It's time for us to go find a place to do what we must do."

"You mean I actually get to get out of this hell hole?" asked the Q'riln. "How truly grand!"

"Out of here, yes, Mistress, but we're going underground."

"Anything," she said, "just to get out from these four walls."

"Fine, put on your coat, leave the hotel, take a right, and then walk to the Arlington Street station. Then we'll take one of those odd trains to that new government complex they're building. That, and the tunnels and cavities I sense leading to and around it. I cannot sense what, if anything, is within those hollows, and we need to know."

Parker House, Boston, Massachusetts

Topaz had been sleeping. She awakened with a start, then trotted to the laptop and began to type, the whole time *meow*ing to attract attention.

Eisen went over to the laptop and looked on as the words slowly appeared on the screen, "The Q'riln is out. She's out and . . . I've lost her. She's gone underground somewhere."

Eisen pulled up his mental map of Boston. "Underground? That probably means Arlington Station. We can't know in advance where she will pop out, but we can be pretty sure they'll come back to the hotel. We might be able to ambush her when she comes out.

"Kids, to your stations; Francesca, get dressed for the cold, arm up, and come with me."

Arlington Street Station, Boston, Massachusetts

"Get back down into the station, Mistress," the cube ordered. "And quickly. They're above, waiting for us to emerge. It would be a great shame to find the spot for our coming deeds and then lose your life and my mobility in the process."

"Excrement!" exclaimed the Q'riln, in her Catherine Branch seeming. "What now?"

"We go back and take the conveyance to the next station down, then infiltrate to the *rear* of our hotel. There I'll change you a bit and we'll climb up the back wall."

"Oh, that's going to hurt."

"Yes, it will, but not as much as getting shot with a *forjin* bullet will."

"Right; I'll hurry. Let's hope the train comes soon."

Arlington and Boylston, Boston, Massachusetts

"It came to the surface again," Juliana said over the radio, "some ways southwest of where you are."

"That would be Copley Square, I suppose; that, or . . . well, hell, could be the next station, Prudential, or could be any of a dozen others, since the line splits into two and then four. Or, if she went north, it would still split into two, if I remember it right. No hope of tracking them."

"Shall we wait here a while?" Francesca asked, "Just in case."

"Forty-five minutes," Eisen answered. "No more than that."

As the time passed and as the cold began to seep through their coats, Eisen thought better of it. "Maybe we should . . ."

"Look," Francesca said, pointing with her nose at the very top of the Ritz-Carlton.

Eisen looked up to see a bizarre creature, and clearly not a human one, staring down at him from the roof.

I'm going to kill and eat you, he heard in his mind. *Before that, your mate will be eviscerated and skinned alive in front of you, for your greater anguish. Your little companions and your small domestic animal will suffer untold torments, all before your eyes, before I eat them, too.*

Eisen, rather than responding, smiled and summoned up a mental picture of piles of shiny silver coins being counted out by hand.

The alien howled in outrage before disappearing back behind the roof parapet.

After it, Eisen sent the thought, "And, do but note, I'm the one here, waiting for you, while you're the one there, running and hiding from me."

In his mind, he heard the Q'riln howl more loudly still.

Interlude

India was everything the cube had promised, and more. Shortly after arriving by ship at Karachi, they'd left to cross the Indus. Before they'd even reached the river they encountered three villages, sacked and burnt by thugs, with children impaled on outskirts and their mothers nailed down to horizontal logs to facilitate forced reproductive behavior. Most of the males of each place had had their throats cut, which waste the cube deeply lamented. Even with that waste, though, there were enough humans still alive and suffering in all three places to provide several goodly meals for the cube.

There had also been more than enough fresh meat for the Q'riln, herself. The only issue was that she had to be careful not to fatally butcher the living, lest her cube be deprived.

With those feasts behind them, the cube had darkened her skin enough to pass as local, while leaving it light enough to be presumed to be high caste.

The cube, after delving into the mind of a woman nailed to a log, had decided, "You are the very Avatar of Kali, a goddess among these people. We ought to be able to turn that into a snack or two, from time to time.

"Collect all the heads here," it ordered her, "while I plot out how most efficiently to bring out your third arm and give you a fourth."

Chapter Nineteen

In Boston the night comes down with an incredibly heavy,
small-town finality. The cows come home; the chickens go to roost;
the meadow is dark. Nearly every Bostonian is in his house or in
someone else's house, dining at the home board,
enjoying domestic and social privacy.
—Elizabeth Hardwick

Ritz-Carlton Hotel, Boston, Massachusetts

It was late, late at night, dark and drizzling, with a typical cold Boston fog hanging low to the ground and filling up the low places. Indeed, chronologically, it was nearly midnight and the trains were about to stop running.

"They've just left their hotel room, Mistress," sent the cube. "It's time for us to go out and meet them."

"Are you sure this will work?" the Q'riln asked.

"As sure as anyone can be of anything. Item one, the cat—who I am becoming convinced is your old quarry, hanged near here—is never with them and yet they know where we are. Item two, after we went underground last time their chief didn't follow us. I take that to mean they depend on the cat to sense us—to sense me, of course, you being largely organic and inert—and are communicating in some way. I am not sure of the way, but that they are communicating somehow, I am sure of.

"Item three, since they probably can't sense you and can sense me, thus, I can become bait for a trap. I'm also small enough that I can be hidden somewhere they won't see easily, if at all; I think atop that statue of a human riding a horse, nearest to this hotel."

"And me?" she asked. "This sounds risky."

"You I will change as soon as we're on site. You will go into the body of water to the east and wait. When they have come to the statue and are totally engrossed in it, with their backs to you, I will call you to attack."

"And it's not riskier than staying here forever."

"The tallest of the humans, he has very quick reactions," the Q'riln observed, a hint of worry in her voice. "And he will be armed, I think."

"I am certain," agreed the cube, "that he will be armed. "I am going to give you an extra helping of ambrosia, to support you while I slow down your perception of time and speed your reactions. You will strike him, kill him if possible, and take the mate, the female—they tend to be the sensitive ones—to the cavern we found. There we will paralyze her and then extract nourishment from her, *my* way."

"As you wish. Now my ambrosia?"

"A double helping, since I'll need to make some serious changes to you when we're near that statue, and you know how those *hurt*."

Parker House, Boston, Massachusetts

The radio beeped before Juliana's voice said, "The Q'riln is out of her hotel and probably waiting for you by what the map says is an equestrian statue of George Washington."

"High Noon then," answered Eisen, "or the shootout at the OK Corral." His coat was a de facto cape, buttoned only at the top with his arms free of the sleeves, his right hand resting on the slung Sterling.

"She's waiting for us in the Garden," he said to Francesca, "near the base of the Ritz-Carlton; at Washington's statue, to be specific."

Nervously, she nodded, then said, "I'm ready."

"Ready you probably are, but I want you to stay well behind me, a good fifty feet."

"All right," she agreed. "But don't expect me to stay there if you get in trouble and there's a chance I can help."

"'All right,'" he echoed. "I understand."

They walked past Old Granary Burial Ground. This time Eisen didn't send any message to the interred.

"Is the thing moving at all?" he asked Juliana, via the radio.

The squelchy voice came back, "No, Topaz and Mary still sense it by that statue."

"Roger," Eisen answered, by force of habit.

To Francesca he said, "I absolutely don't like this. Sure, I infuriated it last night to entice it to come out and play, but it didn't. Now, after plenty of time to reflect, it's willing to fight? Color me deeply suspicious."

"Yeah," she agreed, "I understand. But my girlfriend excuse is wearing thin. I think my mom is only ignoring how thin it is because she's afraid I'm pregnant and am seeing, with an eye to marriage, whoever got me that way. She wouldn't want to interfere with that, if it's a done deal, in case I might bring a bastard into the family."

"Sure, I understand that," he said, "but this just . . . smells."

"More than the stink of a billion corpses if this thing lives and starts a nuclear war?" she asked.

"Good point. All right; we'll proceed."

The pair walked down Tremont past Park, then entered the Common at the Park Street Station entrance. At that point, Eisen became very active, dropping his IR night vision goggles over his eyes and scanning left, right, behind, and above them. The Common was well enough lit, but mostly in a diffuse manner that didn't threaten to overload the goggles.

Stifling a curse, he said, "I wish these were thermals. The fog's interfering with the ones I have to some extent, though at least I can see above us."

"What are 'thermals'?" she asked.

"Shshshsh," he cautioned, then explained, softly, "Night vision devices that use neither infrared nor light amplification, but which, instead, detect heat differentials. The best ones, which are way too heavy to carry on your face, really, can see through a thick pile of sand to detect the hot running engine of a tank behind it.

"Goggles exist in my time, but they're very expensive. I wish I'd sprung for a pair, even so."

"How much are they?" she asked.

"About maybe a thousand dollars, adjusted for inflation." He sighed. "Yeah, I should have bought a pair, even two of them, but I never expected to need them. Oh, well; too soon young, too late wise."

Eisen and Francesca reached Brewer Fountain. He whispered "Hello" to Galatea, then the two passed in front of Father Neptune.

"Any change?" he asked, over the radio.

"No, Grandpa," Juliana answered, "still by Washington's statue."

"Why is it so foggy?" Francesca asked.

Unseen, Eisen shrugged, but answered, "The right dew point, and an inability for any fog that's formed to escape because of Beacon Hill to the north and tall buildings everywhere else. It can escape a little down the streets, but there's a small ratio of street opening to blockages."

"Oh."

They crossed Charles Street and entered the Gardens by the Edward Everett Hale statue. Eisen had considered swinging left or right and coming at the statue from the flanks, but decided against it because the flanks of the statue's base were much wider, affording the Q'riln more cover.

"Anything up ahead, old man?" Eisen whispered, but the bearded and balding statue, hat in one hand and walking stick in another, unsurprisingly said not a word.

With the entrance to the Public Gardens passed and the minute of battle approaching, Eisen felt his heart rate slowing and his pulse dropping, even as his confidence rose.

Francesca seemed to sense that. "Aren't you afraid?"

"Right up until now, I was, at least somewhat. But I'm a little weird and tend to get more calm under more stress. No clue why, but it's always been so."

With each step forward, so Francesca noted, Eisen walked a little bit less like a human being. His knees bent, and then bent more still. His goggle-encumbered head jerked in a random pattern, almost like some out of kilter machine, rarely staying pointed at anything more than a quarter of a second. The Sterling was out with its laser on, closely tracking the movements of Eisen's head. It made her decidedly nervous, though she figured he knew what he was doing.

They got off the bridge on its western side, then, in forty or so paces, reached an orthogonal path, about fifty or sixty feet shy of the ring path around the statue.

Eisen, partly letting go of the Sterling, raised his right hand in a fist, and said, "Standby here."

"All right." Unseen by Eisen, Francesca had her forty-five out and held low in both hands with the grip he'd taught her. She didn't have a lot of faith in her ability with it, so was ready to sprint to his side at a moment's notice.

Meanwhile, Eisen, moving in a snake pattern, approached the base of the statue, checking out both sides as well as atop it.

"Are you sure it's at the statue?" he asked into the radio.

"No change, Old Man," Patrick answered.

"Where's Juliana?"

"She put me on duty and said, 'To hell with it, the old man might need help.' She's coming toward you."

"Shi—never mind."

Insubordinate little bi— No matter; she came by it honestly, via inheritance.

"Now, Mistress, now!" sent the cube. "Take the mate, then kill the quarry!"

Silently, the Q'riln emerged from the southernmost half of the pond. The pond was no more than three feet deep at its deepest, so her rising from it and moving to the edge was very silent, indeed.

In an explosive burst of speed she leapt from the shallow water, and raced for Francesca. Reaching the girl, the Q'riln knocked the pistol from her hand with one arm, slapped her senseless with another, then used that one to tuck her under the third.

Racing toward the statue, the alien was frightened to see her main quarry turning quickly with some weapon—she sensed *forjin* within it—turning with him. The thought of what that might do to her sent her into a panic. A beam of coherent light moved with the weapon. She had been told of these and how some versions could slice an unwary Q'riln in two.

Eisen saw that the creature held Francesca, but high. He got off a single, poorly aimed burst, aimed generally low, one slug of which grazed the left front of the Q'riln's five legs, leaving a small bit of silver behind, and causing her vast pain, as well as partial loss of control of her eight limbs as her previous exposures to silver made her body's surface bubble, blister, and smoke.

Thus, the blow, when it came, was ill-timed and ill-placed. It struck Eisen on the side, damaging several ribs, knocking him to the ground, and sending him sliding along the ground until his head struck the base around Washington's statue.

Unconscious, he didn't see the Q'riln jump high to snatch the cube from its perch, behind Washington's horse's right rear hoof.

"Oh, Grandpa, you idiot," Juliana wailed, as she came upon Eisen's prostrate form at the base of Washington's statue. In an instant, she was beside him, on her knees, trying to ascertain and fix the damage.

"I'm all right," Eisen said, at last, only to have to twist back to one side to retch onto the ground. "Well, maybe not perfect, but still all right.

"Help me up, please."

For some moments after she'd helped him to his feet he swayed unsteadily before saying, "The damned alien grabbed Francesca. The thing must have hidden under the filthy water and the fog."

"What do you need me to do?" asked Juliana.

"Inventory is the big thing right now." Again, he bent to hurl onto the ground. "Well, that and equipment check."

Taking the Sterling in hand, he fired a short burst into the ground around the statue. "Okay, since it still works, I'll presume everything is there. See if you can spot Francesca's pistol," he added to Juliana.

"It's right here," she said, walking a few steps, then bending to pick it up. She'd been well trained by her grandfather, starting at about age five; she automatically flicked the pistol on safe.

"My goggles?" he asked, weakly. "They should be all right; I was wearing them in front of my face rather than atop my head."

Those she bent to pick up, too, testing them on herself before returning them to Eisen. "They work fine," she announced.

"All right," Eisen said. He felt like throwing up again but was sure there was nothing left in his stomach to hurl, hence forced himself to refrain. "Back to the hotel. Don't let me fall."

Scollay Square Station, Boston, Massachusetts

The Q'riln had sprinted back to Arlington Street, then cut left, headed to the station. All the way the girl beat against it with her fists, while trying to kick and bite it, as well. Before they'd reached the station entrance, though, the cube said, "Enough of this," and paralyzed her in a way analogous to the verbal disability it had inflicted on Topaz, centuries before, but much more thorough.

At the station, the Q'riln stopped to glance in all cardinal directions. Then down the long flight of steps she pattered, before turning right to head toward the tunnel leading generally to the northeast.

A drunk was sitting on one of the flat benches with a paper bag-wrapped bottle of Thunderbird in hand. He'd come into the station because, while it wasn't precisely warm down there, it was considerably warmer and drier than the street above. He saw the smoking, bubbling monstrosity emerge into the station with what looked like a skinny girl under one of its three arms. The creature glanced at the drunk for a moment before opening its tripartite mouth, each of the three parts lined with teeth a great white might envy, and snarled at him. Then it sprinted for the dark mouth of the tunnel.

The drunk watched the creature carrying the girl disappear into the tunnel. Then he stood, a bit unsteadily. Glancing left and right, he headed for the nearest green-painted, perforated trash can. Into the can he deposited the bottle of Thunderbird, still in its bag, and carefully, so that some other sot in need could find it, then headed for the exit muttering, "Enough is enough. AA for me and maybe a halfway house while I figure out what to do with myself. But no more of that crap. Ever. I know my limits and I have reached them."

Meanwhile, at a mile-eating pace of about twenty-two miles an hour, the Q'riln raced through the tunnel connecting Arlington to Boylston and then Park Street Stations.

Twice a trolley came rumbling up behind her, causing her to duck into one of the alcoves lining the walls of the tunnels, in which maintenance people could shelter when a train or trolley had to pass. These were, again, trolleys, drawing their power from bare lines overhead, via roof-mounted pantographs. Thus, there were no third rail dangers.

The Q'riln padded almost silently through the system, passing Boylston and Park. Boylston was completely abandoned. There were a few tired souls in the open area of Park Street Station, right near where Eisen and Patrick had bought their collection of men's magazines, but no one seemed to notice the monster rushing through with a girl under one arm. If any had noticed it, they probably chalked it up to a costumed joke from the students of either MIT or Harvard, bearing a mannequin stolen from Jordan's or Filene's.

Finally, the Q'riln came to the currently closed Scollay Square, where she and the cube had previously spied out a place for what was to come. The whole time, Francesca, under the control of the cube, remained silent and still, indeed stiff, so much so that, but for slight breathing, she might have been made of wood.

In what had been Scollay Square there was a mostly sealed off and abandoned two-hundred-foot section of tunnel. It took a bit of weaving, and of moving some barriers that would have been too heavy for a normal, solitary human being, to enter the section.

It was utterly dark, very damp, but not as cold as the air outside. The cube could make the Q'riln see by heat, and there was just enough heat differential to allow navigation.

"Go through that brick-lined tunnel, as we did before, the one with the two upright metal columns, Mistress, and then place her down on the floor," the cube told her.

The Q'riln, obediently, did.

"I am hurt," she told the cube. "My lower locomotory appendage; it was pierced by a small projectile. Based on my body's reaction, there is silver in there. It is going to hurt, fiercely, soon. I need more ambrosia as well as solid food."

Pulsing, the cube replied, "Until I have extracted nourishment from this one, I have no more ambrosia to give beyond what it takes to turn your appearance back into fully human and to remove the silver pellet. Now hang me around the girl's neck, and go back to the hotel. Eat much. Perhaps have some of the humans' wine for your pain. When you return, I will be able to give you more ambrosia again. And I'll be done extracting nourishment from this one, so you can eat her as well. Come back with a carving knife. I sense there is a good place to buy one on Temple Place, just off the Boston Common. Look for 'Stoddard's.' Now get ready for your change."

Parker House, Boston, Massachusetts

"You have a nasty gash on your head," Juliana announced, "over a good-sized goose egg."

"No matter," Eisen said, "I've got to get Francesca back. And slaughter that bitch. So just clean it up so it's not too noticeable."

"But your nausea?"

"Is there any of that whiskey left?" he asked.

"Yes, but you don't drink," Juliana said.

"I don't ordinarily, but this is a special occasion. Please get me a good stiff belt, kiddo."

"All right. I understand."

In a bit over a minute, she returned with a three-quarters full glass. He took it and downed half of it in a series of gulps.

"Once upon a long time from now," he said, his voice distant but firm, "I will have sat on a long flight out of Iraq, on an Oklahoma Air National Guard C-130, flying *inside* ravines, in order to keep under enemy air defense radar—we were, after all, in range and they had no cause to love us—except where the ravines got too narrow and twisty and the planes had to do the up and down elevator routine. In the course of this a female major on the other side of the plane hurled, which set off a chain reaction of people, first on that side, then on mine, tossing up everything they'd eaten for the last twenty-four hours, at *least*. It became a sea of vomit, a tide of the stuff, an inch deep on the flat, but rolling from one side of the plane to the other, sweeping around and over our boots.

"It was disgusting, worse than fields of dead, rotting bodies. Everyone projectile barfed; everyone, that is, except me. Oh, I had to choke down my own puke, but I still didn't hurl. You see, that female major was a Kurd in the U.S. Army Reserve, and she had been a pain in the ass for months before she was tossed out of the country. I'd be damned if I'd let her force *me* to do anything, even inadvertently.

"And neither will that stinking alien."

This was a very different Eisen than the one Juliana normally saw. This one's voice showed he had blood in his eye and murder in his heart. She shuddered.

"Are you all right?" he asked.

"Yes, but I am scared for Francesca, scared for you, scared for my brother and sister, and scared for me."

He didn't tell her not to be, but only nodded his understanding.

Patrick came over and announced, "I've reloaded the Walther.

The Sterling is ninety percent charged—best I could do at my weight—and fully armed. Topaz says the Q'riln is underground somewhere; she and Mary have no clue about just where, though."

"Right," Eisen said. "Great . . . very good job. Now look for Larry Southard's number on the desk and call him. Tell him it's from me and I need to see him, here, right away. Tell him that it's critical."

Despite the lateness of the hour, or the earliness, depending on point of view, Larry Southard smiled pretty warmly at seeing Eisen open the door. "Morning, Captain. Your nephew called, said it was important, so I came right away. You know, you don't look so well."

"I know, Larry; I've got a concussion. I need you to do some things. How would you like to take your wife out for a weekend retreat at the Ritz-Carlton?" Eisen asked, with a brief sly and wicked smile.

"Captain, I can't afford that place, not even with the—"

"Oh, please, Larry! As if I've ever given you the slightest reason to think I won't cover expenses. Tsk! Double tsk!"

"Let me guess; Whitey Bulger is holed up there and you—"

"No, no," Eisen reassured him, "nothing of the kind. I have no idea where that swine went. I just want you to take a room there, actually, two rooms there, one above the other, but reserve and pay for them for two more days after you leave."

"You going to leave another pile of bodies there, captain?"

"Oh, no; again, nothing of the kind. Well, not a pile, anyway. Trust me, though, Larry; you really *don't* want to know what's going on here, if anything does. That's all I can tell you."

"Captain, much as my wife might enjoy something like that, I'm going to have to decline. She's a simple woman, really, a sweetheart. She doesn't have any clue as to the kinds of shenanigans you and I got up to the other week. I tried once to tell her about the war and she fainted. You want me to get you a room, or two of them, I'll do that, but we need to keep her out of it."

"Fair enough," Eisen agreed. "But I don't need just any room. I need one facing the Public Gardens, on the top floor, and I need the one under it."

Southard whistled. "That's going to be a pricey pair of rooms, Captain. Might run fifty dollars or more a night. Each."

"I figure one hundred or more, Top, for the upper one, and something close to that for the one underneath it." Eisen reached into his coat, withdrew his wallet and peeled off ten one-hundred-dollar bills. "Give them a fake name for yourself and use my real one for the room."

"Can't do it until the morning, Captain. Is the timing that critical?"

"No, not really, Top. Tomorrow, which is to say, later today, will be fine. Maybe better, even, since it will take me a little time to set things up on my end."

Once Southard had left, Eisen said, "I'm going to lie down for a while, Juliana. Set an alarm. Get everyone up at eight."

By the time Juliana awakened him, Eisen's brain had come to several distinct conclusions. One was that he really wasn't as up to this problem, alone, as he needed to be. The other was that, even at age fifty or so, Larry Southard *was*, if he could be recruited.

But to recruit him for this, Eisen thought, *I'd better tell him the whys of the thing.*

Thus, when Southard brought the keys at about nine in the morning, Eisen sat him down and said, "Juliana, break out the laptop. Topaz, introduce yourself to Mr. Southard."

While that was being done, Eisen said, "Top, when I reveal what I'm about to reveal, I want you to strain to remember that nothing I've told you has been a lie, even if I haven't been able to tell you the complete truth until now."

"I hope you haven't been lying to me," Southard replied, "since I put the money you gave me into that company you suggested, Berkshire Hathaway."

"Well," said Eisen, "I've..." He stopped them, because to Southard's shock, Topaz had begun obviously typing on the flat device Juliana had laid on the table.

"Southard walked over to read, "Hello, Mr. Southard. I am Topaz. I am from a different world. I advise you to listen to what Mr. Eisen has to say if you want to save this one."

"I will be dipped in..."

"Not if we succeed," Eisen corrected, "but very likely so if we don't."

"Where? What? When..."

"I and these kids came here from about fifty-seven years in the future. I came here partly to show my grandchildren—no, I am not their uncle—what life used to be like and partly to make a good deal of money from prior knowledge. Yeah, it's a bit of a dirty trick but, since the money came from gamblers, bookmakers, and speculators, my sense of guilt over it is, you might say, somewhat limited." Eisen punctuated his indifference with a shrug, then winced as his concussion gave him a stabbing pain in the head.

"After arriving we became aware, largely through the cat on the laptop—and, by the way, there is more computing power in that little flat device, a *lot* more, than in all the computers at NASA and the Pentagon, both—anyway, we became aware that there is a very dangerous alien on this planet. Very dangerous. Slagged cities by the hundreds or thousands worth of dangerous.

"I've been trying to eliminate this bitch—yes, it's female—for some time now. It got the better of me and now has my girl. I intend to go after it, do whatever is needful to find out where my girl is, recover her and kill it."

Eisen closed his eyes, briefly, against a wave of nausea. When he opened them again, Southard was holding out two sets of hotel keys with tags saying, "Ritz-Carlton."

"Any problems with getting the rooms?"

"No. It seemed like it was kinda normal there for someone to make a reservation for their boss. They did ask our relationship and I told them I was your valet, which was the closest lie to the truth."

Eisen then explained the nature of the threat of the Q'riln, not only to him and his grandchildren, but to the world.

Southard nodded, soberly. "Do you...?"

"Need you for this?" Eisen asked. "Yes. And I'll make it very worth your while to come along. It's going to be nasty and—I won't lie to you—dangerous."

Southard looked down, stretched his lips, and finally nodded. "I'm in. Should I bring my M1 carbine or do you..."

"Juliana," Eisen said, "give Mr. Southard Francesca's forty-five." To Southard, he elaborated, "It's nothing different from what you're used to as a pistol, but the ammunition is hollow points with a silver plug in the cavity. These things are extremely allergic to silver, it seems."

Topaz sat half on the laptop, so that her paws could reach the keys. She typed, "I have still not found the Q'riln and the cube. Since they went underground not far from where we recovered Mary, I just lost them. No idea where they went."

"That's all right," Eisen said. "We're going to go to a different hotel, the Ritz-Carlton—no, kitty, stop sneering just because it isn't your hotel—and wait for the bitch. When she comes, we grab her, cube or not."

"Grandpa," Patrick asked, now that the uncle front had collapsed, "What makes you think they'll come if they know you're waiting?"

"Because they're as sick of this waiting game as we are. How do I know this? Because they *were* willing to come out and fight, even if it was an ambush.

"And we learned something important from that ambush. It's not the Q'riln Topaz can sense, at least when it's above ground, but the cube.

"Patrick, figure out how much in silver coinage and gunpowder we still have."

"Why, Grandpa?"

"Because we're going to use the other pair of walkie-talkies to make an anti-Q'riln Claymore mine. Though capture of the alien and recovery of Francesca is Priority One, if all else fails, and we can't capture and interrogate the thing, we'll blow it up and fill its body with silver.

"Also, put the roll of dimes in your pocket."

Ritz-Carlton Hotel, Boston, Massachusetts

Hungry, hurt, weak, out of ambrosia, and demoralized from the recent, agonizing change, with her cube, which was her major sensing device, removed, it had taken the Q'riln well over an hour to limp to Temple Place and buy a good carving knife, and then return to her own hotel. The whole time, a tiny bit of silver tormented her, a small sliver stripped off from the grazing wound in her leg.

Without her cube, which was busy mentally torturing the female for sustenance, she was devoid of any senses but her own as modified by being in human form. Being in human form, for a Q'riln, was not necessarily an advantage.

The elevator raised her to her floor. Slowly, shambling rather than walking, the Q'riln went to her room.

The knife she'd picked up at Stoddard's was in a bag, clutched weakly in her left hand. With her right, she fumbled for her room key.

And then a door two down from hers burst open, and a now all-too-familiar human stormed out, weapon instantly pointing.

The Q'riln was more or less familiar with the weapons of this time and place. Indeed, she never ceased to be surprised at how much more powerful they were than those available to her own people. She had no great fear of their noise nor even of their flying metal balls, bullets, and shards. The weapon in the hand of the interloper, however, had surprised her, and in two ways.

The first way was in its silence. She knew of suppressors but she had never, outside of one of the locals' fantastical two-dimensional entertainments, experienced anything quite this quiet.

The second way was far worse. The slugs from this weapon tore through her legs, made her lose all control of her form, such that the extra arm and all five legs sprouted out, her head redefined itself as a bulb—albeit one with human hair—with a three-part mouth, and her previous silver wounds began to smoke, even as the newly introduced silver slugs imbedded themselves deep in three of her five thighs. The pain was unbearable, so much so that even screaming was out, like a human being stabbed in the kidney.

She was only distantly aware of it when the interloper spread out a plastic sheet and rolled her onto it, then grabbed her hair along with the plastic and dragged her, writhing, into the room from which he'd emerged moments before.

She sensed the evil cat there in the room, sitting self-satisfied atop one of the pieces of stuffed furniture. It gave out a *mreoowww* of complete joy. The Q'riln quite correctly translated the cat's sound as, *Payback time, bitch.*

She didn't notice that the cat was holding a silver coin in her mouth.

Scollay Square Underground, Boston, Massachusetts

Francesca sat unmoving, but for a limited swell of chest for breathing, and some movement in the eyes. No human could have told what was going on with her, in her mind.

But then the cube was not human, nor even from this universe, nor even from the next one over. It knew exactly what was in her mind, because it not only had full access, it was also preparing to plant things within that mind.

Lacking eyes, it did not see the prey. Instead, it sensed her, as it sensed its surroundings, in four dimensions. She sat essentially unmoving in the cold, thin mud at the bottom of this tunnel. She said nothing. Only her eyes darted to and fro in stark terror.

But not as much, thought the cube, *as you are going to experience, my little prey animal. Now let's see, which treatment first? Oh, I know; sympathy for others; this species has it in full measure. So let us conjure up unassailable images of two of the three children she has grown to love . . . and slowly destroy them in front of her.*

Yes, the image of the smaller one, thought the cube, after poking around in Francesca's mind some more, *because that one is closer in age to the daughter this human hopes to have. Moreover, her psychic agony at seeing, she'll think, this girl-child suffering will increase her suffering, the better to increase the energy I can gather, and increase what I can give to the beast of burden who, when I am not punishing her, pretends to be my owner, the Q'riln.*

How fortunate my people were, when escaping our old plane of existence, to have stumbled on a species as tractable as the Q'riln. Of course, it helped that we could addict them so easily to a byproduct of the energy we gathered from the psychic pain of others. Rather, we found we could addict the females. After a thousand gnars of tampering with their genes, while we didn't get males whom we could addict, we did get stupid males that couldn't resist us, as their natural males had once tried to do. That this made the Q'riln females even more stupid than they had been was all to the good, of course.

This was all the more important because, trapped in these cubes wherein are simulated the laws of physics of our home universe, so that we may survive, we cannot get around so much as a crig without some kind of beast of burden to carry us.

Well, time to collect the food. I trust the human will appreciate the thought I have put into her torment. And we'll go slower than real time, for the savor.

Francesca:

I don't know where I am. I don't know how I got here. All I know is that this is a huge undulating sea of sand, with a hot, bright sun overhead. Juliana and Cossima are there and chained just as I am. We start to walk toward each other but our chains won't let us reach. We talk but none of what any of us says makes any sense to the other. In frustration, Cossima looks to her left, my right, and screams.

Her words may have made no sense but her scream does. I hear a buzz, like the sound of a wasp only louder, and louder than there being only one could account for. When I turn I see that there are five giant wasps—well, something like wasps but as big as those old prehistoric dragonflies or bigger—easily two feet across the wings—with dripping stingers, and mandibles that are lined with needle sharp fangs.

Gigantowasps. They look... intelligent. I remember that Cossima is terrified, her only real fear, of stinging insects.

I scream. That, too, is not voluntary. Automatically, unthinking, like an animal, I run to the end of my chain to try to rescue Cossima. It pulls me up short, causing me to fall on my face to the rough sand. I know they're not for me. They're coming for her. I run toward her again but the chain's slack is gone in an instant. I fall on my face again as the wasps get closer to her. Screaming still, I get to my feet and run to my left front until, once again, I run out of chain. Before I can stand up, the wasps are over her.

Their buzzing is deafening.

The five gigantowasps circle over Cossima as she flips over onto her back and puts her arms up defensively. The tone of their buzzing changes, modulates. I find I can understand what they're saying.

"Let us paralyze this creature and lay our eggs on it. Our precious larvae can eat it all to sustain them through their early growth."

Immediately, I see in my mind what their young look like. Small, maybe an inch long, they are half larva, like maggots, and the other half wingless wasps. They have the same mandibles and the same sharp spikes growing inward from them. The wasps swoop down.

Cossima sees it too. She gives off a shriek of terror so heartbreaking that, indeed, my own heart breaks.

One stings her on the neck. A great lump grows. Now I can understand as she exclaims, "It hurts, oh, God, it hurts so much. I cannot move. Please, God, please make it stop hurting."

Her arms flop outward.

The other four then come to rest on her hands and feet. They slice open her palms and the soles of her feet with their mandibles. And then they bend their abdomens toward her wounds and force out twenty or maybe twenty-five of their young each.

Immediately the larvae start to chew on the flesh and bones of her hands and feet. Her little bones are twisted and broken. They tear off small scraps of her flesh and gobble it down. The smaller ones scuttle, chewing all the way, down the marrow of her larger bones. Only the pins and screws in one of her arms—a souvenir of gymnastics—stops one of them. The others feed all the way.

All I can do is fall to the ground, weeping. I cannot any longer even scream aloud, though I hear Juliana's screaming.

But I scream inside, in my brain. When the image goes away, I am still screaming.

Mmmmmm . . . delicious, exulted the cube. *Tender and fresh and wonderfully tasty. I must have more! Although . . .*

Even at this distance, and through this much earth, steel, rock, and concrete, the cube sensed something wrong with its Q'riln.

Silly, panicky creature, thought the cube. *I suppose I'll have to march these prey to her for her to consume them; she'll never have the strength of mind to make her way here. Ah, well, if imperfect, these are still much the best beasts of burden my people have ever found, completely tractable,* especially *after we've addicted them to ambrosia.*

Of course, there was that unpleasantness with the males of the species, until our gene tampering turned them into non-sentient providers of genetic material. Those were good days.

As the prey's torment continued, the cube pulsed and vibrated with sheer joy. *Oh, this is so good, better than any war, better even than twenty thousand of their men, women, and babies impaled.*

I'll let this one suffer for a while, watching the little one being eaten alive in her mind, while I prepare to work on the image of the middle-sized one.

Interlude

With four arms now, and bluish skin, the Q'riln and the cube had taken up, indeed, taken over, a temple of Kali twenty miles into the Cholistan desert, northeast of Bikaner, close to midway between Bahawalpur and Delhi.

To there, in a steady stream, came coffles of Jains, Sudras, Moslem children, and anyone else unfortunate enough to be caught by the devotees of the temple, who specialized not merely in kidnapping, but in slow and artistic live butchery of their victims, to feed the avatar of the goddess.

With regular feeding and close proximity to the agony of the many victims of the temple, the cube was able to keep the Q'riln doped to the gills more or less constantly.

Unfortunately, thought the cube, *she's far too stupid to learn another language, so I have to keep her silly mouth shut and speak directly to the minds of her acolytes. This is hundreds of times more difficult, tiring, and energy consuming than speaking to one or two at a time.*

Sometimes I wonder of it's all worth it . . . sometimes. But then the humans bring me a new feast and I know that it is.

Chapter Twenty

❦❦❦

Bring forth the rack
Fetch hither cords, and knives, and sulphurous flames!
He shall be bound and gash'd, his skin fleec'd off, and burnt alive...
—Nathaniel Lee and John Dryden, *Oedipus*, 1679

Ritz-Carlton Hotel, Boston, Massachusetts

"Close the door, Patrick," Eisen said, calm as could be, as he dragged the last couple of inches of the Q'riln's body inside the room. Fluids, more or less bloodlike, had pooled into the lower folds of the poncho onto which he'd loaded her.

The boy walked in with the bag holding what felt like a knife in one hand, then turned his attention to the wide-open door.

While Patrick shut the door, Eisen rolled the Q'riln over and then he and Southard began taping the limbs with duct tape. Satisfied with that, they taped the creature's mouth to stifle any screaming. Under the circumstances, specifically the need to keep the police from pounding on the door, Eisen had to take a very odd approach to the very harsh interrogation he had planned. He pulled off her coat and cut away all the clothing fixtures, revealing a monstrous creature, half human, half alien, and thoroughly disgusting.

Satisfied with his binding and gagging, he slapped the Q'riln, viciously, several times across the face. The creature emitted a kind of high-pitched keening, but nothing so out of the ordinary as to invite inquiry from others.

"Do I have your attention now, beast?" Eisen asked. "Just nod your head if you understand me."

The Q'riln nodded three times.

"Good, now let me explain what's going to happen to you. I am going to drag you to the sofa and tape you to it. Then we are going to put silver coins on you—and none of those cheap forty percent jobs, oh, no, not for *you*—until I'm pretty sure you're feeling everything Dante showed in Hell. Then, when I think you've suffered enough to be in a cooperative frame of mind, we'll rake the coins off, give you some time to get control of yourself, remove your gag and ask questions. If you don't answer, or I don't believe your answers, the gag goes back on and the coins get dumped on your body again, only more of them and for longer. Then we repeat. At the end, when I am satisfied, we leave you with coins on you, taped to your body, in fact, and will only come back to remove them if the answers you've given me turn out to be true. If not . . ."

Again, the creature commenced high-pitched keening until Eisen slapped it into silence. He dragged the creature to the sofa, then hoisted it on.

"Patrick, push the stuffed chairs over here to make a frame she can't easily roll out of."

Patrick put aside the short twelve gauge he'd been carrying and did so. As he did, though, he said, "I don't think we can leave this monster unattended, Uncle Fitz. We'll have to take her with us."

"He's right, Captain," said Southard.

Eisen considered this for moment before agreeing, "Yeah, the boy's right. Okay, Q'riln, instead of leaving you here taped up with coins on you, we'll take you with us. But first, some questions."

"Topaz," Eisen said, "I think the first honors go to you."

Moving liquidly, languorously, the calico slid from the back of the sofa to sit on the Q'riln's chest. With its tongue, Topaz pushed a silver dime out of her mouth, which coin fell to the cleavage between the creature's false breasts. Immediately smoke began to arise from the skin around the coin, even as the Q'riln writhed and tried to flail its limbs in its torment.

The elevation and softness of the sofa kept almost all the sound from being transmitted through the floor. What little got through stayed in the room Eisen had had Southard rent, below.

At that point, Eisen, without so much as a trace of a smile, took five more dimes and flipped them onto the alien beast's skin. More smoke arose, accompanied by more flailing of limbs and a despairing keen.

Cossima and Juliana watched the process with horror, cupped hands hiding their mouths while already huge eyes widened still more.

Eisen saw this and told them, "Omelets and eggs and I *will* get my Francesca back."

The Q'riln's flailing and writhing eventually dropped to a sobbing shudder. At that point, Eisen picked up all six dimes. He waited another ten minutes and repeated to the Q'riln that he was going to remove her gag and question her, but that any attempt at shouting or screaming would return the gag and recommence the torture, only redoubled.

He barely had the gag off when the alien blurted out, "Underground, down in the old abandoned tunnels under where they've cleared a section of the city."

"Scollay Square?" asked Eisen.

"Yes! Yes! Yes! Now please don't hurt me anymore."

This, thought Eisen, *is not an especially brave or tough creature. Why do I believe her? Because in this case honesty is the only thing she's got to keep her pain to a minimum; any lie means more exposure to silver.*

Scollay Square Underground, Boston, Massachusetts

Francesca or, rather, the image of herself in her mind that had been generated by the cube, having just apparently seen little Cossima eaten alive from the outside in by a swarm of insect larvae, sat on the sand, knees up, arms across them, and with her shuddering head resting on her arms. If she'd thought about it, she might have realized that the sheer volume of her tears was life threatening in the desert.

She didn't think about it. She couldn't think about anything except having seen the girl eaten down to the bones by insects. She didn't even notice that the chain that had bound her had disappeared.

Thus, she didn't notice as the desert disappeared, to be replaced by trees and bushes, with leaves and some grass on the ground. But then she smelled the smoke, strong, hot, and harsh. *That*, she *had* to notice.

Francesca's head whipped up to see smoke and fire and dry leaves twisting in a current of air. The fire was close enough and hot enough to feel the glow on her face. Her eyes darted left, then right, to see much the same thing, only slightly farther away.

She leapt to her feet. A shift in the wind surrounded her with disintegrating leaves and smoke. She coughed, then looked frantically about for an escape.

Behind her was clear, though the walls of flame to either side seemed to be trying to join together, to trap her inside an inferno and burn her alive.

Still coughing, Francesca ran for the gap. She managed to clear the gap, only to discover that the walls of flame had paralleled her flight, and were still trying to seal her inside. A quick look behind showed the fire nipping at her heels, like some vicious animal.

She continued to run, just barely keeping ahead of the flames. She didn't know when she'd begun to scream and only now realized that she had been screaming. Her throat felt as if someone had reamed it out with course steel wool.

Then she saw it, a small crystal lake sitting placidly just ahead. She sprinted for in, in pure panic. Beside her, the fire kept pace. It seemed to be toying with her.

Not bothering to strip off her clothing—*No time, no time!*—she reached the edge of the water and dove in. Around the lake the flames petulantly continued on, striking trees into instant bonfires as if daring her to come out.

Francesca sensed that the lake was shallow, with the bottom not far below her. She stood up and discovered that, in fact, it was deeper than it had seemed. *Or did it change?*

And then she felt two monstrously strong hands grip her ankles. She managed to get out one more scream before the hands pulled her under the water, and she began to drown.

With water entering her throat, Francesca felt her epiglottis close involuntarily. No further water came in, but neither could she get at any air beyond what was already trapped in her lungs.

Her lungs; they screamed and shrieked for more air as the oxygen depleted and carbon dioxide began to build. Her head felt ready to

explode with a headache worse than any she'd ever experienced. Still,
she fought on, trying to kick away the grasping hands. Still, she
struggled on, knowing that unconsciousness would be death. Little
by little, though, in everything but the pain in her lungs and brain,
she began to pass out. The cone of her vision narrowed, then
narrowed, and then narrowed again, until finally all was black.

Francesca awakened on the rocky shore of the lake in which she'd
been psychically drowned. She automatically coughed, but there was
no water in her lungs to expel. Still shaking with stark terror, she
managed to get to her hands and knees, and then to rotate back to see
around her. She didn't know how it had happened, but her clothing
was dry.

But then she heard a rustling to her left. It wasn't a bear's sound
nor anything like that. Terrified, she forced herself to look.

Oh, my God, her mind silently screamed at the sight of a six-foot-
tall praying mantis, its intelligent eyes staring down at her while
something like saliva dripped from its mandibles. Where the "saliva"
touched the ground, it hissed and bubbled. The mantis seemed to be
growing.

A spear shimmered into existence right in front of Francesca. She
automatically bent to pick it up, then rose somewhat unsteadily to
her feet.

Ah, I love it! A little hope, a hope that will be dashed when . . .

The cube ceased congratulating itself when the woman made a
surprise move. Running, but toward the mantis, she raised the spear
almost overhead and back, and threw it with all her might. It took the
now seven and a half-foot-tall mantis in the chest, smashing the
chitin and driving through into vital organs. The insect flopped
weakly to the ground, then rolled over to create a small forest of
writhing legs and fluttering wings.

"Girls Latin Track and Field!" she exulted.

Now that *is not what I had in mind,* thought the cube.

Suddenly, the spear went soft as if . . .

Francesca grabbed the snake with her right hand, then ran her
left up until she had a grip right under its head. Surprisingly strong,
the snake twisted in her arms, almost past her ability to control it.

"A rock," she said aloud. "I need a rock, no, two of them."

Still struggling to keep control over the snake, whose open, hissing mouth revealed glistening fangs, dripping with venom, Francesca bolted for the lake shore. There she glanced around until she found a good fist-sized stone, and a larger one half buried in the soil.

Francesca knelt down and placed the writhing snake's head on the half-buried rock. Then she raised the smaller rock overhead, and brought it down precisely on the snake's head. Its body was still twisting, trying to escape her grasp. She raised the stone once more, once more bringing it down. She thought she felt bones or fangs break under the blow this time, but still the snake's body would not die. Again she lifted and struck, and then again and yet again. Finally, the snake gave an extreme shudder, and then lay still, an exhausted Francesca still holding it in a death grip.

There is something wrong here, thought Francesca, *something either magical or fraudulent. Spears do* not *turn into snakes. People do not drown and then come to on the shore with no water in their lungs. And no wasps like those exist. This is all fake or, maybe better said, real in the mind and only there.*

Well that *certainly didn't work out as planned,* thought the cube. *She thinks she's had it bad so far? She'll learn . . . oh, oh.*

Ritz-Carlton Hotel, Boston, Massachusetts

"There's something odd here," said Eisen.

"Odd?" Southard queried.

"Very odd. I don't think this alien creature is all that bright. It made no attempt at lying to me. It took only one application of the silver to break its will . . ."

"I am a beast of burden," said the Q'riln, in a quavering voice. "Nothing more. I obey the one who can cause me pain."

"Do you think that, after all, you can trust it enough to leave it here?"

Eisen shook his head. "No, not a chance. Patrick was right; and you, too. Despite my initial thoughts it has to come with us."

Two of the Q'riln's natural legs had been shattered by silver bullets from the pneumatic sterling.

"Please, don't," the Q'riln asked, sensing what he had in mind.

"Sorry," Eisen replied, "but there's no choice. And I'm not really sorry."

Again, he bound the creature's mouth, then twisted both the shattered legs upward, taping them so they'd be hidden under her coat. Once more the Q'riln gave off a high-pitched keening, even as it shuddered uncontrollably on the sofa.

"Hmmm . . . now the tail cum fifth leg," Eisen mused. "I wonder, should I just slice it off?"

The sound from the Q'riln changed from agony to pleading. Even through the gag it sounded to Eisen like "nonononononono."

The alien then showed that it could raise that limb high enough and close enough to her torso to keep it from being seen under her coat.

"All right," he agreed, "we'll let you keep your tail for now."

Taking up the Q'riln's knife from Stoddard's, Eisen sliced the tape binding the Q'riln's two human-seeming legs, then pulled her to her feet.

"Put her coat around her, Juliana," he said, while strapping the pneumatic tanks for the Sterling around his torso. Then, with the alien on her feet, and fully armed, himself, Eisen took duct tape, wound it around her neck, then reeled off enough for a good leash, twisting it as he did.

"She still looks like a monster," Juliana observed. "Maybe if . . ." She took the largest doily in the place and draped it over the Q'riln's head. With a "tsk," she added, "Best I can do."

"Can you secure it against the wind?" Eisen asked.

"Yes," Juliana said. "Let me get out some bobby pins."

Eisen looked at the window facing the Public Garden. "It's dark enough. Even the moon's down."

"It's been down," said Patrick, "since a little before five."

"All right. We shouldn't be all that noticeable on the street. Q'riln, remember this; if you give me any trouble, I'll *deluge* you in silver. Patrick, get the door. You and your sisters follow. Topaz, take point. Top, left rear. We're heading to Scollay Square Station, what's left of it. Now march!"

Eisen scorned using the elevators; clothed and veiled or not the Q'riln just wouldn't bear close scrutiny. Instead, with Topaz leading the way, he guided the party to the staircase and chivvied them along until they reached ground level. The stairs were mainly for the use of the maids or, perhaps, for evacuation in case of fire, so they met no one along the way. Perhaps if it had been earlier in the day, and the maids still busy cleaning rooms, they might have.

As it was, since the Old Man had to keep an eye on the Q'riln, Patrick took over opening the doors they encountered, then falling in behind as rear security. He had the short twelve gauge hidden under his coat. That was for human problems, however, not for dealing with aliens. The dimes used on the Q'riln he'd recovered.

In the event, after descending some fifteen flights of stairs, the party found themselves on the ground floor, facing a more or less industrial appearing door. Patrick opened this one, too.

Topaz was out first as the most non-sinister in appearance. Looking around carefully, in the somewhat garbagy-smelling back alley, she came back and motioned with her head that it would be safe to leave. Eisen told the Q'riln, "Forward, carefully. You won't survive an attempt to run away. And you won't die easy."

The alien awkwardly shambled forward on her two human-looking legs, careful not to choke herself with the duct tape wrapped around her neck. Eisen followed keeping a firm grip on both the duct tape leash, with one hand, and the pneumatic Sterling, with the other. Southard followed. Patrick and the girls emerged last. Then they all turned toward Arlington Street.

The one-mile walk should have taken about twenty minutes. Encumbered by the Q'riln and the need to keep her from being seen, the party took an hour, zigging and zagging, this way and that, to avoid other people. If it had been any earlier, with the concomitant business crowds, or the prior month, with the predictable hordes of late-going Christmas shoppers, it might have been impossible to have done at all.

Though it took a detour down Bosworth and across Chapman, which is to say behind their own hotel, they eventually arrived at the shattered residue of Scollay Square.

"Where now, Q'riln?" Eisen demanded.

Without a sound she led them through gaps in the fences, past the ruins and the detritus of construction, to the mostly hidden entrance to the old underground station.

Scollay Square Underground, Boston, Massachusetts

Damn, thought the cube, *the beast is in worse shape than I imagined possible. I'm going to have to extract as much as I can from this woman, then give it all to the Q'riln, keeping nothing for myself. And no more slow time, either.*

Ugh, I can feel *the pain my beast is in. It is* most *inconvenient.*

The lake was gone, though the forest remained, untouched by fire for the nonce. Once again, Francesca found herself chained to a tree, with Juliana and Cossima likewise chained, the three forming a triangle as viewed from above. The dead mantis lay desiccated on the ground between them.

Also between them buzzed what Francesca took to be botflies, furry flying insects, though larger than any she'd ever imagined. Indeed, while normal botflies were, at most, about three quarters of an inch in length, these looked to be at least three times that size.

One of the botflies landed on Cossima's left thigh. Using an apparently razor-sharp claw, it sliced into the flesh, letting blood trickle freely down the child's leg. Cossima's resulting scream broke Francesca's heart. She struggled against her chains, raising a cacophony of metal on metal.

The fly then turned and deposited a single egg into the wound. Another joined it, going for the other thigh. Then another went for the forehead. Still more swarmed over the younger sister, slicing her flesh and depositing eggs in her neck, the top of her head, both of her eyes, her buttocks ... *everywhere*. Soon the young girl's skin was a seething mass of rapidly developing botfly larvae, each breathing through a hole in that skin, while using enzymes to dissolve the flesh in their warm little stolen wombs.

The itching was abominable, worse than the pain by far. Cossima, straining at her chains, begged Francesca to help her or kill her. The older sister, likewise bound, could do nothing but weep and struggle uselessly against her shackles.

Eventually Cossima went silent, slumping down in her chains. Whether she was dead or unconscious Francesca couldn't tell. But from her limp body emerged a mix of huge larvae and fully developed flies. The flies took wing and began to buzz around Francesca's head, while the larvae descended to the ground and began a slow crawl to her feet.

It's the ones coming from her eyes that I cannot deal with even the thought of.

A botfly settled on her forehead. Francesca started to scream, then stopped, suddenly.

Dammit, dammit, DAMMIT! cursed the cube. *How I hate giving up more food to the Q'riln than I must to keep her happy. No help for it, though. If those locals find me here I'll lose my food, my food sources, my Q'riln, and, once they've had a chance to talk to the woman, quite possibly my life.*

I need to wait until the Q'riln is very close before I do the transfer; she'll need everything I have. And, what's this . . . ?

"Hold, Q'riln," Eisen commanded, at the entrance to the underground station. He stopped, too, to put on his night vision goggles and flick on the laser coaxially mounted to the pneumatic Sterling.

"Juliana," he said, "you, Cossima, and Patrick wait here. Mr. Southard and I will pr—"

"No," she answered, and seemed quite certain of it.

"You mu—"

"No," she repeated, shaking her head vigorously. "I'm going with you. I don't know that I'll be of much help but I don't know that I won't, either. No, no sense arguing with me. I'm going; it's settled."

"Patrick!"

"I always do what you say, Grandpa, but in this case, no," the young boy insisted. "That's my future step-grandmother in there and I am going in with you."

Before Eisen could make a reply, Topaz, standing impatiently inside the dank entrance, meowed with a tone of extreme urgency. *We need to hurry; I sense it.*

"You won't see a damned thing!" Eisen said.

"I brought the flashlight," Patrick replied. "No need for your night vision goggles then, is there?"

Eisen stifled a pungent curse, then pushed his NVGs up from his eyes. "Goddamned mutiny, that's what this is." Despite his words, Eisen felt a surge of pride at their defiance.

"Well, hell; Patrick, use the flashlight. Move, Q'riln."

Topaz continued to take point. There was nothing on the ground, though, and whatever there might have been in the air was overwhelmed by the stink of diesel, welding, old mold, and general decay.

At a certain point in time, perhaps a hundred yards deep into the tunnel, Eisen called a halt, ordering, "Patrick, shut off your flashlight."

The boy did so. Strangely, though, the tunnel did not go into complete darkness. Instead, the air itself seemed to glow with two streams of light, one blue, one green. The streams intertwined but did not mix. Instead they eddied and flowed, twisted, lifted, and plunged. It wasn't a strong light, but it was enough to see by.

"And it is not man-made," Eisen observed. "Q'riln, what is it?"

"I've never seen anything like it before tonight," the alien answered, truthfully.

Eisen thought about ordering Patrick and the girls to stay behind, again, continuing with Southard and the cat, alone. But, *Never give an order you know won't be obeyed.*

"Forward, Q'riln."

The alien started forward again, still carefully because conscious of the tape leash about her neck.

"Grandpa?" said Patrick.

"Yes?" Eisen asked.

"The light is ending behind us. I suppose that means it's following us, doesn't it?"

The grandfather risked a quick glance to the rear. "Yes," he agreed, "I think it's following us or, maybe better said, it's sticking around us. Patrick, girls, move closer to me. Patrick, use the flashlight to check out our six."

"Roger, Grandpa."

Francesca's lithe body pulsed with fear and rage. She saw from the corner of one eye that the spear that had turned into a snake was just a spear again. *How . . .*

This is all illusion; it has *to be, but an illusion that can hurt you, for a while. I wonder if I . . .*

She glanced down to where the larvae were about to start munching on her toes and envisioned a set of thin steel boots upon her feet. The crawling maggots reached it and recoiled.

Well . . . isn't that interesting. Let's see about . . .

Suddenly, the chains holding her had grown. Indeed, they'd grown so large that they slipped right over her hands. She reached up and grabbed an oversized botfly with finger and thumb.

"How do *you* like it, bug?" she asked, rhetorically, as she squeezed the bug until its organs erupted from both ends. The other bugs disappeared in soap bubble-like pops.

Freed of the chains, she looked at both girls and said, "You really cannot be here, can you? You're both still safe in the hotel. So . . ."

She walked to where Cossima's apparent body hung in chains, infested with larvae. "No, I don't believe it."

Experimentally, Francesca touched one of the breathing holes left by the larvae and said, "You are fake. Go away."

The hole instantly sealed up. She did it again with the next, then another after that, and still another. Sometime before she was finished, the emaciated form of the little girl began to fade away, along with her chains. Juliana's image, likewise, began to fade and then to disappear.

"I knew it couldn't be real, though, yes, it took a bit to figure it out. But it was all too horrific to be real. And it was *way* too well choreographed to be real."

"Now let's see. I need to imagine a lightweight sword that can cut through diamond, a shield in my own size, light but strong. Add in a suit of armor in just my size with no holes to let bugs through, too tough for a mantis to chew through, weighing next to nothing, fireproof . . ."

Damnation! thought the cube, as one of its bug avatars died in a bilateral gush of gore. *When the Q'riln needs all the power, all the ambrosia, and all the help I can muster, this evil creature continues to annoy and distract me. How* dare *she?*

Interlude

⤜⤝⤞

Their Indian idyll ended with the arrival of six companies of infantry, two troops of cavalry, and a battery of three-pounders, all courtesy of the East India Company and under the command of the daring John Nicholson, already then elevated to the status of living god, with his own following, among some Indians.

Before first light one troop of cavalry had spread out on the far side of, and at some distance from, the temple grounds, to prevent both reinforcement and escape. The other was kept well in hand, as a reserve, to break up any attempt at organization once the attack went in. Their orders were simple: *No escape. No reinforcement. No surrenders. No quarter.*

Meanwhile, the rest of the task force formed up with the three-pounders in the center, two companies of foot to either side of those, and with another company of foot on each flank, *refused.*

The attack began with the three-pounders, firing on the temple with an accuracy and rate of fire sufficient to bring the whole edifice down with a few hours. Outraged, carrying whatever was to hand, Kali's devotees swarmed out and charged the, in this case, medium-thick red line of Company soldiery, only to be shot down in droves.

Three times the temple's community stormed forward. Three times their charges disappeared in smoke, fire, hurtling lead shot, poured blood, shattered limbs, and agonized screaming.

With the recess of the final charge, Nicholson gave the order, "Forward and no quarter!" His soldiers duly marched forward, leaving the battery behind, and finishing off with the bayonet any wounded or shirkers among the windrows of brown and red corpses.

"This game, Mistress, is played out."

"What are we going to do?" the Q'riln asked. "They'll surely kill us!"

"Don't be more of an idiot than the genetic demands of your species requires. Now brace yourself, because this is going to hurt.

And get rid of your clothing. Oh, and hide yourself in that pile of corpses. I will change you, and when the soldiers arrive you will be just ever so grateful for your rescue, but shocked into muteness by the horrors you have seen and endured . . ."

Chapter Twenty-one

❦

Americans: Enthusiastic amateurs with a disposition
to aggression I'd never seen in any other nation's sons.
—A survivor of the 276th Volksgrenadier Division

Scollay Square Underground, Boston, Massachusetts

The light surrounding them suddenly grew much brighter before
disappearing entirely. The impression of all was that it had been sucked
into the Q'riln. When the tunnel had gone almost pitch black, Eisen
heard a sound that struck him as very much like what he'd expect
ripping duct tape to sound like. His immediate thought was, *Oh, Hell.*

That was just before a furry but insectlike limb slapped him
across the head, sending him stunned to the tunnel wall before
rolling down to a sprawl on the muddy floor. His pneumatic Sterling,
torn free of its hose, went flying God alone knew where. Likewise, his
night vision goggles were torn from his head.

Patrick shone the flashlight in the direction of the sound of the
fighting. What he saw, then, was a seven-foot-tall, eight-limbed, furry
monster with a mouth that opened in three directions, set with several
rows of needle-sharp teeth. At the juncture of each, for lack of a better
term, lip, a single large eye protruded on a stalk. He thought the eyes
were red but, by the dim light he had, he couldn't be sure.

Tatters of duct tape hung off several of the creature's limbs. The
limbs, he noticed, were all whole and free now, where a number of
them had been broken, twisted, and bound but short moments before.

The creature continued her attack on his grandfather, where he lay insensate on the tunnel floor. Patrick saw a leg kick him mid chest. Then one of the Q'riln's arms lifted up to strike. Paralyzed, Patrick saw the tripartite claw on the end join into what looked more like a spearpoint than anything else. Almost in a blur, the joined claw lanced down, with the obvious intent of killing the Old Man.

Still paralyzed, with shock, not with fear, Patrick saw the spearlike claw touch the Old Man's chest and penetrate the coat. Before he could even scream, however, what seemed like an explosion erupted from Eisen's chest. This blast was powerful enough to knock the alien silly and send it, in its turn, to smash against the tunnel wall and roll to the floor.

What the blast had done to his grandfather Patrick couldn't be sure. *Must have been the air tanks suddenly releasing all their pent-up energy at the Q'riln.*

At about that time Patrick sensed a short and very feminine form rushing past him. He saw Juliana stand scant feet from the prone Q'riln, draw her air pistol, and proceed to start pumping little silver pellets into the beast's head.

"Stay away from him, you bitch!" the girl shrieked.

Half a moment later Cossima, air pistol in hand, arrived next to Juliana and began emptying her load of silver pellets into the alien, as well.

The silver's not having the same effect as it's supposed to, Patrick realized. *Something's protecting the alien or, based on the smoke that erupts and then stops, something is healing it faster than Juliana can harm it.*

From farther away down the tunnel Patrick's flashlight illuminated a single streak in the form of a small calico cat, bounding for the alien. The cat, with perfect feline instincts, lunged for one of the eyestalks. Sinking her own needlelike fangs teeth into the stalk, she fixed it also with her rear claws, while her front claws raked the eye, slowly tearing it apart.

Unfortunately, the eye healed as quickly as did the slight wounds from Juliana's and Cossima's air pistols.

And then the stunned Q'riln began to stir again.

Clad now in her armor, with frustrated pseudo-insects buzzing angrily all around her, Francesca wondered what to do next. Besides the armor, she gripped a sword in her right hand and had her left arm and hand gripping a shield. None of it felt like it weighed more than a few ounces per piece.

"What now?" asked Francesca of herself.

She looked at everything at ground level, seeing only the unburnt forest, the lake with the gripping *somethings* at the bottom, the annoying bugs, the dead mantis...

None of it makes sense, thought the girl. She looked at the dead mantis and thought, *Go away!* That didn't work, which caused her to think back to her first "trick," when she'd made metal boots appear.

How did I feel then? What was I thinking about? I was terrified, especially after seeing Cossima apparently eaten. But I wasn't able to do anything then. What else? Oh, yeah, I was angry. *I was ready to murder, I was so angry. So...*

She looked again at the mantis, thinking back to how she'd felt when it had come for her, letting the anger and adrenaline flow through her once again.

The mantis popped out of existence.

So, not fear but anger. But what happens when you're angry? Adrenaline!

But then, since it was all in my mind, why should it? I wonder where we are physically. I wonder...

Finished with the surface scan, she began to look up. There wasn't much to see, just some of the taller trees. She looked farther up. There she saw a blue sky but one with neither clouds nor birds.

Nothing to catch the eye, really, except that the sun is a strange color. I don't think I'm actually on another planet, though. Gravity feels perfect, for one thing.

She saw something flicker in the sky but it wasn't lightning. She concentrated on the flickering and saw that it appeared at different times in rapid succession, but always in straight line. She followed the line until she saw another series of flickers, at right angles to the first. This, too, she followed, until it ended in another line at a right angle. From that line, still another set of flickering descended. She looked back to the first line and where it met another. Then she saw still another line of flickers, this one descending from the corner formed by the first two. It was then that she realized...

I'm inside a cube. Now where have I heard the mention of a cube, lately? Oh, I remember; Topaz. Now why would I be in a cube? Because the Q'riln wears a cube, from which a good deal of her power flows.

So I'm inside—or at least my mind is inside—the cube the alien wears around her neck. Let's go find something and destroy it. Like Sean says: "Any offensive action is better than sitting on your butt doing nothing."

Then she smiled and said, "Besides, I want to get even."

Francesca then stopped momentarily, before saying, "I can make armor with my mind. I can make weapons with my mind. I wonder if..."

Slowly, and then accelerating, Francesca began to ascend.

"Oh, yes," the young woman exulted. "Just let yourself get really mad and then defy some gravity!"

With a shriek of outrage, the rising Q'riln tossed the cat fifty meters down the tunnel. Frustratingly, the little beast rolled and came back up on her feet, not obviously the worse for wear. The alien cursed. Then, after shaking her head groggily, she punched Juliana in the stomach, bending her over at the waist. A blow to the back of the young girl's head sent her, stunned, to the ground. The other human female—or small domestic animal—backed quickly out of range while reloading her air pistol.

Southard, meanwhile, took a two-handed grip on his pistol and assumed a solid firing stance. Three rounds in rapid succession half deafened and more than half stunned him and everyone else in the tunnel. The three impacts on the Q'riln's torso staggered it but could not drop it to the muddy floor.

No more of that crap, thought a stunned Southard, just before the Q'riln's swinging tail knocked his feet out from under him, causing his head to hit a chunk of concrete and the man, himself, to lose consciousness.

A staggering Eisen launched himself from the ground directly at the Q'riln. A series of rapid punches fazed the alien not at all. It sent the Old Man flying with a single blow to his chest.

As the alien raised a three-digit claw, again formed as a spear, to strike downward, Topaz appeared out of the darkness to once more latch onto one of the Q'riln's eyestalks, ripping, tearing, slashing, and biting for all her little feline claws and teeth were worth. Eisen was, for the moment, forgotten.

Juliana pulled herself from the ground. She wasn't a coward but she wasn't stupid, either. She knew that in a hand-to-hand fight with the creature she was worse than useless; she'd be in the way. Instead, she bent again and started picking up rocks and fist-sized chunks of concrete, throwing them at the Q'riln with all her might.

"C'mon, Cossima," Juliana shouted. She had to shout, given what Southard's pistol had done to everyone's hearing. "There are plenty of rocks and bricks and chunks of concrete. Hit the Q'riln with them!"

At an elevation she thought was about three or four hundred feet, Francesca willed herself to stop rising.

"I don't want to smash into the ceiling of this place," she muttered to herself, "if it has one. Now let's look around for something out of the ordinary."

It was a long moment before she saw it, some kind of silver cube, off in the distance.

Like a young peregrine, Francesca swooped down toward the silver cube.

I saw this around the alien's neck when she planted the tracker on me, in Jordan's, and again while she was dragging me away from the Public Gardens.

Looking for doors or windows and seeing none, Francesca wondered, "Now what can I do?"

Remembering the torture to which she'd been subjected, Francesca's eyes started to glower while her face seemed almost to smolder. She looked around at the plentiful woods. Then she placed her hands in front of her, palms up. When she looked at her hands, from each of her palms sprang up an eight- to nine-inch flickering flame.

With a wicked grimace, the woman said, "Let's try some fire." The flames flickered slightly lower as she cast her gaze back upon the edge of the woods. Trees began to uproot themselves, then fly to slam against the large cube.

Keeping the Q'riln in the fight against so many adversaries of such different capabilities was proving much more difficult than the creature that dwelt in the cube—normally called "the cube," by itself—had expected. Its ambrosia, its "juice," as the beast of burden called it, was fast depleting.

If I'd had a couple of the local days to torture that female beast in quicktime, I'd have been set. But noooo...

The feeling of something heavy smashing against its home shocked the cube. It was rather like a clapper hitting the inside of a bell, if not so noisy.

What!?!? What in the name of all that's unholy and delicious was that?

With a wave of a tentacle, one facet of the shelter cube turned transparent, allowing the creature that dwelt therein to see the tall female beast laughing uproariously while waving her arms. The shelter shuddered as another tree hit it, splitting then into a pile of kindling, firm up against the transparent wall.

In the creature's view, the prey beast turned toward the pile. She smiled when she saw the transparency, along with the implike creature beyond. The smile grew quite wide when flames leapt from her palms to set the kindling alight.

When it was well aflame, two more trees, in rapid succession, settled down onto the kindling.

The Q'riln shook its head against the stunning pain from the impact of a Cossima-hurled chunk of concrete. With a roar that filled the cavernous station, she arose to greater than normal height, her three arms outstretched and her legs straight.

All three lips curled back, revealing row upon sharklike row of long, needle-sharp teeth. Juliana almost turned and ran, but thought better of it, hurling another piece of shattered concrete with unerring accuracy. One of the alien's eyes was torn from its stalk by the impact, setting the creature to keening and rocking from side to side, while grasping the stalk.

The eye did not return. No new one replaced it.

The flow of juice suddenly stopped, causing the Q'riln to cry out in her own tongue, "Master! Master! Why have you abandoned me!?"

Came the answer, *"I've given you everything I had to give. Now I have troubles of my own. Save yourself, if you can, but smash in the head of the female I have enraptured by the side of the tunnel. Do it or we're both doomed."*

Eisen was pretty sure the last blow from the Q'riln had cracked a couple more ribs. Breathing hurt and movement was an agony. But there were his granddaughters, gamely—and wisely—fighting from a distance. There was the alien-inside-a-cat who had become a close friend, fighting as hard as anyone could have expected. There, too, was a limp but still breathing Southard, who had made their cause his own.

He looked around for his Sterling by the reflected light of Patrick's flashlight, still on the floor of the tunnel.

Doubt I can hook it up to the hose again, he thought. *But a club is better than no club. Aha!*

He only had to bend over to vomit once on his way to his high tech, pneumatic . . . club.

Khawham! With a ring of a battering ram on metal, yet another tree slammed into the shelter cube, dissolved into kindling, and immediately caught fire.

I'm really getting the hang of this! Francesca thought. *See how you like it, you rotten little monster.*

She avoided thinking about the objective reality that this was all in her mind; she'd been shown that what's in your mind can really *hurt*. Moreover, she was afraid that thinking about it might cause her to lose the powers she had here and now, and return her to a state of helpless slavery.

Francesca wondered, *Can this thing be frightened into helplessness?* She summoned up the image of the imp in the cube, a bipedal and symmetrical, ghastly gray colored creature, with a central cluster of eyes mounted in front of the head, and a half dozen or so waving tendrils, each about a foot long, flowing from the top of that head. From the sinuous way it had moved, she had the impression of a creature held upright and in three dimensions by cartilage rather than bone. *Now what's the worst we could do to it? Sean would say . . .*

I have no power, wailed the imp in the cube. *This feral beast has more power than do I.*

The wailing stopped, replaced by a shriek. The imp saw in its mind itself, lying on crossed logs on the ground of the little cubic pseudo-world around the shelter cube. It could not move, as if its back was glued to the logs.

Four sharpened wooden stakes hovered a foot or so from each of the creature's wrists, as well as its heels. It saw those stakes suddenly plunge downward and inward, driving through flesh and cartilage into the wood below. The imp did not feel the agony of the piercings, because it was only a vision. Instead, it *anticipated* what was going to be done to it once this female got control of it.

In its mind, the imp saw the cross being raised up to the vertical. Then, in faster than real time, it saw itself die, a *greetz* at a time, while, stick by stick, a pyre built up underneath it.

The imp fainted.

The injuries were now sticking with the Q'riln, body blows and old silver wounds, a missing eye and another damaged by the damned cat, and its body burning inside from the presence of three small chunks of silver.

The taller female continued to rain rock and concrete down upon it, from a distance, causing bruises, weeping cuts, and pain.

Suddenly, from out of the darkness came the adult human, its projectile weapon held in its hands like a club. It raised the club up, then brought it down to smash the Q'riln's head.

The alien blocked the blow with a limb, which the club broke. The pain of that raised another wail. It lashed out, once again sending the human male sprawling. Then, still realizing that her only salvation lay in killing the paralyzed female, the Q'riln resumed its now ponderous progress to where she sat propped against the tunnel wall.

Patrick hadn't been able to do anything so far. Like Juliana, he'd realized that he was not large or strong enough to do any physical damage with feet or fists. Like her, he'd realized that he'd just be in the way. He also knew that the lead of the shotgun would have little, if any, effect on the alien, while he'd be risking hitting the cat or his grandfather or Mr. Southard if he'd tried.

The boy thought frantically, *What can I do? What can I do? My shotgun is useless, or close enough to it. I can't ... oh, wait, I have the silver dimes, I can throw them at the Q'riln and at least hurt it, without risking Topaz. But . . . there's something else, something I'm missing. Aha! Useless? Oh, hell, no, it isn't!*

Suddenly inspired, from his pocket Patrick drew the full roll of dimes. Like a minuteman of old, if not far, biting off a cartridge and pouring the powder down his musket on a certain warm April day, he bit open the roll of domes, then upended it the muzzle of the twelve gauge, letting a dozen or thirteen of the dimes fall down the barrel.

Then, steeling his nerve, he raced under the arc of his sisters' flying rocks and concrete, causing Juliana to exclaim, "Patrick, no!"

He ignored her, continuing to close on the Q'riln until he stood right beside the alien, who was almost upon Francesca. Then, placing the muzzle of the short twelve gauge nearly against the thing, he braced himself—more mentally than physically—and pulled the trigger.

Inside the shotgun, a firing pin flew forward to dent a primer, causing the primer to explode. The shock, heat, and flame of the primer went to the propellant, causing it, likewise, to deflagrate into a cloud of expanding gases under high pressure. The pressure, in its turn, began to force the cup holding the lead buckshot in the only direction it could go, down the barrel. The buckshot, for its part, likewise drove the silver dimes forward, forward and out the muzzle . . . and deep into the Q'riln, tearing and slashing all the way.

The recoil also spun Patrick around, even as it knocked him to the tunnel floor. No matter; he was young, resilient, strong for his size and age, and quick. In a flash, even though a little stunned—a shotgun blast in a tunnel will stun anyone, even if muffled in a large body—he was back on his feet, shotgun in hand, muzzle up, and pouring another load of dimes down the barrel.

Thank God, thought the boy, *that most of the blast went into the Q'riln. Hate to even think about what would have happened if I'd fired from any distance.*

He placed the muzzle, once again, in close proximity to the alien and, once again, pulled the trigger.

Between the rain of rocks and concrete, the attacks from the teeth and claws of the cat, and the blow of the adult male's submachine gun turned club, the Q'riln hadn't even noticed the boy pitter-pattering up to her.

She noticed the blast of his shotgun, though. She felt the silver dimes as they penetrated her skin and then separated out into a dozen or more poisoned tracks, scattering through her body, not merely damaging and destroying vital organs but setting them aflame wherever the dimes settled inside her.

The pain was analogous to a human being having their kidneys instantly shredded. It was, in short, so painful that the Q'riln could do nothing but look upwards, three-sided mouth agape, while waving its head about in total silence.

For a change, it was the reawakened imp that felt the pain of the passage of the silver through the Q'riln. Connected as they were, by centuries of polite if ruthless bondage and control, it still hadn't imagined that there could be such agony for one of its species. It instantly cut the bond with the Q'riln, leaving itself deaf, dumb, and blind as regarded its surroundings. Ordinarily, yes, it could sense matters outside its shelter. But this was not an ordinary time, the imp being in agony from the Q'riln's wounds, as well as beginning to roast from the flames now flaring on all sides of its shelter.

And hate? The hate that flowed from the human female was intolerable in intensity. Usually, too, the creatures it tortured, mentally or, by arrangement, physically, hated their torment. But they never saw the ultimate cause. This vicious skinny feral female knew what was behind her previous suffering; knew and *hated* the one responsible. That hate became a mental pain, while the mental pain began to manifest itself as oozing sores, breaking out all over the imp's body.

It wept in self-pity. Finally, with the remains of its strength, it cast the mind of the human female out of the shelter, stopping her pains and its.

For a third time, young Patrick lifted himself from the tunnel's damp and muddy floor. The shotgun was somewhere behind him, having ripped itself from his hands. In the dim light from his cast aside flashlight he searched for it, finally spotting its blued barrel against where the tunnel floor met the curving wall. He walked as briskly as the light allowed to it, picking it up.

The boy's hand squeezed the roll of silver dimes. He judged, *Twenty-five, at least, left, I think.* A dozen more of these he poured down the barrel. He then walked to the Q'riln.

It was making a sound now, all sibilant Ss and guttural Ds and Ks and Ts. As he approached it, the incomprehensible sound became quite comprehensible in his mind. It was the Q'riln begging, *Please! Please! Finish this. One more shot to my head and I will be free of the agony and free of my bondage to the cube.*

Perhaps the cat understood, too, because she left off her destructive work and retreated.

Unseen by the alien—at least, Patrick didn't know how it could see him—the boy nodded. He took a few more steps toward the alien, then got down on one knee. He had kept the shotgun's muzzle high through all this—or, at least, everything but the actual shooting—so as to keep the dimes in the barrel. That wouldn't be possible with the Q'riln on the tunnel floor. Reaching down a few times, the boy grabbed a small quantity of mud which he fed down the barrel over the dimes. When a couple of shakes of the shotgun told him that the dimes were held well enough not to fall out, he knelt down and placed the shotgun right against the Q'riln's cranium.

Thank you, the alien passed to the boy's mind. He pulled the trigger for the final time. This time, the shotgun neither flew away nor knocked him to his rear.

Practice, I guess, thought the boy.

Surprisingly, the Q'riln's head didn't just explode the way a human's might have. However its cranium was set up, it allowed the head to expand to two or perhaps three times its normal size, before collapsing again into a misshapen lump. Some of the teeth went flying, and one of the remaining eyestalks jumped to slam against the tunnel's ceiling. The body shuddered a few times and then was still, but for smoke and what was probably something like blood, pouring from the open wounds.

Patrick became aware of his grandfather standing beside him, to his right, holding his damaged ribs with that arm, and the damaged Sterling in his left hand. Juliana was on the other side of the Old Man, helping him to stand with one arm, while holding Topaz with the other.

Southard was rising groggily from the tunnel's damp and muddy floor.

"Well done, Grandson," the Old Man said, a sentiment echoed by Juliana who added, "I saw what you did. It was very brave."

Moments later Francesca appeared to his left, holding out a cube on a chain. She looked down at the corpse of the Q'riln, then over at the shotgun hanging loosely from her future step-grandson's hand.

"Well done, Patrick. Well done."

"What's in the cube, Francesca?" asked Eisen.

"The imp that controlled the Q'riln," the girl replied. "It is evil and must be destroyed."

Don't destroy me! The grandfather heard in his mind, faintly and weakly. *I can make you long-lived, wealthy, powerful! Just see what I can do.*

With that, the Q'riln's body began to combust, from the inside out. Smoke, much denser than before, poured from the holes made by Patrick's shotgun. As the smoke poured out the body shrank in on itself. All the humans present began to cough at the noxious smoke.

"Let's get out of here," Eisen said.

"Where to, Grandpa?" Cossima asked. "Back to the hotel?"

"No," he said, shaking his head. "We're going to Park Street Station, the Green Line level. But first my night vision goggles."

Casting a glance at Francesca, he said, "I think I'll need you to help me."

"Gladly," the woman replied.

They searched until they found the goggles, which were, unfortunately, broken beyond hope of repair.

"No matter," said Eisen, stuffing the pieces into his overcoat pocket. "They were cheap enough. I just want to make sure they don't screw up history for us."

Before they left the tunnel completely Patrick turned around, playing his recovered flashlight over the spot where the Q'riln's corpse had been. There was nothing there but an oily spot with a light haze over it.

Over the Milwaukee Deep, Puerto Rico Trench, Atlantic Ocean

Eisen's first instinct had been to take the cube to the Park Street Station, and lay it upon the tracks for a trolley to crush.

Francesca killed that idea. "We don't know what it will do to crack the case. That thing came across universes; there's no telling what kind of energy is stored there. I mean, I *used* some of that energy. It was immense."

"What do you suggest then?" Eisen had asked.

"Cover it in something heavy and drop it deep into the ocean. Unless you can launch it into space."

"Out of my league, the latter, but I can easily afford a charter boat to take me out of Puerto Rico."

They'd all flown to Puerto Rico, less Francesca, who was already having serious trouble with her parents, trouble that, now, would not end until she was safely married off. The cube was there, too, but buried inside a ball of silver that had, in molten state, been poured around it.

From San Juan they'd taken a well-recommended charter boat, out over the Puerto Rico Trench.

Eisen made himself stand straight against the pain of his cracked ribs, keeping his face stoic. *No sense inviting the attentions of the captain, after all.*

"Which of you wants to do the execution?" he asked the kids.

No, don't, intoned the mental voice of the imp. *Please, please, don't? I beg you . . .*

"Cossima should," Juliana announced. "She's got the mean streak. And Patrick already killed the Q'riln."

"Here, Cossima," Eisen said, passing over the cube in its three-inch ball of silver, its chain sticking out almost a foot.

"Over the side with it."

Reaching out one hand, the girl tipped it over, releasing the still begging and whining cube, rather, its imp inhabitant, to fall to the sea below. It hit with an unremarkable splash and then was lost to sight.

Eisen shouted to the skipper, "We can go back now."

"But there's some good fishing," the captain objected.

"We were here to give something to the sea, not to take it."

"Your dime," answered the captain.

They'd gone perhaps a quarter of a mile when a great bubble arose from the sea behind them, something reminiscent of a torpedo explosion, or a naval mine.

"What the . . ." asked Patrick.

"I think it self-destructed," Eisen replied. "I didn't expect that, though in retrospect, I should have. This being young and immature is not all it's cracked up to be. I should have left you and your sisters back in Boston."

661b East Broadway, South Boston, Massachusetts

It was dark along Broadway, but at least it wasn't raining this time. Christmas was long over now. The goodies gained in their trip, from ornaments to lights to a chess set and weapons, along with everything else in between, all were safely stored in a place that the Museum of Fine Arts had recommended to Eisen. Francesca had both a wedding ring and an enormous engagement ring to show her parents.

It had been Francesca, the aspiring nurse practitioner, who'd said, back at the hotel, when he'd considered going to a doctor, "Ribs heal themselves. The important thing is to keep breathing deeply, even if it hurts, to avoid pneumonia."

They still hurt, some, but, at least, Eisen had avoided pneumonia, a potential killer.

He'd taken one more short walk to 110 I Street, to say goodbye to his dog.

"Suzy," said a kneeling Eisen to the boxer around which he had his arms, "I have to go and you can't come with me. The me that is now needs you more than I will in the future. I don't suppose you'll understand but, go home, Suzy girl, little Sean is crying for you!" With that, Eisen pointed in the direction of home.

The dog made no human sign of understanding. Instead, it licked Eisen's face, then turned and trotted back toward home at 110 I Street, right across from the big rock house where the Great Being lived. She stopped once to look back, at the corner of I and Broadway, right by Morrey's pharmacy. With that, the dog turned and was gone.

Eisen dashed away a few tears, certain at that moment he'd never see his best little four-footed friend again.

The dog hadn't cried or whined. Francesca, on the other hand, was crying freely. As soon as Eisen stood she leaned into him, wrapping her arms around him and quietly pleading with him to stay. "Will you at least promise to come back?" she begged.

"I will," he said. "I do. I have responsibilities I cannot let go and a few things to set up. But I'll come back as soon as I can. I don't really understand the gate but I will come back. I may look older."

With that he planted a not especially chaste kiss on her, albeit on her forehead.

With shallow nods and a good deal of sniffling, she accepted that as the best he could offer, for now.

Hefting the heavy duffel bag they'd been using since coming to this time, Eisen ordered, "Patrick, break us in."

Once inside, Juliana asked, "And just what the hell is going on there, Grandpa?"

"Going on where?" he asked.

She pointed at the front window on the "safe" side of Slocum's Toyland. When he looked he saw his currently young self, holding Francesca very tightly, indeed, and giving her a kiss that was, oh, as far from chaste as it's possible to go. Mr. Southard, off to one side, grinned broadly. Another woman looked on with a warm and approving smile.

"Oh," he said. "That means that taking care of business, uptime, was easier than I'd expected. Well then . . . come on."

One by one, the four of them, plus Topaz, on Cossima's arm, with Mary riding the cat's collar, ascended Old Man Slocum's ladder. Cossima went first to ensure the gate would open. She passed into the vestibule, followed one by one by the others.

Eisen went last. As he entered the vestibule he gave one final thought to Suzy. He was then shocked when a glowing ball struck him and he found a little boxer puppy in his arms, eagerly licking his face.

All he could say was, "I've got my own frien' doggie, Uncle Billy." Then he gave off a laugh such as his grandchildren had never before heard come out of him. Almost shouting, he said, once again, "No Unca Billy; I already foun' my own frien' doggie."

His grandchildren and the cat looked at him oddly, until they saw the boxer puppy.

"Which leads me to a question," the Old Man said. "Who- or whatever is running this thing, can you talk?"

A deep rumbling voice answered, "Do you have any idea how long I've been waiting for someone to ask that? Do you have any idea what it's like to . . . no, of course, you don't."

"You are the gate?" Eisen asked.

"I am the intelligence that controls the gates on this level and the next," was the response, still deep and rumbling.

"You gave me my dog back?"

"I read how much you missed her in your mind and gave her back to you, yes. Only this version is a lot healthier. She'll outlive you, or she could."

"Are you," Eisen asked, "specifically *here?*"

"You mean in this place you think of as the vestibule? No. I am connected to all the vestibules on . . . no, that's not the right way to say it, *under* this system of gates."

"Do you have a name?" Cossima asked.

"No. Do you want to give me one?" the gate asked.

"How about Portia?" Eisen asked. "Portia doesn't really mean gate, but at least it sounds somewhat the same as portal."

"Portia would be fine." For reasons unknown, the deep rumbling voice changed to something much sweeter and decidedly feminine.

"So . . . ummm . . . how specific can you be with the changes you make and the material you provide?"

"Pretty specific," answered Portia.

"Can you return me to my previous age on the outside, but with young, completely serviceable organs, bones, ligaments, and—be still my heart—perfect short-term memory?"

"Yes," Portia said. "Not even hard if I have the power which, at the moment, I do."

"Can you close this entrance, and move it to some other place?"

"Yes, within reason. I can open other gates to you, for different times and places, too, if you like."

"What are the limits?" Eisen asked.

"Power," Portia answered. "It takes an enormous amount to maintain the system. I can only do so much beyond that. And I cannot send you to your own future, not even by so much as a minute, though the cat I can, since she is from elsewhere where they have their own gates. And I can't raise the dead. I can't make anyone fall in love with you. I can't make you as needlessly verbose as William F. Buckley, either. I can't—"

"Wait," Juliana shouted, "something I've been struggling with just came clear. It was seeing you, Grandpa, with Francesca, and who I suspect is Topaz, that was the final clue I needed.

"Portia, please make Topaz—that's the kitty—human again and the age she was when her mate was killed. She'll need to look no different than she was then."

Cossima shouted, as suddenly the cat ceased to be a cat and was far too heavy for a little girl to support. The alien woman settled gracefully to her own feet.

"Why, Topaz," said Eisen, "you are even prettier as a woman."

"You, Mr. Eisen, are shameless," said Topaz, giving him a scolding, wagging finger. "You are now flirting with a being who is not only from a different planet, and a different species, but you knew her most recently as a cat!"

"So?" he asked.

"So." Topaz shrugged.

Turning to the elder of the girls, Topaz, now in fine human female form, asked, "What are you thinking of, Juliana?"

"Yeah, that was you with Grandpa and Francesca. I'm thinking of Mica. We can save him for you."

"How's that? He's already dead. We can't change that."

"How do you know he's dead?" Juliana asked.

"I saw him stabbed several times and then saw his body fall to the ground."

"How do you know it was him?"

"Because . . . what are you thinking?"

"Portia?"

"Yes, Miss? May I call you Juliana?"

"Please do. Can you build a replica of Mica, Topaz's mate, and build it to be controlled by and support Mary."

"Who's Mary?" Portia asked. "I don't know any . . ."

"This is Mary," Topaz said, holding the little spiderlike AI up in the palm of her hand.

"I can do that," the gate said. "Not hard either, or wouldn't be, if I had a model to work with and the power. I'll need a while, perhaps as much as three weeks, to amass the power."

"Everything known about Mica is either in my mind or Mary's drive," Topaz said. "But I don't see . . . what about temporal paradox?"

"In the first place," said Juliana, "my grandfather raised holy hell in South Boston to rescue me. But we didn't disappear. So clearly time is not as fragile as some might have thought. In the second place, though, with Mary playing a perfect version of Mica, you will see Mica, as you think he is, die, but we'll have replaced him out of sight with Mary. Then we rescue Mary from the body and come back here."

"I'm game if you are," Eisen told Topaz.

"To get my mate back? To bear offspring? Oh, yes, very, very yes."

"All right, but you and I, not the kids," Eisen said. "It's time for them to settle down and get ready for school. But, yes, I'm willing to go back and save your mate.

"But first, I need to go and tidy matters up uptime, and take the kids back to their parents."

"Awww, Grandpa," came from three young voices.

"Don't worry, brats; we're going to take a lot more trips together. I foresee it."

In Memoriam

Eric Flint, 6 February 1947–17 July 2022

My friend and colleague, Eric Flint, passed in July of 2022. Yes, he was a communist, specifically, a Trot, I think, or, at least heavily influenced by Leon Trotsky. In any case, he wasn't called "Eric the Red," for nothing. But something people could easily miss; Commie or not, Eric loved the United States of America and her people with a light burning so brightly that no black hole could have hoped to contain that light.

Moreover, though I think he was wrong, deeply wrong, about Communism's prospects and benefits, and never hesitated to say so, Eric took that in *good* spirits, always ready to argue the points. It's also true that he brought an intellectual rigor to the matter that the weak, useless, oversensitive turds of the modern left seem completely to lack. You could *talk* to Eric, disagree completely, argue vociferously, and with no offense on either side. And I quote, "The mere fact, Tom, that someday we may find ourselves shooting at each other in a civil war is no reason not to enjoy a good dinner and discussion now." See? That's a *mensch* in action.

Eric was an atheist. At the moment of passing, I am pretty sure God had a good laugh as his expense. Eric will have laughed at himself, too.

As for me, my world is an emptier place without the patriotic commie in it.

And . . .

Stephen Saintonge, 25 February 1953–17 July 2022

On the same day Eric passed, so, too, passed a Baen's Barfly of longstanding, Stephen Saintonge, sometimes spelled St. Onge.

Steve was, to my certain knowledge, highly intelligent, well read, deeply thoughtful, and with a keen and acerbic wit and, to paraphrase something I once heard General Petraeus say about someone else (me, actually), had "a sense of humor that should be appreciated but not necessarily encouraged."

He'd lost his wife, Kaye, a few years before his own passing. She was terribly dear to him. Many would have given up on life after something like that. I've known a few people who did. Steve didn't. Oh, it hurt. Oh, it left him half empty; yes, that, too. But he never gave up, never lost his sense of humor, and never withdrew into the hell reserved for men who've lost beloved wives and can't cope with the loss.

That's pretty admirable, if you'll stop and think about it for a bit.

He never made a public announcement of the liver cancer that is probably what killed him, that, or at least led to his death. That, too, is rather admirable, if, again, you'll stop and think about it. There was no whining, no, "O, O, woe, O, woe is me!" from him. He went out privately and with as much dignity as a man can hope for.

Saintonge appears as the character, Santiona, in my book, *Carnifex*. Santiona is Spanish for Saintonge. Yes, really.

Sigh. The world becomes an ever lonelier place.

Music List

(Many of the lyrics of which would have been included, were not the music industry such a bunch of tight-fisted, greedy prigs):

The Standells, Shel Silverstein's "Dirty Water"
Bob Dylan, "Like a Rolling Stone"
Jacqueline Steiner and Bess Lomax Hawes, "Charlie on the MTA"
Sylvia Fricker, "You Were On My Mind"
The Temptations, "My Girl"
Smokey Robinson, "The Tracks of My Tears"
The Lovin' Spoonful, "Do You Believe in Magic?"
The Animals, "We Gotta Get Out of This Place"
The Rolling Stones, "(I Can't Get No) Satisfaction"
Petula Clark, "Downtown"
Jay and the Americans, "Cara Mia"

Acknowledgements

So many people gave of their time and knowledge to help with this. I can only hope I have forgotten none of them.

In mostly chronological order:

Brian Wallace, of Southie, who provided the names and locations of most of the businesses on Big Broadway that I'd long since forgotten. My cousins Trish and Lulu, who helped with research. Tom Nee, Deanna Terranova, Kathleen Walsh, Maureen England, Pamela MacKerron Cherry, Mary Ellen Cuddyer, Karen Fahey Ricciardi, Marie Keough Desrosier, Paul J. Sweeney, and Eileen Holmes, all of whom gave a hearty assist with old time geography or facts or both. Vermont Custom Armory that "built" the Sterling to spec. Chloe Tzang for "Topaz." Jake Friend of Vermont Custom Armory for weapons design. Sam Straus for "the money." Robert Ciccolo, Jr.; Maureen Elizabeth Parolin, late of Jordan Marsh; Susan Wilson, House Historian for the Parker House; Dan Manning, elevators; Richie Savicke, for the FID; Marykay Wienezkowsk, for the power transformer; Robert A. "Bob" Hall, Billy B's home town and street, the confessioners; Susan Quigg Lenehan; Betty Ann Snyder; Deb Turner; Donna Santoro Crosby; Louise DiFrumalo Elkaliouby; Patti Noonan O'Brien; Walter Morse; Irene Mahoney; Pat Kelley Connolly; Jerry Judge; Robert Flynn; Diane Glynn; Janice Santosuosso; Kathy Shepard Yebba; Linda Quirk; Rosemary Sullivan; Debbie Logan McDonald; Mary Beth Fahey Moore; Margaret Fogarty; Denise Bognanno; Linda Alice Feliciano; Johnny White; Jane Newton; Ann Perd; Roy Benson; Patricia Constantino; Mary Miller; Bob Healey; Father Erik Richtsteig, theology; Hugh Knight; Valeria Palmer, this, that Heather Knight; David Hause; Rick Holbert; Justin Watson; Kacey Ezell, horror; Anthony Sammarco, S.S. Pierce (pronounced "Purse"); Ben Blatt, Attorney at Law, firearms law and transfers; and Larry Correia, the travails of a Class III.